DOVE
SEASON

JOHNNY SHAW

DOVE SEASON

A JIMMY VEEDER FIASCO

PUBLISHED BY

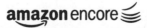

Text copyright ©2010 Johnny Shaw
All rights reserved.

Printed in the United States of America.

Published by AmazonEncore
P.O. Box 400818
Las Vegas, NV 89140

ISBN-13: 9781935597643
ISBN-10: 1935597647

For
Jack H. Shaw
(1925–1997)

The Imperial Valley represented in this novel is an entirely fictional version of a real place.

A hometown is a lot like a younger brother. You can tease him, knock him around, and give him a hard time, but you'll always love him and stick up for him.

I might take some liberties and do some name-calling, but this novel was written with great respect and admiration for the people of Holtville, El Centro, Calexico, Imperial, Brawley, Mexicali, and the rest of the Imperial Valley.

PART ONE

PART ONE

ONE

There is something about the desert that pisses everything off.

It could be the heat. Or the barren landscape. Or the stark desolation. It doesn't really matter the why. The fact is the desert brings out the desperate worst in a thing. In an environment where nothing is meant to survive, life seethes.

In the desert even the plants have chips on their shoulders. They're water-starved and sunburned fighters. Forced to wrestle their way through rock and earth. Cactus, yucca, and saw grass can all draw blood. No one goes to the desert to see the fall colors, mostly because those colors are an unbeautiful shade of brownish.

There are no cute calendars devoted to the creatures of the desert floor. Whether a rattlesnake or a scorpion or a centipede, under every rock some scaly, poisonous monster waits for the chance to bite the next unsuspecting ankle. Even a desert hare will take a finger off the dumbass that tries to pet it. If the desert can make a bunny that angry, imagine what it does to the people.

That's the kind of horseshit that filled my head as I stood in the dark with my father's shotgun in my hands and an involuntary tremor in my knees.

It was quiet at that moment, but there was definitely something in the shed. At first I had heard movement, light banging, loud enough to hear from inside. No wind to blame it on. An animal maybe. One of the chickens, a cat, or a coyote. But when I stepped outside, I had heard something closer to a voice. It was only a fraction of a second. Faint, but human. I didn't know what Pop kept in the shed. But even if it was nothing but rusty tools, they were his rusty tools.

Slow, quiet steps brought me to the shed door. I closed my eyes and listened. The only sound was my breathing. And even that I kept to a low wheeze. I aimed the Winchester at the ground and slowly reached for the looped rope handle of the corrugated tin door. Whoever was inside was in for a big surprise. So why was I the one that was shaking?

I swung the door open and lifted the shotgun tight to my shoulder. The double barrel swept into the darkness.

It had only been a few hours before that I had been driving my pickup eastbound on the 10 freeway. I had daydreamed then, too. Anything to stay awake and avoid the reality that I would eventually have to face. No good could come from analyzing my life. Introspection was for people with interesting lives and money.

I had left Los Angeles at midnight to avoid traffic in Pomona and San Bernardino, hoping to get to the Valley around four thirty or five. By getting in late and waking up at ten, I could avoid wasting a day on the road. In the middle of the night on the freeway, it was Kenworths, Peterbilts, Macks, and my piece-of-shit Mazda.

I had been making good time when I pulled into the parking lot of the Wheel Inn in Cabazon just west of Palm Springs. I needed coffee and something to eat, and the Wheel was eternally open. The food was standard diner fare, but the giant dinosaurs that loomed over the parking lot offered a pleasant wave of nostalgia. Come on, they're giant dinosaurs.

I grabbed a seat at the counter, not bothering to look at the menu. I kept to a strict policy with roadside diners: OOB. Only order breakfast. It was a safe bet and sometimes a pleasant surprise. Lunch and dinner could be a crapshoot. There's always that one entrée that doesn't belong. Whoever orders chicken cordon bleu at Chonchy Joe's Gasoline and Beef Jerky Emporium is asking for the intestinal challenge that they will soon face.

Because I had no interest in health or proper diet, I ordered biscuits and gravy with a side of bacon. I considered bacon to be a digestif.

I wasn't in the habit of chatting with waitresses, so my refueling was unremarkable. The food was above adequate, and the coffee gave me just the amount of jitters that I wanted. I wasn't ready to get in my truck. The gift shop in the belly of the brontosaurus was closed. So I walked underneath the tyrannosaurus, running my hand along the cracked plaster and having a smoke before I got back on the road.

From far away those dinosaurs were roadside behemoths, but up close they were nothing more than shoddy construction, chipping paint, and exposed chicken wire. To be crystal clear, I'm not saying that when we look at monsters up close we find that they are truly fragile. And I'm not saying that strength from a distance can often be revealed as a façade, protecting one's smaller weaknesses. What I'm saying is that those dinosaurs needed some spackle. Simplistic metaphors are for people who take fortune cookies to heart, need something to say at their book club, and believe that love conquers all. Things are never more than exactly what they seem. We all could use a little spackle.

Another half hour on the 10, then I turned off at Indio and headed south on the 86 toward the Imperial Valley. I couldn't see it, but I knew the Salton Sea was just outside my driver's side window. In the daytime the Salton Sea could be beautiful, the cloudless blue sky mirrored on its reflective surface. But at night without the visuals to distract, all I got was the combined smell of rotting fish and some polysyllabic disease that somehow made its way into my truck through the closed window. I lit a cigarette just to freshen the air.

I passed a birdshot-riddled sign: YOU ARE NOW ENTERING IMPERIAL COUNTY. The Imperial Valley was as far south and as far east as you can go in California, on the border of Arizona and Mexico. The towns of El Centro, Imperial, Brawley, Holtville, and Calexico made up the bulk of the population on the American side of the border. On the Mexican side of an imposing steel and razor-wire fence, the city of Mexicali sprawled, a metropolis of a million-plus. Due to Mexico's proximity, a solid three-quarters of the population of the Imperial Valley was Hispanic. Spoken Spanish was far more common than English.

Imperial County was the poorest county in California with an unemployment rate over 30 percent and an illiteracy rate that made rural Mississippi appear erudite. With a quarter of the people out of work, it was not hard to imagine the crime rate. In short, it was kind of a shithole. But I mean that in the most affectionate way.

I touched the back of my hand to the window, feeling the heat of the desert through the glass. Even late at night, it was in the mid-nineties. The days were going to be blistering, topping 110 degrees.

It would be an hour before I got to the house, but I was home. This was my home. Whatever that meant.

Pop hadn't told me when the doctors had first diagnosed him with cancer. He hadn't told me about his first surgery. Or his second surgery. Or about the chemotherapy. Or the radiation therapy. I had been gone twelve years, but we weren't estranged. We talked regularly on the phone and had a mail correspondence that continued even when modern technology made it anachronistically quaint. But apparently all cancer-related events had slipped his mind. For his own reasons he had chosen to keep it from me.

Until a couple of days before my drive. Without prologue Pop had laid it out for me. Everything that he had kept from me about his illness. According to Pop, he was on what he jokingly called "the final push." Not a great joke, but he was dying of cancer, so I cut him a break. No more chemo or radiation or surgeries. No more nothing. He had checked himself into a care facility and was just trying to maintain a level of comfort. He hadn't sounded depressed, but he hadn't any hope either.

I did the only thing I could. I packed up the truck and headed home. The house and the farm needed tending, and I wanted to spend as much time with Pop as I could. If he was dying, I wouldn't let him die alone.

I left everything behind in Los Angeles. Luckily, "everything" wasn't much. I quit my job installing stained-glass windows, a non-taxing, sometimes-fun job that helped me avoid any real responsibility. So far my degree in American literature had not come in handy in the series of labor jobs that I worked only when absolutely necessary. Carpenter, glazier, day laborer, home security installer, Christmas tree salesman, just to name the recent ones. Few skills jump off a résumé like the ability to single-handedly inflate and deflate a thirty-foot Santa Claus.

I hadn't been in Los Angeles for long, just one in a growing list of addresses. I moved around a lot. Since I had left home and then graduated college, I had been constantly drawn to new cities, new faces, and new experiences. The money that I was using to finance this trip had originally been intended for a planned three-month jaunt to Southeast Asia.

I tried not to look too far ahead or too far behind. If your eyes focus on the horizon, you trip over your own feet. I read that somewhere. I think it was on the side of an ex-girlfriend's box of chai tea.

As much as I would like to say that the labor jobs were a way to keep me in frozen burritos while I struggled to make my real dreams come true, I couldn't. I wasn't writing the great American novel. I didn't want to open my own haberdashery. I didn't want to direct (which made me the only one in the greater Los Angeles area). I didn't have a dream. I just was.

I was one of those guys who knows a little bit about a lot. If I could sit around and shoot the shit all day, I would. But there are only so many talk show host jobs out there. Instead, I stuck with drywall. I worked and then lazed, hanging out in bars and coffee shops and opining on the world, art, and my fellow man. I was a shit-shooter extraordinaire. It was cool when I was in my twenties. Unfortunately, when I had recently hit thirty it began to concern me. Not enough to change, but enough to make me feel more losery.

It was about four in the morning when I drove through Brawley. Dirt patches pretended to be lawns in front of houses. A constant haze of dust lingered in the air. Some of the older buildings downtown hinted at better times, but decay, graffiti, and heat had eroded them. Brawley looked like a town that was losing a long battle, exhausted past the point of caring. It was as if the effort to fight off the desert wore on the buildings and plants and roads. Everything about Brawley sagged from the weight of its own slow cessation. I was born in Brawley.

I drove through Imperial, then El Centro, finally making the turn east toward the house. My tires clicked on the caterpillars that crossed the road between two alfalfa fields.

I didn't have a hometown proper. The house where I grew up was on a farm between Holtville and Calexico. "In the country," as opposed to "in town."

I claimed Holtville, as it was where I went to high school (Go Vikings!) and where we shopped for groceries. Holtville was small town quiet, home of the "world-famous" Carrot

Festival. After all, Holtville was officially the Carrot Capital of the World.

On the other hand, Calexico was all border town with an almost all-Mexican population. Calexico was the tip of the gigantic Mexicali iceberg, the small portion surfacing into the U.S. Twenty-five thousand people on this side, a million people on the other. It was mostly just hardworking families, but with the border so near, mischief and the mischievous were never too far away. Calexico was the Knife Laceration Capital of the World. Unofficially, of course.

As I turned off Bowker Road, I could see the house in the distance. A large Spanish-style house, white with a red terra cotta tile roof, it looked like one of the old missions. Surrounded by a sugar beet field, it appeared as an island in the vast flatness of the farmland. Its remoteness was spared by Morales Bar, a Quonset hut field-workers' bar directly across the street. Growing up, it had never seemed strange that my only neighbor was a bar. It probably explained a lot.

I pulled into the circular driveway of the house and parked my truck behind Pop's tired Chevy LUV. There must have been sheep grazing nearby because the sound of the truck cleared a large group of turkey vultures out of a tall pine. I couldn't see them, but their feathers sounded like sheets of metal rubbing against each other. The brief disappearance of stars marked their path in the sky. I got out of the car and stretched. Live trumpet blasted from Morales Bar across the street. I grabbed my bags out of the truck bed.

Almost twelve years and I had never taken the key off my key ring. I unlocked the front door and went inside. It was dark and empty, but not quiet. Country houses make noise. Creaks, groans, and a strange bubbling sound in the basement brought the house to life. The house had the pleasant reek of farm living, a faint combination of dust and stale sweat. In the Imperial Valley, very little changed. And when it did, it changed slowly.

Pop had warned me that the air-conditioning had busted a couple years prior, so the inside of the house was like the inside of a convection oven. It was actually hotter inside, as the house had trapped the heat of the day. I dropped my bags in the living room and turned on two oscillating fans that moved the dust and hot air around.

Crashing on the couch, my ears rang from the drive. I was wide awake, yet exhausted. I stared at the ceiling doing the exact thing I had been trying to avoid. I was back in the house I grew up in, my father was dying, I had no job, little money, and between my head and the heat, I wasn't going to sleep. As I lit a cigarette, I thought, at least I have my health.

About three cigarettes and a half hour later, I heard the sound coming from the shed. The shotgun had been where Pop always kept it.

The moment I saw them huddled in the dark, I felt like the biggest asshole in the world. Why? Because only an asshole would point a shotgun at three unarmed, middle-aged Mexican women and a small boy. They didn't look surprised, although they seemed concerned about the shotgun. I lowered it and tried to smile.

While the boy was all eyes to the shotgun, the women slowly rose and gathered the blankets they had laid out on the dirt floor. Their nonchalant acceptance spoke volumes. I dug into my brain for what little Spanish I remembered.

"Wait. *Espera*," I said. "*Tu puede* sleep *aquí.* It's okay." I even made the universal symbol for sleep, resting my cheek against my hands. Although something was lost in the interpretation due to the shotgun in my hand.

They stopped collecting their blankets and looked at me questioningly.

I knew they were in the country illegally, but that didn't make them criminals. They were only trying to survive, and I saw no reason to treat them as anything but human beings. That's what Pop would have done. I had seen him bring illegals water on more than one hot day.

"*Necessita agua? Yo tengo agua. En la casa*," I said, seeing no water on them.

They nodded shyly.

"*Y* food? Shit, what's the word for food? *Comida*, right?"

They nodded again.

"I'll be right back. *Espera.*"

I went back into the house. I poured out a quarter-full bottle of flat soda and filled it with tap water. The only food I had was a half box of Ding Dongs that I had bought on the drive. It had to have some nutrition, and the kid would be stoked. I even dumped a bunch of ice cubes in a plastic cup. When you've been in this kind of heat for too long, it's hard to remember what cold feels like anymore.

I unloaded the shotgun and put it back in the closet.

When I returned to the shed with my arms full of goodies, they were gone. They must have assumed that I went inside to call *La Migra.* I left the bottle of water in the shed for the next squatter, dumped the ice in the grass, and ate a Ding Dong.

TWO

I woke up to the sound of gunfire. An ominous sound in the city, but in the country just another piece of machinery running too damn early. Among the range of noises that one could rise to, the faint thud of a shotgun from a quarter mile away was far less abrupt than most alarm clocks.

A couple of shotgun reports popped again in the distance. Dove season was a month and a half away, but many of the locals appeared to view the legally defined season as more of a guideline than a rule. Dove season was the calendar event of the Imperial Valley, always starting on September first. It made the Imperial Valley Mid-Winter Fair look like—well, a county fair, which was what it was. I could remember Pop handing me a shotgun when I was ten. Not to hunt, but to patrol the fields. To keep any unwanted bwanas from trampling the crops. Even a prepubescent can be intimidating with a loaded shotgun.

There was a time when people like Ernest Hemingway and Gary Cooper would come down for dove season. Hunt in the day, then drink and gamble down in Mexicali at night. It was still just shooting birds, but something convinced me that it was different back then. The days of Papa and Coop had long passed. If I followed the sounds of the shotgun, I would find a group of drunk-by-noon 'necks sitting in folding chairs on a ditch bank in hundred-degree heat shooting at the bird of peace. The kind of thing that makes frog gigging look majestic.

The house hadn't gotten any cooler overnight. I sat up on the couch, still dressed from the night before. The stink from my sweat-soaked clothes offended even me. I let my mind catch up to my eyes and looked at the clock on the mantel. If it still worked, it was eight thirty. A solid three hours of sleep.

I lit a smoke, cracked my back, and walked to the window overlooking the front yard. The trees and lawn had lost the battle and the war. The grass was shades of brown and yellow, the hedge was spider-infested, and the scattered trees were dying of thirst. One tree had surrendered. It stretched across the lawn on its side, dead roots ripped from the ground. With the cloudless sky and bright, shining sun, it looked like a beautiful day. Looks can be deceiving. It was sure to top one hundred. Egg-frying on the sidewalk was a regular summer segment on the local news. They reserved cats without tails and water-skiing squirrels for the winter.

I grabbed one of my bags, went into the bathroom, stripped down, and jumped in the shower. The water pressure was weak, and there was no hot water. Not that I would have used it. I made a mental note to start a to-do list of things to fix around the house, starting with the air-conditioner and the water. I knew my home maintenance chores would be infinite, but I had the time. The house was broken, almost overwhelmingly nonfunctional. What had once been a beautiful house was now closer to an enormous lean-to.

A dozen years ago, when it was just me and Pop, this place was never going to make the cover of *Architectural Digest*. Two men living together, contented pigs in our own mud. However, I had my chores, and they kept the house from getting past a certain point. It was apparent that after I left, Pop had no reason to keep the place up even to that minimum degree. The house would be laughed at by *Mediocre Housekeeping* magazine. If something hadn't bothered Pop, he hadn't bothered fixing it.

The air-conditioning was busted, the water pressure was weak, the hot water heater didn't work, the basement was flooded, the flooded basement was plagued with frogs, the paint and stucco were chipping, some kind of animal was living in the crawl space, some other kind of animal was dead in the air ducts, the electrical system was spotty, the roof leaked, and I was pretty sure there was a beehive in one of the walls because I could feel the humming vibrations with my hand. All that under stacks of magazines, catalogs, books, and ten-year-old mail that was covered in a quarter-inch of dust.

It couldn't hurt to keep busy. Might as well clean, organize, and repair. I liked to believe that I was doing it so that when Pop got better and came home, he would have this great house to return to. But that kind of rationalization only reminded me of the truth. It was better if it was just a hobby and a way to pass the time.

I got out of the shower and toweled off. Looking into the mirror, I decided not to shave my four-day growth. I'd shave it when it started to itch. With dark hair to my shoulders and a stubbly not-quite-a-beard, I wasn't winning any beauty contests. But what I lacked in looks, I more than made up for with a complete absence of style. I got dressed in jeans, a frayed T-shirt, and my beat-up steel toes.

I made a pass through the house. I wasn't looking for anything, but convincing myself that I was back. Every piece of furniture and every book on the shelf was the same as it was twelve years ago. I could remember when Pop brought home the couch, brand-new and seventies orange. It was ugly, but comfortable. Now the stuffing was poking out and every edge was tattered. The objects were the same, but worn and dusty. It was like I had woken up in a museum dedicated to my childhood. Not a good museum, more like a back-of-a-gas-station roadside attraction dedicated to Spam or yarn.

I decided to grab a bite to eat in Holtville before heading into El Centro. Driving down what used to be Orchard Road, but was now a four-lane NAFTA truck route, I let the fields of lettuce, alfalfa, and wheat blur past me. It's about seven miles into town, a familiar straight line.

Counting the rows, I was reminded that I had to check in with Mike about the farm. The moment Pop got sick, my cousin Mike had stepped up and took over the day-to-day of Pop's crops. A helluva thing to do, considering he was my cousin on my mother's side and my mother died when I was born. We weren't close. We barely knew each other. But down here, family is family.

I decided to put off seeing him until the next day. It's not like farming held any urgency. And I wasn't sure what I was going to do anyway. I hadn't worked the fields since high school, and I wasn't particularly a good farmer then. My friends in different cities found it charming, even romantic, that I grew up on a farm. It was neither. Ask a farmer.

In my youth, Holtville had fought off the decay and erosion of the desert better than its neighboring towns. With only four thousand people, it had been able to maintain its all-American appearance. A big white gazebo shared space with large cedars in the two-block park that made up the center of town. Despite the box stores in El Centro and Calexico, the locals had still shopped at the small independent stores that circled the park. The older generation had been willing to spend a few extra bucks in an effort to keep their town from losing its personality.

Not anymore. Times were tougher. Sammy's Hardware, Walker's Barbershop, Good Health Pharmacy, and the five-and-dime, all important parts of my childhood, were gone. Driving down Holt Road, there wasn't much that I remembered. There weren't many businesses still open, except the bars and churches.

Luckily, one mainstay persevered. The J&M Café. From the outside, it looked like just another grease pit truck stop. And in the interest of full disclosure, that's what it looked like on the inside, too. Because that's exactly what it was. But to the truckers and locals, it was a social center. I had never been inside J&M without seeing someone I knew. Which isn't saying much, as I knew all the waitresses. And these were waitresses that I would happily chat with, more like family, like great-aunts.

The waitress with the big red wig seated me. She had been working there since I was a kid, and I'd never known her name. I called her "Ma'am." I always imagined that her name was in the Gertie or Flossie family. I could have easily asked, but I didn't care that much and Ma'am was a good nickname. Flirtatious and sassy with the truckers even into her seventies, Ma'am was the heart and soul of J&M. She poured me a cup of coffee without asking. It was morning.

I was a man. What else was I going to drink? I wondered if she would recognize me.

It didn't take long to get my answer.

"You're Big Jack's boy. I heard about the cancer. Sad. How's he doing?" she asked. Not chatty, but sincerely interested. I realized how removed I had been, the last one to learn of Pop's condition. It made me feel like shit.

"I'm going to see him. After breakfast," I said, not really answering her question.

"I'll bet he's giving them nurses hell. Big Jack, always with a joke and a smile."

"That's my Pop, Ma'am." I smiled.

"Well, you tell him I said hey there. You tell him I'm keeping the coffee hot." As if she knew I didn't know her name and didn't want to reveal it now after all these years. I was onto her sick game.

I ordered a short stack of pancakes and a side of bacon, and then I grabbed a copy of the *Holtville Tribune* from the rack in the front. The *Tribune*, Holtville's weekly newspaper, was always worth a look. In the summer with school out and no high school sports to report, the paper was stretching to fill its voluminous twenty pages. Digging through the padded and boring city council news, I found two of my favorite newspaper columns on the planet: the Finley Elementary School Lunch Menu (Friday—Pancho Villa Salad?) and more importantly, the Police Briefs.

The Police Briefs were a roundup of everyone who had called the Holtville Police Department during the preceding week. From petty theft to locking your keys in your car, it was a glorious page of embarrassment and amusement.

July 17 – 4:12 pm – Gladys Wells of Walnut Street reported two strangers walking through her neighborhood. A patrol car was sent to the scene, and after a brief interview, it was determined that the two men were visiting relatives in the area.

July 19 – 11:07 pm – Pinky's Bar and Grill reported that an altercation between two women had broken out in the parking lot. Officers were sent to the scene. No arrests were made. Officers instructed the management to clean up the broken glass.

"Here you go, sugar." Ma'am set my food in front of me. I dug in, saving the bacon for last. Some people "accidentally" let their syrup touch their bacon, ashamed of the combination's deliciousness. I pour the syrup right on top of the bacon. That's the kind of rebel I am.

As I took a bite, a hand came down hard on my shoulder. "We ain't partial to no longhairs 'round these here parts."

It wasn't the first time I had heard this kind of statement. But it was unusually early for shit-kicking and so shockingly cliché that I was more amused than threatened.

I looked up at the smiling face of Bobby Maves. "You ain't from around here, are you, boy?" He affected his best redneck accent on top of his normal redneck accent.

"Holy shit" was the only comeback that came to mind, so that's what I said with a laugh and a smile. Bobby Maves. Mexican on the outside, hillbilly on the inside.

I half-stood in my seat and shook Bobby's hand. With a nod I offered him the booth across from me. Bobby sat, his eyes on me the whole time. He had to lean his head back to see through the slits under his sagging lids. I couldn't tell if he was drunk or tired. Maybe both.

Bobby was maybe five-eight, wiry, and looked like he didn't have an ounce of body fat on him. The most striking aspect of Bobby was his hair. It was already completely gray, almost white, styled in a high pompadour. It contrasted sharply against his brown skin. He could easily be mistaken for a Mexican Elvis impersonator.

His father was German Swiss and his mother Mexican. But despite his dark skin, Bobby didn't consider himself Mexican. As he had told me once, "Down here, if your parents speak Mexican in the house, then you're Mexican. If your parents speak American, then you're white." It wasn't important to me, but to Bobby there was a distinction. It was a way to separate the fifth-generation California Mexicans from the recent arrivals.

Bobby had the familiar look of a night of irrigating: bloodshot eyes, spatters of mud on his shirt and shorts, and his feet only in socks. He had left his boots outside. By the time he was done with his breakfast, the heat would cake the mud and he could just knock it off.

"How you been, Bobby?" I said, genuinely interested, but coming out a little generic.

"I still live in Holtville—how good could I be?"

"Yeah, but it's a dry heat" was the best I could come up with. It was still early for me.

Bobby gave my mediocre joke more of a laugh than it deserved. Not because he was humoring me, but because

Bobby thought I was hilarious. He always had. Growing up, I was the funny kid and Bobby was the bully with the giggles. It was a perfect symbiotic relationship. I could run off at the mouth and Bobby was always there to pull me out of the fire and enjoy doing it. I had never seen anyone more at peace with violence than Bobby Maves. He didn't have a mean bone in his body. He just liked to fight. And he was good at it.

"Heard about your old man," Bobby said, his laughter dying down and his face doing its best to display sobriety. "I was thinking about going to see him, but I didn't know if they'd let me or if I should bring flowers or shit like that. I don't even know what I'd say or if he wants to see people." Bobby was definitely drunk, swaying a little in his seat, grasping pauses between sentences.

"Pop'd get a kick out of seeing you. Anytime you want to go."

"I like your dad. Big Jack never treats me like a fuckup. Never tells me I drink too much or I got to be more responsible, not like the other old-timers. Always makes me feel smarter than I am 'cause he talks at me like I'm smart."

It was nice to hear Bobby talk about Pop in the present tense. People could get in the habit of talking about the dying in the past tense, as if they were already gone. It's easy to see someone as a dying person, not as a living person facing death.

Bobby turned back to me. "Cancer, right?"

"No, I'm an Aries," I said, trying to lighten the mood. I still had the whole day and didn't want the conversation to get too serious. Ten o'clock was too early for maudlin.

The corners of Bobby's mouth rose, but he couldn't muster a laugh. The topic was serious to him, and he couldn't make the turn that quickly. I kept it short. "Yeah. In his gut. Nothing left to do, from what I'm told. Another surgery would kill him."

"Sucks." Bobby stared ahead, summarizing the situation perfectly. We bobbed our heads, nodding like idiots at nothing.

"Weird being back?" Bobby asked.

"I'd say yeah, but I still haven't got my head around it. Nothing's changed and everything's changed."

"How long has it been? Since we seen each other?"

I thought about it for a minute. "At least five years. When you got married?"

"Yeah. That didn't take, did it? Fun wedding, though."

"The parts I remember."

"Why haven't we kept in touch?" Bobby didn't sound hurt, just interested.

"Sorry, man. I don't know. You get absorbed in your own shit, you know. Hard enough keeping your present-tense shit in order. But you're right, I should've called more."

"Should? No. Shit, I know how to work a phone. On me too. Just saying, you know, would've been nice to catch up or whatnot. A fucking laugh, right? You're in the city with shit to do, having fun. I live here. I'm bored as shit. I missed you, fucker."

"Yeah. Same here," I said, wondering why I hadn't called.

I didn't have many friends like Bobby. Even if I hadn't seen him in years and didn't really know who he was as an adult, I knew that some things didn't change. I knew that Bobby was someone I trusted without reservation. I knew that face time wasn't a necessity of our friendship. And I knew that the trust between us ran deep, the product of teenage violence and secrets.

"You want anything, Bobby?" Ma'am shouted from near the register.

"Just a night on the town with you, beautiful," Bobby hollered back.

"Soon as my husband kicks, I'll take you up on that," she laughed.

"Well, in the meantime, I'll settle for some coffee and a Denver ommy. Thanks, hon." Bobby blew Ma'am a kiss.

Bobby turned to me. "Hey, man. What's that waitress's name? I can't never remember. Always just call her beautiful or honey or sexy or some such."

"I don't think she has a name."

Bobby raised an eyebrow, but didn't bother to ask. "When you heading back to—I don't even know where you live. When you heading back?"

"I ain't. I'm here. At the house. For a while. Until…for a while. For as long as need be. I'm back."

Bobby slammed both hands on the table, startling me and splashing my coffee onto the tabletop. "Jimmy fucking Veeder is back," Bobby shouted, turning most of the heads in the J&M.

Bobby and I shot the shit for another half hour. I had kept up with Bobby through Pop, my conduit for all Imperial Valley news. I had heard about his divorce, but I didn't know if it was a good one or a bad one, so I didn't bring it up. We kept it light. We talked movies. Our tastes were the same. Music—our tastes had a little overlap. And books, which was a new topic. Bobby hadn't been much of a reader in the past, but in his words, "I was so bored one day, I picked up a book. Kept picking them up. I'm still that bored."

When Bobby started to fade from too little sleep and too much drink, we pledged to continue our conversation another time. We exchanged cell phone numbers and agreed to meet up and grab a beer or ten. I could use a bender, and some of my best drunks had been with Bobby, at least six of my top ten.

I paid, gave Ma'am a wave from across the room, and walked out into the heat of the morning. The steering wheel and gearshift on my truck burned my hands as I made the drive into El Centro to see Pop.

THREE

The twelve-mile stretch between Holtville and El Centro was mostly fields and power lines until the El Centro city limits. For a mile stretch east of town, truck yards and packing sheds lined the road. Even though the road was paved, a continual cloud of dust hazed the air from the tractors returning from the fields.

I drove past the spot where Nathanael West died, an unremarkable intersection with a fifty-acre scrap yard on one corner, a John Deere dealership on another, and abandoned hay sheds on the other two. The tragedy was in his death, but driving past the desolate anonymity of the site made it more regrettable. If West had avoided the Imperial Valley, he wouldn't have died in that car accident. There's a lesson to be learned somewhere in there.

I passed the WELCOME TO EL CENTRO sign, a cartoon sun wearing sunglasses welcoming me to "The Largest U.S. City Entirely Below Sea Level." When I had been a kid, El Centro had thrived. But as I drove down Main Street, I saw more empty storefronts than open businesses. A mass of concrete, dirt, and scattered palms, El Centro was the kind of town that needed a bath. Even the buildings seemed to sweat. Still it was "The Center." And if you lived down here, you had to go to El Centro or Calexico eventually. When you've got the big stores, the movie theaters, the hospital, the Sears, and the courthouse, you don't have to get all dolled up.

The house was too hot in the summer and hospice was only available on a temporary basis, so Pop had made arrangements. He had wanted to stay close, so the best he could do was Harris Convalescent Care. I knew a few people's grandparents who died there, seemingly satisfied customers. I got off Main and headed down Ross past the hospital.

Sadly, there were plenty of parking spots in the Visitors Parking Area. My truck was one of two cars. Before going inside, I paced and smoked a cigarette. I hadn't seen Pop in a while, and I didn't know what to expect. I accepted that a certain amount of mental preparation was necessary. As much as I was looking forward to seeing and talking to him, a nervousness sat in my stomach. It felt like the first sentence of a final chapter.

I tried to concentrate on the positive. I was looking forward to prodding Pop to tell me stories of his youth. It seemed like an appropriate time for that kind of thing. Beyond a few repeated army stories that were probably lies, I knew very little about my father's life before I was born. And he was fifty-four when I clocked in. That's a lot of life. A lot of questions. Born in the Depression, drafted into World War II, and everything before and after, you'd think he'd have a story or two that didn't involve a weekend pass, a half bottle of applejack, and a USO singer in a shit-brown dress.

Of course I'd known him my whole life, but I left home at eighteen. And not a particularly mature eighteen. This was to be the most concentrated amount of time together in our adult relationship. That was important. I knew who Pop was, but not who he had been. The story felt incomplete. We had the chance to get to know each other as father and son, as friends, but mostly, as grown men.

I crushed my cigarette underfoot, took a breath of hot, less-than-refreshing air, and headed into the pink-stuccoed building. The air-conditioning made me light-headed when I walked through the glass doors. I leaned one hand against the wall, needing a two-second break to avoid passing out. From one hundred degrees to sixty in one second could not be good for the body.

I was greeted by an angry woman's voice.

"Where the fuck have you been?"

I looked up. Behind the reception counter, dressed in lavender scrubs, Angela Torres was trying to kill me with her eyes. She clenched her face in a fist, eyes squinting tight, lines burrowing into her forehead. She looked pissed. She looked beautiful.

"Angie?" I had never pegged Pop for that kind of treachery. If I hadn't known better, I'd think that he had set up this situation. "Wow. How're you doing?"

"You haven't answered my question," she demanded. "Your father has been here for weeks. You're just showing up now?"

"I didn't know you worked here." Then I realized she had asked me a question. "He didn't tell me he was sick until a couple days ago."

"Yeah, why would he. You're only his only son."

"I honestly had no clue. Ask him. Came straight when I heard."

"Okay, go see him then," Angie said, pretending like she was reading a piece of paper she had picked up at random.

"It's good to see you, Angie. You look great."

She did. Even in scrubs and with her hair spilling out of a knot on the back of her head. The twelve years that had passed since I last saw her had only made her more striking. Barely five feet tall and with curves in all the right places, Angie could turn some heads. But it was her face that made you fall in love. Big brown eyes and full lips set on smooth brown skin, Angie had the kind of face that made men stupid.

"We haven't talked in like ten years, Jimmy. That's a long time. Nice to see you, whatever, but we're not really friends anymore, are we?"

"Fair enough, Angie. But if you're mad, you're mad at someone I'm not anymore."

She held up a finger, shutting me up. She continued to fake read. Then she said, "I'm not angry, Jimmy. It's just not something I think about."

"I've thought about you," I said.

Angie stared at me, biting the inside of her cheek. I'm pretty sure she was trying to decide whether to punch me in the face or not. In high school, she had been a little hitty.

"Go see your father," she said, clearly dismissing me. "Room eighteen. Down the hall."

I began to walk down the hall, and then I turned back.

"Don't say anything," she said. "If you've been thinking about me, it still wasn't enough for you to call. It doesn't matter what you felt or thought. It's what you did. Or didn't do."

"I know, but I'm going to say it anyway. I'm sorry. I'm not going to piss you off more with excuses. I'm sorry, Angie. Really. That's all. I don't expect you to forgive me."

"Good," she said. "Because I don't."

I walked slowly down the hall with a feeling very close to being punched in the stomach. The past could be one hell of a stalker, lurking and ready to pounce. But for all the conflict, seeing Angie had brought a lot of good memories back, too. Even if she hated me, I couldn't help but smile at the surprise of seeing her again.

Convalescent homes, like hospitals, are a heterogeneous goulash of odors. Underneath the dominant cocktail of urine and disinfectant is the pleasant latex smell of Band-Aids, wafts of sweat, something close to tapioca, and that musty mildew that seemed out of place in such a dry climate. It smelled like someone just finished shampooing a three-month-dead cat.

I found room eighteen, took a deep breath, put a big stupid smile on my face, and knocked on Pop's door lightly as I let myself in.

"Where are the strippers? I wouldn't've come if I'd known there weren't any strippers," I announced.

Pop turned his head from the propped-up position in his bed. His smile was weak, but his eyes were bright. He had lost so much weight that the shape of his skull was prominent around his eyes and cheekbones. The skin hung loose under his chin. His bald head was mottled with dark spots and a couple of scabs. The deep laugh lines at the side of his eyes reminded me of the man I knew.

In better days, Pop was a wiry six-foot-six farmer of Norwegian and German stock. He had always been thin and muscular, and I had never seen any amount of weight that he couldn't lift. His strength hadn't come from his frame, but will. He could lift tons because he believed he could. I once saw him carry a full beer keg up two flights of stairs. Granted, he had been pretty drunk and feeling no pain, but still a feat. Now he looked like he could barely lift a napkin to his face.

I grabbed a chair from against the wall and moved it to the side of the bed. I gave the room a cursory glance. It appeared to be clean and livable, yet had the anonymity of a hotel room. No pictures or personal items decorated the room. The small stack of books and crossword puzzles at the side of the bed were the only indication of identity.

"How was the drive?" Pop asked. His voice was strong, although rough from silence.

"No adventure. Straight shot down. Steady daydreaming," I answered, trying not to react to the noticeable change in his features. I focused on the bloody pieces of toilet paper stuck to his chin.

"Shaving yourself, I see. What'd you use? Whipped cream and a plastic knife?"

Pop smirked. "If they gave me the whole hot towel treatment, I'd let them shave me. But I ain't going to give up my routine for a nurse with a ten-cent disposable."

I remember watching Pop shave when I was a kid. The straight razor across his face sounded like sandpaper on glass. It looked so dangerous for so little reward.

"You ever thought about growing out your beard? Might give you the respectability that you've always craved," I said, smiling.

Pop laughed. "Yeah, I considered growing a goatee and playing folk music in beatnik bookstores and coffee shops, but it's a real son of a bitch finding mandolin strings this time of year."

"It's never too late. Big Jack Veeder and the Literate Farmers."

And that's how it started. For the next twenty minutes, Pop and I came up with names for his imaginary folk band and their playlist. Bad puns and idiotic humor would often fill our hour-long phone conversations. Pop chimed in, "Thank you. That was Jack Veeder and the Bed Sores playing, 'Cancer? I Didn't Even Know Her.'" The worse the band name, the harder we laughed: The Colostomy Bags, The Atheist Catholics, and my favorite, Jack Veeder and the Fuck You I'm Dying Tropical All-Stars.

As Pop was doing his best deejay voice to introduce the song, "The Only Thing the Army Taught Me Was How to Shit While Someone Watched," a nurse who wasn't Angie came in to give Pop some pills, breaking up our rhythm.

It was a shame. When Pop and I were joking and laughing, it was like he wasn't sick. A large part of our relationship was centered on our attempts to make each other laugh. I couldn't think of a stronger foundation for a friendship. I suppose some people would find it superficial, but they're just not funny enough to understand.

Many of our phone conversations over the last dozen years were predicated on our attempts to find "The Big Laugh." That elusive, once-a-year laugh that was so rare. The contagious laughter that hurt your face and sides, but you couldn't stop through the pain. Hell, "The Big Laugh" wasn't even fun. Didn't mean it wasn't our goal. It had been too long for both of us. I could see Pop's face in my mind, memories of the pain and laughter of "The Big Laugh." It didn't look like he had it in him anymore.

As the nurse changed Pop's colostomy bag, my mind raced with jokes, but they all seemed inappropriate or stupid. All of them in the "you're full of shit" family. Pop would have laughed, but the nurse would have judged me insensitive.

After the nurse left, we watched a couple of hours of television, which gave Pop an excuse to steal a short nap. Around one, an orderly brought Pop his lunch and meds. Due to his condition, Pop ate slowly and deliberately, concentrating on every bite. Eating was work, but I could tell he took pride that he didn't have to be fed through a tube. Over lunch, we watched a rerun of *Macmillan and Wife*. Neither of us particularly liked the show; however, there was a certain non-offensive ease to how the plot played out, a familiar and affable time-eater. We were both pleasantly disappointed when we couldn't figure out the who in the whodunit in the first five minutes. I don't know if it was the medication or the food, but after lunch Pop seemed a little more energized.

"I need a few things from the house," Pop said.

I got a small pad from my back pocket and found a pen on top of one of Pop's crosswords.

"I got some fingernail clippers. They should be on the nightstand next to my bed. The ones here tear my nails out." He reached for a folded piece of paper and handed it to me. "And I wrote down a couple of books. If you can't find them in the house, Book Nook in town might have some of them." I glanced down at the paper, Pop's inimitable block print showing eight or ten titles.

I knew the function of the list. Pop had talked about this for a long time. He was an avid reader. But if he liked an author, he never read everything that author wrote, particularly if they were dead. Pop claimed that the disappointment in knowing there wasn't any more work out there was depressing. So he always kept one book on the shelf, unread. Each of those books had potential energy, one more story just when Pop needed it. Possibly saved for just that moment.

"You need any more crosswords?" I asked.

"Not yet. They're getting harder to concentrate on. Even with my glasses. I can read, but they only make the easy ones in large print, and those bore the hell out of me. What's the point of doing a crossword you know you can finish?"

"Hey," I said. "Did you know Angela Torres worked here?"

Pop went poker faced, which told me more than whatever bullshit he was about to say. "Torres? Torres? Pretty Mexican girl, right? Was she in your year?"

"You can do better than that. I went to prom with her. Don't act like you don't remember Angie."

"She works here?"

"You're diabolical."

"I knew it didn't end quite right. What's the harm? I'm an old romantic."

"What makes you think I care?"

"The look on your face."

I shrugged, wondering what my face looked like. I tried to think of something else to talk about.

Pop and I didn't have the kind of relationship that necessitated discussing our feelings. Even though we talked for hours, emotions and personal matters never came up. We didn't hug. We didn't tell each other "I love you." And I had no need or desire to ever sing for my father. We didn't need to do those things because we knew them, and saying them would be redundant and would cheapen an implicit understanding.

So it surprised me when I asked, "Are you disappointed I didn't take over the farm?" I honestly have no idea where it came from. But I'd never had much of a filter. My mouth was like the end of a construction chute, dumping out whatever garbage my brain manufactured.

"Hell" was Pop's mumbled response, as if that was answer enough.

"We don't have to talk about it." I felt my face flush, embarrassed that I had drifted outside of our unspoken boundaries.

Pop laughed. "Afraid I'm disappointed in you or something? I thought you had a little more confidence than that. I thought you'd be smart enough not to give a damn what I think. What anyone thinks."

I shrugged, still not knowing why I asked and now not knowing what to say. My mouth and my brain really needed to get on the same page.

Pop used his arms to prop himself higher in the inclined bed. "Everything I did raising you was to make sure you didn't become a farmer. When you graduated college—hell, when you went to your first class—I couldn't've been prouder."

"Don't want to burst that bubble, Pop, but that degree hasn't really done me a hell of a lot of good."

"The hell." Pop almost showed anger, but anger wasn't a strong emotion in his palette. It came out as annoyance.

"By my standards, you're a success. And I'm proud to have been an accomplice in your escape. You know how it goes. You could've easily knocked up some girl in high school, did 'the right thing,' and married her. The right thing? What horseshit. There's an order to it, and one small mistake would've put you in line. You would've leased eighty acres, planted some alfalfa. It would've been tough, but slowly you'd work more acreage. Knocked out a few more kids. Then, in fifty years or so, you'd die. The fact you avoided any of that means you won."

"Come on. Farming ain't that bad," I said.

"Maybe. For you, back then, it would've been. Anything can be a curse if it ain't a choice. If it's all you know. If you do it because your father did it. And you do it because it's familiar and safe and you're afraid to do something else. Even if all you want to do is anything else.

"You know how many books I've read where farmers are the salt of the earth. The salt of the earth. Backhanded compliment if I ever heard one. You put salt on the earth and nothing grows. Farming is a noble profession is what they'll tell you. It ain't any more noble than coal mining or meat packing or grave digging. If having a shit job is all it takes to be noble, then I'm the Queen of Norway. They may exist, but I ain't never met a first-generation farmer."

Pop paused, staring me directly in the eye, his breath rapid. The sad look of his sunken eyes made me a little uncomfortable. He spoke slowly and seriously.

"I didn't really want to have the dying father/loving son mortality talk, but I suppose we should." Pop looked at me, more somber than I'd ever seen him. "Let's get this straight. We're going to do this once. Once. Then we're not going to talk about it again. Then this bullshit seriousness is done and we get back to it. It's too ordinary. I taught you to be funnier than this."

I nodded, my throat instantly dry. I needed a glass of water, but I didn't want to move. I leaned in close to Pop, as if we were sharing a secret.

"I'm dying and I'm scared to death. Well, not 'to death,' I guess." He couldn't help a small smile. "But what good would panicking do? What good would complaining or crying or hiding under the covers do me? It's going to happen, and from the way I feel, soon. Dying is a bitch when you don't believe in God. But I ain't going to start now just because I'm scared. I'm afraid, and the only way I know how to kill that fear is distraction. I want to die happy. I want to die laughing."

I just listened, trying not to move.

"It's about the time left. It's about this time. It's about watching crappy TV with my son. It's about laughing in the face of that fear, and I can't do it without you. I know why you're here. I know you've made sacrifices to be here. That means a lot. I know. But for you and for me, let's not let this get dark and sad and morose. Leave the crying to the women."

Pop dropped back onto his pillow, as if that had taken everything out of him. He reached out and took my hand. The intimacy of the moment sent a chill up my spine. I could feel tears welling up in my eyes. In those few moments, it had all become real. I thought past the tears, clearing my head and forcing them down.

Pop allowed an abbreviated grin. "You got that look like you think you should say something. You don't have to. In fact, I don't want you to. Let's sit. Let's just sit."

Pop let me off the hook. If I had tried to talk, I would have blubbered like a drunk frat brother. And nobody wanted to see that.

We sat together for a while. Pop's eyes focused on a spot in space. Not drifting, but alert and intense. I don't know where I was. After maybe an hour, I gave Pop a nod and stood.

"You should have told me when you got sick," I said.

"And use up all my favors?"

"That's a big thing to keep from me."

"Everyone has secrets," Pop said.

As I moved the chair back to its place against the wall, Pop chuckled under his breath. It was the kind of laugh that comes out of your mouth when you don't think a joke is funny.

I turned to him, curious. "What?"

"Damn it," Pop muttered to himself.

"What is it?"

Pop shook his head and then seemed to come to a decision. "I need you to get one other thing for me."

I didn't hesitate. "Anything."

Pop grinned, but his eyes were serious. "I want you to get me a prostitute."

FOUR

"You need my help to do what?" Bobby's voice was groggy on the other end of the phone. I could hear country rock and what may have been a female voice or a small dog in the background. I didn't ask.

I was standing in the parking lot of the convalescent home, lighting one cigarette off the next and pacing the length of my truck. There was no one around, but I kept my voice low.

"Pop asked me to get him a prostitute," I said as matter-of-factly as I could. As the words left my mouth, I couldn't believe what I was saying, let alone that I was enlisting Bobby's assistance.

"I've got company here, buddy. Good joke, but bad timing," Bobby said. "I'm going back to bed."

"I'm serious, Bobby. No joke," I said in my most sincere tone of voice, which actually sounded a bit sarcastic.

"You're not fucking with me?"

"I couldn't make this shit up."

There was five seconds of nothing but tinny guitar twang on the other end of the phone. As I was about to say something, Bobby's roar of laughter nearly blew my ears out. And even after I'd pulled the phone away, I could hear his distinct machine gun wail.

I kept the phone away from my ear, yelling into the receiver, "Bobby. Look, man. This is embarrassing. I don't know. Not embarrassing, just fucking weird. Forget it. I'll do it myself. Go back to sleep. I shouldn't have called. I just thought we could. Pop asked me, so I'm doing it. Go back to sleep."

I could no longer hear Bobby's laughter, so I dared to listen. Bobby was laughing, but the volume was replaced by a chuckle and heavy breathing that quickly turned to coughing. You know it's a good laugh when you choke on your own spit. Between gasping hacks, Bobby was able to get out, "Sorry, man. What do you need me for?"

"I thought you'd know where to find prostitutes."

Bobby stopped laughing. His voice got quiet. "Wait a minute. You haven't seen me in fucking years, you barely fucking know who I am anymore, and you just assume that I have some line on where the hookers are? Now I'm the tour guide driving the Muff Bus down Pussy Road? Is that what you fucking think of me?"

"Yeah. Something like that."

"Sounds about right." Bobby laughed, not able to keep up his feigned anger. "It just so happens that I have a little experience in this area. When you want to do this?"

"The way Pop's looking, sooner's better than later."

"So, let me get this straight. Just to make sure. Just so that I can hear myself say it." Bobby cleared his throat. "Big Jack wants you to find him a hooker. He wants you to find him a hooker and bring her back to his room."

Hearing it said to me, I let out an involuntary snort. "Yeah, well, not exactly. That would be easy. Pop doesn't want any hooker, he wants me—I'm sorry, us—to find a specific hooker. Some Mexicali bar girl named Yolanda. Probably not even her real name."

Bobby cut in. "You ain't in LA no more, brother. Besides, you're thinking of strippers. Mexican hookers tend to use their real names. Fun fact."

"Anyway, Pop says she sometimes used to work weekends at Morales. I got a kind of description. I figured we could start there."

"He say why he wanted to see her? Her specifically. Beyond the obvious."

"None of my business," I answered brusquely.

"Good enough. Fucking Big Jack." Then Bobby didn't say anything for a few seconds.

I used the silence to try to absorb the fact that I was going to find a hooker for my dying father. The few seconds weren't nearly enough. I had the feeling I was going to need a few years.

Then Bobby's voice roared from my phone, "Your dad is fucking awesome. I am so in on this. Beats the shit out of bringing flowers. Jack wants a piece, let's tear him off some chonch."

"Delicately put, Bobby."

"I am excited about this. I mean, this is fucking awesome. Let's do this." Bobby was positively giddy about the whole idea.

"You free tonight?"

"I'm supposed to be irrigating, but I can get Buck Buck to change the water. He owes me a favor."

"Meet me at the house. We'll walk over to Morales," I said.

As I shoved down my second Pine Market tamale, I heard Bobby's Ranchero pull into the driveway. I left my plate on the table and was out the door. I walked through the front gate as Bobby was getting out, beer in hand.

The sight of Bobby's car made me laugh. The same car he drove in high school. A late-seventies Ford Ranchero. Orange with a red and yellow racing stripe that had come stock when the car was new. I wish I could say that Bobby keeping such an ugly car cherry was a testament to something, but I can't and I won't. Even when we were young, it was sad how much he loved that car.

The smile on Bobby's face said it all. It had probably been there since our conversation a couple hours before.

We shook hands. "Thanks, Bobby," I said, gripping his shoulder in a manly alternative to a hug.

"No, thank *you*. I am honored. That I can do something this awesome. Seriously. For Jack. It's awesome."

I was starting to worry. I looked Bobby square in the eyes. "I don't want anybody to know what we're doing. Pop doesn't usually give a shit what other people think, but this might be an exception. You know that, right, Bobby? Nobody else is ever going to hear about this, okay?"

"Of course." Bobby smiled. "You know what they say— what happens in El Centro stays in El Centro."

"I mean it. You can't tell anyone."

Bobby's face got serious. That's how you knew Bobby was serious. He made his serious face. "I'm not a fucking idiot. You think I don't know that? This is between you, me, Jack, and—what's the name of the *señorita?*"

"Yolanda."

"Between you, me, Jack, and Yolanda. Nobody else'll ever know." Bobby held up his hand as if swearing an oath. "You got a plan of some kind?"

I shook my head. It hadn't even occurred to me. A plan would've probably been a good idea. "Don't know. Play it by ear. Make it up as we go?"

Bobby nodded. "Kinda what I figured. How hard could it be to find one Mexican woman in a city of a million people? We know her first name and everything. Piece of cake."

Bobby and I started walking down the driveway toward the bar across the street. Bobby gave me a light shove. "What was it you used to say? Slapdash, but not half-ass, right?"

"That's the Veeder promise."

We walked across the road onto the dirt patch that passed for a parking lot next to Morales Bar. Ford, Chevy, and Dodge pickups parked wherever there was room with no visible sense of order. Morales Bar was a field-worker bar with no sign, just a couple of neon *Cerveza* lights in the darkened windows. The Ash Canal ran along the back where an old corral had been transformed into a cockfighting arena, then abandoned entirely. Lettuce fields were on one side with a few salt cedars lining the road on the other. Once a windbreak, now their acid needles rusted out the abandoned cars below them.

Bobby and I kicked past a few stray chickens that had been trying to catch some shut-eye by the front door. I reached for the handle, but Bobby held the door.

Bobby said, "I forgot to tell you. Last time I was here, there was some trouble."

"Trouble?" I asked, not really wanting to know. My hand dropped from the door handle.

"A smidge." Bobby shrugged.

"How long ago?"

"While. I ain't been back. Maybe like three, four years."

"That's a long time. You really think anybody'd remember or care?"

"It was a lot of trouble." Bobby looked like a seven-year-old who just got caught stealing candy. "I ain't pussin' out. I'm still going in. Just thought it fair you knew is all."

Bobby reached past me and opened the door, careful not to pull the rickety piece of plywood off its hinges.

It was just as hot inside, except the air was stagnant, dead, and smoky. The whole place smelled like a hangover—alcohol sweat, cigarette ash, and stale beer.

In a movie the music might have stopped and everyone might have stared us down. The six-foot-four longhair and the Mexicanish dude with a white pompadour walking into the desert hard bar. Luckily this was real life, and in a real bar people were there to drink and not give a rat's ass who came in. We didn't warrant a single glance. There is something to be said for the aggressive indifference of the plastered and soon to be plastered.

There wasn't a single woman in the place. Not even a slightly effeminate guy prettying up a barstool in the corner. A couple dozen Mexicans were scattered at tables, mud still on their boots, playing cards and drinking. They yelled and laughed over the *banda* tune that blared on the jukebox. There were a few white faces in the back keeping to themselves, most likely because they were underage. They looked like high school kids in their letterman jackets and store haircuts. Probably brothers or even sons of the guys I used to come here with in high school. Some traditions never die.

Bobby found a table just to the side of the vacant pool table. He grabbed a seat against the wall, wiping off whatever was on the table with a sweep of his forearm. He gave me a nod, holding up two fingers, and then ducked his head into his chin in a ridiculous effort to look inconspicuous.

The one face I did recognize was Mr. Morales. I probably looked completely different. He looked exactly the same. A short, powerful man with massive forearms and a barrel chest, Mr. Morales was built like a Pemex oil drum. A bushy mustache and deep crevices made up the terrain of his face. I'd never once seen him smile. But I'd also never seen him angry. A good neighbor, I'd known him since I was a kid. I remember walking across the street, and for a quarter plus the deposit, I would buy a bottle of 7-Up. Mr. Morales would put salt on the rim of the bottle, a detail I could only appreciate in hindsight.

Morales Bar didn't have beer on tap. Mr. Morales would buy cases of beer in Mexicali and then sell them by the bottle. When you have to piss in a hole out back, why bother with a liquor license.

"What'll it be, Jimmy?" Mr. Morales said, as if I had been in just the other night rather than twelve years ago. He pulled a weathered half of a cigar out of the breast pocket of his checkered short-sleeve shirt and lit it. Not the only bar in California that you can smoke in, but probably the only one that doesn't know it's against the law.

"Four beers. *Gracias*, sir."

He dug his bare hands deep into the ice bucket behind the bar. "How's Big Jack doing?"

"Could be better. You know."

Mr. Morales set four wet beers on the counter, his dark arms burned red from the ice water. "Jack's a tough son of a bitch, don't you worry. Never seen him lose a fight in the fifty years I've known him. A few he didn't win maybe, but he never lost. Anyone kick cancer's ass, it's him. You need anything, you ask."

I nodded, having no interest in getting further into the conversation. If only the optimism of an old Mexican could cure cancer.

I held up a ten. Mr. Morales shook it off. "It's good you came back down."

He squinted past me, spotting Bobby against the wall. Bobby caught Mr. Morales's eye line and quickly looked in the opposite direction at nothing. Mr. Morales cursed softly to himself in Spanish, and then he looked at me with his stern stare. "You tell that Maves boy the only reason I'm letting him in here is because he's with you. Remind him I got a shotgun behind the bar."

"Bobby said there had been some trouble."

"That what he said?"

"Three, four years ago though. That's a long time."

"Uh-huh."

"Maybe he's changed. People change. I've changed."

"I doubt it," he replied.

I nodded and then began to ask whether he was talking about Bobby or me or both of us. But Mr. Morales was already on his way to the other end of the bar, getting a couple of beers for one of the letterman jackets.

I brought the four beers over to Bobby, two in each hand. Bobby finished leveling the table with a folded napkin. He gave the table a shake, satisfied with its stability, and reached out, grabbing his two beers. He quickly drained half of one by the time I sat down.

"Mr. Morales still seems a little miffed at you," I said. "What happened?"

"Things just got a little out of hand, that's all," Bobby said. "You remember Tomás?"

I nodded. "Tomás Morales? Mr. Morales's grandson? Yeah. Last time I saw him he was maybe fourteen. He's like four, five years younger, but we hung out a lot. The only two out here. Good kid. You get in a fight with him?"

"No. I was trying to change the subject." Bobby smiled. "Trying to get back to business. We're here for the dying father whore hunt, remember?"

"Very tactful, Bobby. What does Tomás got to do with it?"

"Tomás is in his twenties now. Obviously. That's how time works," Bobby said. "Anyway, he seems to have built a bit of a border business. Last time I was here, he was the guy who brought the girls from Chicali. Girls like Yolanda. Bar girls, strippers, hookers—whatever, all the same. And there you have it. Saturday night entertainment. Six ladies doling out blowjobs in the shadows of the walkway to the shitter. It turns a sandwich into a banquet."

"Are you telling me what happened to you, or are we discussing Yolanda?"

"I'm getting to it. Word is Tomás has moved up. Bigger, better, illegaller. His hand in a lot of *galleta potes*. That's 'cookie jars' to you."

"You and Tomás have some beef?"

"Don't think so. Maybe. Probably not. Who knows? I drink a lot."

"So?"

"So. When there's booze, Mexicans, and hookers, trouble is whistling around the corner. Not some maybe or outside chance, but probably definitely something's going to happen. On the nights it's too hot to fuck, it's never too hot to fight.

"Maybe some lonely *campesino* gets drunk enough to fall in love, sees *el pocho cabrón* getting friendly with his future bride he met a half hour before. Maybe a lettuce knife makes its way out of a boot, then maybe a pool cue gets broken over a head and maybe it's no longer fun and it's six against one and the only way you see of getting out alive is to forget about looking stylish and get creative."

"That can't be good."

"I accidentally lit Mr. Morales's pool table on fire."

"Accidentally? How does that even happen?"

Bobby shrugged, almost embarrassed. "I had a bottle of 151 in my hand. Broke it over a guy's head. He must've been smoking, 'cause 'Flame on!' The splash of the alcohol soaked into the felt. Fire-face fell onto the alcohol-soaked table. Whoosh. The place filled with smoke. It happened pretty fast."

Bobby took a big pull, polishing off bottle number one. "Mr. Morales can't really blame me. It was self-defense. I sent him money for the table, but he probably took a ton of shit from the law. They never came out to my hut, so I know he didn't mention my name."

"You ever thank Mr. Morales for that?"

"I was afraid he'd shoot me. He keeps a shotgun behind the bar, you know?"

"Yeah, he told me to remind you."

"No rock salt load either. Morales don't fuck around." He nodded seriously, as if he was giving me sage advice.

We sat drinking our beers. I lit a cigarette and looked at the corrugated tin ceiling above the pool table. Sure enough, a black Rorschach scarred the metal.

Bobby belched, staring at his empty beer bottle. "So, what I was getting at is, we got to talk to Tomás. Don't know if he still brings girls, but he's connected. He'd know where the ladies come from. Mr. Morales don't know where the girls come from, but he knows where Tomás is, right?"

I nodded. "Okay, here's what you do. Go apologize to Mr. Morales, and then make up some story and see if you can find out where Tomás is."

"Why me? You go ask him."

"He ain't going to shoot you. Least not with me here. Take the chance to square it. Talk to him. Make it right, and then find out about Tomás while you're talking."

Bobby stared at me, trying to think of a good reason not to. Failing, he stood up.

"And grab a couple more beers." I sat back in my chair smiling, sticking my pinkie out as I drained the last of my beer.

Bobby walked to the bar. I lit a cigarette and watched. Bobby stood at one end, head down, waiting for Mr. Morales. He made no motion to call him over, allowing Mr. Morales to take his time.

I hadn't thought about Tomás Morales in years. We had lost touch, but there was a period of five or six years when we were kids that he was like a little brother. His grandfather raised him. But with Mr. Morales running the bar, Tomás mostly played outside. When I wasn't doing work for Pop, I'd go across the street and hang out with him. Play catch, help him make a ramp for his bike, that kind of thing. I taught him how to play chess and poker, but we stopped playing when he started embarrassing me.

He hadn't been your average kid. A Mexican nerd wasn't that common in the Imperial Valley. When he was eight or nine, if you asked him what he wanted to be when he grew up, he would've said a businessman. He even carried an old briefcase around. I don't know where he found it, but he carried it everywhere. Home and school and church, always at his side. All he had in it was an old copy of the *Wall Street Journal* that someone had left at the bar, but it represented his dreams. The same way as when I painted my bike to look like Evel Knievel's.

I did my best to keep an eye on Tomás, knowing that the other kids picked on him. An eight-year-old with a brief-case better be prepared to catch some shit. I had gotten him out of some trouble here and there, but we went to different schools. He wasn't much of a fighter, so he did the only thing he could. He learned how to take a beating. That can be as important a skill as learning to fight.

Eventually, Mr. Morales sauntered to Bobby's end of the bar. Mr. Morales said nothing. Bobby did some talking. Mr. Morales did some nodding, still silent. Bobby did some more talking, annotating his story with broad hand movements. Mr. Morales only nodded. Eventually, Bobby and Mr. Morales shook hands. Then, Bobby motioned for Mr. Morales to lean in. He whispered conspiratorially in his ear. Mr. Morales's eyebrows rose more than once.

At one point, Bobby pointed back at me, and Mr. Morales nodded. Mr. Morales said a few words, put another two beers on the counter, and walked back to the other end of the bar. Bobby put five dollars on the counter and walked back to our table with the beers. He stood over the table, smiling. I reached for my beer, but Bobby shook his head and motioned to the door.

"Road beers. We're going to Mexicali."

FIVE

The history of Southern California is the history of water rights. And the residents of the Imperial Valley know it. When you live and farm in the desert and get your water from the longest man-made canal in the U.S., you don't need to be reminded of the importance of water. Many of the older farmers moved from the Owens Valley after the city stole their water. Back then, they only had guns to protect their land. Now, they had lawyers. And guns. Still the feeling remained among the farmers that it was only a matter of time before the city made a grab for its water. The city had the voice and votes. Historically, the city always won. But until they outlawed swimming pools in San Diego and LA, they could get their water somewhere else. Farming is hard enough that you have to deal with that kind of bullshit.

To create an agricultural community in the middle of the desert, all of the fields in the Imperial Valley are irrigated by a series of canals from water that comes from the Colorado River forty miles away. To the disdain of the cities on the coast, the Imperial Valley has the California rights to the Colorado River water, and the district and subsequently the farmers are allotted a certain amount of acre feet at a reasonable rate based on acreage. The Colorado dumps into the All-American Canal, which then delivers the flow into secondary canals, then down to the individual ditches that line the fields.

When it is time to irrigate one of the fields, the farmer orders the water from the IID, the Imperial Irrigation District. They fill the ditch, and then the irrigator lets it onto the field. However, you can't let the water onto the field all at once. You'd immediately lose the water level, and the furthest part of the field wouldn't get any water. So, the ditch has a number of gates that must be opened a few at a time. A night of irrigating consists of opening and closing gates every two or three hours, depending on the lengths of the rows. At its best, it's boring as hell. But when something goes wrong, it's just hell. And something always goes wrong—a gate gets busted or stuck, overflow, or the water spreads to another row. It could often be a night of muddy, frustrating work made worse by lack of sleep. Because the water has to be changed every couple of hours, you can't sleep more than an hour and a half, and you can't go too far away. What you can do is get someone to do it for you. Which is what Bobby did.

Before going down to Mexicali, Bobby decided to check and make sure our old high school buddy, Buck Buck, did like he said and was out irrigating Bobby's alfalfa.

"Why don't you just call him?" I asked.

"If I call him and he's not there, he'll just lie and say he is. Don't matter that I'll find out later. Buck Buck's like a kid—he don't know consequences," Bobby said.

It was fine with me. I was in no hurry to be in Mexicali. I didn't feel the invulnerability that I once had in high school. Back then, we'd go down to Mexicali almost every weekend and get in trouble. I was older now, wiser, so less likely to get in trouble, but more wary of the trouble that I might find. Mexicali made me nervous.

I looked to the south at the orange glow of the city. We were miles away, but the bug-light-yellow border lights were brighter than the moon.

"What did you say to Mr. Morales?" I asked.

Bobby smiled. "I thanked him for keeping my name out of any police report and apologized for the fire and such. Told him I'd bring him some new cues next time I was in. A peace offering. Never hurts to pay double on a debt a person didn't want to loan you in the first place."

"Then you asked about Tomás?"

"He said he hadn't seen him in a while. That he spends more time on the other side. I felt kind of weird asking to talk to him 'cause I don't really know him so good. But I said that I remembered that he used to bring the girls up and does he still do that."

"What'd he say?" I was really holding up my end of this conversation.

"He said yeah, he still brokers the girls, but now he has one of his boys bring 'em. Apparently Tomás has got employees. Didn't sound like Morales liked the new dude, called him a punk. Got the feeling there's some bad blood between Mr. Morales and Tomás, but you can't get nothing from that face."

"Then he gave you his address?"

"Do I look retarded? Don't answer that. I was undercover, remember? Had to be subtle. Have a plausible story," Bobby said. "What I told him was that you hadn't been laid in five years, and I was worried that you were edging toward queer. Mr. Morales agreed with my assessment, saying something about your long hair. We both agreed it was pretty gayish. He gave it some thought. And seeing that the situation was desperate, he told me where Tomás holds court. Didn't know if he'd be there or not. But if he is, he said we go there, Tomás should be able to find you a *señorita*, set you back on the path to Mantown. Or away from Mantown, I guess. One of those."

"You're kidding, right? You didn't say all that."

But Bobby just laughed.

Bobby pulled his Ranchero onto the shoulder. My side was so close to the ditch bank that I had to slide across the bench seat and get out on the driver's side. Bobby reached into a cooler in the truck bed and pulled out a six-pack of Coors Light tall boys. He didn't allow smoking in the Ranchero, so I lit a smoke to get my nicotine fix.

There was a small fire a few yards away, and two figures huddled around it. It was ninety-something degrees. What kind of idiots build a fire?

These kind of idiots. Buck Buck and his brother Snout had a gopher turning on a makeshift spit. They sat on the ground in nothing but boxers and rubber boots, facing the fire. They looked up as we approached, their crooked smiles screaming booze. Bobby handed Snout the six.

Buck Buck shrugged. "You making sure we're here?"

Bobby ignored him and turned to me. "You remember Buck Buck and Snout, right?"

Everyone I went to high school with, I also went to grammar school with. It was hard to forget anyone you'd known that long. In the short time I'd been back, I felt like I recognized every face on the street. Like I never left. But I did leave. I knew the faces and the names, but I didn't know the people anymore.

Buck Buck and Snout Buckley. Buck Buck was a year ahead of me, Snout a year behind. They came from a good farming family and appeared to have accepted their fate with ease. They looked like I remembered them only more so, thirty pounds apiece mostly around the midsection.

It was obvious that they spent their lives outdoors, their skin tan to leather. Buck Buck had always been the leader of the two. He smiled more than he should, often to the point of pissing people off. And Snout—well, he didn't get the name because he had big ears. Although he also had big ears. But his nose was glorious, starting at the middle of his forehead and making its way to his upper lip. His face was aging into his nose well, giving him a stately appearance. He could be on a nickel.

"Hey, Jimmy," they said in unison. They turned back to the gopher.

"You're going to burn it, dumbshit," Snout yelled at Buck Buck, reaching for the spit. "Let me do it."

Buck Buck slapped the back of his hand like an Italian mother.

Bobby squinted at the field. "Anything I should know about?"

"You got a low spot on that southeast corner. It's either going to flood or not get water," Buck Buck answered, concentrating on the slow-turning rodent.

"Yeah. Scrap land. Thirty-five good acres and five crap. Got to eventually get it retiled, leveled. Thanks for doing this. I owe you."

"No, you don't." Buck Buck smiled. "I'm baling hay in a couple of nights, and it just so happens I need a couple of strong, young men like yourselves."

Bobby looked the question at me. I nodded. I've always liked hard work.

"Just give me a holler and we'll be there," Bobby answered.

Snout leaned into the fire, trying to smell the singed gopher. He looked up. "You want some? I think it's done."

I answered, walking back to the Ranchero. "That's okay. I had gopher for lunch."

"You go down to Mexicali much?" I asked as we neared Calexico. The millions of stars in the sky dissolved in the artificial glow of Mexicali.

"After the divorce, I was down here all the time. Too much, probably. Bad as I was at being a husband and father, I missed it when they were gone. I'm not so good at change. Guy like me, take away the wife and kids, and I'm trouble on a stick."

"And lately?"

"Maybe once a month. When I'm in the mood for Chinese or I need to get something reupholstered, you know. Not so much for the drinking and ladies." Bobby smiled as if that wasn't the whole truth.

But it was no joke that Mexicali had some of the best Chinese restaurants. La Chinesca, Mexicali's Chinatown, was one of the largest in Latin America, and the fusion complemented the cuisine. Shark fin tacos and chorizo chow mein.

"Mexicali the same as I remember?"

"I don't know how you remember it, but the answer is no. Don't you read the papers? Mexico is all fucked up. Got to flip to the back pages. That's where they put news about Mexico. It's way worse. It's always been a shithole, right? But in a totally different way. Maybe we didn't notice it, but with drugs and illegals and the *maquiladoras*—them's the factories along the border."

"Yeah, I know. They were here when I left," I said.

Bobby continued. "They had that 'Operation Gatekeeper' up in SD. Alls it did was move the shit east. Move it into the desert. Made it more dangerouser for the illegals. But shit, San Diego got the votes, right? They're happy 'cause the wetbacks ain't a problem no more. Same time, we're scraping bodies off the hardpack. People can be fucking dicks. Their idea of taking out the garbage is probably dumping their trash on their neighbor's lawn and congratulating themselves for a job well done.

"It's getting nastier. Too many people. They got a slum on the edge of town that looks like how I imagine parts of India look. Hell, there's gangs in Calexico. Not like we remember. Not a bunch of pachucos in hairnets and that top button. But real, honest to God, Crip/Blood, Mexican Mafia gangs. With guns and shit. You can see their tags all over the place. It ain't Tijuana bad, but it could get there."

A green Border Patrol SUV passed us, followed closely by a white Homeland Security SUV. We had entered Calexico and drove past the edge of town with all the box stores and a surprising amount of freshly built industrial parks.

The lights of the border crossing approached. It had definitely changed. Now a NAFTA route, there were six lanes instead of two, and it looked more high-tech. More lights, newer building. Trucks lined both sides of the road waiting to change countries.

Bobby turned off the main road before the border crossing. He drove up Anza, then down First, and found a place to park in front of a *mercado* that looked like it specialized in creepy dolls and Tupperware.

"We're walking?" I said, suddenly aware that I was going to have to get out of the car.

"You don't take a car this cherry that far south," Bobby responded, not kidding.

"How far is it?"

"Relax. Cachanilla's, that's the place, is only a few blocks from the tunnel. Less than a hundred yards. Easier to walk. Faster getting out."

I nodded, reaching for the door handle.

Bobby grabbed my arm, stopping me. "Where you going? You ain't ready. Give me your wallet."

"No. What for?"

"Just give it to me," Bobby said, reaching over insistently.

I rolled my eyes, but took my wallet out of my back pocket and handed it to him.

"Put your passport in your boot. On the bottom, under your sock."

After we left Morales Bar, I had stopped by my house and grabbed my passport. Times had changed. You couldn't just walk across without ID anymore. Scratch that. You could still get into Mexico, but you couldn't get back into the U.S. without a passport.

"In my boot? Isn't that a little paranoid?"

"We're going to a third-world country to find a hooker. We ain't going to be looking in churches and museums. It's better to be safe than stupid."

I took off my boot and tossed my passport in it, and then I put the boot back on. As I laced it up, I watched Bobby pull the cash from my wallet and stuff it in his pocket. "We'll leave the credit cards here."

"They're maxed anyway. Can I at least have some of my own money? I promise not to spend it all on candy."

Bobby reached into his pocket and pulled out my wad of bills. He picked out a twenty and gave it to me.

"Very generous."

"You still carry a knife?"

I nodded. Part of the country boy in me. I'd carried one since I was a kid. I felt naked without a knife in my pocket.

"Let's see it," Bobby said.

"I really doubt that I'm going to get in a knife fight." I pulled out the small, two-inch folding Buck knife from the front pocket of my jeans.

Bobby let out a snort. "I don't want to get all Crocodile Dundee on you, but that's for cleaning your fingernails."

He reached past me and unlocked his glove compartment. After he tossed my wallet inside, he rummaged around the maps, tools, and pencils. He found a watermelon knife, a thin, six-inch, folding pig-sticker. When open, a watermelon knife is like a small, foot-long sword. I took the knife and put it in my sock, wedged tightly against the inside of my boot. It gave me no comfort, just more unease.

Bobby smiled. "Now we're prepared."

SIX

All the fun stuff is in Mexico. And when you live on the border, it's always tempting. Mexico has a lenient drinking age and booze aplenty. Drugs are everywhere. Women are available and willing. And for the kids, firecrackers, switchblades, and Roman candles are abundant. Hell, you can buy Cuban cigars. You can go to a bullfight, a dog fight, or a cock fight if that's your pleasure. What is fun and illegal in the U.S., Mexico gladly offers in a semi-legal, slightly dangerous way. If the law looks the other way, then is it really illegal?

Mexicali is a fairly normal city in the day. A great place to shop, grab a bite to eat, and see the sights. It could be trouble, but it didn't have to be. Nighttime was a different story. Most of the activity was a varied form of trouble. In high school, we used to call twenty-dollar bills "Get Out of Jail Free" cards.

I could vividly remember the last time I was in Mexicali. Not coincidentally the closest time I had ever come to being thrown in a Mexican jail. I was in the back of the police car in handcuffs and everything. Of course, I hadn't done anything. I had been there to rent a tuxedo for prom. The "crime" I committed was running a stop sign that didn't exist. The real crime was that I didn't have any money on me.

I don't blame the Mexican cops. They're underpaid and underappreciated, so they built the *mordida* system into the economy. *La mordida* means "the little bite," and that's usually all it was. The real mistake I had made was getting angry. Drunk, I would've been meek. But sober, I was self-righteous. As I refused to pay for a crime I didn't commit, they knew they had me.

When I realized my steadfast protest was only going to get me pain and more pain, I gave in. All in all, it had ended up being reasonable. They took my Maglite, an old *Playboy* (Mensa edition), my Leatherman, and a Billy Joel CD that some girl had left in my car. Only the Leatherman pissed me off. It had been a gift from Pop.

Back then Mexicali was fun and scary and dangerous and welcoming. Now, it just felt scary and dangerous. I reminded myself that it was a city like any other and that most of its residents were just regular people. It didn't help. I was glad Bobby was with me.

Bobby and I walked down the steps of the tunnel that crossed the border. Half the dim fluorescents were out, and the shadows implied movement. There were a few businesses in the underground no man's land, but only the magazine stand was open. At the end of the long tunnel was a turnstile, the identical design used at the exit of amusement parks. Once you leave the U.S. into Mexico, you can't return the same way. It's just like leaving the fun park and emerging in the harsh reality of the parking lot.

A fat Mexican border agent barely looked up from his skin mag. A small wall-mounted fan made his mustache dance on his upper lip. Sweat poured from his face and over the thick flesh that spilled over his too-tight collar. He didn't ask to look at any paperwork. He didn't ask us where we were from. He didn't say a single thing. Not a word. I'll hand it to Mexico. It was not a country that lived in fear of the people who crossed over its borders. Maybe they felt like they had nothing to lose.

We walked through the turnstiles and Bobby and I were in Mexico.

Walking over the border can elicit culture shock for people whose Mexican excursions have been limited to getting off the plane in Cancún or Puerto Vallarta. For most tourists, the only concern is whether or not the cab driver overcharged for the ride to the all-inclusive resort. Walking into Mexicali, there weren't any welcome signs. No *bienvenido*. No tourist board. Just a crumbling set of concrete steps that led you out of a tunnel and onto the bustle of Avenida Francisco Madero.

The air felt different—thicker and dustier with a hint of burnt meat. It might have been in my head, but the difference was acute. We'd walked fifty yards, but it may as well have been fifty miles. I immediately wanted to be back on American soil.

As we climbed the steps, I watched the buildings of Mexicali rise in my field of vision. Not hindered by building codes or common sense, the architecture was a hodgepodge of cinder block, concrete, link fence, and corrugated tin. All covered in slapped-on stucco. Odd angles jutted from roofs made from the accumulation of makeshift repairs. Nothing looked new. Every surface appeared weathered and worn. Wires crisscrossed overhead, cutting the hazy night sky into an irregular grid.

The moment Bobby and I reached the street, we were mobbed by a half dozen *chicle* kids. Dirty faces and sad eyes.

Bobby reached into his pocket and without looking threw a handful of change against the nearest wall. The kids bolted for the coins, their little fingers scraping at the silver, then the pennies.

"Can't stand them kids' faces. And I ain't chewed gum since Little League," Bobby said, almost to himself.

On Avenida Madero, we made our way along the narrow sidewalk, squeezing between *turista* stands and the dense crowd. Clothes, shoes, candles, CDs, DVDs, hats, food, postcards, magazines, books, rosaries, pornography. You name it, you could buy it on the street.

More than once I felt a hand on my back pocket. Either there were a lot of fresh Mexicans, or I was disappointing a whole mess of pickpockets.

I accidentally made eye contact with a young guy leaning against a wall. He gave me his curt sales pitch in heavily accented English. "Hookers? Cocaine?" I continued walking.

Bobby was right. The bar was close, but also closed. We stood in front of a pair of doors with heavy chain wrapped around the handles. Next to the door, painted on the wall in swooping red on green letters, was the name of the place. Cachanilla's. And beneath it, block letters stated, "Bar and Girls—Floor Show" in English.

"Well, shit," Bobby said, looking at his watch. "Probably don't open 'til ten. We got shy of two hours to blow."

"We could come back another night," I said, trying not to sound as anxious as I felt.

"Relax, Jimmy. You need to find your sea legs. We ain't looking for trouble, means we ain't going to find any."

"When has that ever been the case?"

"Always a first time." Bobby smiled.

"It's been a while. When we were younger…"

Bobby interrupted. "Yeah, yeah, yeah. Alls you need is a couple of drinks in you. Help knock some of the sand out of your vagina."

"I don't know if I belong here anymore," I said, but Bobby hadn't heard me. He was already down the street. I quick-stepped to catch up. A couple of drinks might do me good.

Bobby opened a door that I hadn't seen. What appeared to be a wall covered with posters was actually a door with a small *Abierto* sign hidden in plain sight. Below it a handwritten scrawl read, "*Se prohibe la entrada a mujeres, uniformados e integrantes de las fuerzas armadas.*" Loosely translated, "No women, soldiers, or anyone in a uniform." I followed Bobby into the darkness of the bar.

The dark hallway opened into a dark room lit by neon beer signs and some Christmas lights that lined the ceiling, walls, and half the bar. An old man played guitar quietly in the corner. Thankfully, he didn't stop playing when we walked in. There were a dozen customers, all but two of them over sixty. Those two sat in the far corner dressed in Mexican cowboy gear: hats, jeans, rhinestone snap cowboy shirts, and matching boots. One in red boots, the other green. They both gave me the stink-eye, or so my paranoia told me. Bobby either didn't notice, which I doubted, or chose to ignore them. I felt a cold drip from my armpit land on the skin over my ribs. I could've blamed the heat. It was stifling in the dark room, but I knew it was more than that.

Bobby smiled broadly at the approaching bartender. "*Hola! Qué onda! Cuatro cervezas y dos tequilas, por favor.*"

"*Cuatro? Más vienen?*" said the bartender, looking behind us for more people.

"*No. Tenemos sed,*" Bobby said, laughing and turning to me. "Really thirsty."

"*Dólars o pesos?*"

"American dollarinos," Bobby said too loudly. "*Cuanto?*"

As the bartender loaded up the bar with our four beers and two shots of tequila, he added in his head. "*Diez.*"

Bobby turned to me, taking my money out of his front pocket. "Ten bucks. I bet this would cost forty in LA. Another reason to love Chicali." He dropped fifteen on the bar, grabbed the four beers, and nodded for me to grab the shots.

"*Gracias,*" I said more meekly than I meant to.

Bobby found a table. We sat with our backs to the wall, facing the relative darkness of the bar. Bobby took one of the shot glasses and tapped mine. We downed them together. It tasted like it had been made that morning, but the burning felt good. I washed down the shot with half my beer. I started to feel more relaxed. In two hours, I was going to feel right at home, if I could feel at all.

In an effort to ease my mind, Bobby took control of the conversation. I concentrated on drinking and smoking. He talked work and farming and his experiment with marriage and the subsequent divorce. He mentioned Griselda, the woman he was currently seeing, but stopped short. "It's good. She's cool. Don't want to jinx it." Finally, he moved on to his kids. It made me realize how much of a child I was and how little responsibility I had. Is it better to have responsibility and fail or to choose to remain irresponsible?

"Stacy is in Riverside," Bobby told me. Stacy was his daughter. She was probably around five by now. "With her mom. And probably some dude who's not me."

"What about Julie?" I asked. That was Bobby's other daughter, born when we were still in high school. A mistake he hadn't even known he had made until years later. Probably for the best since it kept him from doing the wrong thing by doing the right thing.

"Still in Twentynine Palms. Becky's with some jarhead stationed there," Bobby said.

"You see them much?"

"Never. Once, twice a year." He drank down a whole bottle and started another one. "I send 'em money, birthday presents, Christmas presents, Valentine cards, like that. Make sure I know how old they are, what grade they're in. I'd say I miss 'em, but hell, I don't know 'em really. They're good kids, I think. And their mothers are good mothers. I know that. Probably better for them they're not around a guy like me."

"A guy like you? What's that?"

He ignored my question, continuing. "I like getting the Father's Day cards, I'll tell you."

He took a look down the neck of his bottle. "I know it sounds cliché, but you ever feel like you were born in the wrong time? I should've been born in Conan's time."

"Wait, what? You mean Conan the Barbarian?"

He turned to me, no smile. "Yeah. I'd've been a good barbarian."

"You know, Conan isn't real. He's a fictional character."

Bobby gave me his best *shut up* look. "Yeah, Jimmy. I ain't a dumbass. I went to college, too. I also know that it's impossible to be born in a different time. Why you got to ruin it? Why you got to mess up my barbarian fantasy thing? Why you got to be the guy sitting in the back of the movie theater when the monster shows up, you say, 'That would never happen?'"

"Sorry, man." I had touched a bit of a nerve about his kids, and I should have just let him change the subject. Bobby sat and brooded, his eyebrows suggesting that he was working out something in his head.

"Fuck this," Bobby shouted, smiling his crazy smile and slamming his hands against the table. I wasn't ready for it, and my waiting beer crashed to the floor. Loudly. Shattered glass and foaming brew. At that moment it was the loudest sound I had ever heard.

The old man stopped playing guitar. Everyone stopped talking. The bartender walked to the edge of the bar, one hand out of sight. He said, "*Esta bien todo?*"

Bobby got to his knees and began picking up pieces of broken glass. "*Esta bien. Lo siento. Un accidente.*"

The bartender slowly raised his hand and grabbed a rag off the bar. I reached for it. "I'll do it. Let me clean it up."

He stared at me blankly.

Bobby translated for me. "*Permitalo. Limpiaremos esto arriba.*"

The bartender shrugged and tossed me the gray, wet rag. It smelled like vomit, but I wasn't worried about the quality of my cleaning job. It was the principle. We were their guests.

The bartender pulled a plastic two-gallon bucket from behind the bar and set it next to Bobby. He dropped his handful of glass shards into it. Bobby reached into his pocket, pulled out one of my twenties, and handed it to the bartender. "*Cuatro cervezas más, por favor. Y uno para usted.*" The bartender took it and walked back behind the bar to get our drinks.

While wringing some beer into the bucket, I caught Red Boots and Green Boots out of the corner of my eye. They were staring at me. One turned to the other, nodding his head toward me and saying something. The other one laughed and nodded.

That couldn't be good.

An hour, five beers, and a couple of shots later, I was beyond caring. It felt good to overdo it. I wasn't thinking about Pop, which had been dominating my thoughts. I was no longer uncomfortable in Mexicali, joking with the bartender like I was a regular. He acted like he liked us because Bobby was throwing my money around, but that was good enough for me. When he gave us a shot on the house, I teared up.

I stood uneasily and slowly made my way to the bathroom in back. It was my fourth trip, so I was familiar with the route through the dark hallway. I congratulated myself on only bumping into two chairs and the edge of the bar on my not-so-straight way.

Thinking the bathroom was empty, I kicked open the door with too much force and walked in. The cowboy with the red boots was standing over the toilet. He gave me a surly look over his shoulder and went back to his business.

"Sorry," I said, embarrassed, and waited.

With just a sink and a seatless toilet, the bathroom was surprisingly big. Because of all the space, it was easy for me to stay the maximum distance from Red Boots. I examined the fixtures on the sink and gave him ample personal space. I thought about waiting at the bar, but we were grown-ups and I had to piss.

Finished, Red Boots didn't bother to flush the toilet. He just walked to the door, bypassing the sink. I was in too much bladder distress to lecture him on hygiene. I hurried past him to the toilet and unzipped my pants. And just stood there. Even though I felt like I was going to burst, nothing came out. Fucking stage fright. I closed my eyes and waited for Red Boots to leave, thinking of waterfalls, the ocean, and dripping water.

I heard the door close behind me. My body relaxed. I took a deep breath and counted to ten. On four, I was pissing. But then, instead of the silence that should have been in the room, I heard footsteps. Bootsteps, to be precise. I half-turned my head, trying to maintain my drunken aim. Red Boots and Green Boots stood with their backs to the closed door.

In the half second that my brain had to register and assess the situation, I couldn't imagine a more defenseless position. While Green Boots hovered near the door, Red Boots took small steps toward me, malice in his crooked smile.

I did the only thing that I could think of. I took the offensive, turning quickly and pissing all over Red Boots's red boots. He jumped back, but I moved forward, aiming to get as much urine on him as I could. If he would have had a chance to collect his thoughts, he would have punched me in the face. But when you're dodging piss, that pretty much consumes the mind. I even roped the stream toward Green Boots, forcing him to do a little dance. I felt like an Old West gunfighter.

"Come on," I yelled, my drunken bravado making me invulnerable. I was actually having fun, laughing boisterously.

Then my stream began to weaken. I used whatever muscles I could to force more out of me, but it slowly reduced to a dribble and then drained to nothing. And I was left standing with my dick in my hand and two pissed-off and pissed-on Mexican cowboys staring at me with murder in their eyes. In retrospect it was a pretty funny image, but at the time I couldn't see the humor.

I probably should have rushed toward the door. But if I was going to get in a fight, my first priority was to get my pants buttoned up. It's kind of an unwritten rule in street fighting not to have your penis exposed. I had the first couple of buttons done when Red Boots threw a haymaker that caught most of my shoulder and some of my jaw. I fell backward, the back of my legs hitting the toilet behind me. Tripping over the bowl, my head hit the wall and my body got pinned awkwardly between the toilet and the wall. My legs were draped over the bowl, one arm underneath me and the other sticking straight up.

I clawed at the side of the toilet, my eyes on the approaching Red Boots. Panic started to overtake me. I struggled harder, unintentionally wedging myself further into the tight space. My only consolation was that I had just seen Red Boots take a leak. At least he wasn't going to piss on me. Only beat the shit out of me.

Sure enough, he kicked me. The point of his boot connected with the back of my thigh. My own piss sprinkled my face, droplets from the top of his boots. The irony of it all.

"*Dinero, pendejo,*" he said, thoughtful enough to use Spanish that even I could understand.

"Fuck you," I replied, extending him the same courtesy.

He pulled a big folding knife from his back pocket and opened it slowly. He showed me both sides of the blade. It was a well-used knife stained with black splotches. I could even smell the faint odor of fish coming off it. It would have been bad enough if it was clean.

"Okay," I said, holding up my hands and pointing to my front pocket. "My money is in my pocket. *Dinero esta aquí.*"

He nodded.

Using the opportunity to try to stand, I slid away from the toilet. I was stalling, knowing Bobby had all my money. I reached into my pocket anyway. That's when the bathroom door swung open.

Bobby took two steps in, his melon knife in one hand. Before Green Boots could turn, Bobby had kicked him right behind one knee with the flat of his foot. Green Boots folded backward with a yelp. The moment he hit the floor, Bobby brought his foot down on the guy's wrist and then kicked him in the cheek. It took all of two seconds.

Red Boots turned in time to see, but hadn't moved. The two of them stared each other down. Bobby looked at the knife in Red Boots's hand. Red Boots looked at the knife in Bobby's hand. Bobby smiled. Red Boots didn't.

Bobby glanced at me. "Get up, man. We've got to go."

"No shit," I said, wiggling out of the space and sliding across the urine-puddled floor. I kept my eyes on Red Boots's knife, waiting for him to do something stupid.

Reading my mind, Bobby said, "He ain't going to try nothing. He came in here for the easy buck. That's you. He might be a dumb Mexican, but he's smart enough to see that I ain't easy. I'm too much work. Nobody ever wins a knife fight. You both get cut." Bobby looked at me, the floor, and Red Boots's legs. "Bro. Clean up on aisle five."

We backed out of the bathroom. He closed the door and hurriedly stacked cases of beer in front of it.

"The door opens in," I said.

Bobby shook his head, set down the case of beer, and walked past me toward the front.

SEVEN

I kept looking over my shoulder as we walked quickly away from the bar. The neighborhood still bustled with activity. Food vendors were out in force, and the smell of the street was intoxicating. Or maybe it was all the beer and violence that was intoxicating.

Bobby smirked. "They don't teach that in karate class."

"The guy came at me. I was taking a leak. What am I going to do?"

"Stop pissing, maybe?"

"I couldn't. I didn't. It wasn't conscious." I couldn't believe I was getting defensive or even discussing it. "When did you become such a kicker?" I said, trying to turn it on him.

Bobby laughed. "You smell like diaper."

I didn't notice that Bobby had stopped until I was a couple of steps past him. I turned. "Come on. Why you stopping?"

"We're here," Bobby said, pointing to the painted Cachanilla's sign.

"Bobby, those two cowboys are going to be looking to kick our ass. Do this some other time. I need a shower. We're out of here."

"First of all, they would be coming to kick your ass, not mine. Secondly, who gives a shit?"

"I don't want any more trouble."

"Why not?" Bobby asked, as serious as I'd seen him. "We used to come down here all the time. It's no big deal.'"

"Bobby," I said, defeated.

"We're here. We're right here," Bobby said. "Nothing is going to happen. Well, probably nothing. If something was going to happen, it already would've."

"It did. I got attacked in a bathroom. Jesus Christ, I'm a fucking grown-up now. I don't get drunk and in fights every weekend."

Bobby laughed. "That supposed to be some jab at me? Shit, like I care a dog fart what you think. For all the places you've been and all the shit you've seen, how can you be such a puss? 'I'm a fucking grown-up now.' What the fuck does that even mean?"

"I'm covered in piss. My own piss. I want to go home."

"Fair enough on that front. Chalk that one up to experience." Bobby shook his head. "But this prom date ain't over 'til you put out. You're here for Jack. Your father, not mine. You asked me, remember? I shouldn't have to convince you. We're friends, and I'm going to back you no matter how stupid you are and no matter what stupid you do. But as a friend, the last thing I'm letting you do is quit. We started this together. We're going to finish it together. So sack up, put all your personal shit away, and let's go find a hooker for your old man."

Bobby walked to the door of Cachanilla's, not waiting for my response. I nodded abruptly and followed him.

Very few people can pull off a purple velveteen suit. The guy working the door at Cachanilla's might have been one of them. He was dressed like Superfly by way of Cantinflas, deep purple down to his snakeskin shoes. It was hard to tell if it was fat or muscle under all the ruffles of his frilly shirt, but he had size. Luckily he was one of the friendliest guys I had ever met.

He looked at me and Bobby, did the math, and smiled widely. Two Americans standing outside of a Mexican strip joint didn't make for that complex of an equation. He smelled money. And after the doorman gave me a whiff, he obviously smelled piss, too. To his credit, he didn't say a word. It takes one hell of a salesman to ignore urine. He went straight into his patter. "Best floor show in *México*. Beautiful *chicas*. Cheap tequila." He turned to me, smiling. "You like Mexican pussy?"

I smiled and laughed under my breath. His Mexican accent sounded slightly affected like he was exaggerating it to sound more like the Mexican that he thought we thought he was.

He didn't wait for my answer. "You come in, you have a drink, another drink, you watch the girls, talk to them, have fun, buy the girls some drinks, you know. You like to have fun, no? *Sí? Sí*. Some drinks, some more drinks, you find a girl, you like her, she likes you. You think maybe I want to be alone with her. She wants to be alone with you. Another drink just to be sure. That's when you talk to Guillermo."

"Who's Guillermo?" I asked.

"I am Guillermo. Whatever you need. Talk to Guillermo," he said, pointing at his inflated chest.

"Thanks," I said, taking small steps inside. Bobby had already squeezed past and was leaning against the hall wall, laughing at me.

Guillermo kept up his patter, leaning in closer to my ear. "One hundred dollars. Any girl. All night. Guaranteed. Only one hundred. Nothing to a man like you. All the girls, they're clean. Doctor did the full check two days ago. *Bueno.* And these girls." He whistled. "They do it all. Everything. Whatever you want. They love it all. In the mouth. In the pussy. In the *culo.* They love it."

I finally got past him and made my way inside. Behind me I could still hear him. "Weekday special. Three for the price of two. Whatever you want. Talk to Guillermo."

As strip joints go, Cachanilla's was a bit of all right. It was a big room with a large stage jutting out of one wall, stripper poles at each corner. Harsh, bright light illuminated the stage, but the scattered tables and booths quickly receded into shadows and darkness, the corners black with depraved potential.

A nude-except-shoes, mid-thirties Mexican woman was on the stage not quite dancing, but gyrating her hips in uncoordinated spasms that made a mockery of eroticism. It quickly grew on me. There was something splendid about her bored lack of effort.

Bobby pointed to the bathroom door against the far wall. "Go clean up. I'll get us a table and some drinks. That scuffle made me dangerously close to sober."

The bathroom was filthy, but empty. A toilet, a urinal, and a sink all against the same wall with no dividers between them. I felt a noticeable rise in the humidity. The walls and floor were wet from I don't know what. I didn't want to touch anything, but I washed my hands and tried to pat down my pants with a wet paper towel.

As I was giving myself a failing sniff test, a plump woman walked in pulling a short Mexican man in his fifties behind her. She sat down on the toilet, nonchalantly crossed her legs, unzipped the man's pants, and began working his shank with the same motion and interest as someone inflating a bicycle tire.

In an effort to look in any other direction, I stared at myself in the polished steel that passed for a mirror. My kingdom for a partition.

When I glanced back, the Mexican man had one of the woman's breasts in his hand. He squeezed it as hard as he could without moving a muscle. The woman continued her violent pumping, staring directly at me with a shrug and a face that said, "It's a living."

What is it with me and Mexican bathrooms? My pants were clean enough.

"Dude, you still smell like piss," Bobby said as I sat down.

"I was kind of a third wheel in the john."

There was a shot and a beer waiting for me and the same in front of Bobby, but Bobby waved the girl over anyway. "*Una cerveza más. En una taza, por favor.*"

"Do you see Tomás?" I asked.

Bobby nodded his head toward the back without looking. My eyes drifted toward a very dark booth in the corner. Tomás was in his twenties, looking good in a suit, button-up shirt, and no tie. He held court with two bar girls and a hard-looking guy in a cowboy hat. A giant stood in front of the booth.

Tomás had a stack of American dollars on the table in front of him, probably twenties. I watched the cowboy sitting next to him peel one off and bring it below the table toward one of the girls. She feigned a sexy smile through her discomfort. Eventually he brought his hand up from under the table, gave his finger a quick sniff, and took another drink. Tomás stared at the man for a second past comfort and then returned talking to the girl next to him. So much for the kid I taught to ride a bike.

The girl handed Bobby his glass of beer. Bobby paid, and the girl walked back to the bar. Bobby said, "I'm not going to apologize."

"For what?" I asked.

And Bobby threw the full beer into my lap.

"What the fuck?" I half-yelled, half-standing.

"Rather you smell like beer than piss."

"I'm fucking soaked," I said, pulling the dripping pants away from my wet skin.

"You'll thank me later."

"Well, fuck you now."

I wasn't quite ready to talk to Tomás. I needed a break. I'd had more excitement in the last hour than I'd had in some time. I was beginning to embrace it, but it was definitely exhausting. So I did what you do in a place like Cachanilla's. I drank and watched the ladies on the stage.

The woman on stage was dancing to her first song. It was a *corrido* that I didn't recognize, but they all sounded the same to my ethnocentric ear. She was in her thirties and danced fully clothed in what looked like a circa 1985 gold lamée prom dress. No tease, she danced with concentrated disinterest, watching herself in the mirror on the far wall. She swayed and turned like she was displaying merchandise, which appropriately she was. She didn't take a stitch of clothes off during the length of the song.

The second song was "Ace of Spades." But even with Motörhead's increased tempo, she maintained her slow sashay. At the very end of the song, she took the dress off. Not slowly, not seductively, but awkwardly, unzipping the back and letting the heavy fabric drop to the ground. It was so workmanlike that I found myself looking at the crumpled dress instead of her naked body.

The third song was, of all things, "Baby, Baby" by Amy Grant. She danced in the nude except for her clear plastic high heels. Full bush and real tits, it was only sensual in its total lack of effort.

I turned to Bobby, who kept his focus on the woman on the stage. "Look, man," I said, "I'm sorry if I've been a drag. It's just been a long time since I've been down here, and I can't get comfortable. I don't got that thing you got, to do shit like this so easy."

Bobby shook his head and grinned, the kind of face you make when you're frustrated with a small child or a dog. "What in the holy fuck are you talking about?" he said.

"I can't cross a border and just see people differently. Can't see Mexicans and Americans as different. People are just people to me," I said.

The song ended, and the woman walked off the stage. Bobby turned to me. "I'm officially calling bullshit on that. You're as much a racist as me."

"It ain't racism. I ain't explaining right. It's Mexico, the country. Look at where we are. What we're doing right now. I enjoyed her dance. You think she did? Or do you think she's doing it to have some money to send south or to save up to get to *El Norte* or to just feed herself? Or her kids? I can't help think of that shit when I'm down here.

"Like those kids on the fucking street. If I was anywhere in the U.S. and a six-year-old came up to me, I'd immediately ask where his mother was or find a cop or do something. Here, it's not just that I don't ask. I don't need to ask 'cause I know. There's no point. In doing anything."

Bobby held up his hand. "When'd you turn all hippie? Christ. You guilty for every starving child in the world? They're out there whether you see 'em or not, you know. What are you going to do about it? You going to take all the little kids in and save them? Save the world?"

"No. That's the thing. I ain't going to do nothing. I ain't even going to try. And it makes me feel like an asshole."

Bobby sat up. "Look, man. Mexico is like a house that's caught on fire. And as an American, you're outside, standing on the sidewalk, right? You're watching it burn, but you see people inside. You see them on fire, burning alive. But you can't save them. There's nothing you can do. You got only two choices. You can stay and watch, or you can say to hell with it and walk away. Don't matter none to the people in the burning house. Either way, they're fucked."

"We're participating. I came down here to find a prostitute."

"For a good cause," Bobby interjected. "And don't tell me you never got some Mexican tail. Never came down, hit the whorehouses."

"Not proud of it, but yeah, once. But when I went back to her room, the room she lived in, slept in when she wasn't fucking, and she took the stuffed animals off her bed before we were supposed to screw, I realized how fucked up it was. How human and vulnerable and tragic that poor girl was. How I was about to use her. Like that was why she existed. I couldn't do it."

"Dude, you're making me feel bad for being in a strip club. Don't ruin titties for me. I'll go vegetarian before I let you ruin tits for me. You got no right."

"I stopped coming down here because I got tired of seeing people get used. Being back just reminds me that nothing has changed." Listening to myself, I wondered how I had gotten so maudlin and introspective, and then I remembered that I was on my umpteenth beer.

"You're spinning this whole 'if you're not a part of the solution, you're part of the problem' bullshit. It makes a great bumper sticker for your shittily painted VW bus, but sometimes there ain't no solution, so you just enjoy the problem.

"You see that youngish lady over there." Bobby pointed at a girl talking to a couple of older Mexicans at the bar. "She's going to fuck someone for money whether you like it or not. She could grab one of them rough-handed *campesinos*. Or maybe she lucks out and ends up with a sensitive fella like you who gets all guilty and gives her all your money as you cry into her pillow about how unfair the world is. No matter what, she'll be back the next night, throating some dude in a back booth. For all you know, this place is an improvement from the shack she grew up in and the father who beat her three times a day."

"That's your thesis? Some people are just fucked?"

"And if you believe different, you're the most naïvest fucker on the planet. There's a large population of this country where hooker work is a step up. Didn't the last line of *Chinatown* mean anything to you?"

"Forget it, it's Mexico," I said, cracking a smile.

"Exactly, Jake. So go talk to Tomás and stop thinking about shit you can't change." Bobby downed his beer.

As I approached Tomás's booth, the giant took a few steps toward me. He put his hand up like a traffic cop. Taller than me and built like the Michelin Man, he looked completely immovable.

"I need to talk to Tomás," I said, smiling and attempting to appear as nonthreatening as I could.

He shook his big rock head, his face expressionless.

"I know him. He knows me. Ask him."

Not even a head shake, just a bored stare.

"Look, I've had a lousy night. Do you speak English? I smell like piss and I'm ready to go home. But I came down to your shit sewer of a *ciudad* to talk to your *patrón*, so I'm going to talk to him. Get the fuck out of my way, *cabrón*," said Mr. Tough Guy.

At least that got a smile.

"Hey, Tomás," I yelled over the giant's shoulder. As Tomás squinted through the darkness in my direction, the giant gave me a straight-arm to the chest. He probably thought that he pushed me lightly, but it sent me tripping backward. I *Dick Van Dyke Show*-ed over the top of the table behind me, my hands grabbing at air. The table tipped, sending me and three empty highball glasses flying ass over tits. Glass crashed around me. I landed hard, but unhurt.

I got to one knee. Out of the corner of my eye, I saw Bobby getting up from his chair. His eyes focused on the giant. I whistled over the music, and he turned to me. I shook my head. Bobby sat back down, visibly reluctant. He shrugged, smiled, and pulled the nearest stripper onto his lap with a big laugh.

I stood up and walked back to the giant, who surprisingly didn't apologize. Behind him I saw Tomás staring at me. I gave him a nod and yelled, "I must've read you *Billy Goats Gruff* one too many times when you were a kid. You hired your very own troll."

Recognition lit Tomás's eyes. He pushed at the girl, rushing her out of her end of the booth. He slid to his feet, his eyes never leaving my face. He smiled. "*Hijo de la chingada*" was his summation of the situation.

He rushed over and cuffed the giant on the back of the head, not maliciously but as a form of instruction. The giant showed nothing. He moved to the side, his face the same expressionless mask.

Tomás held out his arms. "Jimmy!"

As I stepped in, he held me away from his body. "You smell like beer piss."

Tomás walked me back to his booth. The cowboy stood at the edge of the booth. His turquoise silk shirt would have been loud on a gay jockey. I didn't let the clothes fool me. The guy's face was stony with tough guy disdain.

"Jimmy, this is Alejandro. He works for me. And yes, he's as mean as he looks."

Alejandro gave me an almost imperceptible nod. The formality of a handshake seemed overly audacious for the particular moment and setting.

Tomás gave Alejandro a slap on the shoulder. "Why don't you check on the room?"

He was being dismissed, but Alejandro's face only allowed the slightest sign of insolence before he walked away.

Tomás and I sat down. Without any instruction or command, the two women slid in on either side of the horseshoe booth. It was a tight fit, everyone pushed close together. The girl next to me rested her hand on my crotch.

"It's good to see you, Jimmy," Tomás said. "Been a long, long time. Good to see a friend from the past. Seems lately I'm only around new people."

"What about Mr. Morales?"

"*Mi abuelito*? I don't see him as much as I should. I don't think he approves of my lifestyle." Tomás smiled.

I looked around the place and at the two women, then back to Tomás. "What exactly is your lifestyle?"

Tomás opened his arms wide. "This is it, Jimmy. Or at least part of it."

"You own this place?"

"Not on paper. Never on paper. I use it as a form of office."

"And what's a day at the office like?"

"It's like ruling the world," Tomás said, putting his arm around the girl next to him. She dutifully laughed.

When he had spoken to Alejandro and the giant, Tomás had a hint of a Mexican accent. But as he spoke to me, I couldn't help notice the accent fade, except when he chose to pepper in the occasional Spanish word with newscaster inflection. There was an ease to his voice, but a control in his language. Every word was enunciated and selected for its purpose.

"I guess that makes you upper management. I don't know if you know this, Tomás, but most businessmen, you know, suit and tie guys, they don't have henchmen." I pointed over my shoulder at the giant.

"Little Piwi? He's security."

"Little Piwi. That's clever. Because he's a big guy. The old switcheroo. He's big, but his nickname makes him sound small. I get it."

"*Sabihondo* smart-ass. I didn't name him. That's the name he had when I picked him up at the pound."

I looked toward the bar and saw Alejandro talking to one of the dancers. He rested his hand on the back of her neck. It wasn't an affectionate gesture, but an unsubtle expression of dominance. When he sternly jerked her toward him, I physically flinched. I turned back to Tomás.

"And that other guy? He security too?"

"He's necessary. A bit of trouble, but necessary. He serves a present purpose. Watch him long enough, he'll do something that'll make you want to kill him."

"Yet he works for you?"

"I'm an equal opportunity employer. I even hire my enemies when necessary. He's helpful for what I do."

"So what is it you do, Tomás?"

The smile left his face. "*Pinche cabrón,*" he muttered under his breath.

"I didn't mean to get personal," I said, seeing something in his eyes that warned of potential violence. Something that I immediately knew I didn't want to face.

"Is that that white-haired freak, Bob Maves?" he asked.

I looked over my shoulder at Bobby, who was laughing with the stripper on his lap. She had her top comfortably off. They shared a bottle of tequila, passing it back and forth.

"He's here with me."

Tomás turned to me. "Talking of trouble. That *cabrón*'s dangerous. You know he tried to burn down my *abuelito*'s bar?"

"They worked it all out. He apologized a couple hours ago."

"Bob likes to fight too much. He'll get you in trouble."

"Or get me out of it. You have a hired goon. You should understand," I said. "Who do you need protection from?"

Ignoring my question, Tomás turned to me. "You know how I wanted to be a businessman? When I was a kid, young, how that's all I talked about?"

"Yeah, I worried about you a little bit. But if a kid wants to carry a briefcase around, let him, right?"

"But being a kid and all, I didn't know that being a businessman wasn't really a job title. That all things were business. That there aren't any classified ads asking for just 'businessmen.'" He air-quoted the word. "But that's what I am. That's what I've become. I'm a businessman. I see opportunities and I take them."

"Legal or not?"

"This is Mexico, Jimmy. Nothing is illegal—if you have the money."

Tomás gave a nod to the woman sitting next to him. She slid out of the booth, followed by the other woman. When we were alone, Tomás caught me up.

"The day after I graduated Holtville High, I got on a Greyhound with one hundred and fifty-eight bucks and the worst hangover of my life. Got the hell out. I was in San Diego for two years. At first, working for an uncle at his *taquería*. But eventually I got a job at this investment firm, Statler & Moore. Mail room, but I was in. I'm smart. Ready to learn. I was taking classes at Grossmont College at night. Learning business, accounting, marketing. But people like you and me, we go into the city, we still have the desert in us. We have the border in us. You ever feel one hundred percent right anywhere else? Even in LA. I mean, completely like you fit? I worked hard, but I saw quick that I wasn't going to be anything more than 'the Mexican.' I could have worked harder, but I couldn't work whiter.

"When you close your eyes and picture a Mexican, is he wearing a suit?

"I learned what I could've guessed. Nine to five is pointless, unless it's nine at night to five in the morning. I found different businessmen that I could learn from. And they had no problem working with me. It was good money, but I didn't care about all that gangster, macho bullshit. I wanted to go into business for myself. I wanted money, not some skewed idea of respect. Nothing against them. They have a strong business model, but too much unnecessary violence.

Not for me. I'm not a tough guy. I'm more—what did you call it? Upper management.

"When I got back down here, back home, I found any opportunity I could. I did a little smuggling, a little coyoteing, a little pimping. It's like there was a dollar in the wind and I was chasing it in whatever direction it blew.

"Here's the most important thing I learned. The harder the government in the North tries to stop something from getting in from Mexico, the more money there is to be made from it. Doesn't matter what it is. Seems like the demand is always getting bigger and the supply is getting smaller. Makes prices go up. Makes people like me rich.

"Used to be, back in the day, the *campesinos*, the farmers, ran the heroin trade out of Sinaloa. Steady trade, everybody was happy, everybody made money. Then, boom, Reagan. The War on Drugs happens, and the narco-cowboys take over and turn Tijuana, Ciudad Juárez, and Mexico City into war zones.

"Used to be, being a coyote was a fifty-, hundred-buck-a-head, low-end job. Barely worth it. But now with all the fences and sensors and *La Migra* agents, fucking Homeland Security. Now you can get two, three grand a head to get someone over. It isn't inconsequential money anymore. And when there's real money, there's real competition. And when there's money and competition, that's when the guns finally come out. And that's not for me either. Although I've been known to dabble.

"I knew I wouldn't last long if I tried to compete with *La Eme* or the Sinaloans or the Colombians or Mara Salvatrucha. They're all chainsaw crazy with a serious amount of blood on their hands. I needed my own thing. And I knew that they couldn't own all the financial opportunities that a guarded, but leaky border provides. I was about to go legit, open up a T-shirt stand or something—steady, not flashy—when I figured out what it was I could do. Had a what-do-you-call-it—epiphany.

"I'm a people person. While I do run some of my own businesses, my strength is as an arranger. I do favors. I make friends. And sometimes, my friends need help from my other friends, and people come to me. I've introduced smugglers to border agents. I've sold baby urine to the Mexican police. I even helped the Mexicali Zoo acquire a new tiger from a recently incarcerated drug lord's holdings.

"The businesses make me money, but people give me power. Most gringos don't think Mexicans are smart enough to work a computer, but there's a whole new generation down here. There's tons of kids that can do things on the computer, Web pages, digital shit. Put your face on a body-builder's body, make it look like you're a muscleman. For real.

"It's like computers and the Internet were made for one thing. *El Porno.* All of a sudden, porn from all over the world could be sold anywhere else in the world. No more videotapes, no more copying, no more warehousing, no more shipping. And like religion and drugs, it's recession-proof. No more borders. It's all just information. And no taxes to Uncle Sam if production is in Mexico. *La mordida* is a bargain compared to self-employment tax. Low overhead, high return. And Mexicali has all the talent I need. Fresh talent coming in every day.

"Like Anna, the *señorita* that was sitting next to you. She speaks no English. Tiny, sweet thing. Same story. She came to Mexicali from some village in the south. Paid her money to some coyote. Probably every dime she earned or stole to get to *El Norte.* Coyote left her in the desert. *La Migra* brought her back. Now she's far from home. In a strange and dangerous city. She has no money. She's desperate. And that's where I can help her. She's got marketable assets, and I got the market. She does some work for me, I help her get to Los Angeles. Between movies, she works here to pay for her room and board. Her own room, instead of some cardboard and tin shack in one of the *colonias.* Everyone wins.

"I maintain over a dozen Web sites. Credit card orders. New movies every week. I got a director that went to film school at UCLA. He uses lights and sets and everything. Makes it look nice. It's all about a good name: *Spanish Flies, Latin Lessons, Toss My Taco Salad.* Most popular site I got is called *Brown Bagging.* Good, huh? In it, there's a guy in a Border Patrol uniform, and we shoot it like he just caught the girl, and he tells her that he'll let her go if she has sex with him. Then they do it, of course. And at the end, he still sends her back to Mexico. The site didn't get popular until we did the switch ending. It's like unless the woman is completely used, the customers can't get off. But it's all acting anyway, so who cares. Give the people what they want. Even if those people are repellent.

"Makes a good net profit. Only reason Little Piwi is around is because I like to carry cash and there's a lot of *pinche ladrónes* in this city. Lots of bad people with no sense of right and wrong."

I really didn't want to hear any more. Hadn't I just finished talking to Bobby about not wanting to see this kind of shit?

I knew that the world could be a fucked place, but to have someone throw it in your face was a little much. Especially with the amount of alcohol I had in me and on me. It seemed that everyone in Mexicali was either predator, prey, or both. I wanted to say something, but I kept reminding myself that I was down here to find a prostitute, so who was I to judge. I wanted to make Pop happy, and right now, more than anything I wanted to crash on that ugly, orange couch back at the house.

"I need to find a prostitute," I said, not waiting for an opening.

Tomás paused, absorbed what I had said, and then laughed loudly. He said, "You need a girl? That's why you came to see me? Why didn't you say so? I'm talking and talking and you just want to get laid. Take your pick. Take a couple."

"No, that's not it exactly. I ain't looking for just any prostitute. I need to find a specific woman. She used to work for you, I think. Your grandfather told me you used to bring girls up to the bar on weekends."

Tomás laughed nostalgically. "I haven't done that myself in a long time. One of my early entrepreneurial endeavors. Made a lot of people happy. These days, Alejandro handles the girls directly. They're scared of him, which is important."

"You think I could talk to him?"

"We go through girls quickly. Don't be surprised if he doesn't remember. A couple of years? That's a long time. Especially in Mexicali. You know if she's still here?"

"I got no idea," I said. It hadn't occurred to me that she might not be in Mexicali anymore.

"What's her name?" Tomás sat up, becoming interested.

"Yolanda. I don't got a last name. She's about twenty-five. Like five foot eight or nine, so she's tallish for a Mexican. She has long, black hair and big, brown eyes, but I guess that doesn't help. And she's got a mole or birthmark on the left side of her neck. Like about this big," I said, holding my fingers in a circle about the size of a nickel.

"Yolanda, tall, birthmark, got it. Sounds familiar. Why you want to find her?"

"Why do you think?" I had decided to keep Pop out of it.

Tomás said nothing for ten seconds, just staring at me.

"I ain't the kid from across the street no more, Jimmy," Tomás said, his eyes serious but still friendly.

"I kind of got that." I held his gaze.

"So don't treat me like a kid is what I'm saying. You come to me, ask a favor, but don't trust me," he said, looking almost hurt.

"I just need to find this Yolanda. It's private. I can use your help. But if you don't want to, I'll find another way. I didn't mean to bother you," I said, sliding to the edge of the booth.

"I didn't say I wouldn't help. I just didn't want you to think you were getting away with anything. It's your business. I'll respect that."

"Can you find her? I can pay."

"No money. I'll ask around. If she's in town, I'll find her. Give me your phone number. I'll call you when she's found."

"Let me pay. You're out your time. Might be a lot of work."

Tomás smiled. "Does it look like I need money?"

"No, but it looks like you'll always want more."

Tomás laughed and waved the girls back to the booth.

EIGHT

Tomás insisted that I stay, have a few drinks, and give the bar girls a go. Even if they weren't Yolanda. After some back and forth, I was able to convince him that I was done for the night. We finalized our arrangements, Tomás promising to call me as soon as he heard anything about Yolanda.

I slid out of the booth and leaned over the table to shake Tomás's hand. Walking past Little Piwi, I gave him my toughest glare, which didn't even warrant a grin. I dragged my simultaneously drunk and hungover ass over to Bobby's table.

Bobby's face was buried deep in a two-hundred-pound woman's ample cleavage. His laughter bubbled almost inaudibly, complemented by the platinum blond-wigged dancer's seemingly sincere giggling. She squirmed on his lap, grinding into him in a playful, but probably painful way. Bobby gripped her ass with one hand in a constant struggle to maintain balance and leverage.

I stood over the table, waiting for Bobby to look up. He didn't. I gave him a light kick in the shin. Nothing.

"Time to go," I yelled over the music.

Bobby answered, his voice muffled by the woman's flesh. It sounded like, "Candy bee's inner tube knew French." But I doubted that's what he said.

"What?" I yelled, starting to get annoyed.

Bobby leaned back, frustrated. "I said, can't you see I'm busy entertaining my new friend? Marguerita, Jimmy Vee. Jimmy Vee, Marguerita."

"Come on, man. I'm spent and I stink."

"You're such a crybaby. I ain't going to be long," he said, pinching Marguerita's ass. Her squeal pierced.

I walked to the exit, yelling behind me. "I'll wait for you at the car."

"It's a truck," Bobby said, knee-jerk defending his Ranchero, and then he returned his attention and face to the woman's chest.

I lit a cigarette as I hit the street in front of Cachanilla's. I inhaled deeply, wishing I still got the same light-headed buzz that I had gotten when I first started smoking. Thankfully, the night had turned the desert heat from crushing to pleasant. A warm breeze curled the smoke around my head. The thought of taking a nap in the bed of Bobby's Ranchero didn't sound half bad.

Alejandro walked over, giving a chin nod toward the pack of smokes in my hand. The international symbol for "Can I bum one of them there cigarettes?"

I handed him a cigarette and lit it.

"I didn't know Tomás had friends," Alejandro said, trying to sound casual, but there was something serious below the surface.

"Sounds like he has a lot of friends to me."

"He knows everyone, yes. But who he trusts?"

"Okay," I said.

"I watched you. I watched you talking. He trusts you."

I didn't like where this was headed. There was threat spiked in his voice.

Alejandro continued. "I don't know you. Never seen you. In five years. Who the fuck are you?"

"I'm nobody. An old friend."

"Nobody," he repeated. Then he stared at me through the length of his smoke. He tossed it on the ground and crushed it underfoot.

"*Gracias*," he said and walked back into Cachanilla's.

I got my bearings and pointed myself in the direction of the U.S. Immigration Building three blocks away. The top of the modern bunker was visible and out of place among the older, run-down buildings along the border. I headed down the street. The alcohol and exhaustion were catching up to me. I wanted to sit down and take a nap right there.

Ask and you shall receive.

I had just reached the end of the block when something hard crashed into the side of my face. From experience I was pretty sure it was a fist. I turned in time to see that I was correct, as another fist (possibly the same one) hit me square in the mouth. It shoved my lit, now-broken cigarette into my mouth and sent me flying toward the stucco wall behind me. I hit my head hard and scraped the skin off my arm as I slid to the ground. The taste of tobacco, ash, and blood made me nauseous. I caught the sight of two red boots through my blurred vision.

Red Boots stood over me, Green Boots behind him, and three other cowboys behind them. I'm not sure what color their boots were. Serves me right to think I could piss on a guy's cowboy boots and get away with it. I wondered what he'd do if I puked on them. I owed Bobby a big "I told you so."

I made a futile attempt to get to my feet and reach for the knife in my boot. But what felt like fifty boots came flying at me. And all I could do to stay alive was curl up in a ball and take the punishment, one arm protecting my face, my other hand cupping my balls. It sounded like ten cursing Mexicans hitting bread dough with baseball bats. I made very little sound. It's hard to yell when you can't breathe. The pointy boots hit me at all angles. Luckily when the pain is distributed all over one's body, it's impossible to concentrate on any single location. Each new pain took my mind off the last one. Either way, the pain only lasted for a short time. Pretty soon I was unconscious. Passed out, knocked out, fainted, or all of the above. It doesn't matter. I wasn't feeling any pain.

When I woke up, it took me a long couple seconds to figure out what had happened. Unfortunately, the pain quickly reminded me that I had gotten my ass kicked. It made sense that my whole body would hurt. What I couldn't figure out was why I was upside-down and moving.

"What the fuck?" came out of my mouth, slurred and drippy.

"Thank fucking God," was the response I got.

Bobby eased me off his shoulder and set me on the ground. I pressed my face against the cool tile floor. I had never felt anything better in my life. I opened my eyes. I was inside. Somewhere lit by harsh fluorescents. I looked up at

Bobby, his nose dripping blood and one eye almost completely swollen shut.

"What the fuck happened to you?"

"You should take a look in a mirror," he said. "You going to live?"

"The tile feels good. It's cold. Get down here. Put your face on the tile. It feels amazing," I babbled.

"Great. They kicked you retarded," Bobby said, trying to get me to my feet. "You never could take a punch."

I tried to keep my face pressed against the tile, but Bobby pulled me up. I had trouble focusing, but pretty soon I had my weight underneath me. Shaky and swaying, but I was standing.

"What the fuck happened? Where are we?" I asked.

"Second question first. We're at the border building. About to head back into Calexico. Your first question is more of a story. You okay to walk?"

"We'll find out, won't we?"

We were in the Mexican-side lobby of the U.S. Immigration Building. It was a large room built to accommodate hundreds of people. The room was furnished similarly to a train station or an airport with bench seating and scattered potted palms that replaced the need for urinals. At this time of night, there were only a few people using the lobby to catch some shut-eye. A rowdy group of drunk teenagers hung out in the corner vocally comparing their pornographic discoveries.

Bobby and I walked the length of the lobby to the long hall that led to the "Welcoming Station." I kept one hand on the wall for balance, running my fingers along the lines of a faux mosaic mural. I couldn't tell what it was. Maybe a fish or a snake. Whatever it was, it felt out of place in the sterility of the government building. It looked like Quetzalcoatl as done by the guy who did that children's book *The Very Hungry Caterpillar.*

There were two Border Patrol agents on duty. The white one working the desk looked like the kind of guy who works out three hours a day, but can only do it if he's looking in the mirror while he pumps up. Upper body show-muscle. The Hispanic agent had a solid boiler for his age. I was impressed. A tight potbelly at twenty-five takes some extra work. They both looked mean and dumb.

Bobby put on his best dumb smile. "Hey, guys, how you doing tonight? Bet you'd rather be drinking, right?"

The white one gave us both a look, focusing his attention on Bobby's face, then mine. "Jesus, what the hell happened to you two? You get in a fight with a cheese grater?" He hit his partner lightly on the shoulder, prompting some laughter.

"Good one," Bobby said. "We got jumped. You know how it is. Head down to Chicali for a couple of drinks. Couple cowboys didn't like the way we looked at their *chicas.*"

"Can we just get this over with?" I said, tired and frustrated.

Bobby gave me a light elbow. But considering that my entire body was a giant bruise, I couldn't help but yelp.

"Obviously we're done for the night. Time for bed," Bobby said.

The two Border Patrol agents looked at each other. The Hispanic who hadn't said anything gave him a nod. "Let's see your passports."

Bobby pulled his out of the back pocket of his jeans and handed it to the man.

"Where were you born?" the agent asked. He held the passport up, his eyes going back and forth between the photo and Bobby's face.

"Right here in El Centro. Imperial Valley Regional Medical Center is what they call it now. Back then, they just called it 'The Hospital.'"

The agent shook his head and grinned. "All right. Go ahead." Then he turned to me. "Passport."

I reached into my back pocket and then remembered that I had put my passport in my boot. I sat down on the ground and untied my boot, tugging at it to get it off. It was gone. I looked up at the Border Patrol agents and Bobby. They were all shaking their heads.

"Try the other one," Bobby said.

I took off my other boot and shook it. My passport dropped to the floor. I put my boots back on. I had trouble getting the thin passport off the slick tile, sliding it around for a while. Eventually, I got a fingernail underneath and handed it to the agent. It felt like it took me a full, painful minute to stand back up.

"Where were you born?" the agent asked. He squinted at the photo and then flipped through the array of stamps in the back.

"Brawley. California. Here. What's the point of this? You know we live here. You know we're Americans. Can't we just get back in our country?"

"You travel a lot. Been to a lot of places."

"Yeah," I said, getting even more annoyed.

"You bringing back anything I should know about?"

"Why didn't you ask him that?" I said, pointing at Bobby.

Bobby rolled his eyes, indicating his assessment of me as the stupidest asshole in the world.

"Do you have any drugs, alcohol, fireworks, produce, or anything else that I should know about?"

"Produce?"

"Fruits or vegetables."

"I know what produce is. No, I don't have any drugs, fireworks, or produce, but I have some alcohol. I'm not sure if this counts, but I bought a couple of drinks and now I'm attempting to smuggle them into the U.S. in my stomach. Should I declare that?"

"Look, smart-ass. You want, I can call the cops, have them bring their breathalyzers, give you a drunk and disorderly."

I was about to tell him that I was, in fact, acting drunk and orderly, and also that he could go fuck himself, but the face that Bobby made stopped me. I stuck with "Yes sir. Sorry. When I get tired, I get punchy."

"I can see that. Punched in the face-y is more like it," he said with a snort for a laugh. He turned to his partner, who joined in.

"Good one," I said.

"All right. Go ahead. But next time you head across the border, I suggest you drink a little less or learn how to fight a little better."

Bobby smiled, looking at me. "Sound advice, sir. I've been telling him that for years. You officers have a good night."

"What the fuck was that?" Bobby said, walking back to the Ranchero. "You had to fuck with that dude. All night you're made out of pussy, but as soon as it's time to shut the fuck

up, the time to be 'yes sir,' 'no sir,' then your balls drop and you got to be Rickles?"

"I liked your Eddie Haskell. How many times did you call that douche 'sir'? Shit. I was going back into my country. The country I'm a citizen of. Fuck them."

"They're doing their job."

"Being assholes isn't in their job description. They were assholes. Don't matter the job. If a waiter is doing his job and acts like an asshole, I'm going to call him on it. Their job isn't to dick with me because they're pissed they aren't cops or FBI agents or some shit. Assholes like that crave that tiny bit of power. Sure they got a crap job, but it's the one they chose. The one they're pissed they settled for. The one that ensures them the daily duty of fucking with people, whether those people need to be fucked with or not. They get off pushing people around. They're probably having a hearty masturbate as we speak."

I took a breath and then continued. "I'm sorry. Am I out of line? No, you're right. They're heroes. American heroes. Keeping us safe on the front lines."

"Bro," Bobby said, "maybe wine coolers or appletinis are more your drink. Who knew beer and tequila made you self-righteous?"

"I'm fucking exhausted" was all I could get out.

"You want to go to the hospital or home?" Bobby asked, not joking.

"Home."

As soon as my ass hit the bench seat of Bobby's Ranchero, I dozed. The warm haze of sleep crept over my skin. But not for long. Bobby punched me in the arm.

"You probably have a concussion. To complement your preexisting brain damage. Better stay awake for a while," he said.

"Tell that to all the alcohol you pumped into my system." I slapped myself in the face, immediately regretting it, but waking up. I was tempted to flip down the sun visor and check out my face in the vanity mirror, but I decided to save the surprise for later.

Bobby said, "It's just that I'm going to be a little embarrassed if you die. I'll have to tell your dad and everything."

"Yeah. That'd be a real bummer for you."

"Exactly," Bobby said, starting the car. "Let's get the fuck out of here."

We drove back a different way. Bobby took the car slowly through the quiet residential streets at the east end of Calexico. Even though it was late, a few people were sitting on their steps. The smoky remnants of barbecues wafted through the air. It's never too late to have a couple of beers with your neighbors. The peace of the blue collar Mexican neighborhood was refreshing. It reminded me that most people led quiet lives and not everyone had just gotten a world-class beating.

"So, what happened?" I finally asked Bobby as we left the city limits and drove onto the back roads. The sweet pungence of a distant skunk and the sticky, grassy smell of the alfalfa fields felt like home. Back in the country.

"You mean, while you were taking your little beauty sleep?" Bobby said.

"The last thing I remember was getting jumped. When did you show up?"

"When last we saw our hero, he was entertaining a young damsel named Marguerita. Man, I don't know about you, but don't matter who the chick is, there's nothing better than making a woman laugh. Don't care if she means it or not. I was telling Marguerita knock-knock jokes in English. A language she knows about three words of, but I taught her how to say, 'Who's there?' and, you know, the 'Who?' part at the end. And every time, didn't matter what I said, didn't matter if it made sense. Every time I said the punch line, she laughed her ass off. And she had an ass. 'Knock-knock.' *'Who there?'* 'Shorty.' *'Chorty who?'* 'Shorty Fuckadoodle.' Big laugh. *'Ha, ha, ha, ha!'* You got to respect that. That's a professional. A whore who takes pride in her work.

"Then our buddy, Guillermo. You remember, 'Talk to Guillermo'? Dressed like Cesar Romero. He comes bouncing in, saying there's a fight outside, thinks it might be my friend, you. I get up quick, accidentally drop Marguerita to the floor. But of course, she laughs more. They don't make enough of 'em like her.

"I hit the sidewalk. It takes me a couple of seconds to find you. You ended up kind of around the corner. But I see the cowboys, and I hear the thuds. You might want to take it up with Mr. Turquoise, that dude that was sitting with Tomás, 'cause he was leaning against a wall watching and smiling. I don't know what you did, but he was enjoying himself.

"I hit a couple cowboys before they even know they're fighting me. Couldn't give you details, just swinging at everything that moved. You weren't one of those things. You were out. They got a few licks in, but I took most of the heat off you and I was definitely giving better than I got. I put my back against the wall, my head down and kept my punches short, letting them come to me. Punishing them when they did. My shins are bruised to shit from those boots. Talk about kickers.

"Then the cops show up. First time I've been glad to see a Mexican cop. These three local *federales* shove everyone apart. One of them, probably the new guy, got to his knee and checked your pulse. Of course he checked your back pocket for a wallet once he knew you were alive. I was honestly relieved when I heard you moan. I mean, you were crumpled up in a weird-ass position, one hand squeezing your junk.

"So I'm bleeding all over myself and what do our pals, the *federales*, do. They roust me. Completely ignore the five fucking cowboys. Five against one and it's my fault. Like I would start some shit. They come at me with rapid-fire Spanish. And the cowboys ain't going anywhere. Just waiting. Smiling.

"This ain't my first cage match. I know the deal. It's always about money. I give the lead cop the rest of your money. Problem is, it's only like twelve bucks. Bro, we bought a lot of booze. He took it, but I'm pretty sure he was insulted. I do my best to explain that that's all I got. *Todo dinero.* He nods, steps back, and says something I don't hear to one of the cowboys.

"I know then, I'm super fucked. One of the cops points at me and holds up some money, yelling, "*Treinta pesos.*" Another gives him a nod, digging into his pocket. They're betting on me. Or against me. It's like a fucking cockfight or some shit. The cowboys circle me again. The cops are laughing and betting. I get my fists up, ready to go.

"But before the cowboys have a chance to make me into a squishy pile like Beetle Bailey after the Sarge jumped on him, the Incredible Hulk, that big dude that works for Tomás, the one that threw you over the table, he starts grabbing guys and throwing them left and right. Throwing them like a midget toss. The cops just watch. Me too. We're stunned. And in like ten seconds, less, all the cowboys are on the ground, hurt, moaning. One of them is shaking in a really freaky, disturbing way. Like a seizure, you know. Then the Hulk turns to the cops. I don't know what he was going to do, if he was going to do anything, but they sure thought he was. Because they all drew their guns.

"Man, you missed some shit. I don't how you slept through all of it.

"Now the Hulk and me are standing there. He's breathing hard 'cause, Christ, it's got to be something just hauling all that weight around, let alone beating serious ass. And I'm bleeding. Pretty much all I'm doing. Bleeding as quietly as I can. And there's like the three *federales* pointing guns at us. They're scared absolutely shitless. I mean, guns-shaking, piss-stinking terrified. Full disclosure, the piss might have been you, I don't know. I concentrate every ounce of energy on not moving. I know if I move, one of these mothers is going to freak, shoot, then the others are going to unload. Red light. I'm frozen. And I'm hoping the Hulk gets it, too.

"We're like a what-do-you-call-it? One of them scenes in a museum. Like with a stuffed mountain goat. That's what we are, like in a museum. Nobody's moving. Nobody's saying anything. The only sound is the Hulk's breathing, which is deep and steady with a nose whistle. Actually kind of nice. Soothing. I couldn't help it, I started breathing with him. We were on the same side kinda, so it was like we were bonding.

"A diorama, that's the word. We were like a diorama.

"Oh yeah. You'll never believe this. I look down. There's a knife sticking out of the Hulk's ass. One of the cowboys stabbed him in the butt. Some blood running down the back of his leg. Deep in the meat of his cheek. I don't even know if he knows. Didn't make a move to take it out. Didn't seem to bother him. He was just breathing.

"And then, '*Amigos.*' Someone says, '*Amigos.*' I hear the word, I know what it means, but I don't know why I'm hearing it. Then again, '*Amigos.*' We all turn our heads. Real slow. Nobody moves their bodies, just the heads. And we all see Tomás standing on the sidewalk. And he's got a fistful of twenty-dollar bills fanned like he's Biggie fucking Smalls. And he's smiling 'cause he knows he owns the situation.

"The tension immediately fades. The cops, they slowly put their guns back in their holsters, although they keep looking at the Hulk like he's going to smash. Tomás peels off a couple of bills, pays each one of them, but not before he says something in each one's ear. I don't know what he said, but if they were scared of the Hulk, they were terrified of Tomás.

"And right there in front of our eyes, I watch everything change. The cops start kicking the cowboys awake. Four of them slowly get to their feet. The other one won't wake up. So, two of them drag him by his feet as the cops hold them at gunpoint and walk them down the center of the street. To jail or a ditch at the edge of town, I don't know and I don't want to know.

"Tomás knelt down next to you, checked your pulse, your eyes. You kind of woke up, but then dropped back out. More passed-out than knocked-out, I was thinking. I told him I would take care of you. And without a word, Tomás went back into Cachanilla's.

"When did Tomás turn into Tony fucking Montana?

"The Hulk followed Tomás. And as he walked, no shit, he reached behind him and pulled the knife out of his butt cheek. Just dropped it on the ground, barely missing a step. I wanted to watch him turn back into the Mexican Bill Bixby, but I figured it was time to get you home.

"I carried your ass three blocks. You are one heavy sleeper.

"But that settles it. We have got to go to Mexicali more. The weird shit always happens when you're around. I missed you, man."

Bobby dropped me off at the house. I decided that I would rather die in my sleep from my probable concussion than stay awake. I didn't try to reflect on the events of the evening. I didn't want to think about the fact that I'd only been back one day. I didn't even take my shoes off. I just dropped on the couch fully clothed. And through the spinning, I let myself pass out.

NINE

Ow.

I knew I was going to be in pain, but—ow. Ow all over my body.

The morning sun woke me, searing light ripping through the living room windows. I had been awake for a half hour, but remained motionless on the couch. I knew if I moved it would hurt. How did I know? I wasn't moving and it hurt. I seriously considered avoiding any kind of movement until sometime next week. Or next winter.

I kept time with my pulse, counting each pounding heartbeat that echoed in my head. I hadn't lost a fight that decisively in a long time and was quickly remembering why I had put it off so long. A hangover was bad enough. Pile on an A-plus ass-kicking and it made you forget that life was precious and every day a miracle.

I sat up slowly, holding my ribs for fear that they would shatter inside my body. I may have screeched in pain, making a sound not dissimilar to a cat fighting a pterodactyl. It's hard to recall. I was alone. There were no witnesses. So let's just say I manned up and silently took the pain.

I rubbed my hand gently across my right side where I had taken most of the punishment. My ribs were definitely bruised, a couple probably cracked, but none felt out of place. You know you're having a rough morning when the most you hope for is to not piss blood.

I sat up. That was enough for the moment. I went back to not moving, my teeth pressed so tightly together I thought the enamel would crack. I lit a cigarette and smoked two before I made the effort to stand and make my way to the bathroom.

I stood in front of the mirror and stared at my face. I looked like the parachute hadn't opened. It was an impressive array of injuries. I had a mouse under one very bloodshot eye, a fat lip, and a greenish bruise on one cheek. Coagulated blood filled my inflamed nostrils, and the entire length of the right side of my face was scraped with thin, red scabs. Some caked blood covered my forehead, having dripped down from where I had hit my head. I could feel the cut under my blood-matted hair, the wound still wet.

The skin on my right arm was almost completely scraped off on one side. I had speckled bruises and cuts here and there. But it was when I took off my shirt to get in the shower that I almost cried. My chest and stomach had so many dark bruises I looked like a Dalmatian. It didn't look real. It looked like some teenage *Fangoria* magazine fan's first attempt at gore makeup. Little spots, big spots. I was an Appaloosa. And my legs weren't any better, my thighs patched dark purple. I poked my right quad because I'm an idiot. It felt soft like a bad apple and hurt like hell.

The cold shower would have felt a lot better if there had been any kind of water pressure. The light drip was more frustrating than soothing. It took me forever to get the blood out of my hair.

I dried my body, continually hitting spots that made me shriek, swear, and then breathe deeply. I doused my body in Bactine, the stinging so severe at one point I started laughing. Getting dressed was like playing Operation. I tried to get my clothes on without the clothes actually touching me. Unfortunately my nose kept lighting up red.

Before I left the house, I chewed on three aspirins with two shots of tequila as a chaser. The tequila almost came up, but through concentration and practice I kept it down. The warmth in my stomach took some of the edge off. I thought about bringing the bottle with me for medicinal reasons, but decided against it. Two shots were helpful. The whole bottle would be twelve steps in the wrong direction. Besides, I was meeting Mike, and he might have frowned on it.

Mike Egger is my cousin. His mother is my mother's sister. Here's the thing. I never knew my mother, so I never got close to that side of the family. I knew Mike enough to say hi to him on the street or if I saw him in J&M's, but we didn't spend holidays together or even exchange Christmas cards. The most I could say is that we were aware of each other.

But apparently marriage was as good as blood. Because when Pop got sick, Mike immediately offered his help. I spoke to him before I drove down and asked him why. He just said, "That's what family does—what family is for."

Mike had been farming Pop's land for the last year and a half. For anyone else, taking over the land would have been a big deal, but Mike farmed close to six thousand acres. So he just absorbed it into his workload and massive workforce. He made sure that the alfalfa was irrigated, mowed, and the hay stored and sold.

I didn't ask him why he hadn't called me when Pop first got sick. I assumed it was because he had promised not to.

There are people who say that they'll do anything for you. And there's the people who actually do. Mike had stepped up when he knew he could help, and as much as I would like to believe that's common, my experience was that it was a rare gesture.

The simplistic way in which the media portrays people would suggest that Mike and I shouldn't like each other. He was a Red Stater. I was True Blue. As usual, the media was full of shit. Nothing is black and white. People can be different and get along.

Mike was an easy guy to like. Two hundred and fifty pounds of burly, big guy. Bear hugs and slaps on the back that knocked you five feet forward. A family man and a good Catholic, Mike had four kids, never thought about cheating on his wife, donated time and money to the church, rarely complained, and never judged the people around him. He believed in what he believed and wasn't afraid to express it, but he never thought I was stupid because I didn't agree with him.

I drove my pickup down a dirt road toward Mike's shed, an enormous corrugated tin barn visible in the distance. The deep tractor ruts made my truck bounce and swerve, mocking my day-after agony. I drove as slowly as I could without stalling. Each bump felt like someone was hitting me in the head with a shovel. Dust blew into the slit in the window meant to let my cigarette smoke out. I was forced to stub out my smoke when I started having a coughing fit that made my ribs burn.

I pulled my Mazda next to the more manly pickups next to the shed. The Dodge Rams and Ford F-150s made my four-banger look like a child's toy. They were bigger, badder, and filthier. Mud spatters shot up the sides of every fender.

Walking into the shed, I gave a wave or head nod to the couple of familiar faces that I recognized. Guys who had done some work for my father or guys I had worked along-side in the fields when I was a teenager. There were no titles in farming. No managers. No foremen. Just guys.

Daniel Quihuis, an ageless Mexican man, was Mike's main guy. Rail thin, Daniel had one of those faces that had always looked old. Deep laugh lines and leather skin. Now that he was old, it finally fit him. He ran the day-to-day that Mike didn't handle himself. Daniel had worked for Mike's father, my Uncle Frank, but I never saw him treat Mike like a kid.

"Jesus Christ, Jim. What the hell happened to your face? You get in a fight with your boyfriend?" Daniel asked as we shook hands. Years ago, the first time he had seen me with long hair was the beginning of a long series of jokes about how much of a girl I was. It never got old. At least for him.

I gave him a smile, acknowledging that I got his joke. "Mike around?"

He nodded toward the back. "How's Big Jack doing? Marta brought some tamales by a couple days ago. Not sure if he was allowed to eat 'em, but at least he could smell 'em. She said he looked okay. Thinner."

I shrugged. "Thank her for me. How you doing? You must be like a hundred years old by now, right?"

"Some days it feels like it." He laughed. "But I'm just a seventy-three-year-old youngster."

"You ever going to retire?"

"And give up all this?" he said, holding his hands out to his side.

One of his guys yelled his name from the other side of the shed.

"Good to see you, Daniel," I said.

We shook hands.

"You too. Oh, do me a favor. Ask Jack something for me?"

"Sure. What?"

"Ask him if he wishes he had a son," Daniel said, cracking himself up. I walked to the back, Daniel's laughter trailing behind me. All I ever wanted to do was make people happy.

Behind the shed, rows and rows of heavy equipment filled the two acres of packed dirt. Tractors, caterpillars, threshers, plows, and other monsters with enormous, dirt-caked tires filled the yard. Some were operational, some antiques. In farming you never threw anything away. You never knew. There might yet be a need for that rusted-out horse-drawn plow.

I found Mike underneath a thresher. His boot heels pushed him further out of view as he tried to gain leverage in the dirt. I could hear the banging of metal on metal and the grunts that accompanied it. Two of his guys stood over him. An array of tools littered the ground.

Mike slid out and stood up, shaking the dust off his pants and shirt. He turned to his guys. "All right, I give. You were right. Bent to hell. I can't fix it either." He saw me out of the corner of his eye. "Hey, Jim, that you? I'll be right there."

I nodded, but he had already turned back to his guys. "I bring it to the shop, they charge me two grand. That ain't happening. This ain't a sports car. Don't need to run fast. It don't even need to run good. Just needs to run."

"*Qué quieres hacer?*"

"Talk to the other guys. See if anyone has a brother, a cousin. Someone that's a mechanic or a welder. In Mexicali or here. Tell them I'm offering five hundred to whoever fixes it. And a hundred for the guy who finds him. But only if it runs for at least six months. They do a good job, I'll shoot them more business. No gypsies."

The workers nodded and picked up the scattered tools off the ground. Mike walked to me and gave me a crushing, one-handed shoulder squeeze. "You want something cold to drink? A steak for that eye? Let's go to my office. It's cooler in there."

It wasn't. The small fan was overmatched. Its blades moved so slowly you could track them with your eye. It may even have been a little hotter inside, the air thick and stale. Mike's wood-paneled office was all function, no frill. A desk, a water cooler, a mini-fridge, a filing cabinet, and a couple of chairs. And stacks and stacks of paper everywhere. Each stack with a different makeshift paperweight to keep the paper from blowing away. Although I doubted that the fan was capable of moving even a single sheet of paper.

As Mike took a seat, I moved a large stack of paper off the only other chair and set it at my feet. The stack had been held down by a box of shotgun shells, which I set on top of the stack. I didn't want to mess up Mike's system.

Mike grabbed a couple of bottles of Coke out of the mini-fridge. He handed me one and gave my face a squinting once-over. "You never learned how to fight? What's the other guy look like?"

I felt the bruise on my jaw, immediately self-conscious. "I went down to Mexicali last night with Bobby Maves."

Mike laughed, explanation enough. "I thought Bobby got married. Settled down."

"Didn't take."

"That's too bad. Hate to hear that. He has a daughter, right?"

"Two. They're with their mothers. Not in the Valley no more. He sees them when he can." I didn't know why, but I felt the need to defend Bobby.

"He'll settle down. Has to eventually realize he's a grown man. Act like it. Did he start the trouble last night?"

"Trouble found us."

He nodded, taking a big drink of his Coke. "So, what can I do for you?"

"I wanted to talk to you about Pop's land. Make sure it's cool. Not giving you too much extra work. It's a big load."

Mike interrupted me with an embarrassed wave of his hand. "Yeah, yeah, yeah. It's nothing."

"So. I'm down here for a while now. I don't think I'm ready to take over the farming completely. I don't know if I'll ever be. But if you tell me what needs to be done, I'm sure I can do some work. I can irrigate, mow, you know, bale. I know how to do the stuff I did in high school. I'm ready to work, but I ain't really ready to take charge."

Mike smiled and nodded. "It's all alfalfa now. Just been mowed, I think. I'll check. But next time I need an irrigator, I'll call you."

"I hope you're not paying for anything yourself. You're keeping track of all the expenses, right? Take it out of the hay sales."

"Labor's on me. No way I'm charging Uncle Jack for my work or my guys. But real expenses, I keep track, got it all figured. It's in one of these stacks. Don't worry about it."

"Thanks, Mike."

"How you doing for money?"

"I'm okay. I got a little. Hadn't really thought about it, you know. I just knew I had to be down here," I said.

"I can always use a hard worker. If it ain't an insult to a college boy like you." He smiled. "When do you usually see Jack?"

"I'm going to try to see him every day. From like ten to three or four. But I'll take work if you got it."

"All right. I'll see about some irrigating, mowing, digging, whatever. If not, maybe some work here, around the shed. During the summer, we're not in the fields midday, so your schedule fits." He sat up in his chair and looked for a spot on his desk to set down his empty Coke bottle. Failing, he settled on the ground.

"I don't want to step out of line or get personal or nothing, Jim. If I do, you tell me. But do you have any kind of plan? I don't mean now. Now you spend time with Uncle Jack. That's important. I mean later, you know. Do you know what you're going to do?"

"You ain't out of line, Mike. I haven't thought about any of that. I know I should plan stuff, but I can't or haven't or

I don't know. Like if I start, I've made a turn I'm not ready for. And I don't care if it's smart or not. Pop's still alive. That's my focus."

Mike nodded. "Good enough. When you coming over to the house, get yourself a home-cooked meal? Annie and the kids would love to see you."

"Soon. Still getting settled. Only been back a day. After my face heals a little. How about next time she makes that thing with the Fritos in it, you call me?"

"Everything she makes has Fritos in it." Mike shook his head. "She likes Fritos."

"I'll come by soon," I said, getting up. "Thanks for the Coke. Thanks for everything."

"Tell Uncle Jack not to worry. He's got family."

"Jesus Christ, Jimmy. What happened to you?" Angie said, her hand instinctively going to the bruise on the side of my face.

Considering how our last encounter had gone, I was a little surprised to receive any sympathy. But I hadn't made it ten feet inside the door before she was on me. More than a foot shorter, she simultaneously pulled my head down and tilted it back to angle better light onto my battered face.

"Hey, that hurts," I said, but bent to her will.

"What did you do?"

"Why is it I had to do something? Couldn't this just have happened?" I said, immediately defensive.

"Yeah, it was an accident. You had nothing to do with it. You accidentally hit your face on someone's shoe. The bruise on your forehead is shaped like a boot heel."

I hadn't noticed that when I had looked at myself in the mirror. It made me want to take another look, curious if it was that sharply defined.

"Face doesn't hurt like my body, just looks worse."

"You're kidding. It gets worse? Jesus, Jimmy."

"It's fine. I'm fine," I said, attempting to sidestep her. "I'll be honest. It kind of surprises me that you care. I thought you hated me."

"Lift up your shirt," Angie said. She stepped back and put her hands on her hips, blocking my path.

"What? No. I'm going to see my father." I tried to walk past her.

Angie slapped my side. Right where my ribs were most likely cracked. I jumped back with a squeal.

"Okay, you're coming with me." She grabbed my wrist and pulled me down the hall. I didn't try to resist, feeling like some ne'er-do-well being taken to the principal's office.

Angie found a vacant room and pulled me in behind her. "Strip down to your underwear," she demanded.

"No sweet talk? No dinner?"

"Don't push your luck," she said. "And I don't hate you. I just don't know you. You don't know me."

"Mr. Morales told me last night that people don't change."

"That doesn't work in your favor."

"What I'm saying is I'm still your friend. Even if I haven't seen you. You never stopped being my friend. Whoever you are."

"Okay, I'll give you the benefit of the doubt. It's not easy, but it's fair. Now, get your fucking shirt off."

Very slowly, I took off my shirt. I couldn't really lift my arms high, so it awkwardly got stuck on my head.

Angie's reaction sounded like a combination between a laugh and a shriek.

I got the shirt off. "Look, it's all bruises and maybe a couple of cracked ribs. What's a doctor going to do? Nothing. Tell me to get some rest."

"And tell you to stop fighting until you learn how."

"There were five of them. Winning is surviving when it's five against one. Technically, I won. A doctor would probably prescribe me some pain pills, right?"

"Yeah, but then how would you learn your lesson?"

"I've learned it. Trust me."

"Doesn't look like there's any permanent damage. Is there blood in your urine?"

"I love it when you talk dirty."

"I'll take that as a no. Like you said, the only thing a doctor would do is give you something for the pain."

"Exactly."

"Pain is God's way of telling people to stop being an idiot."

"I'm not so up on the Bible, but I don't think it says that anywhere. Unless of course it's from the Book of Crazy. I'm serious. Can you score me some pills? It hurts."

"I'll rephrase. Pain is God's way of telling me to tell you to stop being an idiot. Stop being an idiot."

Angie insisted on disinfecting and stitching up the wound on the top of my head, which was probably a good idea as it was still oozing. She stopped scolding me after a while, but only because she ran out of clever and cruel things to say. I thanked her when we were done. And as we walked down the hall, I got a shake of the head, a corner of the mouth grin, and an honest chuckle.

I couldn't help myself. "You want to grab some dinner sometime?"

"No."

"It would be good to talk."

"Probably, but not yet. I'm going to do my best to treat you like a human being. We'll take it from there."

Pop was asleep when I came into his room. I set the fingernail clippers and books I had brought from the house on his nightstand. I grabbed the chair, moved it close to the bed, and leafed through the book on top: *Seven Slayers* by Paul Cain. I had just finished reading the first short story when Pop stirred. He gave a weak stretch, pushing at the mattress with both hands and scooting himself up a few inches in the bed. He blinked himself awake and then turned to me, taking a second to register my face.

"You drop your left?" he asked nonchalantly, staring at my bruises.

I didn't want to tell Pop it had anything to do with finding Yolanda. I didn't want him to feel responsible. "And my right. It was a misunderstanding."

"A misunderstanding did that to your face?"

"No, I did. Made a mistake. Pretended I was someone I'm not anymore."

Pop laughed. "Look at my boy getting poetic. Don't worry, you don't got to tell me. You're a grown man. But can you take my objective opinion? You ain't changed as much as you think you have. Nobody does."

"How you feeling?" I asked.

"I feel about how you look," he said.

"Yeah. Dumb question."

"I'm just playing with you," Pop said, reaching his hand out and weakly squeezing my shoulder. I acted like he hadn't caught one of my bruises.

"You awake enough to play a little 'Walks into a Bar'?" I asked.

"You really want more pain?" he said, talking a little smack.

"Bring it, old man."

"Walks into a Bar" was a game that Pop and I had started playing in our phone conversations. It was based on a joke: "A mushroom walks into a bar. The bartender says, 'We don't serve mushrooms here.' The mushroom says, 'But I'm a fungi.'" ("Fun guy," get it?)

The point of the game was to pick a subject and then make up as many bad puns or wordplay punch lines that you could think of. Unlike the original joke that made sense (or of course, the classic "I'm a frayed knot"), it was less important that the punch line completely worked than how you incorporated the theme.

I challenged, so Pop picked the subject. "A boat," he said.

There was no preparation time. One of the challenges was to see if you could come up with the punch line while you were reciting the setup. We always said the joke in its entirety.

I started. "A boat walks into a bar. The bartender says, 'We don't serve boats here.' The boat says, 'But I'm about to keel over.'"

Pop gave me a condescending smile, and then he gave his response. "A boat walks into a bar. The bartender says, 'We don't serve boats here.' The boat says, 'I'm just here to pick up a couple of oars.'"

"Round one to the old man," I laughed. "You've been sitting on that one, haven't you? When did you think it up?"

"A couple of days ago. Knew you'd eventually challenge me." He smiled.

"Give yourself a point. How many boat punches do you have in the bank?"

"That was the only one." He crossed his heart. "It popped into my head. Too good to pass up."

"One, nothing. A boat walks into a bar," and the game continued.

We played for the next half hour, Pop winning by a landslide. Fifteen to six. He usually won, this time coming up with "I heard you served schooners here," "Looking for a small port," and "If I'm not wanted, I can shore leave," among many others. The best I could do was "I thought you were having a sail," "Is that pier pressure?" and the embarrassed-as-I-said-it, "Just one drink, I'm full of seamen." I'd blame my aching head, but Pop just had a quicker mind. The point wasn't winning. The point was laughing. And in that way, we both won. But really, I lost.

"Your face got something to do with the snipe hunt I sent you on yesterday?" Pop asked.

"Nope," I lied.

Pop turned toward me and looked me in the face. He reclined, his head in the center of his pillow, staring up at the cottage cheese ceiling. "I appreciate you lying, but you've never been good at it. You've never gotten away with it. Not with me. I know you think you have, but you haven't. When you were in high school, every time you came home drunk, I knew. When you used to sneak out to raise hell with Bobby, I knew. You got good grades, were responsible, I trusted you. I mean, I trusted you to get in the right amount of trouble. I didn't trust you to believe every word you said. I don't mind you lying to me. I'd just hate to die knowing that you thought you got away with it."

"Did I lie that much? Or that poorly?"

"No more than most."

"You sound pretty sure of yourself. Every time? Odds say I got away with it a couple times."

"Every time. Sorry about whatever happened to your face."

"This was essentially unrelated. I said I'd find her, and I'm on it. Got someone tracking her down. I should be getting a call soon. If she's in Mexicali."

Pop nodded.

"When I find her—and you'll notice I said *when*—should I bring her here? Or I guess you could come out to the house, right? They'd let you?"

"Let me? They don't have any say, but I don't think I'm up for an overnight. You just bring her here and give us a little time."

"Okay."

Pop nodded, drifting somewhere else. After a moment he said, "Why haven't you asked me about Yolanda? Aren't you curious? I'd be if I were you."

"None of my business. If you wanted to tell me you would."

"I suppose."

"So, do you want to tell me?"

"No."

I headed out early. I was feeling a little better, although my ribs gave me reminders in the form of sharp pains every fifteen minutes. I probably should have gotten some rest and spent the day in bed, but I wanted to get some work done. Back at the house, I took four aspirin and went straight out to work on the water pump.

The water for the house came directly from the Ash Canal that ran behind Morales Bar. Not water you'd want to drink, but good enough for bathing, cleaning, and cooking. From the canal the water flowed through a pipe with no filtration system and filled an open cistern, essentially a buried concrete water stand that held the water and maintained the water pressure for the house, such as it was. It used to have a concrete lid, but that had cracked and fallen into the water below during one of the bigger earthquakes in the late seventies. It had been covered with a plastic tarp, and it was still covered with the same tarp, a little worse for the thirty-year wear.

Not knowing what I was doing, I looked at the ancient system for a while and tried to get a feel for the mechanics of it. I shook a few hoses and gave some connections the once-over. At one point, I gave the pump a solid bang with a wrench, hurting my hand. It was all procrastination and I knew it. I was avoiding the real problem. The most likely culprit was the pipe that connected the cistern to the house. To the best of my knowledge, it had never been cleaned, meaning it was probably filled with mud and gunk and Lord knows what. A clogged artery giving the house a heart attack.

Eventually I would have to get a ladder and climb down into the cistern and clean it. But looking into the dark well, it was eight feet down to the water level and I had no idea how deep to the pipe. I could snake it, but it was definitely a two-man job. And I didn't want to be one of those men.

I tried to summon up my learned work ethic. According to Pop, you never hired someone to do something you could do yourself. His house, his rules. But I decided I could put this off a little longer and concentrate my attention on a nap. There was plenty to do. No need to prioritize. It would all eventually have to get done.

I had plenty of time.

TEN

It took a week for me to get the call about Yolanda. I was beginning to think that Tomás had made the promise, but never bothered to follow up. I wasn't angry. I didn't blame him. It was a crazy request. I was relieved and surprised when I got the call. The alternative was a return trip south of the border that I didn't want to make. If I never went to Mexicali again, that would be dandy with me.

At nine o'clock that morning, I was calf-deep in the dark, flooded basement trying to fix the sump pump when my cell phone rang. I had already slipped once on a hidden frog under the murky water and wasn't in the best of moods. The sludgy water smelled like rural Florida, and my flashlight was flickering on and off. Not surprisingly, Yolanda wasn't the first thing on my mind when I answered.

"Hello?" I answered curtly, slipping on something slick and moving under the murky water.

"Jimmy?" the caller said. I didn't recognize the accented voice.

"Yeah, this is Jimmy."

"We found Yolanda," the voice said.

It took a second to sink in. "Great. Who is this? Tomás said he'd call."

"Tomás is filming today. You're talking to Alejandro. Tomás told me to call this number. Tell you."

"Should I arrange everything with you?"

"Tomás told me to help you," he answered.

I carefully made my way to the basement steps so I had somewhere to sit. My foot hit frog and I slid about three feet, but maintained my balance.

I sat down on the steps. "Should I bring her down or can you bring her to me? I want to take her somewhere. On this side of the border. How do I do that? Do I pick her up? Or do you bring her? What do we do?"

"Tomás told me to bring her to his *abuelo*'s cantina tomorrow night. Wednesday. If that is what you want."

"Sure. Is she…does she know why she's coming? You're not forcing her, are you?"

There was a long silence on the other end. The only sound I heard was something moving in the water at the far end of the basement. I shined my flashlight in the direction, but only saw the rippling of the water. The basement was starting to creep me out. At the first sign of tentacles, I would run upstairs.

Finally, Alejandro spoke. "Tomás does not force women. He asked. She agreed. She is a worker. This is her work."

"What time on Wednesday?"

"Ten. Eleven, the latest. Depends on the border. The traffic."

"That late, I'd need her to spend the night," I said.

"Tomás told me that would be what you'd want. You can bring her back. Same time, same place, next day. If a day is enough." He said the last sentence as if he were making a joke, but I didn't get it.

"More than enough. Thank Tomás for me."

"*Sí. Mañana.*" He hung up.

I held the phone to my ear, frozen. I stared over the brown water that filled the basement. Where did all the water come from? I was in the middle of the desert and there was a wading pool inside the house.

I looked up the stairs. I should probably do a little more cleaning. I was going to have company.

During the previous week, I had divided all my time between visiting Pop and working on the house. A heat wave had hit the Valley. Temperatures rose into the 120s. Believe it or not, there is a big difference between 112 degrees and 122 degrees. Ten degrees, to be exact. I focused my attention on the inside of the house: cleaning, picking up, and organizing. If I kept all the curtains closed and kept the fans running, it was bearable. Heat or no heat, my injuries kept me moving at a snail's pace. Luckily, I wasn't in any hurry.

I worked slowly and inefficiently. I would start to organize the books, but end up reading for a couple of hours instead. I'd begin to throw away a stack of thirty-year-old catalogs when I'd realize that thirty-year-old catalogs were fascinating. Every room was like a sunken pirate ship filled with weird treasure. Pop's pop had built the house, and Pop had lived in it his whole life. Every room was filled with layers of dust-covered history. Even in the bathroom, I found some electric-blue aftershave that was in an unopened cut-glass bottle shaped like a Dachshund. I sloshed the Slurpee-colored liquid around, fashioning a story in my head about how one ends up with a wiener dog full of cologne. It had to be a gift. From whom? I could see why it was so hard for Pop to throw anything out. Everything Pop owned was a story.

When organizing Pop's closet, I accidentally stumbled on his porn stash. It was just two magazines. Thankfully nothing extravagant or creepy, just a couple of skin mags. They were twenty years old and probably had been forgotten. I put the magazines back exactly where I found them, making sure they were in the exact same position. I consciously avoided looking inside them. Those were Pop's tits, not something I wanted to share.

I only saw Bobby once during that week, although I talked to him a couple times on the phone. I had forgotten that we agreed to help Buck Buck and Snout bale hay, but it's not like my dance card was full, so I put in a night's work.

It felt good to be working in the fields. It had been such a long time. Hard work, laughing with friends, getting filthy and sweaty. It reminded me that while I was focused on my dying father, the rest of the world continued happening. It was a reminder that the real world would still be waiting when my personal bubble finally exploded.

After the call from Alejandro, I went into a cleaning frenzy. Yolanda was going to have to spend the night. I wanted to make sure that at least one of the bedrooms was presentable. It didn't matter whether or not she lived in worse environs. She was going to be my guest, and I wanted her to feel comfortable. I washed some sheets by hand and hung them on the line in the back. Desert perk, they were dry in ten minutes.

As he was integral in the trip to Mexicali, I called Bobby to tell him about Yolanda.

"Tomás came through. Good deal," Bobby replied to the news.

"Yeah, I think he felt like he owed me. From the past."

"That's awesome. You got your dad the hooker he asked for."

"Can that be the last time you say that sentence?" I laughed. "Thanks again, Bobby. For your help. I'll buy you some beers next week."

"Anytime, brother. I like beers."

It had been too late in the day to call Pop with the news. So the next day, Wednesday, I dropped in on Pop earlier than usual. He was eating his breakfast.

"You want my oatmeal?" Pop asked in the form of a greeting. He didn't seem surprised to see me, but I'm not sure how aware of time he was, having no real use for it.

"I ate breakfast. And I hate oatmeal," I answered.

"Yeah, so do I," Pop said, pushing the tray away from his body and then taking a piece of dry toast and biting at its corner. "They honestly don't care what I want. It's like they think old people eat for texture, not taste. If they put a soft turd in front of me, I think they'd expect me to gobble it down. Hell, I don't know what's worse, eating something I hate or the cooks ruining something I like."

"You want me to get you something else?"

"Wish I still had some of those tamales Marta Quihuis brought by," he said, looking disdainfully at his toast.

"I could get you some more tamales. Sneak in a Special Q."

"If my doctor saw me eating a Special Quesadilla, she'd shit herself." Pop laughed. A Special Quesadilla was an Imperial Valley original. I've never seen it served anywhere else. Where a quesadilla is melted cheese inside of a tortilla, to make a special quesadilla you fill tortilla dough with cheese, crimp the ends, and then deep-fry the whole magilla. The melted cheese and doughy inside offset the crispy exterior. Artery-cloggingly delicious. It made a Luther Vandross Burger look healthy. Even without hot sauce, I broke a sweat eating that much saturated fat, my heart pleading surrender.

"How about a *chile relleno* from Camacho's?"

"No. It's not a big deal. I'm just in a complaining mood, I suppose."

"Well, I got good news. I found Yolanda. Going to bring her by tomorrow. What do you think about that?"

Pop took another bite of his toast, chewing slowly. He dusted a couple of crumbs off his chest and waited until he swallowed before saying, "Where did you find her?"

"I didn't. Not really. I got someone to find her. Mr. Morales's grandson, actually. You remember Tomás. I'm picking her up tonight. She spends the night at the house. I bring her here tomorrow morning."

"So you haven't seen her?"

"No. Not even a picture."

"But you're sure it's her?"

"I gave the description you gave me. They seemed to know her," I said, feeling some slight apprehension that maybe I had screwed up.

"She's beautiful," he said.

"I figured she would be."

"Don't bring her by until noon, the earliest. I have some things to do in the morning."

Now I was curious. "Sure. Anything I can help with?"

Pop shook his head. "I should have it under control. Just things I've been putting off. No more time to procrastinate. The upside of dying, better time management."

I nodded. Death jokes from the dying were generally not funny, but I didn't want to appear uncomfortable.

"And you're sure it's her?" Pop asked.

"Not anymore. But they seemed sure. If it's not her, then we'll go from there."

"Yolanda," Pop said, not to me.

"I'm going to take off. I just wanted to tell you in person," I said, sensing that Pop wanted to be alone. "I need to get the house clean. Run some errands. Stuff like that. You going to be okay without me?"

Pop nodded, although I wasn't convinced he heard me. He was somewhere else. And from the look on his face, it was somewhere better. Somewhere where hookers cured cancer. Heaven, maybe.

I found Angie at the nurse's station. She was talking on the phone, the receiver cradled in the crook of her neck as she thumbed through what were probably insurance forms. Or something just as boring. She looked up when she saw me. I gave her a nod.

She let the receiver drop away from her mouth. "I'm on hold. You want something?"

"You got five minutes?"

"Son of a bitch cocksucker," she yelled. Angie had always had a potty mouth. But in my experience, nurses have the foulest mouths of any profession. Ask one. They'll fucking tell you.

"I thought we were past that," I said, holding up my hands in surrender.

She laughed. "Not you, stupid. The ass monkeys at the insurance company hung up on me." She set the phone in its cradle. "So, what do you want?"

"It's a little embarrassing."

"You're not going to tell me you love me or some bullshit like that, are you?"

"No. Here goes. Can you score me some Viagra?"

Angie took a second to let my question sink in. Then she lost it, bringing her hand to her mouth to hold back her laughter.

"Is there somewhere we can talk? Somewhere more private?" I said.

She kept a chuckle going. "You're not going to convince me to steal dick pills for you. So there's no reason for us to go anywhere."

"It's for Pop. Why would I need Viagra?"

"Maybe you can't get a boner. That's usually the reason. If so, using your sick father as a front for your droop is sad."

"Even if I couldn't get it up, which I assure you I can, it's not for me. And if I was asking for Viagra to jerk it with, then that's so goddamn pathetic, I would think that pity would command a couple of pills."

"Why would your father need Viagra?" Her voice dropped off. Her eyes lit up. "Five minutes. I want to hear this." She stood up and walked from behind the nurse's station. I followed her down the hall until we reached a door with a small placard on it. The chapel. Angie gave a chin nod at the word. "Nobody ever comes in here."

I could see why. We entered the crappiest chapel I had ever been in. There were four pews facing a poorly spray-painted black metal music stand that acted as a low-rent altar. Thumbtacked to the wall, posters of stained glass were spaced evenly, failing at the weak illusion they were trying to create. A potted palm sat in the corner, adding nothing and dying silently. Its dry, brown fronds littered the ground beneath it. Angie and I sat down in the nearest pew. Our knees briefly touched before we both pulled away.

"What's going on?" she asked. "I'm not getting anything for you until I know what's going on."

"Here it is. Pop asked me to find him a prostitute. I'm bringing her by tomorrow."

Angie didn't say a word. She stared at my mouth as if the words hadn't quite registered.

"Pop didn't ask for the Viagra, but I thought he should have it. In case he needed it. I mean, he can barely walk. So I didn't know what else, you know, how well stuff was working." Now I was babbling. "I actually need another favor. I know it's a lot. Could you make sure they aren't interrupted when she's, you know, when they're both here? When they're, you know, together? So no one walks in on them."

She said nothing, staring at me like I was insane. She exhaled loudly. "Wait. Go back. You're bringing your father a what now?"

"A hooker."

"A hooker. Here. You're bringing a hooker here. To a convalescent home?"

I nodded.

"And you want me to help sneak her in?"

"No, no, no. Nothing like that. Why would I need to sneak her in? This isn't a prison. She's like any visitor. We'll go to Pop's room together, but then I'll leave. I just don't want to have to stand guard by the door. I don't want to have to hear anything that I don't want to hear, that I won't be able to unhear. You can keep the nurses out. Give them privacy."

"Do you know how ridiculous that sounds?"

"Of course I do. Jesus Christ, of course. But I honestly don't give a fat shit. Pop's dying. He's going to be dead soon."

I stopped. I had never said that out loud, and it hit me all at once. Tears welled up in my eyes. I felt a little sick.

I continued, speaking in a slow, staccato rhythm to get the words out evenly. "Why is this such a weird thing? He wants some human contact. Where else is he going to go? What other options does he have?"

Angie said nothing, staring at the music stand. I squeezed the bridge of my nose with my fingers. It hurt like hell, but it helped me get control. I wiped my face with my hand, feeling the wetness on my fingers.

"Okay," she said, nodding her head in short, quick movements.

"Thanks."

She took my hand and squeezed. "There's a conversation that we haven't had yet. It's not time. You've got your father on your mind. I'm sorry about Jack, about what you're going through. I should have told you that earlier." She turned to me. "When I'm here, when I'm working, I can't get close. I turn something on. Or off, I guess. People die here once a week or more. I keep a distance. I like your father. And shit, Jimmy, I like you. I'm sorry to see what you're going through. Sometimes I forget that the people here are people."

"You have to," I said, trying to give her an out.

"But you're my friend. You were right. Despite the time, despite our issues, despite everything, we are friends. No matter if I'm mad at you, you're still my friend. It should hurt me to see you in pain. It's fucked up that it hasn't until now. It's fucked up that I haven't even realized how much pain you're in."

At that moment, I wanted to hold her. I wanted to kiss her. I did neither. I just sat with her in that shitty chapel, holding her hand. Holding her hand and wishing things were different. Wishing the impossible.

The house looked marginally presentable when I left the house that night. My primary method of cleaning consisted of piling boxes and boxes of stuff into the extra bedrooms to the point of ridiculousness. As long as Yolanda stayed in the living room, kitchen, or my old bedroom, the house would pass muster.

It was about eight thirty when I walked across the road. I was bored with cleaning and a little antsy, so I decided to head over early and knock back a few drinks. I hadn't had a drink since that night in Mexicali, and I was due.

I immediately spotted Bobby's Ranchero parked between a couple of mud-covered pickups in front of Morales Bar. Hopefully the relaxing drinks that I planned on having wouldn't end up as a bar fight. One can dream.

"What are you doing here?" I asked Bobby.

"I bought you beers," he said, darting his eyes toward two bottles on the table in front of him.

I gave his shoulder a squeeze and sat down across from him. I held the bottle in front of me for a second, looking at the liquid inside, and then I took a long, cold pull. "You come to see Yolanda?"

"Of course. You fucking kidding? What am I going to do, read a book and stop before the last chapter? No way I was going to miss it. No fucking way," he said, grin in place.

"Don't let me get drunk, okay?"

"I'm probably not the best person to hold that responsibility. I'll grab a couple more beers."

Two hours later, I was buzzed, but not drunk. I had willed myself to nurse my drinks rather than gulp them. With the heat as it was, it was hard not to just guzzle every liquid in front of you. But the last thing I wanted when Yolanda showed up was to be shit-faced and falling over.

A little after ten thirty, Little Piwi entered Morales Bar, his massive bulk filling the door frame. He glanced around slowly and then entered. Alejandro followed him. They were immediately accompanied by five women, all of them dressed in what looked like discarded maid of honor gowns. A lot of ruffles and taffeta. The men in the place perked up. I even caught a couple of muddy-booted field-workers adjusting the collars of their plaid work shirts and taking off their sweat-stained caps. Next thing you knew, they were going to lick their fingers and straighten their eyebrows.

Alejandro made eye contact, gave me his best shark smile and a nod, but walked to Mr. Morales, who moved to the end of the bar to greet him. They shook hands and had a few words, leaning in and speaking directly into each other's ears. From a distance it looked like they were necking. The girls stayed close to Little Piwi near the back door. The younger ones peered wide-eyed and scared at the leering men who surrounded them. The older ones, their age obvious by the amount of makeup that caked their faces, looked too tired to care.

None of the girls fit Pop's description of Yolanda. They were all short, under five foot five. Bobby read my mind.

"I thought you said she was tall? A couple of these girls look they snuck over the border of Oz, not Mexico."

"You think he's trying to pull something?" I said.

"I don't know what he'd be pulling, but I guess we'll find out, won't we?" Bobby nodded up toward Alejandro, who was walking to our table.

"*Buenas tardes, amigos,*" Alejandro said, one hand on each of our shoulders.

"Where's Yolanda?" I said, starting to believe this was a big waste of time.

Alejandro smiled. "Yolanda is outside in my van. I bring her in, everyone thinks she's available, for sale, for them. I leave her outside, no confusion. No trouble. Everyone knows who everyone is for. She, your Yolanda, is for you."

I started to stand, but Alejandro put some light pressure on my shoulder. Enough to make me sit back down. "Finish your drinks. I have small business. Make some money. Money always comes first."

I decided not to push it. After all, Tomás was doing me a favor. And in a sense, so was Alejandro. Although it appeared to be through some reluctance. But he was right. What was the hurry?

I watched Alejandro walk the girls out the back door past Little Piwi. He gave Little Piwi some last-minute directives as the men in the bar lined up. They acted like nervous children, hats and caps in hand and wonder-filled eyes anticipating the fun just outside. Alejandro stood back and watched as Little Piwi took the money from the first five men. Satisfied the transactions went smoothly, Alejandro whispered a final message, rubbed the bald monster's head, and walked to the front door. When he reached the door, he turned and gave me a "What are you waiting for?" shrug. Bobby and I looked at each other. We downed our almost full beers.

I had to give Alejandro one thing. He had an efficient workforce. As I exited the front door, I caught the first customer returning from the back door out of the corner of my eye. He appeared more relieved than happy, but I guess that's what you get for thirty-five seconds of love.

Alejandro's van was parked under the salt cedars a little up the road. It was an orange late-seventies Dodge family van with a small, bubbly, heart-shaped window on the side and dingle-balls visibly hanging at the top of the windshield. Alejandro unlocked the van and whipped the sliding side door open.

Yolanda woke, her body curled catlike on the shag interior. She yawned, stretched, and sat up, looking at the three of us, waiting and ready for whatever was next. She was beautiful. Long dark hair, big dark eyes, smooth dark skin. I guess what you would describe as dark features. But there was something else. Three men, two strangers, were staring at her from the open door of a van. And she didn't look afraid. Her neutral expression communicated a confidence and an acceptance that there was nothing we could do to her. That there was nothing to take.

"*Estás lista?*" Alejandro asked, holding out his hand to help her out of the van.

"*Sí,*" she replied, her voice surprisingly deep. She ignored his hand and slid on the carpet until her long legs struck ground outside the side door. The move pushed her skirt high up her thigh. Bobby gave me a look that said what I was thinking. Wow. She was a tall glass of *agua.*

Alejandro gave her a hard squeeze on the ass. No pleasure in it. A demonstration of power. Bobby took a step forward, but I held up my hand. He stopped. Yolanda turned toward Alejandro and made a face that should be reserved for the first time one cleans a fish.

She pulled an overnight bag out of the van and turned to Bobby and me with a big smile. "Hello," she purred with a rehearsed lack of accent, as if that might be the only word she knew in English. She turned to Alejandro, her eyes on Bobby and me. "*Cual?*" she asked.

"Me, I, me," I babbled like an idiot, momentarily forgetting that she wasn't actually for me. A part of me wished she was. I took a breath and suppressed those thoughts.

She cocked her head and approached me slowly. The smile never left her face. Her eyes danced up and down me, not giving Bobby a second glance. It was as if everything else had dropped away except the two of us.

She set her bag down and held out her hand to shake. "Yolanda," she said.

"Jimmy," I answered, shaking her delicate hand.

"Jimmy," she repeated, making a conscious effort to pronounce the J.

"Bobby," Bobby chimed in.

I turned to Bobby, giving him my best "shut the hell up" look.

"Okay, okay," he said, walking back to the bar. Yolanda and I stared at Alejandro until he got the hint and followed. We silently watched the two of them walk back to Morales Bar.

"*Donde está su carro?*" she asked as she took a few steps toward the row of pickups on the other side of the bar.

"*No carro,*" I answered. "*Mi casa,*" I said, pointing across the street. I picked up her bag and took a step onto the road. Yolanda stopped, the smile leaving her face. "*Su casa? No. Señor Veeder vive allí.*"

"*Sí.* I am *Señor Veeder. Yo Señor Veeder.* I mean, *Señor Veeder es mi padre. Yo soy* his son, his *muchacho,*" I said, mangling not only the language but its pronunciation.

"*Su hijo? Jaime?*"

"Yes. *Sí.* His *hijo.* I'm his son, Jimmy."

"Jimmy." She said my name again, but this time with a hint of recognition and affection. As if she had remembered some shared anecdote from the past. She walked up close to me, her nose inches from mine. I could feel her breath on my lips. Then she kissed me on the cheek and stepped onto the road toward the house. I watched her, came out of my trance, and ran three steps to catch up.

ELEVEN

I woke up to the smell of coffee.

I'm not sure what I had expected when I stumbled into the kitchen. But I hadn't expected Yolanda cooking at the stove and wearing Pop's apron over a flower-print sundress. I'd only seen Pop wear the apron on the birthday I had bought it for him as a joke. "Quiche and Fondue Me" was printed on the front. It looked better on Yolanda.

She turned, gave me a brief smile, and then went back to her frying eggs. "*Buenos días. Hice café. No habia comida, pero las gallinas tuvieron huevos,*" she said casually, but too quickly. I got the gist of it. Good morning, coffee, no something food, the *gallinas* something the eggs. What the hell was a *gallina*?

"Morning. *Buenos días,*" I answered. "*Qué es un gallina? Un pollo?*"

"*Sí.*" She giggled, realizing she had taught me a new word. "*Una gallina es un pollo.*"

"*Gracias,*" I said, pouring myself a cup of coffee from the full pot. "*Café?*"

"*No.*" She smiled. She had made the coffee just for me. And she was cooking breakfast. I had to give Pop credit. He had excellent taste.

"Can I help?" I said, and then I took a second to translate in my head. "*Puedo ayudar usted?*" I winced at how bad that must have sounded, hoping I communicated something. I held out my hands in an effort to pantomime cooking and then pointed at myself.

"*Gracias, no.*" She skirted past me and walked directly to the silverware drawer. She pulled out two forks and then opened the cupboard above and took down two small plates. She squeezed past me again and brought the plates to the edge of the stove. She snapped her fingers as if remembering something and reached for the salt and pepper shakers hidden behind the sugar bowl.

She knew where everything was. She knew her way around the kitchen. Not any kitchen, but this kitchen. I didn't even know where the salt and pepper shakers had hidden themselves. When the toast popped up in the toaster, I jumped a bit. I was staring so intently that I had lost myself in her.

She dished the eggs onto the two plates and pulled the toast out, smelling each slice before putting one piece on each plate. She held up both plates and walked past me to the dining room, turning in the doorway. "*Desayuno,*" she said. Then in rehearsed English, "Breakfast."

The night before I had been worried that the language barrier was going to be a problem. My Spanish was obviously awful, and Yolanda's English appeared to be close to nonexistent. I was concerned that she would misunderstand and come on to me before I could fully explain that I wasn't the customer. It had ended up being far easier than I thought, as if she already had a good idea of why she was there.

"*Tú no es por mio. Tú va a Señor Veeder mañana,*" I had explained. My high school Spanish teacher, Mr. Huerta, would have cried or hit me on the back of the head with an eraser in disgust.

"I go to Jack. *Mañana. Sí. Donde está Jack?*"

"Jack, *Señor Veeder es enfermo.* He has cancer. Cancer? *Entiende?*"

"Cancer. *Sí, entiendo.*" Her eyes had dropped to the ground, the smile leaving her face for the first time.

"*Señor Veeder puede para tú.* He asked for you. He's dying," I had said, not knowing the right words.

And with that, she kissed me on the cheek and walked down the hall. I watched her until she disappeared into the bedroom, giving me a weak, uninspired smile and a small wave before closing the door.

Breakfast was pleasant. We said almost nothing to each other while eating our eggs and toast, but it wasn't uncomfortable. It was that kind of silence that old couples earn after being together forty years. A mutual peace. I was eating breakfast with the prostitute that I had found for my father, and it felt perfectly normal. Better than normal. Yolanda looked up at me from her food, smiling in a way that made the rest of the world go away.

I smiled back and said, "*Bueno huevos,*" because I'm an idiot.

"*Gracias,*" she answered, and then she reached over and pushed the hair away from my face. "*Muy guapo. Parecido a tu padre.*"

I'm not a blusher. I'm just not. But at the moment, I could feel my face flush. I looked down at my plate. The three minutes of silence that followed didn't have the peace from before. Yolanda made me nervous in the way a crush makes you nervous around a woman you barely know.

Eventually, Yolanda said, "*Me gusta su padre. Me gusta Jack.*"

I like your father. I like Jack. That's what she said, but this is where any subtlety of the language was completely lost on me. I like your father. I like Jack. Is that *like* like or just like? They knew each other. That was pretty obvious. But knew how? I knew Pop liked her. He had asked me to find her. It was like I had no idea what the word "like" meant anymore. I answered in the best way I could think of. I shrugged and jammed my mouth full of eggs.

Yolanda refused to let me wash the dishes, going so far as to slap the back of my hand playfully when I reached for a plate. I showed Yolanda the bathroom and shower and tried to explain to her about the cold water/water pressure issue. It occurred to me that Yolanda, depending on where she grew up, might be used to cold showers. For fifteen minutes I mangled the Spanish language by stupidly repeating, "*Agua frío.*" I tried to decipher her words until I realized that she was trying to tell me that she had already showered while I was asleep. What is life without a little comedy?

After I took my shower and dressed, Yolanda was nowhere to be found. Walking from room to room, I kept expecting to see her sitting in a chair or thumbing through a book, but she wasn't in the house. For a brief moment, I panicked, convinced that this had been some elaborate scheme and she was just here to rob Pop. But then I looked around the house and came to my senses. Who was I kidding? There might have been a few things worth stealing, but good luck finding them in the mess.

I found Yolanda outside walking along the side of the house and eating pomegranate seeds one at a time from a cracked open pomegranate. She daintily took each seed out of the husk and put it in her mouth. I could see the subtle motion of her jaw positioning the seed and then grinding it between her front teeth. One seed at a time. At that rate it would take her three days to finish that pomegranate. She turned to me, smiled, and held out the pomegranate to me. I shook my head as I walked to her.

She sat down on the concrete slab next to my nemesis, the water pump. I gave it a wicked sideways glance, reminding it who was boss. (It was.) Yolanda continued to eat the pomegranate, her fingers stained red. I sat down next to her. And for the next hour, we just sat. Yolanda worked through one seed at a time and I watched her. Talk was even cheaper when you didn't understand each other. All in all, Yolanda was excellent company. I hadn't had a morning that pleasant in a long time.

We got to Harris Convalescent around twelve thirty. I had called Angie on the drive to give her fair warning that we were on our way. She had assured me that Pop and Yolanda would not be disturbed.

Angie was at the front desk when Yolanda and I came through the double-glass doors. Yolanda wore the same sundress and carried her small overnight bag over her shoulder. Angie gave a noticeable eyebrow lift when she saw Yolanda. Angie gave me a smirk and an overexaggerated flourish and bow, with an elaborate, "You may enter." I was going to introduce Yolanda and Angie, but it not only felt unnecessary, but inappropriate. I kept it to a nod and headed down the hall. Angie caught up to me and without a word put a blue pill in my hand.

At Pop's door I motioned for Yolanda to wait. She nodded, switching her bag from one hand to the other. I gave the door a light rap and entered as I usually did, not waiting for permission.

There was another man in the room. A man in a suit. He sat next to Pop's bed. Papers littered Pop's tray and covered the man's lap. Pop saw me and said softly to the man, "We'll finish this later. Tomorrow maybe."

The man turned and I recognized him as Clem "Red" Fidler, Pop's lawyer and one of his closest friends.

"James, how you been?" Red stood, holding out his hand. "Your father and I will take care of this some other time." Red might have had red hair at some point in his life, but he had been completely bald the whole time I had known him, his pate speckled with dark spots. I had always liked Red. He was a straight shooter. And as lawyers go, that was rare.

I shook his firm grip. "Thanks, Red. Doing good. How's Bertha?" Bertha was his oldest granddaughter. We had gone to high school together. I wasn't that curious, but I thought it polite to make small talk.

"Married to a preacher. Four kids, if you can believe it," he said proudly. Pop shuffled the pages in front of him into an orderly stack and handed them to Red. Red stuffed them in his open-top briefcase and headed for the door.

"Jack, I'll come by in the next couple of days to get the last few signatures," Red said. "It's good to see you back down, James." He walked out the door, almost bumping into Yolanda. He gave her an extended stare. He looked back at me and Jack, then at Yolanda, then disappeared down the hall. The door closed. Yolanda remained outside.

"I thought you got all the paperwork finished months ago. Or did you think better of it and take me out of your will?"

"I didn't tell you? I'm a Hare Krishna now. Leaving everything to the ashram." Pop smiled. "Had to cross some t's, dot a couple of i's, and umlaut a few o's. Is that Yolanda in the hall? My eyes were too far."

"Sure is. How long should I skedaddle for? A couple of hours?"

"What time is it now?" Pop asked, squinting at the clock on the wall.

"About twelve thirty."

"How about three? You entertain yourself until then?"

"I'll be waiting in the lobby at three." I silently set the blue pill on the nightstand and walked to the door.

Yolanda with her ever-present smile walked into the room as I exited. As the door closed, I watched Yolanda approach Pop in his hospital bed. Life returned to his eyes and smile. I saw something special happen, something important, and I was glad that I was able to give Pop that moment. All week, I had failed to give him the Big Laugh, but somehow Yolanda's presence gave him something more real.

Angie was still at the reception desk. I strolled up, knocking on the counter. "They're in there," I said.

"I can't believe you talked me into helping you," she said. More as conversation than any real complaint.

"You're not helping me, you're helping Pop. But both of us thank you, Angie," I said, meaning it.

She waved it off, pretending to work.

"Do you want to go to the movies with me?" I asked.

She looked up.

"I know you can't play hooky right now, you're working, but we used to go to movies together all the time, and it was fun, and I thought maybe, you know, we could see a movie together and then talk about it after, over coffee or a drink, just a movie. Not dinner. Dinner seems too much. A moving picture," I said, realizing how ridiculous I sounded as I said it. But for whatever reason, I couldn't stop the flow of words coming out of my mouth.

"Maybe," she said after a few seconds.

"What? Really?" said Mister Cool. "Really?"

"Maybe."

"Thanks. I don't have many people down here. People I really know, you know. And as much as I like Bobby, we always end up hammered or worse."

"He's a good friend."

"The best. No question. Shit, Angie, I'd just like to spend some time with you. We're different people now. Like to see how we've both changed."

"Just friends."

"Just friends," I lied.

And Angie and I left it at that. Not making any real plans, but opening up the possibility of seeing each other outside of the building where my father was dying.

I drove through El Centro. Just crisscrossing streets and getting nostalgic over different buildings that sparked forgotten memories. Because gas isn't free, I parked downtown and walked among the mostly vacant storefronts. I tried to remember what businesses had been there when I was a kid.

El Centro Jewelers was gone. And so was Sports Mart, Valley Music, the Central Buffet, the Fashion Boat, and Desert Office Supplies. There had once been a magazine shop where I had bought comic books every Sunday as a kid, the name escaping me. The storefront was now being used as an office for the United Farm Workers.

Luckily, Book Nook was still around. The only used bookstore in the Imperial Valley and air-conditioned to boot. I browsed the stacks and picked up a couple of mysteries and a Hubert Selby book I had never seen. I remembered a conversation I had had with Pop, him telling me that he had never read Nathanael West's *A Cool Million*. He had made the mistake of reading *The Dream Life of Balso Snell*. And due to his policy of not reading everything by an author, he had never read it. I picked up a copy.

El Centro is not an easy town to kill a couple of hours in. There is nothing to do. Especially when it's hot. Luckily, I liked to drink. So I went to the Owl Café to join the lunch crowd for a couple of beers. The interior of the Owl is unique. It is a long, thin building, with a long counter running along each wall. On one side was the restaurant counter, and the other counter was the bar. When the Owl was full, it was almost impossible to squeeze between the backs of its patrons. Many of the regulars would just shift their weight from one stool to another, depending on when it was time to eat and when it was time to drink.

The lunch crowd looked like they may have also been the breakfast crowd, only a couple of people at each counter. Two Mexicans scarfed down burgers at the lunch counter, while a couple of barflies that I recognized by sight, but not name, stared at the labels of their bottles of Coors Light at the bar. When in Rome. I order a Coors Light, sitting two stools down from the nearest barfly.

About halfway through my beer, I noticed that the barfly closest to me was staring. His weather-worn face looked like an overused catcher's mitt with eyes. From five feet away, I could smell his sour alcohol breath as it wafted toward me. The overhead fan was too weak to dissipate its weight.

"You're Big Jack's boy, aintcha?" he slurred, practically one word.

I nodded. "Yeah, that's right."

"Look like him. I know your pa, Veeder."

"I'll tell him you said hello."

"You do that, you do that. But, and this is important, you tell him Squatty ain't found it yet."

"Okay, Squatty." Then out of curiosity, I asked, "Found what?"

"The fucking fort," he shouted, his voice piercingly high. He wasn't angry, just uncontrollably excited. Nobody reacted, save for the bartender, shaking his head in that "now you've done it" way.

I would've let it go, but what the hell else did I have to do. "What fort?"

Out of Squatty's sight line, the bartender held his finger to his head like a pistol and fired, miming suicide.

"Out there in the dunes. Out past Buttercup. Where nothing lives. That's where they filmed *Beau Geste*. You're too young."

"*Beau Geste* with Gary Cooper. I've seen it."

Squatty laughed, although it sounded more like he was dying. The kind of laugh that is nauseating to hear, thick and viscous.

I took a cigarette out and held it up to the bartender, raising my eyebrows in question. He nodded and shrugged. I lit the cigarette and listened.

"Was a time, used to be able to see the fort from the I-8. They built a full-size fort for the movie, you see. Used to be able to see it from the highway. 'Til about the sixties. See it on the way to Yuma. Then the dunes, the sand, swallowed her up, buried her. But it's still out there. That fort's still out there. And I'm going to find her."

"If you could see it from the highway, don't you know where it is?"

"That was some time ago. Before you were born. Do you remember anything from that long ago?"

"Do I remember anything from before I was born?"

Squatty thought about it for a few seconds. "Exactly. Do you remember when you were five years old? Do you remember it right? I remember it, but I don't remember it right. I remember it sorta. The dunes, they play tricks.

They change, they turn, they're alive. You can't draw a map, 'cause it'd just get you loster."

"I don't mean to be a jerk, but why look for it? It's just an old prop building, right? Just some wood and nails and plaster under the sand. Probably collapsed. You just looking for something to do?"

"You don't understand. It's *Beau Geste*. It's Gary Cooper. It's a classic. It's important. It's more than you. More than me. It's history. We're people. We die and it's done, but history is always. History is forever or at least for longer. Nobody knows it's there, nobody but the old-timers, nobody but the dying, nobody but the dead. If I don't find it, nobody will. If I don't look, it's gone. Forever. If nobody finds it, then it's lost. I ain't ever done nothing important, but if I do this, if I find that fucking fort, then I can. We ain't who we are, we're what we do."

Squatty drained the rest of his beer and then shook the bottle, looking at the liquid at the bottom. Did he really go out to the desert? Or did he just talk about it? It didn't matter. He was what he did.

I crushed out my cigarette, finished my beer, and threw a ten on the bar, pointing at Squatty to the bartender. The bartender set another Coors Light in front of the one and only Squatty, the Finder of the Fort and the Keeper of History.

"I'll tell Pop you're still looking." I opened the door, blinded by the harsh white light of the midday sun.

It wasn't quite three, but I had completely exhausted all forms of entertainment that El Centro had to offer, so I headed back to Harris Convalescent. Angie wasn't at the reception desk to bug, so I parked myself on the couch in the small waiting area.

It was probably half an hour and two issues of *Woman's Day* later when Yolanda walked into the front. Her smile was radiant. "*Siéntese?*" I asked, motioning toward the chairs. I pointed to myself and then down the hallway. "*Yo quiero dice adios a* Jack, my *padre. Sí?*" Yolanda nodded her head and sat down on the chair, her overnight bag in her lap like a schoolgirl holding her lunch pail and waiting for the bus.

Pop was asleep when I opened the door. I thought about waking him, but he looked peaceful. That's really all I needed to know. I noticed the pill still on the nightstand when I set down the copy of *A Cool Million*. Good for Pop. I backed toward the door as quietly as I could.

When I reached the door, Pop's faint voice said, "Thanks, Jimmy."

I just smiled and said, "See you tomorrow, right? Back to the regular grind."

"Sounds good," Pop said, turning his head to the ceiling and then closing his eyes again.

I had to pick up some stuff, so it was five by the time we got back to the house. Bobby was in the drive, sitting on the hood of his Ranchero when we pulled up. Yolanda gave me a look, her eyebrows knitted in concern. She gripped her bag tighter, but when she saw me smile, her face and hands unclenched.

"*Mi amigo*," I said to her.

I got out, grabbing a bag of groceries from the bed of my truck. I picked up the two Hungry-Mans that had slid to the back of the bed and turned to Bobby. "What's up?" I said, in the form of a greeting.

"I need a favor," Bobby said.

"I'm kind of busy," I said, glancing at Yolanda.

"Doing what? Mission accomplished, right?"

He had me. I wasn't actually busy. In fact, I had no idea what I was going to do until night when I had to bring Yolanda back across the street. "What do you need?" I asked.

"Take about an hour. Two, tops. I ordered water on the forty I got down off Holt. The plot by the big tree. I had a guy that was going to dig out the gopher holes. He didn't. If I irrigate with that system of tunnels, the water is going to go all flibberty-gibberty, fuck up everything. But I already ordered the water. I'm stuck. Snout and Buck Buck, I can't find. Probably looking for Bigfoot again. I try to do it myself, I'll kill my back. I don't do it, I'm throwing money in a hole. It's a lot of digging, but not for two people. I got a fuck-ton of beer in a cooler and a bottle of to-kill-ya."

"Bobby, I'd help you," I said, "but I'm supposed to leave Yolanda here?"

"She can come. I got three shovels." He smiled and then went to his serious face. "Look, man. It's fucked up. I know. But I'm screwed. Like every farmer down here, I'm playing it close to broke. I work my ass off and still might lose money. It might be good money after bad, but I could use your help to try to get to break even. You don't know how much it sucks to work your ass off and not get paid. The farmer's fucking life."

I glanced at Yolanda, who smiled at me, still sitting in my front seat with her overnight bag in her lap. I may have been a bad host, but she should be happy that I trusted her.

It took Bobby and me four hours to dig up all the gopher holes. Fucking things had an underground system that made the Chinese tunnels in Mexicali sound like an ant farm. I officially hated all rodentkind.

Bobby asked me relentlessly about Yolanda and Pop. I took the fifth, and when I say the fifth, I mean the fifth of tequila that Bobby used to try to loosen my tongue. Luckily, I had no real information to reveal.

I did, however, make the mistake of mentioning that Angie worked at Harris Convalescent.

"You going to make the big move?"

"I have enough bruises all over my body, I need to provoke that kind of violence. It's great to see her though. Brings back a lot of memories."

"I thought the two of you would be together forever. You never told me how you fucked that up."

"I never talked to anyone about it. Don't matter now, I guess. In high school, we never thought about it ending. Hell, we survived senior year, even when she missed her period and for a horrifying four weeks we thought she was pregnant. Scared my shit. We didn't do it again for three months. I'm talking teenage libido and I was too scared to fuck.

"After we graduated and every day the end of summer got closer, we started getting further apart. We both knew I was going to college and she was staying at IVC, and I think we both knew that it would be the end. Two years and in a couple weeks it would be over."

"Did you try?"

"Until first Christmas vacation, but we were fucking kids. I finally had my freedom. We never really broke up, we just slowly stopped writing, slowly stopped calling. We both just let it go."

"That sucks. Least with a big blow-up you know where you stand. I like to end a relationship with explosions. Sometimes literally."

"I always regretted how it ended—didn't fit how we felt. We were just too young to know what the hell to do with it. I think about her more than I should."

Maybe it was the liquor, maybe it was just the need to hear it aloud, but it felt good to tell someone.

Yolanda had cleaned both the kitchen and dining room by the time I had returned. She had swept, mopped, organized papers, and even found some flowers and a vase for the center of the dining room table. I didn't even remember seeing flowers anywhere outside. They smelled horrible, but they made the table and the room glow. They made it look even cleaner.

By the time I took a shower and got dressed, it was time to take Yolanda back to Morales Bar.

"*Estás lista?*" I asked.

"*Sí,*" she said, standing from the couch and walking to the door.

"I want to pay you. *Pagar tú, por favor,*" I said, taking out my wallet and the ten twenties that I had decided to give her. I wasn't sure if that was low or high or insulting or not, but I wanted to pay her. It felt right to me. Pop would have wanted me to, I was sure.

"*No,*" she said with a smile, not angry or put off, but strong. "*Ya está pagado.*"

"I want to," I said, holding out the money to her.

"*Gracias, no,*" she said and walked to the front door. I put the money back in my pocket and followed her across the street.

Alejandro was waiting by his van. "She work out okay? She what you wanted?"

I nodded and glanced at Yolanda, who stood at the open door of the van, one long leg stepping in.

She put her foot back to the ground and walked to me. She stood close enough for me to feel her breasts brush my chest. She stared into my eyes until I smiled and looked away. She kissed me on the cheek and then wiped off the lipstick with her thumb.

"Thank you," I said. "*Gracias.*"

She closed her eyes and kissed me softly on the lips. And then she was in the back of the van and gone.

TWELVE

Immediately after Yolanda's visit, Pop's health slid downhill at a quicker clip. It was as if there was nothing left to live for. Nothing more for him to do. Like he had been falling off a cliff and been in the air so long that screaming or struggling no longer made sense. He just let gravity take him. Doing his best to enjoy the plummet.

I tried to imagine cancer as a small army invading and spreading throughout the body. Little green army men frozen in familiar poses trailing through the bloodstream, pillaging organs and leaving antibody corpses on a fleshy battlefield. But that's not what I saw most of the time. Whenever I heard "cancer," I imagined it as a cottage cheese–like substance oozing over mounds of meat. A bubbly, chunky white mass spreading over the cells of the body and leaving decay and disease in its wake in the form of a slimy black jelly.

I used to date this girl who wouldn't take regular medicine. She was into Chinese herbs and natural remedies. She did acupuncture, saw a chiropractor and a naturopath, and trusted homeopathy unquestioningly. If she got a headache, she'd boil up some twig tea that made her apartment smell like the last day of Burning Man. She held the belief that because something was natural, because something came from nature, it was better. I let her believe what she believed.

She was gorgeous and erotically flexible. Who was I to tell her there was no Santa Claus?

I wanted to tell her that just because something is natural, just because something came from her precious nature, that didn't make it good. Snakebites are natural. Poison is natural. Influenza is natural. And cancer is natural. Sure, flowers are pretty. But for every flower, there is a disease or a disaster or a monster. Nature is beautiful only if you find cruelty beautiful. The true beauty of nature is in the tornado, brutally destructive without conscience or remorse.

Since his arrival at Harris Convalescent, Pop hadn't gotten out of bed that much. He had tubes in his body that took away the necessity of getting up to go to the bathroom. He had his meals and medicine brought to him. He only walked when he wanted to. And the only time he usually wanted to was every other Friday when they had bingo in the cafeteria.

As Pop had told me, "Boredom brings out the bingo in every old fart."

I think he found bingo both tedious and lacking in skill. But every other Friday, he hobbled down the hall and gave it a go. He walked shakily, resting every dozen steps with a hand on my shoulder.

It was about two weeks after Yolanda's visit. I had decided to stay late and play a little bingo with Pop. I had asked him what the prizes were, but he just laughed and said, "It doesn't get much past bragging rights and an extra cup of tapioca. Officially." Then Pop looked around conspiratorially. "But Dallas Lowrie won fifty bucks last month. On a side bet. It's all about the side bets. A couple of the long-timers talk about some grudge matches from five years ago like it was Chacon-Limon."

When Pop left his room, he never wore scrubs or a robe. If people were going to see him, he wanted to be dressed "like a man, not an invalid."

So there I was, helping my father get dressed.

He shifted his weight and used his hands to help move his legs to the edge of the bed. I helped him put on a pair of loose-fitting pants. He got the shirt himself. He had a hard time with the buttons, his fingers fumbling with each one. I could tell he was getting frustrated, but I could also tell that it was important he did it himself. A pair of athletic socks and tennis shoes later and Pop and I were ready to head to the other side of the building and play some Big B.

Pop eased himself further along the edge of the bed, his feet tentatively touching the ground. Testing the water. Toe tips first, then feet flat. Then he stopped, both hands clutching the thin blanket on the bed. He turned to me. And the look in his eyes. I had never seen Pop look so sad. Never in my life. Not even close. He looked devastated. Like something had shattered inside him. The look of a boy who just watched his dog killed by a speeding car.

"I can't walk," he said, his voice more confused than sad.

I put my hand on his elbow and braced him upward. "You can do it," I said.

"No, Jim. I can't. My legs won't do it." Pop looked down at his feet as if they were traitors. "I need a wheelchair, I think."

I quickly raced into the hall. It was empty. I quick-walked to the front and finally flagged down a nurse as she exited a room. She told me where the wheelchairs were on the other side of the building.

I had taken too long.

By the time I got back with the wheelchair, Pop was on the ground. He had slid off the bed. Why hadn't I put him back? I heard "wheelchair" and latched onto the one thing that I could actually do.

I moved to him. Pop shook me off with a weak hand. "I'm fine. Just fell. Nothing broke." An honest smile told me he really wasn't hurt. "You missed a solid pratfall. My slip leg went high into the air. More Keaton than Chaplin."

I picked Pop up. I was in such a hurry that I almost threw him through the ceiling. I had expected him to be heavier, but he weighed next to nothing. And his skin, I could feel his loose and soft skin between my fingers. It felt like warm, raw chicken skin seeping between my fingers, dripping off his body and filling the gaps in my grip.

I smiled like it was nothing and set Pop in the wheelchair. But I wanted to scream. I wanted to cry. I wanted to run out of the room and never come back. I wanted to punch a stranger in the face. I wanted to erupt.

Nobody should have to carry their father. You want your father to carry you.

It's hard to admit, but at that moment, when I was holding what felt like the ghost of my father, some horrible shit entered my head. I wanted Pop to die. I tried to tell myself that it was because I no longer wanted Pop to be in pain. That I no longer wanted Pop to suffer the indignities of dying. I'm sure that was part of it. I saw only the decline of worsening days. But I'd be lying if I said I didn't also want to stop the suffering for myself. I had my own selfish reasons that ate at me. I didn't know how much longer I could watch him wither.

We made it to bingo with Pop in the wheelchair. I think I even won a game, but I can't be sure. The rest of that night was a blur. I tried to steer my thoughts away from Pop, but my brain kept pushing them forward. I wanted my mind to be in neutral instead of that spinning sickness that felt like an attack.

Over the next couple of weeks, I sank into a kind of depression. Not noticeably. Not around Pop. We still joked and laughed, although the Big Laugh seemed far out of reach. We invented new games to play. Wordplay. Jokes. It was a challenge, but I found I had it in me to put on my game face and sit with Pop. The problem for me was that at the end of the day, I had left it all on the field. When I left Pop's room, I had nothing left. I was completely spent.

Then Pop's eyesight went.

To that point for all his suffering, I had never heard Pop complain. He treated the nurses and employees with respect and reverence. He was always polite, raised as a "sir" and "ma'am" kind of guy. But when he lost his eyesight, I finally saw his frustration. Not being able to read or do his crossword puzzles, that was Pop's personal hell. We could talk, but I didn't expect to see him laugh again. When I wasn't there, all he could do was lie in his darkness and listen to the radio.

When I left home for college, Pop had given me only one piece of advice. He told me that the lowest points in my life would be the times when I lost my sense of humor. He had told me that if I could keep my sense of humor, I could survive anything. That was the whole point of my visits. I wanted to remind Pop of his own advice. I wanted to tell him to lighten the fuck up, that it wasn't so bad. But when he had given me that advice, he was talking about getting a flat tire or breaking up with a girl. Not something real. Not something serious. Not something terminal. There was nothing funny about what was happening. There was nothing to laugh at.

I spent more time reading to Pop than talking to him. It was easier on both of us, I think. I didn't have to manufacture good cheer, and Pop didn't have to participate, which I could tell was a struggle with his ebbing energy level. But that day, after reading a chapter of some pulpy Frank Kane story (*Trigger Mortis*, I think), Pop spoke up.

Pop's voice was just above a whisper, raspy from disuse. "I know I said I was only going to have the one dying father talk, but I'm half liar. So we're going to have an encore."

"Sure," I agreed, leaning in to make sure I heard and was heard.

"Ain't never believed in God. Wasn't how I was taught. And those lessons were only reconfirmed through my life. I never saw no evidence. But now, this close to being done, I've realized something."

I waited.

"I realized I was right. And how sad that is. I know there ain't no God. I know, because God ain't no asshole. And God ain't no hypocrite. It would be a pretty sad perfect being that would accept faith from a dying man. That's like letting a murderer go because he cried on the electric chair. If I suddenly found God now, I would hope God or St. Peter or whoever would laugh in my face and send me straight to hell. What kind of sucker god would let anyone into heaven on desperation and a loophole?

"All that God stuff forces everyone to play their hand to the end. But that's not how poker works. That's not how a good poker player acts. If the winning hand always won, poker would be a lousy game. It would be a game of luck. The fact that any player can fold anytime is what separates poker from other games. You can quit on each hand. You can quit whenever you like. You can quit the game in the middle. You can quit up. You can quit down. It's your choice."

"In poker, you can fold, because you know there's another hand to play," I said, not comfortable with where the conversation was going. I was even more uncomfortable that Pop was talking in metaphors, which he generally made fun of whenever he had the chance.

"And in poker, you can win with bad cards, but it's a lot easier to win with good ones. I got a losing hand, Jim. I've been bluffing for months. That's all I'm saying. I'm holding jack high, Jim. I can't win."

"You want to fold?" I asked.

Pop didn't answer, and I didn't press him. It took about a minute before Pop broke the silence.

"You been prodding me for war stories. I'll give you a war story. Don't worry none about the details. Going to try to make a long story short. Just know that while I saw some action, I wasn't no hero. There's no such thing as heroes.

"I was dug in with this kid. Just a kid. Hubie something. Don't know if I ever knew his last name. Wasn't in my unit.

It was the end of three days of fighting. Nobody giving any ground. Me and this Hubie, we were in a foxhole taking some fire. Couldn't move, but okay where we were. Waiting for the cavalry. Trapped, but safe.

"At some point in the night, when things had been quiet, Hubie makes a break for it. Got scared, took off. Like you'd expect, the shooting started up, clipping at his feet. I jumped from the foxhole, tackled the boy, and threw him into this ditch that provided just enough cover. Fool thing to do.

"For the rest of the night lying in that ditch, he kept thanking me for saving his life. Wouldn't shut up about it. He was ashamed that he got scared, and that I could've got killed. Shit, I was scared too. He kept calling himself a coward, but he was just a kid. Mostly he kept on about how I had saved his life.

"The next morning, we were still tucked in that ditch, more of a wide truck rut. A Marine unit found us, drove back whatever force was shooting at us. We joined them, ready for a fairer fight. Two seconds in, Hubie took a bullet in the face. Soon as he stood up.

"I didn't save his life. I didn't save shit-all. I postponed his death. By eight hours. Goddamned pointless. I gave him eight terrifying hours. That's all I gave him. We're all dying, Jim. From the moment we're born. That ain't some deep philosophy, just a fact. Nobody can save no one. You can only postpone the inevitable.

"Or hurry it along."

We sat in silence for two or three minutes, until it was my turn to break it.

"I thought of a new game," I practically shouted, not subtle about changing the subject.

"Yeah?" Pop said, barely interested. "Are we done swapping war stories?"

"Is that what we were doing?"

Pop turned to me, his glassy eyes looking past me. "Go ahead. You got a new game?"

"You know Mister Wiley a couple of doors down. His hearing is completely shot, right? But he won't admit he's deaf. Well, every time I talk to him, he misunderstands me, but he never asks me to repeat anything. The other day I was looking for Angie, and I asked him, 'Have you seen the head nurse?' I'm not sure what he thought I said, but he answered, 'No, my wife never wanted to.'"

Pop chuckled despite himself.

"So I was thinking we could come up with some things to say to him. See how he reacts. See if we can get him to ask us to repeat it. What could he misunderstand completely wrong? Like I was going to tell him, 'The other day, I parked my Explorer in your daughter's carport.'"

Pop laughed. I could immediately see the wheels spinning. "Nothing like making fun of the handicapped."

"I'm not making fun of him—I'm exploiting him for my own amusement. Completely different. And they prefer to be called disabled," I said.

"And secretaries prefer to be called administrative assistants. Don't mean they don't make the coffee."

"Touché," I said, thankful that we were back on less serious ground.

He quickly said, "How about, 'I heard that politician polled the electorate in the southern region.'"

I laughed and then responded, "My wiener dog bit that shih tzu."

"I forcefully popped my shuttlecock in Virginia," Pop said.

It took me a second to ingest that one. But when it finally sank in, I started laughing. And I couldn't stop. Then Pop joined in. I could feel it starting. It was the beginning of the Big Laugh. Pop's laugh made me laugh and the same back. Pop let out an uncontrolled snort that sent me over the edge. Tears rolled down my face. My side ached on top of my already aching ribs. I almost fell out of my chair.

I tried to squeeze words out, but I was laughing too hard. I had a good one. But every time I started, my words were quashed by a wave of laughter. The fact I couldn't get it out made it even funnier to me. I took three deep breaths. Pop did the same. A brief moment of silence. Both of us wiped the tears from our faces. When I got out my next punch line, "I lost my cumquat in the Holy Father's rectory," it was all over.

We laughed hard. For five minutes. Pop and I laughed through our deeper pain until we could only feel the physical agony of extended laughter. We laughed past cancer. We laughed past death. And every time it felt like it was dissipating, another round of laughter arose.

Through his laughter Pop said, "I don't want to play anymore."

"You can come up with a few more," I said, massaging my painful cheeks.

Pop took in a few gasps. "No, Jim. I'm done," he said and then snorted loudly.

"What do you mean?" My laughter slowed.

"I fold," he said, his laughter uncontrollable to the point of hysteria. His smile both real and grotesque.

And while we both laughed with tears streaming down our faces, I stood up and walked to the side of Pop's bed. Pop reached out his hand and even without the benefit of sight found my hand and clutched the top of it. The skin on the back of his hands looked paper thin, the veins deep blue under his darkly spotted skin. I reached past Pop and took the extra pillow. Pop laughed. I pressed the pillow over Pop's laughing face with one hand, holding his hand with the other. He didn't resist. Almost imperceptibly, he clutched my hand a little tighter. And I held the pillow, laughing and crying.

I could feel Pop laughing underneath the pillow. Laughing as I held the pillow tighter to his face. His shoulders shook. Laughing the Big Laugh. The once-a-year laugh. Pop's final laugh.

And then nothing. Ten seconds or ten minutes, I have no idea. But it wasn't until my own laughter died down that I realized that Pop's had, too. I lifted the pillow from his face and set it at his feet. He was smiling. Pop was dead.

I stayed in the room for another half hour, sitting and holding Pop's lifeless hand. His fingers still warm on my skin. Trying to lose myself inside it, I stared at a spot in space. I didn't want to think about what had just happened, but I wasn't ready to leave. I hadn't been ready to say good-bye. I didn't know how.

When I eventually walked into the hall, I felt like I was in a trance. I grabbed the nearest nurse and told her that my father had stopped breathing.

She rushed into the room, took his pulse, and felt his breath. At the base of Pop's bed was his chart. She read it, and then her movements slowed. She had read that he had a DNR request. She glanced at the clock and made a note on the chart. She didn't cover his face. I remember thinking, *Don't they usually do that?* She took the extra pillow off the bed and set it on the chair. She pressed the sheet down around him, smoothing it out. Was that procedure, or did she just not know what to do? It was as if she was trying to make the room more presentable.

Realizing I was still there, she turned to me and said what I already knew.

"He's gone. I'm sorry."

She had no idea.

THIRTEEN

The rest of the day was a haze. In fact, the rest of the week felt like bits and pieces of barely conscious activity.

I vaguely remember talking to Angie that day. Her getting me a cup of water and sitting with me on a bench by the parking lot. I remember her talking, but I don't remember a single thing she said. I smoked a pack of cigarettes. She put her arm around me once. I remember that. I put my head on her shoulder. Her hair smelled like dandruff shampoo. I know I didn't cry, but my eyes hurt later. I don't think I blinked enough.

I remember Bobby showing up and tossing me a fresh pack of smokes. Angie must have called and told him I was low. He drove me home and hung around the house, keeping a sharp eye on me. We drank beers. I smoked more. We talked. I remember holding up my end of the conversation. But again, I have no idea what I said. I was so comfortable around Bobby that we could talk without thinking. It was automatic. It could have been baseball box scores, horror movies, or my dead father. I have no idea what our conversation was about. I know I didn't tell him that I had killed Pop.

I don't remember falling asleep, but I woke up the next morning in my bed. Bobby had stayed the night. So protective that he had slept on the floor in the same room.

By the time I finished my first cup of coffee, I was better, but still in rough shape. I went from borderline catatonic to raw nerve. I had it under control, but it wouldn't take much. It was hard to think about anything beyond what I had done. The thought was a constant distraction. Pop's death wasn't a surprise. It was the punch line to a very long setup.

I had done some mental preparation for Pop's death. But I hadn't mentally prepared for killing him myself.

I wouldn't describe what I felt as guilt. Maybe it was my remarkable powers of rationalization, but Pop had asked me. It was what Pop wanted. It hurt because it had become necessary. It hurt because I was the one that could do it. Cancer would have killed him soon enough, but I couldn't feel anything past that pillow.

The "Christian" thing to do would have been to let him suffer. Do we want people to suffer that much? We must, if we don't accept that there is ever a reason to end life early. There were plenty of good reasons. Was I supposed to believe that there was no amount of pain that justified an early death? What was the point of living if life was torture?

Pop deserved better. I knew that. Pop deserved less pain. Pop deserved some dignity. Pop deserved a lot of things that I could never have given him. All I could give him was a hooker and a way out. That was the most I could do. I did something that I hated to do, because it was the right thing to do. It was his decision and my only choice. But there was still a part of me that felt like I had failed him.

Bobby left in the morning, promising to check in later that day. I made a joke about him acting like my mother, but I was glad I had a friend like him.

Earlier while we were having coffee, I almost told him how Pop had died. I came close. But before I confessed, I decided to keep it to myself. I wasn't afraid of what he'd say or do. I knew he'd keep it to himself. I knew he wouldn't judge. But if I told him, it would be his, too. It wasn't. It was mine and Pop's. Nobody else needed to know. Nobody else needed to live with that. Not even Bobby.

Mike called just after Bobby left. After expressing his condolences, he told me that his mother, my Aunt Phyllis, was on her way over to the house. "Let her take over. Let her do it. You shouldn't have to deal with that stuff, and you don't need to. I know what you're thinking. You're thinking, *I don't want to be a burden.* Trust me. You won't be burdening her. She lives for this kind of stuff. I think she likes planning funerals more than weddings. And she loves weddings."

"She doesn't have to," I said. "Pop isn't really her family."

"But you are. Down here, we don't draw lines that hard. Funeral ain't for Uncle Jack, may he rest in peace. Funeral is for everyone still around. But for you, mostly. To give your father a good send-off. Let her do the work. She'll handle the flowers, the food. You still decide on the big stuff, just let her throw the party. So to speak. Sorry, I know it's not a party, you're not celebrating, but…aw, hell, I'm sorry, Jim. I liked Uncle Jack."

"Don't worry about it, Mike. I think Pop would've wanted it to be a party. We ain't Irish, don't mean it can't be a wake."

Aunt Phyllis came over about a half hour later. She was a stout woman in her mid-fifties with strong, defined biceps and a bouffant hairdo. She was a farmer's wife, meaning she worked twice as hard as most people. She split her time between doing the books, managing the paperwork, keeping a household, and volunteering all her spare time to the church and school. She was accustomed to a hard day's work. She was also a talker on par with some coke addicts I've known.

After a warm bear hug and some real tears, I led Aunt Phyllis into the living room. We both sat on the couch, and she began her spiel.

"Just put your faith in me. It'll be beautiful. I get my flowers from Mexicali, so it won't cost so much. And don't worry about money—I already got a collection going. Your father, he was in Rotary, they'll help out. I called Tony Garewal. He'll pit some beef for the reception. Everyone else already knows what to bring. Food is never a problem. Margie makes the potato salad. Jeannie, the beans. Doris, the rice. We've done this so many times, we could write a book. Speaking, I brought you a lasagna. It's in the car. Forty minutes on three hundred. You eat meat, right? You didn't become one of those, did you?"

I shook my head and gave her a weak smile.

"Did your father make any arrangements, tell you what he wanted?" she said, back to business.

"He didn't want to be cremated. Never explained why, but I suppose a lot of people are creeped out by the idea. He has a plot in Holtville at Terrace Park. It's already bought."

"Next to your mother's," she said, crossing herself and looking to the floor.

"Yeah, he bought them together."

Aunt Phyllis looked up, slamming a smile onto her face. "That's good. Makes it easier. Jack was a veteran. Army'll give you a headstone and a flag you can keep. For free. He paid with his service. That's nice they do that. Do you want to have the service at the Catholic church in Holtville or El Centro?"

"Pop wasn't Catholic, just Mom. I don't think he would have wanted it at a church."

"Oh," she said, and then after an uncomfortable moment, she continued. "That was Jack. He did his own thinking. Don't you worry. If anyone's going to slip into heaven sideways, it's going to be your father."

I laughed and nodded. "I was thinking of having a small memorial at the funeral home. I'm going to head over there today and figure out the details. I don't think Pop wanted anything extravagant. Something simple, a reception afterward."

"You using Tanner Brothers in El Centro?" she asked.

"Yeah, unless you know better. Only one I could remember from the couple funerals I'd been to."

"They're good. Know their business. I helped with Sammy Alvarez's funeral a month ago. They did a wonderful job."

"Thank you so much for all your help," I said sincerely. "It means a lot to me and the memory of Pop, of Jack. It really does."

"Well, I'm sure you've got a lot on your mind. You need your time to mourn, too. Least we can do is help about the piddly things. Consider that work done. I'll get the girls together, make some calls and the arrangements. You go meet with Tanner Brothers."

"Keep the receipts and I'll pay you back for everything."

"We'll talk about that later."

"Aunt Phyllis. I want to pay." I tried to sound stern.

"Did your father have a lawyer?" she said, clearly closing the subject.

"Clem Fidler," I said.

"Red? Sure. They were friends. He'll have some paperwork for you, I'm sure. Oh, if you write the obituary, I can get it in quick at the *Post-press*. Or I can write it."

"No, I'd like to write it."

I couldn't remember if the preferred term was funeral home, funeral parlor, or mortuary. Whichever it was, I walked into the air-conditioned foyer. I was immediately greeted by a small man in a traditional black suit. He was about twenty-five, but his slick-backed hair was already gray at the temples.

"I'm Mister Carney. How can I be of service?" He spoke in a whisper that was slightly affected and filled with faux comfort. That kind of "there, there" voice one used when speaking to a crying child, but not really giving a shit.

He was younger than me, so I wasn't about to call him Mister anything. "I'm here about Jack Veeder. I called about an hour ago." I wanted to get this over with as soon as possible.

Carney walked me to a small vestibule that smelled like rotting candy, the product of some off-brand air freshener that probably advertised itself as "Spring Meadow" or "Summer Potpourri." He lifted a clipboard off one of the chairs and handed it to me. There was a pen on a string tied to the top, and "Tanner Brothers" was written in large letters with a permanent marker on the back. Apparently Tanner Brothers had some issues with clipboard theft.

It took about twenty minutes to fill out all the forms. And even then, I had to leave a lot of spaces blank. It hadn't occurred to me that I would need Pop's social security number or his army information. There wasn't a bell or anything, so I wasn't sure how I was supposed to inform Carney I was done. Yelling down the hall seemed inappropriate for a place with dead people.

I wandered the halls looking for Carney. Every door I peeked my head into, I expected to find a corpse or a zombie, but it was just offices or empty viewing rooms. Eradicating any zombie issues was probably first priority with any funeral home. On my sixth door, I found Carney's office. He was behind his desk, eating a sandwich. It smelled like liverwurst, which was an unusual choice. It smelled a little corpsey.

"Sorry to interrupt your lunch." I stepped into the small office and held out the clipboard. "I'm going to need to call you with some of the information. I should have it at the house."

"That's normal," he said, setting his sandwich aside and taking the clipboard. He picked something out of his teeth with his fingernail.

We set a day and time for the memorial (they would handle all the necessary arrangements), music (I would supply it), flowers (Aunt Phyllis), and who would perform the eulogy (I had no idea). I decided on a closed casket, but allowed for a viewing the day before for those who just needed to see a dead body. Due to the heat, I chose to make the burial itself a private affair the day after the memorial. And finally, it was time for me to decide on my choice of coffin.

Carney walked me to their showroom. It was a long room with about a dozen coffins, some closed, some open. It was no different than a car dealership. Last year's models were pushed to the front for quicker turnover. Sheets taped to each model listed all sorts of extras: water sealers, moisture retardants, satin, silk, even a pillow would set you back an extra hundred bucks. The children's coffins were to one side—in two sizes, one for babies, the other one for three- to twelve-year-olds, although dwarfs and larger pets would probably fit. It appeared that children's coffins only came in powder blue or pink.

I quickly learned that coffins were not inexpensive. They had less pricey coffins, but they looked glue-gun cheap. They looked like they were made out of recycled cubicle partitions, down to the tweedy, blue fabric that lined the exterior. Those coffins still cost six hundred bucks, but nothing compared to the three grand for the Lady of Guadalupe model that looked like an East LA pachuco's van conversion. There was no middle ground, only two choices: buy the cheap model and display one's tightwaddery at the most delicate of moments or pay through the nose for something that is going to be permanently buried in the ground.

"Where are your mid-range models? Something nice for about a grand?" I asked.

"I'm sorry, but what we have here is our entire stock."

"These are my choices? Just these? You don't got cheaper ones in the back that don't look like crap? Factory seconds, maybe. Returns? One with a couple of scuffs?"

"There are payment options, if you can't afford it," Carney began.

I ignored him. "Pop would have been okay with a pine box, but I don't really have the time or energy to build it now. Who has the energy to haggle when they're grieving?"

"We have models in a number of price ranges," he said, guiding me toward the nasty fabric coffins.

"You work on commission, don't you?"

"I am only trying to help you in this, your time of need."

I laughed. "You didn't answer the question. You get a commission on coffin sales?"

"Yes sir, I do. And we prefer the term *casket*."

I slammed the lid of one of the coffins. "There is no good goddamn reason why these coffins should be so expensive. Does it eat at you when you up-sell the higher-end model to the parents of some dead kid? Hell, the kid's coffins cost as much as the grown-up ones. They use half of the materials."

Carney leaned in, having to look up. The soft sweetness in his voice was gone. "Look, man. I know it's bullshit. I'm just trying to make a living. The boss here is an ass-hole. The customers are all sad and shit. Give me a fuck-ing break. My job is depressing enough. You're the first person to complain. Ever. It's fucked up, but everyone else is happy to pay."

I took a little under a minute, scanning the coffins.

"Yeah. Sorry. I didn't mean to take it out on you. Doing your job and all that shit."

Carney stepped back, giving me room. "It's okay. Your dad just died. That blows."

"Now sell me a fucking coffin," I said.

Red Fidler came out from his office the moment I walked into the lobby. He took my outstretched hand and gave me a hug with the other. "I'm sorry, James. I considered Jack my best friend—don't know if you knew that. He was a good man. I'm going to miss the son of a bitch."

We walked back to his office.

"Thanks, Mr. Fidler. I'm still absorbing it. Feel a little numb, you know. I knew that this was how it was going to end, but…," I said, not finishing the thought.

"Natural. Perfectly natural." He gave my shoulder a hard squeeze. "I'll do what I can to help from my end."

"If it weren't for you and my Aunt Phyllis, I think I'd be a little lost."

"Phyllis Egger? That's right, she's your mother's sister. She does a nice funeral. You're definitely in good hands."

I took a seat opposite Red. He handed me a manila folder. "I marked all the places you need to sign. Jack made you both the executor of the will and the trustee of the trust. The Jack Veeder Family Trust was the best way to protect the assets: the land, the house, all that. He also wrote up a kind of biography. I think that was to help with the obituary."

"Thanks, Mr. Fidler. I'll read it all over, sign it, and bring it in tomorrow. I've got to write the obit tonight."

"It should all make sense."

"I was going to ask you. Would you speak at the memorial thing? You knew Pop. You were his friend. I'd say something, but I got the feeling I'd just get all blubbery."

"I'd be honored to say a few words."

"Thank you. Pop would have liked that. This is going to sound like I'm some kind of vulture, but how quickly can I get into the bank account? I just dumped the last of my money on an overpriced coffin."

"Should've went to Costco."

"They sell coffins at Costco?"

"They sell everything at Costco. I'll call the banks and get the paperwork started."

I thanked Red and stood to leave.

"James?" Red said, hesitating a bit.

I waited.

He didn't say anything for almost ten seconds, just stared at me, and then he looked at his hands. "Don't be surprised if not too many people show up at your father's service. Your father was a good man, but he kept to himself. Put some people off. Just saying, if not a lot of people show, don't take it personal is all."

Bobby called in the early evening. He tried to sound casual, like he wasn't checking in on me. "How's it going?"

"Okay. Doing all the to-do shit. Probably good, keeping busy with little chores, keep my mind off things," I said.

"You want me to come over? Have a few beers?"

"No, but I do need a favor."

"Name it."

"I want Yolanda to know about Pop. That he died." My throat caught when I said the word *died*. Saying it aloud was a lot different than thinking it.

"Yolanda Yolanda? The Yolanda we found? The tall, hot…"

"Right. Her. I want you to find her and tell her. There was something between Pop and her. I don't know what it is—was—but she should know."

"Done and done. I'll head down tomorrow. Hell, I'll head down tonight, find Tomás or that other guy. Not the Hulk, but Cowboy Dick."

"Alejandro."

"Right. Find one of them. They'll know where she's at."

"Thanks. I just want to know she knows."

> A memorial service will be held at 4:00 p.m. Thursday, August 31, at Tanner Brothers Mortuary in El Centro for John "Jack" Veeder who died August 25 at the age of 83.

> Jack Veeder was born in Oakley, California, in 1927, the only child of James and Emma Veeder. A U.S. Army veteran, Jack served with honor in World War II and the Korean War. He was decorated with both the Silver Star and Purple Heart. After his service, he settled in the Imperial Valley, where he began his lifetime career as a farmer and vegetable packer. A

member of Rotary International, Jack was active in the college scholarship committee.

He is survived by his son, James Veeder.

There were quite a few things that I quickly got tired of hearing at the memorial service. "I'm sorry." "He's in a better place now." "Things happen for a reason." "It was his time." "At least he didn't suffer." "He had a good, long life." "The Lord works in mysterious ways." "He's no longer in pain." The fact was, there was nothing anyone could say that didn't grate. The sentiment might have been sincere, but the repetition and execution was torture. I wanted one person to say something original rather than Hallmark me.

Bobby came close, keeping to a terse, "Fucking sucks. Shit, man." What it lacked in delicacy, it made up for in profanity. He also handed me a flask full of tequila, one of the few quantifiable efforts to comfort me.

One old man that I didn't know said to me, "I guess that means I'm next." Which was pretty good. It got a smile, but ended up being a little off-putting because he appeared to be serious.

It was a decent turnout. Some empty seats, but after Red's prologue, I hadn't known what to expect. Too hot for a suit, slacks and button-up short-sleeve shirts were the uniform of the day. The flowers were beautiful. Aunt Phyllis's Mexican connection had done her right.

Red spoke eloquently of Pop and his friendship. He told a hilarious story about the time they got stuck out in the

Heber Beach dunes, abandoned their truck, and walked back to town with the worst sunburns of their lives.

I turned around at one point during his eulogy, craning to see any familiar faces in the crowd. I saw Bobby, Aunt Phyllis and Uncle Frank, Mike Egger and his family, Daniel and Marta Quihuis, Angie, Mr. Morales, Buck Buck, Snout, a few familiar faces from high school, some old men whose names I couldn't remember, and standing in the back were Tomás, Little Piwi, and Yolanda.

Aunt Phyllis had arranged for a reception at the Elks Lodge. The food was great. Funerals and weddings were the only time I got to eat pit beef. The beans were always prepared in a certain way, too. It was like it wouldn't have been a funeral without each specific menu item. The staples of mourning. I was sad, but I had seconds.

I kept to myself, occasionally shaking a hand or listening to a story. Bobby's tequila kept me slippery. Before I knew it, the flask was empty and I'd probably drank another six beers on top of it. I tried to pass drunk off as grieving, but I didn't really care whether or not I was pulling it off.

By the end of the reception, I was liquored. Mr. Morales suggested that anyone who wanted could continue the wake at his bar. What could be more convenient? Bobby drove, and the last thing I remember from that night was walking through the door into Morales Bar.

FOURTEEN

An eruption of shotguns blasted all around me. Bright sun pounded down on my sensitive eyes. I turned on my side and tasted dirt in my mouth. It felt like someone was pinching me on my arm, neck, and stomach. I wanted to go back to sleep, but the shotgun blasts kept roaring. My ears rang, my eyes throbbed, and my skin burned.

I sat up slowly, trying to figure out where I was and what was happening. It didn't take long. I was on the ditch bank behind my house, and I was covered in fire ants. I stared in fascination at the trail of red ants that made their way over my shirtless torso. Most of them just went about their business, but a few stopped to bite. I stood up and brushed my body frantically, dancing like a crazed lunatic. My hungover brain wasn't having any. I had gotten up so quickly that I fell back down and almost passed out. My light-headedness waned, but then a pounding took its place deep in my skull.

Another shotgun went off. And that's when it occurred to me that today was September 1. It was the first day of dove season.

"What the fuck?" I heard from the ditch below me.

Still brushing ants off my skin, I peered down into the ditch. Bobby lay on his back and looked up at me. He smiled, shielding his eyes with one hand. "What the fuck are you doing?" he asked.

"Ants," I said.

Bobby looked down at his body. "Not down here. You should've been smart like me and slept in the ditch."

"They're biting the shit out of me," I said, running toward the house.

"Hey, Jimmy! Put on a pot of coffee," I heard behind me.

I ran into the shower and turned on the water. Nothing. Not even the weak stream I was used to. Not even a drip.

"Come on," I screamed at the inanimate son of a bitch. I hopped out of the shower and tried the sink. Nothing there either. The water was completely out.

I stripped naked and rubbed my dry body down with a towel for ten minutes until I was positive there were no more ants on me. Even without the insects on my skin, it still felt crawly.

I really wanted that shower. My skin felt uncomfortably warm from sleeping in the sun. I put on a pair of shorts and a tank top, and then I washed my face with some tonic water from the refrigerator. It was ice cold and cooled my face, but it made my skin feel sticky. I found my sunglasses and went back outside.

I headed out to the water pump, determined to fix the fucking thing once and for all. That's what I got for procrastinating. The first thing I noticed when I got out there was that the pump was running. It sounded like it was working hard, so there should have been pressure to the house. The pipe had to be plugged.

Bobby approached from the ditch bank, half his body and face covered in dirt. "You make coffee?" he said.

"Come over and help me with this," I said.

"I'll take that as a no."

"There's something blocking the intake to the house. Probably in the pipe down at the bottom of the cistern. I'm going to see if I can fix it the dumbass way. I'm going to drop a ladder down there, get whatever gunk is in there out."

"I hold the ladder. Got it."

"You're here to make sure I don't die. Like a swim buddy. That's your job. Make sure I come out of the water alive."

"Will do."

Bobby and I got the rickety wooden ladder from behind the house and carried it back to the water pump. I lifted one end of the ladder to the concrete edge, looking down into the cistern. The catch in my throat echoed from the vacuum below.

Yolanda stared up at me from the depths of the cistern, her mouth open and full of black water. Wet hair stuck to the side of her face. Mosquitoes feasted on exposed skin. Her body floated on the surface, joints twisted in unnatural directions to fit within the confined space. She looked like a string puppet at the bottom of a toy box. I turned away when I could no longer stand the clouded vacancy of her dead eyes.

PART TWO

PART TWO

FIFTEEN

Not counting Pop and a handful of open-casket funerals, I had only seen one other dead body in my life. At fifteen I helped pull a week-old, fish-pecked and bloated body out of a canal. The poor bastard's grayish skin was so misshapen and frayed that it looked like tattered rags. His faceless face continued to resonate. In discordant surroundings the once-alive shell of a human being carries tremendous weight.

Movies and television give the impression that a dead body is no big deal. We are so inured to bad guy extras doing the machine gun dance that death on the screen has become mundane. Villains die from increasingly original projectiles. Sidekicks quietly close their eyes after saying something glib. Blue-veined models lie on steel slabs, the nude centers of a coroner's investigation. It looks like she's sleeping. She's not. She's acting. She's pretending to be dead, and it looks nothing like death. Nothing like a corpse.

A fear-eyed corpse has lost all vanity. Life has quickly turned to rotting meat. Personality to stagnation. Beauty to nothingness. The eyes are shockingly empty, but it's the skin that tells the truth. The flesh goes slack. The body no longer resists gravity, melting downward away from bone and muscle. The effect is subtle, almost unnoticeable, yet unmistakable.

I had never been afraid of dying, but I was scared shitless of becoming a corpse.

I sat on the grass smoking a cigarette and staring at the unremarkable concrete cistern. I found myself slowly following the web of surface cracks with my eyes. At the top the fissure was thick and defined, but like a river it branched out and thinned as it ran along the weathered exterior.

"I called the sheriff's office," Bobby said.

I turned to see Bobby returning from the house with a pitcher full of some frothy red liquid and two empty glasses.

He said, "With dove season starting today and all, might take a while for them to get out here."

"You made Bloody Marys? You really think now is the right time for cocktails?"

"No. I made Barrio Marys. Clamato and beer. I tossed a couple of aspirins at the bottom of each glass. Best hangover remedy in the world."

Bobby handed me one of the glasses. I poured the three aspirins into my mouth and dry-swallowed.

"I can't believe you made drinks," I said as I held out my glass and Bobby filled it.

"It ain't like we're celebrating. This is medicine. Hang over's only going to get worse if it goes unchecked. Drink up."

"Did you see her?" I looked back at the chipped cement lip of the cistern.

"Fucked up," Bobby said.

I took a drink of my Mary. "That's disgusting," I said and then took another drink.

"That's how you know it's working."

An hour later Bobby and I were still sitting in the grass waiting for the sheriff's department to arrive. The dry heat of August had made way for the sticky humidity of September. The muggy air made me feel like I was covered in hot grease. An army of Apache cicadas buzzed in a nearby tree, intermittently interrupted by a volley of shotgun fire.

Bobby and I both stared silently at the water pump. We drank and stared, not a word spoken between us for the length of the hour. I wouldn't assume what was going through Bobby's mind, but the image of Yolanda's dead face haunted mine. I couldn't close my eyes without seeing her. I knew if I took another look, there would be no change in her frozen expression. Fifteen feet away, Yolanda was trapped, her body lost in the water and the darkness.

I couldn't fucking stand it anymore.

I carefully slid the ladder into the cistern. The wooden ends broke the surface of the water and slipped past Yolanda's body into the black murk. The morning light shimmered on the wet, satiny surface of her black dress, making it hard to tell where her dress began and the dark water ended. A splinter of wood caught her dress, pulling it tighter to her body and turning her to one side. A shake of the ladder and the material was free. Slowly the ladder crept lower. As I was about to pull the ladder up and search for a longer one, it found some unseen, semi-solid mass at the bottom.

"Last time I'm going to say it. We should really wait for the cops," Bobby said.

Bobby had spent the previous fifteen minutes trying to talk me out of it. He brought up a number of excellent and surprisingly logical reasons to leave her in the water, but I couldn't leave her down there.

"I can't sit in the grass and wait while she floats in that water," I said, my voice a little shaky.

Bobby nodded. "Okay. I tried. I don't get many opportunities to be the voice of reason—thought I'd give it a go. I can take bottom, if you're not up for it."

"I should." I wasn't sure why it was important, but it was.

I emptied my pockets, took off my boots and socks, and climbed onto the ladder. It immediately sank about a foot and half straight down. I held on for the ride until I was convinced it had settled.

"Hey," Bobby said to get my attention. "You're going to have to climb into the water. Like waist deep. Right next to her. Enough to get a grip. Even with the water making her heavier, don't look like she weighs nothing. Then I climb down, you lift her, and we walk her up together. Sound like a plan?"

I nodded, following Bobby's eyes to Yolanda. I was relieved to find that she was no longer looking at me, her face having rolled to the side. Her black hair hid her eyes.

I must have been staring at her for some time, enough to prompt Bobby to speak up.

"You all right?" Bobby asked. He started to rotate onto the ladder, frozen with his leg up like a pissing dog. "I can still take bottom."

"I'll be okay," I said after a violent shake of my head to snap into focus. I took a deep breath and let it out. I kept my eyes on Yolanda. Wooden splinters poked my bare feet with each tentative, downward step. The damp mildew filled my sinuses.

When one bare foot touched the water, I instinctively jumped back. Considering the heat, I thought it would feel refreshing. But it was warm and thick and felt nothing short of glutinous. I had mentally prepared myself to have to touch Yolanda's corpse, but the soupy ooze of the water on my skin felt like I was stepping into a vat of saliva.

"Don't think about it. Just do it," Bobby shouted above me.

Through gritted teeth and closed eyes, I climbed two steps into the water. I felt like I was being enveloped by its weight. I had to push Yolanda's body along the surface with one hand in an effort to get my body under her for leverage. She moved across the water with little effort, her body seemingly weightless.

All of a sudden, it got considerably darker in the cistern. For a second I thought Bobby was playing a joke on me and had replaced the tarp. But when I looked up, I saw that it was only Bobby's body blocking the light. He was on the top rails of the ladder, looking down and waiting for me.

"I'm going to drop down one more step, try to get my arm around her waist and lift her rightways-up so you can get under her armpits. Then we take her a step at a time, you under her arms, I'll have got her feet," I said, trying to picture the plan and convince myself it would work.

I descended one more step, almost waist deep. With one hand still on the ladder, I reached out my hand, tugged on

Yolanda's dress, and pulled her close to me. I got my hand around her waist, relieved to only feel the slickness of her dress and not her skin. I pressed her slack frame to me as best I could and looked up at Bobby.

"Ready?" I said, not sure I was.

"Right here." He hooked his foot in the ladder and held both hands down to me.

I jerked Yolanda's body up. My foot slipped off the rail of the ladder. And before I knew what had happened, I was underwater. In my immediate confusion, I illogically clutched at Yolanda's body, pulling her down with me, above me, on top of me. The momentum and the weight of both our bodies forced me to the soft, muddy bottom. The surprisingly cold pudding squished between my sinking toes. Grasping at sanity, I let go of Yolanda and kicked off the bottom, but I only sank deeper into the semi-solid goo.

That's the closest I came to panicking. I kicked at the bottom, trying to free myself from the calf-deep sludge. The darkness and silence overwhelmed me. The only sound was my heart pounding in my head. I found the concrete side of the cistern with my hand. I knew which way up was. I used my fingertips to crawl to the surface, forcefully pushing Yolanda's body out of my way. The material of her dress caught my arm and covered my face. I shook violently to untangle myself. I had no air left in my lungs when I broke the surface of the water.

Bobby's hand grabbed my shirt at the shoulder and pulled me toward the ladder. I got my foot on a rail and gasped for air, hugging the ladder close to me.

Bobby kept his firm grip on me. "You all right?"

I nodded, not ready to talk. I tried to steady my breathing. I looked down at Yolanda. She was face-down. Her dress had shifted to one side, revealing too much pale leg.

"That was fucked up," Bobby pontificated.

I gave him a look.

Bobby said, "Let's leave her. Pull the ladder. Wait for the cops."

"No," I said too loudly, my voice hollow within the space. "We're not leaving her down here."

"Dude, she's dead," Bobby said. "It's fucked up, but what's the difference? More respectful to let someone knows what they're doing handle this."

"She wasn't a stranger. Maybe you leave a stranger in the water with all that filth and bugs and shit, but not someone you know," I yelled back at him. I still felt disoriented from my undersea adventure.

Bobby stared at me for a ten-count and then gave me a short nod and a hard slap on the back. "Round two."

Our second effort was less of an abortion. After the ten minutes it took me to regain my composure, I climbed back down and according to plan lifted Yolanda's body high enough for Bobby to get a grip. We weren't delicate about it, her head bobbing from side to side with no support, her arms limp at her sides. We twice scraped her body against the slimy concrete walls, leaving green-black smears on her skin. One step at a time, we carried her up the ladder, draped her over the edge of the cistern, and then climbed out ourselves.

We laid her on the high weeds next to the water pump. Her black dress stuck to her skin, her hair to her face. Her dress had shifted, exposing one of her breasts. Her skin looked white. Not Caucasian white, but white like a lily. I readjusted her dress. The dead might not be modest, but they deserved respect. Bobby got a blanket out of his Ranchero and covered her.

Bobby refilled our glasses with the remainder of the Barrio Mary. He sat on the ground and lifted his glass to the body under the blanket. I lit a cigarette, and we sat quietly through the length of that smoke and the next one. The cicadas and shotguns continued their cacophonous background score. As I lit my third cigarette directly from the second, Bobby spoke.

"Well, that happened. Fucking Christ," Bobby said. "Feel better?"

"No, but I'm glad we did it. Is there anything else we should do?"

"We should do nothing. What we done so far, we shouldn't've done. Makes us one past what we should've."

I turned to him. "You would've left her in the water? You were here alone, you would've left her?"

"Didn't know her." Then Bobby thought about it and shook his head. "I don't know. Just saying, they're going to tell us we shouldn't've. That's all. I've been trying to act like more of a grown-up lately."

"Nothing we can do about it now."

Bobby nodded, his eyes glued to Yolanda's covered body. His cell phone beeped. He took it out of his pocket, looked at the face, and then slipped it back in his pants. "Griselda will be here in about fifteen minutes."

"Isn't that your girlfriend? You called your girlfriend?"

"Yeah."

"Sometimes, I don't know what the fuck you're thinking," I said. "A woman is dead. Someone I spent time with. Someone who was important to Pop. And it's nothing but some big party to you. Cocktails, now a 'plus one' on your guest list?"

"Griselda is a sheriff's deputy," Bobby said. "When I said I had called the sheriff's, I called her. I thought under the circumstances, it'd be a good idea to have someone we knew. Someone I trusted."

"Oh" was the best I could do by way of apologizing.

"She'll keep Jack out of this. If you decide to tell her about their thing. I'll talk to her. No reason no one should know about your old man and her. And offhand, just because a situation is serious don't mean you get to be a dick about it. So I made drinks. Most of the time when I really need a drink, it ain't any kind of party. Just the opposite."

"Sorry," I said. "It's just…sometime last night while we were drinking, while I was getting shit-faced drunk, while I was doing I have no idea what, she died. Something happened and she ended up down in that water. We were right across the street."

"Don't mean it's on us."

"No, you're right. It's not on you. But it's on me. I found her. She wouldn't've even been here if not for me."

"Don't be a fucking retard. That's like driving someone to the airport and then blaming yourself when the plane crashes. Next you'll be blaming yourself for your dad's death."

Taken off guard, a short, abrupt laugh escaped my mouth.

Bobby blurted out, "Did you kill her?"

"What? No," I responded, surprisingly defensive. "Just the same, I can't remember a thing from last night."

"Trust me, you didn't kill her. You're not capable of it. You couldn't kill a fly."

Pop's face flashed into my mind. My hands on the pillow. I said nothing.

"So forget about it. No matter what you do now, no matter what you think, it ain't going to make her any less deader. Guilt is for assholes. Particularly guilt for something that you haven't any reason to be guilty for."

At a distance, Imperial County Deputy Sheriff Griselda Villarreal looked all of fourteen years old. But as she neared, it became obvious that she was a couple years older than me. Griselda, at five foot three (if she was standing on a something that was three inches), must have worn heels to make the height requirement. She had that cop walk, a taurine stride with an extra hitch in her hip. On her frame, it worked. She wore her hair in a ponytail, never took off her hat, and always seemed to have a knowing grin on her face.

As Bobby and I approached her, she looked past us to the blanket-covered body.

"Hey, Gris," Bobby said. "Thanks for coming out."

He leaned in to kiss her, but she backed up a step and pushed his face away with an open hand.

"When'd you get shy?" Bobby sounded hurt.

"He knows about us?" Griselda asked, not acknowledging me past the pronoun.

Bobby nodded.

"Let's get some things straight, Bob," Griselda said. "I am here on official business. I'm treating this like any other investigation—and the two of you like any other witnesses."

"Sure," Bobby said. "I was just saying hi. Your job's important, I get that. Don't mean I can't give my special lady a little sugar."

Griselda rested her hand on her sidearm, only slightly casual. "No, that's exactly what it means. No sugar. We've talked about this."

"It kind of hurts me that you don't want no one to know we're going out. Am I that bad?" Bobby flashed his puppy eyes.

"Should I let you two talk?" I was already backing away.

"Yes, Bob, you are that bad. You have a reputation with the sheriff's department. Also with the El Centro Police Department, the Holtville cops, most of the city of Brawley, that dog catcher out in Plaster City, the Border Patrol, the I-8 CHPs, and I wouldn't be surprised if you were on a Homeland Security watch list. I'm not going to let you impact my job. I'm a short Mexican woman. That don't put me exactly on the fast track in the department. I can't let you make it that much harder."

"Baby," Bobby tried weakly.

"Baby? That's what...?" She stopped and took a deep breath. "You called me because you found yourself a dead body. That's serious. Treat it that way. Most cops' boyfriends just try to get out of traffic tickets. Moment I stepped out of my car, this became my case. You got to treat me like any other cop."

"But I hate cops," Bobby said.

She walked the couple of steps to where I had retreated. Griselda nearly crushed my hand and introduced herself as "Deputy Sheriff Villarreal," but I had already decided that I liked the name Griselda too much.

"How much did Bobby tell you on the phone?" I asked.

"That you two found a body."

"Might as well put me down as the one that made the call. If it doesn't matter. I mean, I'm not trying to lie or nothing, but Bobby—his reputation."

She nodded. "Name?"

"Jimmy Veeder. James. It's my house. Now. My dad died. Natural causes. I live here," I said, nodding my head toward the house.

"Bob told me about your father. I'm sorry."

"Thanks."

"Tell me what happened."

I gave her the rundown of the morning. How I woke up, no water pressure, went to the pump, found the body. She took notes and cut in with a couple of time-related questions, but mostly just let me tell it.

"Was she alive when you found her?"

"No, she was definitely dead."

"Then why is she over there? If you weren't trying to save her, why did you move the body? Why did you take the body out of the well?"

"It's not really a well. It's more like a standpipe."

"Why did you move the body?"

"It didn't seem right to leave her down there."

Deputy Griselda's disappointment laced her slow, steady voice. "You should know better. Don't you watch TV? Haven't you ever seen a cop show? You should know. Everybody knows. You don't move a dead body. Little, stupid kids know that."

"Bobby told me to leave her. It's on me. He was the voice of reason."

"That would be a first."

"Didn't seem right. We waited and nobody came. What else can I say? I did what I did."

"Yeah, and what you did was not only stupid, but illegal. I could cite you." She shook her head, looking up from her notepad. "I'd tell you, 'Next time, don't let that happen,' but let's hope there isn't going to be a next time."

Griselda and I walked to the body together. When we got within twenty feet, she slapped a backhand into my stomach, making a loud *smap*. It stopped me in my tracks.

"Hang out. I've got more questions for you and Bob." She pointed to where Bobby was sitting on the low stucco wall. I shrugged and joined him.

Bobby and I watched Deputy Griselda put on some rubber gloves. She grabbed a corner of the blanket and took it off the body, setting it to the side. She seemed to know what she was doing. But since I had no clue what she was doing, appearances could have been deceiving. She looked at the hands and then concentrated her attention on the face and head, turning it from side to side, spending a lot of time on the back of her head. Twice she walked to her car to get supplies. She put each hand in a paper bag, holding the bag in place with rubber bands at the wrists.

Her preliminary look at the body completed, she walked to the water pump, yelling to us on the way. "Was there any ID? A wallet? A purse? Anything?" Bobby and I shook our heads. She pointed a flashlight and looked down into the cistern. She kept a hand on the ladder, but didn't climb in. She squinted her eyes, looking around the tall grass that surrounded the water pump and the side yard, and then she walked to me and Bobby.

"I'll need to get official statements from you and you. Also, I'm going to rope off this area until I can make a thorough search. Including the water pipe she was in. It doesn't look like there's a way to drain it, but we can fish the bottom. We may find something. I contacted the coroner's office on the way here. Someone will be out to retrieve the body. On their time."

She walked to her car. I followed.

"Can I ask what you think happened?" I said.

Griselda popped her trunk, took a digital camera from a case, and fiddled with some buttons on it. "Too early to say. She's got a big divot on the back of her head. My guess is that's what killed her. But hard to say if it was from the fall or before. Not like the edge of the well is low, so it seems like it would be hard to fall in on accident. Does it have a cover?"

"Yeah, usually, but the tarp wasn't on it this morning."

"Coroner will get an ME to determine cause of death, autopsy, but that'll only tell me so much. Whether it was the knock on her head or the water, not much more. Doesn't look like there was any kind of struggle, but they'll check the fingernails. It looks suspicious to me. Like someone was trying to hide her."

"Her name was Yolanda."

Griselda raised her head from the camera and turned to face me. "You knew her? Yolanda what?"

"I don't know her last name. I could maybe find out. She was a Mexican. From Mexico. She was...sometimes they have women across the street." I pointed to Morales Bar. "Mexican girls come over here to make some money some nights."

"I know what hookers are."

"I've known Mr. Morales since I was born. Don't want no trouble for him."

"I'll ask him some questions, but I'm not concerned about his side business. Did you have a relationship of some kind with this Yolanda?"

"Relationship would be a pretty generous term," I said. "I knew her."

"Bob and you were across the street all last night, right? Bob invited me. I was on duty. Some kind of makeshift wake?"

I nodded.

"Was Yolanda present?"

"That's the thing—I don't know. She was at the memorial, so I assume she came out," I said.

"I'm going to need you to tell me what you remember from last night."

I let out a big breath. "Nothing. I had already drunk too much by the time I got to the bar. I remember walking in the door and waking up on a ditch bank. Other than that, I can't help you. I was blacked out."

She nodded. "Luckily Bob drinks like he gets paid for it. If I know him, he'll have remembered every detail. I have to secure the area, take photos, and essentially do my job. When I'm done, I want to sit down with you and Bob and try to establish a timeline. Get an idea of who was there last night."

I nodded, looking at the sun still low in the sky. It wasn't even nine o'clock yet.

"Place was packed. Hunters, locals, the funeral people for Big Jack. Most of the Valley was at Morales. Might save time if I just told you who wasn't there."

Bobby had been talking for a while, trying to settle his memory and get the events of the night into some semblance of an order. He closed his eyes and moved his hand slowly from left to right.

"Not everyone who was at the reception came out to Morales. And there was like a ton of people at the bar that had nothing to do with Big Jack. Here's who I remember. Jimmy and me were there. Mr. Morales was behind the bar, a given. His grandson, Tomás Morales, was there too. He had this massive Mexican dude with him. Don't know his name. Good luck trying to talk to them, but they were the ones that brought Yolanda. Mike Egger was there with a bunch of his guys, like Daniel Quihuis, Israel Ramos, Tony Villalobos, and some other guys who I know by first name or nickname, but you'd have to ask Mike to get their whole names. There was a group of like a half dozen high school kids, four boys and two girls. They weren't Holtville kids or I would've known them. They were mostly white, so probably not up from Calex. Maybe El Centro. Probably figured who's going to card anyone at a wake, right? So figure them for smart kids. Some random field-workers trickled in and out. Guys with their straw cowboy hats and muddy boots. It's not like the bar was closed. Mr. Morales was running business as usual.

"With dove season, there were even a couple of out-of-towners ballsy enough to brave Morales. Kind of dudes that wear those pants with like eight, ten pockets on them. Some of me and Jimmy's high school buds were there: Kirch, Gweez, Scrote, Gooch, Buck Buck, Snout, Thorn, The Train. Maybe a couple more, if I keep thinking. Some of the older generation: Red Fidler, Fritz Rubin, Felipe Zabala. Give me a couple pieces of paper and I'll make you a big-ass list.

"Mr. Morales drinks steady behind that bar, but I ain't never seen him drunk. Not once. He knows everybody and forgets nothing. You charm him, maybe flash a tit, he'll remember real good for you. Between my list and his, you should be able to name most everyone we know. Everyone except them high school punks and out-of-towners."

SIXTEEN

I let the water hit the back of my head and trail down my neck. I watched the gray grit of the morning run down the drain of Bobby's shower. It would be quite a while before I would feel comfortable using the water back at the house.

I scrubbed the slimy black remnants of the cistern from my skin until it burned, but I didn't feel clean. I closed my eyes, only to see Yolanda floating just below the surface of that black water. Her lifeless face replaced Pop's final laugh haunting the disquiet of my mind. Worst-case scenario, the two would eventually merge just enough to drive me bananas. At least I had that to look forward to. I wished I hadn't seen her dead boob.

What could have happened that ended with Yolanda in the water? She couldn't have fallen in. Griselda was right. The standpipe was too high to fall in accidentally. Suicide? She didn't seem the type. Like I knew her enough to make that call.

The more I spun it, the more I was convinced that someone had put Yolanda in there. Not necessarily killed her, but at the least put her in the cistern. Probably killed her, but definitely probably put her in there. Who would do that? Why?

It didn't really matter. Nothing I could do about it.

Griselda had kept at Bobby and me with questions for another hour. She had searched the scene and photographed every inch of the side yard. She seemed smart, yet realistic. The Imperial County Sheriff's Office wasn't big enough to warrant a homicide division, so Griselda was it: the first responder, the evidence technician, and the investigator all rolled into one. I told her everything I knew, except for Yolanda's relationship with Pop. I didn't see how that could matter, and I didn't see how it was any of her business.

Griselda only allowed her pessimism to show through once or twice. She confided that the dead body of an illegal alien didn't rate that high. Dead Mexicans were too common to chart on anyone's priority list. However, Griselda was a pro and would let the evidence dictate the investigation.

"All victims deserve the same. Dead is dead, and a crime is a crime. If someone did this, I'll do everything I can to find them," she said.

An ambulance arrived while Griselda and Bobby were fine-tuning his list and trying to put some names to some faces. The driver and medical examiner waited in the ambulance with the engine (and the air-conditioner) running until Griselda approached them. I found out later that Imperial County doesn't have its own pathologist, but farms it out to a few local doctors or brings them down from San Diego. The coroner shares an office with the sheriff, too. I wondered if Andy and Barney let Otis sleep in the jail.

Griselda and the medical examiner toured Yolanda's body. The ambulance driver turned off the engine and took the opportunity to have a smoke. Having burned through all of mine, I bummed one. He was in his mid-fifties with a red nose that suggested he had a flask within reach. He wore his uniform sloppily and treated his job like most people, counting time, trying to get to the end of the day. I let him talk.

"Soon as it cools down, there'll be plenty more of 'em. Dead Mexicans. Weird to think that they're already dead, some of 'em. But they're out there. Desert's full of bodies. Out there drying in the sun. Leathering up. In the dunes. In the desert.

"Don't know what them poor bastards are told when they slip the border. What kind of advice they get. But it's all bad. 'Cause from the border to the nearest road, it's fifteen, twenty miles in most parts. In this heat, on a day like today, it's impossible to carry enough water to travel that distance.

"They're out there, all right. Gets nice, drops down to low nineties, weekenders'll start hitting the dunes in their quads, finding corpses left and right. Folks from the city'll find a family stuck to each other and coyote-chewed. I'll be out there trying to pick 'em up without them falling apart. 'Fore they turn into dust. They make like a crackling sound when you move them. Smell like pork rinds. Skin like deer jerky, most of the time. You got no idea.

"Here's something you wouldn't guess. For being in the desert, we get a lot of drownings. Probably as many drowning as from the sun. From the All-American mostly. Got a wicked undercurrent from what I hear. Some in the Alamo or the New River. Damn nasty. Whenever they find a body in the New River and I'm supposed to go out, I fake a stomachache. Make up a dead relative. Anything. I ain't going to swim through a river of puke and diapers for no dead Mexican. Give it time—they'll just dissolve in that toxic shit.

"Remember that flash flood five, eight years ago? Tore through west of the Valley. Out in the Yuha. Like a river rapid, no time for the water to soak into the sand. When the rain finally stopped, we found fourteen illegals in a dry wash just north of Mount Signal. Their bodies stuck and sunk in the mud. Some you could only see a hand, sticking up like that. It looked like a fucking battlefield. Bodies strewn. That's what they were, strewn."

I put on my unwashed suit and tie for the second day in a row, doing my best to shake the dust from the ditch bank off the jacket. It stank of alcohol sweat, but I only owned the one suit and there was no time for dry-cleaning. I was the only invitee to the burial and Pop wouldn't have cared, but I felt better in a wrinkled, smelly suit than my other option: jeans and a T-shirt.

I walked through the first floor of Bobby's house. His bachelor pad was surprisingly clean for a guy like Bobby. I made a mental note to give Bobby some shit for owning throw pillows that matched the armrest covers. I found Bobby making some cold burritos in the kitchen.

He looked over his shoulder and said, "If you're not careful, you're going to forget to eat."

I took a seat on one of the folding chairs at the table. "I can't believe I completely blacked out. I got nothing from last night. Not even images."

Bobby put a burrito in front of me, went to the cupboard, and found a bag of tortilla chips. He tossed them on the table. He grabbed two beers from the fridge, cracked one open and took a long pull. I left mine on the table. I looked inside the tortilla to find *carnitas*, cilantro, onions, guacamole, and salsa.

Bobby said, "I remember, but only what I saw, you know. Just my angle. I'll probably remember more stuff when I stop trying to remember. Hard to say. The place got pretty crazy as the night went on. Lot of people. Lot of stuff happening in each corner. I got a better memory of who was there than what happened. I was making my own mischief."

"What do you think happened to her?"

"She didn't fall in. No fucking way. She may've jumped, but she couldn't't've fallen. Even jumping is kind of ridiculous. The Ash runs right behind Morales, and that's a huge canal. She wanted to drown herself, why'd she ruin your bathwater? My guess, someone chucked her in there."

"But who would do that?"

"Some asshole. Who knows? Could be anybody. Doesn't take much. Everyone's capable of killing."

"You really believe that?"

"Maybe not you, but you're a puss." Bobby laughed. "Most people? Yeah, they could kill. Why would you think any different? You ain't one of them people that think people are basically good?"

I bit into my burrito. The cold meat was delicious. I wasn't up for a philosophical debate with Bobby about the nature of man, so I changed the subject. "Her family should know. Know she's dead. Know what happened."

"Griselda got her name. Her first name, at least. Probably more than they got for most of them they find. The county does a pretty good job. Best with what they got. There was a big thing in the *I.V. Press* about how they work with Mexico, tracking people down. Dental records, DNA, all that shit."

"I'm going to call Tomás. Him or that Alejandro guy might know her full name. Or could maybe find out. Might know her people. Tell me how to get hold of them."

"Tell you? You mean tell Griselda, right? This ain't on you, Jimmy."

"She was found dead on my land. She was up here because of Pop. It may not be on me, but I had something to do with how she ended up."

"You looking for a hobby? You got a farm to worry about now. Griselda's good at her job. Don't get all *Rockford Files* on me."

"Just thought if I could help, I would." I finished the last few bites of my burrito. The meat hit the spot, filling a void I hadn't been aware of.

"You're going to have to tell me eventually. How did you and Deputy Sheriff Villarreal get so chummy?" I gave Bobby a big grin.

Bobby laughed. "She busted me. No surprise. I was on an official Bobby Maves escapade. I deserved it. I'll be the first to tell you when I got it coming, and I had it coming. She was cool about it though. Too long a story to start from the beginning, but a series of unfortunate and escalating events led me to the point where Griselda pulled up next to me in her roller. Me, bare-ass naked from the waist down, being chased by a three-legged German shepherd through a sugar beet field. Her, laughing her ass off and making fun of my dangle."

"If I hadn't lived through some of them, I'd think all your stories were bullshit."

"Ask her. She saved me. Three legs or no, that dog had it in for my junk. Thought it was a kielbasa."

"Or a Vienna sausage."

"She loaned me a pair of county-issues and let me sleep it off in the drunk tank. Didn't file charges, which was cool. So I took her out to dinner."

"And what does she see in you exactly? She appears to be an intelligent, focused, and serious woman. In law enforcement to boot."

"What can I say? Opposites attract. Least for now."

"The novelty of dating a cop wearing off?"

"No, I'm not even bugged by her whole 'you can't tell anyone we're dating' thing. That makes total sense. Look at me."

"So, what is it?"

"It's her," Bobby said, looking to the photos of his two daughters on the wall. "Dude, as much as you think I'm some kind of alcoholic child—which is mostly right on—I'm half a grown-up. I work. I pay bills. Shit, I got two kids. Even if I never see 'em. The kids scare Gris more than my rep. When she came over here the first time and saw them pictures of me with the girls, it queered the deal a little. I think she's got a thing about commitment. I like her. I hope it works out. But shit, I ain't exactly got a winning record."

From the way Bobby ended the story, I took that to be the end of that conversational thread. I nodded and gave Bobby a manly slap on the shoulder. A pathetic excuse for camaraderie, but it's all I had.

Bobby had to check on his fields, so I asked him to drop me off at the cemetery.

Terrace Park Cemetery would not have been my choice as a final resting place. First off, no grass. Also, no trees. Finally, no flowers save for a twisted wall of oleander on the northern edge. Overlooking a scrubby ravine formed by the Alamo River, Terrace Park looked like a fine place to dump a body, but a strange place to put a headstone. A modern Boot Hill for the dead that don't care and the families that want to make visiting a one-time affair.

My pant legs gathered dust as the Bobcat excavator's claw started a fresh hole in the hard, dry earth. Dissonant scraping sounds echoed within the shallow canyon until the shovel finally found purchase and began digging Pop's grave. Pop's plot was right next to my mother's, and I glanced at her stone with curious ambivalence. Barbara Veeder. I wanted to feel more, but I had never met her. My mother was a name and a photo on the living room wall. No memories. Only stories. We had no shared past, except for the tragedy of my birth.

I stood with four Mexican men, all of us with our hands in our pockets. We watched the Bobcat's progress. Five men staring at a hole. Pop's overpriced coffin sat in front of us. I felt hungover, hot, and overdressed.

"*Su familia?*" one of the Mexican men asked.

"*Mi padre,*" I said.

"*Mi más sentido pésame.*" He crossed himself. The other men nodded.

"*Gracias,*" I said, acknowledging each man with eye contact and a nod.

The Bobcat finished its work. A textbook empty grave, four by eight by deep. An organized pile of dirt and clay to one side. The digger lit a smoke, but remained in the small seat of the excavator, his job half-finished.

The men ran two thick canvas straps under the bottom of the coffin and used them to carry it. At the edge of the grave, they stopped and looked to me. I could see their muscles straining.

Realizing they were waiting for permission, I nodded. Slowly they lowered the coffin into the ground. I wanted to tell them to lift with their knees, as it seemed they were letting their backs do most of the work. But I remained silent in the spirit of the moment.

While it felt final, it mostly felt empty. For lack of a better word, it felt dead. All the ceremony one attached to death didn't make dead any different.

I would've watched the gravediggers fill in the grave, but watching the Bobcat do it lacked gravity. I chose to walk around the cemetery until the job was done. Glancing at headstones, I recognized a number of last names. Nobody I knew, but ancestors of classmates and neighbors, many and most still Holtville residents. New generations had cropped up, but it was obvious that if one was born in the Imperial Valley, the odds were that the person was still there. Whether alive or dead.

A path cut through the wall of oleander at the northern edge of the cemetery. Having never been to that section and naturally curious, I walked down the path, avoiding any direct contact with the poisonous vegetation. Every part of the oleander plant is toxic, so of course it would be all over the Imperial Valley.

The path opened to a forty-acre field, an isolated extension of the cemetery proper. There appeared to be graves, but no headstones. Instead, single red bricks marked each plot. I leaned down and picked up one of the bricks. It read, "Doe M-9-28-08-004." I set it back in the exact position that I had found it, matching the corners to the displaced dirt. There were hundreds of bricks and room for hundreds more.

"*Cementerio de pobres,*" a voice behind me stated. "What they used to call a potter's field."

I turned and was surprised to find a uniformed man holding a rifle. "This is where they bury the ones they don't know their names. Unidentified illegals, mostly. Got to put 'em somewhere." A closer look at his uniform told me he was with the sheriff's department. Corrections Division.

"How many are there?" I asked.

"Three, four hundred, I suppose. Maybe more. Seems like we're always digging."

Behind him a dozen women in bright orange prison uniforms filed out from the path. Four women carried well-worn picks, while the remainder hefted shovels on their shoulders. Two more guards followed, rifles pointed casually to the ground, laughing from some joke.

"You use lady prisoners to dig the graves?" I asked.

"Border Patrol finds the dead, but it's all on the county to stick 'em in the ground. Feds don't give a shit. Not like the county's got extra money to foot the bill. We use what we got. We got plenty of prisoners. Men and women. The ladies like the exercise. Keeps 'em fit."

The guard joined the others, barking directions to his prison labor force. The women with picks went to work, the force of their blows making little progress in the packed ground. They were definitely going to get a workout.

I headed back up the path, turning to look at the expanse of land and innumerable bricks laid out in rows. They didn't just represent the unnamed dead, but the questions that remained for the living. The families that would never know what happened. People that would never know their loved one's fate. This is where Yolanda would end up if nobody found out who she was. An anonymous corpse in an unmarked grave. A numbered brick.

The Bobcat had completed its job. The low mound of fresh dirt was Pop's current marker. The army had told me that it would take four to six weeks to get his headstone. I told them to take their time.

I walked back toward the road, up the hill and past the shooting range. The range was quiet, everybody out shooting birds instead of paper targets and clay.

Just as it occurred to me that I didn't know how I was going to get back home, I saw a wonderful sight. Angie sat on the hood of her F-150, her toes stretching to touch the bumper. She smiled when she saw me.

"Bobby called me." She slid off the hood.

"Why do you think he did that?"

"Because you wouldn't've," she said. "He said you needed a ride."

"I need a lot more than that."

"You okay? With your father and all? Burying him, you know? I'm sure it's emotional."

"I guess. My brain's spinning on top of my hangover. So, right now, I'm just trying to get through the day with as little pain as possible."

We were halfway to El Centro, speeding down the Old Highway in Angie's big truck.

"Are we going to talk about what happened last night?" Angie said abruptly.

"If you want to," I answered. "But I don't know that much. Bobby and I just found the body. The sheriff…"

"Body?" Angie interrupted. "What body? What are you talking about?"

"What am I talking about? What are you talking about? Wait…"

"You found a body? Like, you mean, a dead body?" She whispered the last two words. Distracted from her driving and staring at me instead of the road, her truck hit the shoulder and kicked up a huge wake of dust. Angie glanced ahead for the fraction of a second she needed to steer us back onto the road. Then she was back to staring at me.

I nodded.

"Why does shit like this always happen to you?"

"Shit like this doesn't always happen to me. Shit like this has never happened to me. Back up a second. What happened last night that you need to talk about?"

"Whose body was it? Do you know?"

"It was Yolanda. The girl I brought to Pop."

"Jesus. Her? She was young. What happened?"

"All I can tell you is what I know—which isn't much."

By the time I finished the tale about the morning's misadventures, we had arrived at Harris Convalescent. She parked her truck and stared straight ahead, her hands at two o'clock and ten o'clock.

"What a waste" was her final assessment. "What a fucking waste."

Angie insisted on helping me box up Pop's belongings. Even though we both knew it was a one-person job. She took the books, boxing them slowly and carefully, reading each title and on occasion skimming a few pages. I took the personal items, as scant as they were. We worked in silence.

Looking at the stripped pillows on the bare bed, I was brought back to Pop's final moments. Trying to shake it off, it occurred to me that a conversational stone had been left unturned.

"Angie? What happened last night? What happened that we should have to talk about it?"

"You don't remember?"

"I told you—I don't remember nothing. I was blacked out from the moment I walked into Morales."

"You want to guess?" she said, with a head tilt that toyed with me.

Oh shit, I thought. "Oh shit," I said.

"No," she said. "Give me a little credit. You would have remembered if that had happened."

"Then what?"

"You kissed me."

"I did? Are you sure?"

"We had been at the bar talking for a half hour, standing near the back door. You were super drunk, but being kind of charming. I was in mid-sentence talking about my life or my job or some other bullcrap, and you just leaned in and kissed me."

"I was drunk. You said it. Really drunk."

"Yeah, you were." She stopped what she was doing and turned to me. "But I wasn't. I kissed you back."

"Oh" was all I could think to say.

"If you took away the alcohol and cigarette breath, it was nice," Angie said. "There was something about it. Something intimate. I know it was a kiss and kisses are usually intimate, but this—it was just intimate. It felt like it was supposed to happen."

I said, "I don't know what to say. Everything that comes to my mind to say sounds stupid in my head. I want to say something, but I want to say the right thing. I don't want to say the wrong thing. I know I sound like a child, but I am a child, and I say stupid things. Every day I do stupid things, too. All the time. If this is the beginning of something, I don't want to mess it up. "

"Yeah, neither do I." She returned to the task of boxing Pop's books.

"Is this the beginning of something?"

"Maybe."

"I'm going to not talk now. Just so long as you know that I'm not talking not because I'm uncomfortable, but because I'm actually very comfortable with where we're at. I want to keep it that way for a while. At least until I say something stupid."

"That shouldn't take too long," Angie said with a smirk.

"Exactly."

I avoided the temptation of talking to Angie again for the rest of the time we were at Harris and during the entire ride back to the house. It was Angie who finally spoke.

As I was stepping out of her truck, Angie asked, "Do you think they'll find her family?"

"I've been thinking about that."

I could see her looking out the windshield, her eyes focused on the water pump and the yellow tape that surrounded it.

"They should know. Her family should know," she said.

"I know people that knew her. People that the sheriff and coroner won't be able to talk to. People in Mexico that don't like any kind of cop. I'm going to talk to them. See maybe if I can find her people."

"Can I help? I'd like to help."

"Pop knew her. And I'm thinking he knew her pretty good. There may be something in the house that can help me find out more. With the state of the house, I could use any help you want to give. I'll warn you, you're looking at the haystack and there may not even be a needle. If there was something Pop didn't want me to know, I doubt he left anything for me to find."

"What about finding out what happened to her?"

"Someone should pay. If someone was responsible, they should pay. But what the hell could I do? What do I know about that? That's for the cops. They'll handle that. I just want to find out who she was and where Pop fit in."

"You got any kind of plan?"

"Grab Bobby and head to Chicali. Talk to the people I know. See where it leads us."

"I could go with you."

"You could," I said. "But better you stay. There's a lot of house to cover, and the sooner we start the better."

She turned off the ignition and smiled. "Let's get to it."

SEVENTEEN

I had never received better driving directions than the ones Tomás had faxed me. Each turn, street name, and landmark was clearly defined. Adequate warnings for each change of direction left nothing to chance. As I drove, Bobby read the directions. Both of us marveled at the level of detail and accuracy. I usually hated driving in Mexicali. Most streets are unmarked, and the grid chaotically devolves. But driving to Tomás's porn shoot made the Mexicali streets as pleasurable as a Sunday drive to a porn shoot.

"He's a details guy, I give him that. The next turn, he even drew a picture of like a weird, bent arrow. So I'll bet…" Bobby looked up and out the window. "Sure e-fucking-nough."

In front of us at a fork in the road, there was a shuttered gas station that appeared to have sold its last drop in the mid-sixties. Its sign was a rusted, bent arrow pointing to the stripped frame of the garage.

"Left, right?" I asked.

"Right. Left." Bobby smiled, pointing to the left to make sure I wasn't confused.

"You're in a good mood," I said.

"Jimmy. Jimbo. We're going to a porno shoot. They're making a pornography. And I'm going. I'm going to get to watch. Porno. Maybe for you that ain't a big deal, being

Mister Bohemian world traveler guy. You've been to Amsterdam, diddled European chicks, eaten snails. But for a farmer from Jerkwater U.S. of A., who considers Yuma the 'big city,' it's a fat, fucking deal. All my favorite actresses are porn stars. And the ones that ain't, I wish they did porn. And that includes Dame Judi Dench."

The shadows stretched across the road, but it was still a long way from sunset. It was hard to believe that we had found Yolanda's body only that morning.

"Tomás said he had someone that knew more about Yolanda. We aren't here to hang out on the set."

Bobby gave me a serious nod. "Don't think I forgot this morning. Yeah, I'm excited and all, but that dead lady's fucked up. I ain't ever going to forget carrying her body out of that water. It's been a hell of a shit day."

"Understatement of the year," I said.

"Why didn't you get whatever on the phone? Don't get me wrong—I'm glad you didn't. I'm down with the plan. Give me some time to soak it all in, so to speak. Not literally—that would be gross."

"Tomás said this would be faster."

"Tomás could have killed her," Bobby said, more thinking aloud than anything else.

"Maybe. From what little I saw of Tomás the other night, from talking to the grown him, he's definitely capable of it. No motive I know of. But of the people that were at Morales, Tomás is the only criminal, far as I know."

"Other than me."

"Right. Other than you. But you're more a bumbling no-goodnik. Like the Frito Bandito to Tomás's Keyser Söze. Whoever the Mexican Don Knotts is, he'd play you in the movie," I said. "I am curious to see how he reacts when I tell him she's dead."

"You didn't tell him she's dead?"

"No, only told him I had questions about her. If he knows she's dead, he didn't act it, didn't mention it. Just told me I should come down."

"So you have no idea what we're walking into?"

"I'm not scared of Tomás," I said.

"Maybe you should be."

Sadly, Speedy Gonzalez stands as the only frame of reference for many Americans when it comes to Mexico. To them the Mexican landscape is all cactus, adobe, and bullrings. One trip to Señor Frogs in TJ does not an international journey make.

In reality most Mexican cities aren't that different from Phoenix or Tucson, similar businesses and industry. And compared to most Mexican cities, Mexicali enjoyed a fairly well-represented middle class, due in large part to the profitability of agriculture in the Mexicali Valley. The further south you went, the nicer the neighborhoods. The district we drove through had groomed lawns and squat palms, far nicer than the nicest neighborhood in El Centro.

The ranch house was a stucco and terra cotta job with a rock lawn and a few succulents scattered for color. Concrete discs led through the pebbles to the front door. I rang the doorbell and waited. Bobby stood behind me, a huge smile on his face. He excitedly bounced up and down, barely able to contain himself. He quietly repeated the word *porno*.

Little Piwi swung the door open quickly. Before I could say a word, he held a finger to his lips. With abrupt seriousness he signaled for us to enter.

I silently mouthed, "Sorry." Which he silently ignored. Little Piwi led us into the modern living room and motioned for us to take a seat on the red leather sofa. He took a seat on the armrest. We sat and stared straight ahead, forced to eavesdrop.

The sound of sex from somewhere deep in the house played as soundtrack while the three of us waited. A woman's staccato scream, insincere male grunts, muffled Spanish direction, that unmistakable rhythmic slapping sound, and uninspired dialogue. "You like that? Take it. Fuck yeah," all from the man.

"But I...we..." Bobby pointed toward the sound. Little Piwi held up his finger. Bobby fell silent, severely disappointed.

We had probably only waited for five or ten minutes, but sitting in a room and listening to two people fucking through a wall was surprisingly monotonous. Aside from some pauses for what I have to assume were position changes, they just kept at it. Finally after a crescendo of male bleats, the house fell silent.

"And cut! *Corte. Bueno,*" a powerful voice boomed.

Little Piwi stood and gestured for us to follow.

Bobby tried to crane his neck over Little Piwi's bulk as we made our way down the long hall. The shag carpet was so thick underfoot it felt like wading in melted marshmallows. Bright light leaked below the door at the end of the hall. I turned to Bobby. His beaming face was ecstatic. When

Little Piwi opened the door, we were momentarily blinded by white light.

It took a few seconds for my eyes to adjust, but the smell was immediate and palpable. Cheap aftershave, sweat, something mediciney, and burnt dust filled the air. I could taste it in the back of my throat.

There were too many people and too much equipment in the small room. Behind a tiny digital camera on a tripod, two men watched the small foldout screen. They commented to each other in animated Spanish. Smoke drifted from the colored filters taped to the barn doors of the lighting gear. Through the forest of light stands, I saw Tomás in a director's chair in the corner. He smoked a thin cigarillo and flipped through a three-ring binder.

A naked white man with a flattop, arm-sleeve sea monster tattoos, and shaved balls leaned against the wall at the head of the bed and chatted with Alejandro. Flattop was oily with sweat and comfortably unashamed in his nakedness. Alejandro went with a lime cowboy shirt and matching boots. He was a walking bad decision. Flattop and Alejandro were laughing to the point of tears. When Alejandro saw me and Bobby, his laugh turned to a scowl. What the fuck did we do?

I turned to Bobby. His eyes darted through the room. He looked baffled by the scene, then horrified as he focused his attention on the center of the room.

I followed his eyes to the queen-size mattress resting directly on the carpet. The naked girl we had been listening to for the last ten minutes lay spent, trying weakly to cover herself with a single sheet. She was Mexican, tiny, and crying. Nobody made any effort to acknowledge her, let alone comfort her.

As I stared at the black lines of mascara running down her cheeks and the smeared lipstick on her face, I felt my face grow hot and my fists clench.

Bobby leaned in and whispered in my ear. "If you don't get me out of this room in the next five seconds, I'm going to beat the shit out of everyone in here."

I walked to the girl on the bed and did my best to wrap the sheet around her. "Let's go. *Vamos.*" I helped her to her feet. Her face sank into my armpit. My arm around her practically lifted her tiny frame off the ground.

Alejandro put his hand on my arm. "What the fuck you doing?"

I shook his hand loose and continued walking her to the door.

I could hear Alejandro behind me, but I shut out whatever he was saying. Mostly Spanglish threats. I would have walked her straight out the door, but another voice rose.

"Jimmy." It was Tomás. The calmness in his voice chilled me. Way too fucking calm, especially in comparison to how amped I felt. I stopped, still facing the door.

"You can't take her, Jimmy. We aren't finished. Film production is a complex process. There are what are called pickups. Reaction shots. Over the shoulder. Close-ups. Part of the business. So the editors have sufficient material to work with. I have an arrangement with Minerva. We have not yet wrapped her, as they say."

I turned. Alejandro had taken an aggressive stance in front of me. Bobby angled himself next to me.

"Back off, asshole," I said to Alejandro.

"She's not yours to take," Alejandro said.

"*Cállete*," Tomás said. His voice cowed Alejandro for a moment, but his scowl returned quickly.

Tomás turned to me. "I can't let you take her. You know that. I can't let you come in here and disrupt my business. You reacted—I understand. You're accustomed to a different world. A world with clear rules. Mexico isn't like that. I appreciate your perspective. But stop. Think. Jimmy. My friend. You are on dangerous ground. You are on my ground. Be very careful."

I nodded in complete and total agreement. "Tomás, I know what I'm doing is stupid. I know. But I don't think I can *not* do this."

"Some battles you can't win."

"I like a good battle," Bobby said, always ready with an action movie one-liner.

Tomás gave Bobby a smile. "The worst of what Minerva agreed to do has already happened. If you take her now, she would miss out on her end. Her compensation. You would be taking from her, not helping her. Making her performance for nothing. And it was an enthralling and enthusiastic performance. Her work and any pain would be wasted." Then to her, softly yet forcefully, he said, "*Venga a mi.*"

"Bobby, take her out to my truck," I said, my eyes steeled on Tomás.

"You are thinking with your heart. A common mistake. Use your brain. What will you do? Where will you take her? You think you are saving her, but you're taking away whatever chance she has. Sometimes you have to do the wrong thing because it's the right thing to do. Because it's the only thing to do," Tomás said.

He was right. I knew it. I hated him for it.

"*Venga a mi*," Tomás repeated.

We stood motionless for what seemed like an eternity, but was probably about five seconds. I turned to Bobby.

He said, "Your call. Sucks any way you cut it."

Then the girl peeled my fingers from her arm. She nodded to me and walked to Tomás, turning for a moment to say, "*Gracias*." Tomás opened his arms for her, and she let him embrace her. Her arms stayed straight down at her sides, present but not responsive.

"Next time you challenge me, you should be better prepared." Tomás smiled.

"Next time I will be," I said, disgust sitting in my stomach like a fucking brick. I was pissed, but not so much at Tomás as the world he lived in. Tomás hadn't made this girl poor and desperate; he'd only exploited her like everyone else.

"I'll make sure she's treated well," Tomás said. "I am a businessman. We have an informal contract, and I guarantee that it will be respected."

"You might say they have an oral agreement," Alejandro said, laughing at his own lame joke. And with that, I dropped Alejandro with one punch to the jaw. A haymaker from nowhere that landed square. Alejandro crumpled, unconscious before he hit the ground.

Time momentarily stopped.

The film crew grabbed the camera and scrambled out the door. Flattop jumped into a fighting stance out of instinct, but thought better of it and put his hands down. He grabbed a robe, but didn't put it on. He left the room naked, softly saying, "Woulda fucked you up," as he passed me. If ever someone deserved a kick in the dick, there was a strong candidate.

"Oh shit," I said, summing up the situation.

Tomás's cigarillo smoldered between his fingers. "What the fuck?" he said, more curious than angry.

I felt Bobby edge closer to my side.

Tomás said, "You have any idea what this means? What you've started? I told you, Alejandro is batshit loco. My warning was not subtle. One guy in the city of Mexicali that I warned you not to fuck with, Jimmy."

"Dude's an asshole. Fuck him," Bobby said.

"He's going to want blood when he wakes up. He's going to wonder why I didn't kill you," Tomás said, and then he whistled loudly.

I turned to see Little Piwi materialize in the doorway. He held a revolver, probably a .45, but it was hard to tell lost in his enormous paw. The gun was pointed at the ground, but it was one more gun than Bobby and I had. We were officially fucked.

"Easy, Tomás," I said. "It was an accident. I snapped."

"You can't hit someone on accident," Tomás said. "You've forced me to do something that I really don't want to do."

"You going to shoot us?"

"*Cállete*," he said. "I'm thinking."

Tomás looked at Little Piwi, then distractedly down at the girl. The whole time she had quietly let him hold her to his body. He took a pull off his cigarillo, letting the gray smoke drift slowly from his mouth.

"All these years I've known you," I said, "and like that, for this, you're going to shoot me? Shoot us?"

Then Tomás laughed. A big mad-scientist laugh with his head back, looking up at the ceiling. My balls retreated inside my body.

"Of course I'm not going to kill you," Tomás said. "You're my friend. Who do you think I am? Some kind of murderer?"

I exhaled.

Tomás pointed at Alejandro's prone body. "I am going to have to kill *him* though."

Alejandro moaned and stirred on the ground. Tomás nodded at Little Piwi, who put the pistol away, walked to Alejandro, and gave him a rib-shattering kick to the midsection. All that from a nod.

"You can't kill him," I said.

"Yes, I can. Of course I can," Tomás said. "It's easy."

"I don't think I can let you."

Tomás stroked Minerva's hair, the same as he would any pet. "You don't have a choice. I don't have a choice. If not now, I would be forced to six months from now. He's ambitious. He'll eventually try to take over my operation. This was going to happen eventually. Soon. He has to be put down. Nice punch, by the way. You laid him out, Jimmy."

I shrugged, taking the compliment with embarrassed pride.

"You're about to murder someone," I said. "How can you be so fucking calm?"

"How else would I act?"

"It's wrong."

"I know Alejandro. The world will be a better place without him."

"Would the world be a better place without you?" Bobby asked.

Tomás laughed. "Better? Maybe. But far less organized."

"What's going to happen to her?" I said, nodding my head at Minerva, but too ashamed to make eye contact.

"As per our agreement, she will fulfill her obligations and then receive the agreed upon compensation and an all-expense-paid trip to Modesto to join her family. You did right by not taking her. She would have had to start from nothing."

"I fucking hate this country," I said.

Tomás nodded. "Who doesn't? Americans hate Mexico. Mexicans hates Mexico. Strangely, Germans seem to like it. I don't want to be impolite, but I still have a lot of work to do. And with this mess, I'm going to have to cancel my dinner reservations. You came down here for a reason. Something about Yolanda."

Apparently any conversation about Alejandro or Minerva was done.

"She's dead," I said.

"What?" Tomás's eyes widened in what appeared to be sincere surprise.

"Last night. While everyone was at your grandfather's bar. Found her this morning. Murdered, it looks like."

"*Qué desmadre*," Tomás said, his mind drifting. "I liked her. We had a nice talk on the drive yesterday."

"I'm trying to find her family. Her last name. Anything. Her people should know what happened. Someone who can bury her right."

"Murdered? Who did it? Do they know who killed her?"

I shook my head.

"She came with you last night. Weren't you her ride home?" Bobby said, behind me.

Tomás nodded, thoughtful. "When I left, she wasn't around. Figured she found some profit. In her line, you're always working. Looking for opportunities. I wasn't worried about her getting home. Nothing easier than a Mexican finding their way back to Mexico. That's what I thought. Little Piwi and I left without her."

"What do you know about her?" I asked.

"Nothing. Less than you. Alejandro runs the girls. I have very little contact. I was going to have you speak to Alejandro. He's the one that'd know, but I don't think he's going to tell you anything now."

We all looked at Alejandro. Out cold on the ground and sentenced to die.

"Is there anyone else I could talk to about Yolanda?" I asked.

Tomás glanced at Minerva. A soft smile crossed his face as he spoke softly to her. "*Yolanda? La conoces? Una de las chicas de Alejandro? Una mancha de nacimiento aquí.*" He pointed to his neck where Yolanda's birthmark had been.

"*Sí. Yolanda Palomera? Muy alta. Sí, la conozco. Vivimos en La Ciudad Perdida.*"

Tomás pointed at Alejandro. Little Piwi picked him up and threw him over his shoulder. Blood and saliva dripped from Alejandro's open mouth. Mumbling sounds escaped, not quite words. Little Piwi carried him out of the room.

With a fresh set of detailed directions, Bobby and I drove away from the middle-class neighborhood toward La Ciudad

Perdida, a *colonia* near a group of *maquiladoras* at the western edge of the city. La Ciudad Perdida was a makeshift slum filled with mostly migratory residents. Some waited for their chance to cross the border, but many just survived on hope remaining in their own country.

While nowhere near the size of the slums in Tijuana, the western edge of Mexicali swelled in constant growth with haphazard structures made from wooden pallets, corrugated tin, garage doors, weathered plywood, street signs, blue tarp, and whatever other discarded or stolen materials were available. A wall of old tires stacked ten high acted as the informal barrier between the road and the *colonia*, each tire painted a different bright color. It was almost pleasant. Until you saw the confinement of pain and poverty that it concealed.

I parked my Mazda in the muddy truck ruts that ran alongside the road. The smell of sewage rose from the stagnant water that trailed into a low ditch. Three naked children chased a half-starved dog, laughing as they ran. Bobby and I followed them into what could only be described as the main drag, a wider expanse with a series of boards zigzagging over the watery filth of the district's runoff.

Bobby rarely looked up from Tomás's directions as he acted as guide. "Go straight. At the house with the Coca-Cola billboard for a wall, jog left. If the path is flooded, see below. If not, head toward the house with a small satellite dish on its roof. Just after the house, turn right. The path will narrow."

"Sorry about what happened back there," I said.

"What?" Bobby looked up from the paper.

"Sorry to get you into this—put you in the middle of my mistake."

"You hadn't punched Señor Shithead, I would've. I got your back no matter what. You know that."

I noticed that we were getting some attention. Two young men followed us. As we approached the narrow path described in the directions, I had some concerns about our safety. My face had finally healed from our last trip to Mexicali, and I liked to think that I had learned my lesson. Bobby read ahead on the directions, his lips moving silently with each word.

"Bobby," I said. "We got company. Couple of townies been following us since we got here."

Bobby gave them a look and then smiled. "They're just curious. Bored, probably. Not many gringos come in here. Least none that aren't reporters or Christ types. You don't look like either. They're harmless. Don't got the look."

"All of a sudden you got Spider-senses? You can just tell whether someone is trouble or not?"

"Six of one. If they want to start something, we can take 'em. Bro, after that shit at Tomás's, I'm ready to throw down. Got a lot of steam in me. If I don't fuck or fight soon, I might explode. These boys want to tussle, take it ringside, 'cause I'll do damage."

We both gave a smile to the young men. They made an effort to look hard and indifferent. Bobby was right. They were only curious. They followed us to our destination, but never got within twenty yards.

The door was one of the few doors that was actually made out of door. I knocked, but I didn't expect an answer. If Minerva was right and this was Yolanda's house, who was supposed to be home? I knocked again anyway. Nothing. I grabbed the door by the knob and hinge edge, lifted it out of the way, and set it against the side of the shack. You can't lock a door if it's not attached to anything.

One of the young men spoke behind me. "*Oye. Salga de ahí. Esa es la casa de Yolanda.*"

Bobby turned. "*Yolanda esta muerta.*"

"*Muerta?*" He glanced at his friend, surprised. The other boy shrugged.

"*Sí,*" Bobby said.

The boys spoke softly to each other. They gave us one last look and then walked back the way they had come.

I gave Bobby a look and entered the one-room house, ducking my head at the low eave. It was still light out, so it hadn't occurred to me to bring a flashlight. My first step in the dark room, I tripped on something and flew its length into the opposing wall. The impact shook the whole structure.

"You okay?" I heard Bobby through a laugh. "I'd blame it on clumsiness, but it's like you're allergic to Mexico."

I turned to see Bobby's silhouette in the doorway, squinting his eyes and examining the interior. He took slow, deliberate steps to my left and picked up something.

"There's a lantern. Toss me your lighter," he said.

The room was so small that I only had to crawl a few feet to hand my lighter up to him. He shook the lantern and then lit it. The room filled with flickering orange light. Shadows danced on the walls, funhouse-distorted by the ripple of the corrugated tin.

The dirt floor was covered with two thick Mexican blankets. A bed, a small desk, a single stool, and a dresser made up the furnishings. Not much room for anything more. The furniture was third- or fourth-hand, dinged and paint-peeled, but everything was clean and the room felt organized and cared for. I scanned the floor to see what I had tripped on. A big, red ball. The kind we played kickball with as kids.

"What are we looking for?" Bobby asked, already flipping through papers on the desk.

"I don't know. Mail. Can you even get mail here? An address book. Anything that might tell us more of who she is—or, I mean, who she was. Where her family is. You'll know when you see it."

"I will?" Bobby studied a piece of paper for a few seconds and then set it aside. He sat down on the stool.

I took the dresser. Clothes filled the top drawer, stacked neatly. My hand searched underneath the dead woman's dainties, hoping to find I'm not sure what.

As I reached to open the second drawer, a three-year-old boy burst through the open door, screaming, "Mama!"

Both Bobby and I jumped, surprised by the loud exclamation. My heart raced from the shock. The child stopped in his tracks. His eyes grew wide, filled with fear and confusion at the two men rifling through his mother's belongings.

"Holy shit," Bobby said slowly. "She had a kid."

"Or we're in the wrong house," I countered.

And with that, the boy took off running.

Bobby and I looked at each other for a second, and then Bobby ran for the door. I scrambled to my feet and followed as quickly as I could. I could hear Bobby hollering. "*Niño, soy un amigo de su madre.*" I looked down the muddy path just in time to see Bobby scoop up the kid in his arm. The boy kicked and screamed as Bobby carried him back toward Yolanda's home.

"Shhh. *Calma. Yo no le dolere. Calma,*" Bobby said softly into the child's ear. But the kid wasn't having any. He was a fighter. And after a few near misses, his heel connected with Bobby's groin. A nauseous smile crept onto Bobby's face. His eyes teared up, but he held his grip.

He looked up at me. "Square in the *cojones.* Center shot. I'm lucky I have kids, or I wouldn't be as practiced at the nut shot. When you become a parent, your balls are a big bull's-eye. It's like they know." He even managed a laugh, going back to shushing the boy.

We had created quite a commotion, as a few heads popped out of doorways. A middle-aged woman with a powerfully squat Mayan build stomped toward us. She shouted Spanish too fast for me to absorb. Bobby spoke calmly, trying to get his words through her barrage with little luck. She reached for the boy. Bobby had no choice but to hand him over. She turned her body protectively, continuing what I can only assume was a scolding. She stood her ground unafraid. Bobby tried to calm her, and after fifteen minutes, more out of exhaustion than convincing, the woman allowed Bobby to speak.

The Spanish was too fast for me. But when I heard Bobby say "*muerta*" three times in thirty seconds, that apparently hit home. Her face changed, and she muttered "*no*" a few times.

Her sympathy turned to the boy. She stroked his hair. There was something familiar about the boy's face. Had he been one of the *chicle* kids from weeks ago? That would be a hell of a coincidence. Couldn't be. Maybe I was becoming one of those white guys that all Mexican children looked the same to me. That wasn't it. I knew this kid.

I was concentrating so hard on the boy's face that I only just heard Bobby say to me, "She'll talk to us. She'll help."

Carrying the boy, the woman entered into Yolanda's house. I was about to follow when Bobby grabbed my arm.

"You see it?" Bobby said, studying my face in an unsettling way.

"What are you talking about?" I asked.

"Bro, that kid looks just like you. When we met in kindergarten. That kid is the Mexican version of you."

I knew I'd seen that face before. The kid looked like photos I'd seen of myself. Not someone I'd met, but images that I grew up with. Pictures on the mantel. Pictures in scattered photo albums. Pictures of me.

Bobby slapped my shoulder. "Looks like you got yourself a new *hermano*."

EIGHTEEN

"That's not Pop's kid."

"Whatever." Bobby shrugged. "Just saying, he looks like a browner version of you. But I'm sure it's just a coincidence. A woman Jack was plowing ends up with a kid that looks just like you. Call Ripley's. You're right. Impossible."

"No way Pop had a kid and didn't tell me about it."

"Everyone has secrets."

"Why wouldn't he tell me?"

"It's funny how quickly this became about you," Bobby said. "Jimmy, think. Maybe Big Jack wasn't so proud of his Mexican mistake-bastard. He was old-school. Probably thought you wouldn't never find out. What good does it do to tell you? Other than make you feel responsible for the kid."

"That's not his son," I said.

"The lady said the boy's name was Juan. In the olden days, wasn't Jack a nickname for John?"

"I can't believe he wouldn't tell me. What the fuck do I do? If that really is Pop's kid? Christ, that'd make his parents both dead. Probably make me…"

"His closest living relative. You wanted to find her family," Bobby said. "Easy as looking in the mirror. You cracked the case."

I gave Bobby a stare that attempted to convey the complete lack of humor in the situation. He smiled goofily, communicating silently that he would find humor in any fucking thing that he damn well found funny.

"It's possible Jack didn't even know he had the kid," Bobby said.

"That's true, I suppose," I said, doubting it.

"You want to put a side bet on it?"

I ignored Bobby and walked into Yolanda's house.

Bobby did his best to translate. He let me ask the questions, only occasionally following up to clarify details. Both of us stared at the young boy who played in the corner with some faded multicolored wooden blocks. He even had the same haircut I had at that age. He did look like a brown me. A good-looking kid.

"Where is the boy's father?" I asked.

Bobby gave me a face, but asked and listened for her response.

"She says he's an American." Bobby smiled. "She doesn't know his name. A farmer."

"We'll get back to that. Does she know Yolanda's family?" I said.

Bobby spoke to her, and then he relayed, "Yolanda has people in Guadalajara, but she doesn't know their names or where they live. She thinks her parents are dead and all there are are uncles, aunts, and cousins."

"It's a start. Gets us a little closer. We got a last name. Now we got a city."

"I've been to Guadalajara. There's like three, four million people there," Bobby said.

The woman continued without any prompting, and Bobby listened and relayed her words. "Yolanda had told her that she had plans to take Juan back to Guadalajara. Mrs. Ruiz, this nice lady, met Yolanda about five years ago. Said Yolanda came to Mexicali to try to earn enough to cross to California. But after she had Juan, she decided to stay in Mexico and earn enough to go home. Yolanda told her last week that she had raised the money. Enough to take care of Juan and open a dress store in Guadalajara."

"Did she say how much money that was?" I asked.

"*No*," Mrs. Ruiz responded after Bobby asked. "*Probablemente miles.*"

"Probably thousands," Bobby unnecessarily translated.

"Did she talk about any of the men she met?"

The woman listened to Bobby, crossed herself, and then nodded. She spoke conspiratorially to Bobby, glancing at Juan to make sure he didn't hear. Bobby relayed, "On nights when Yolanda wasn't working and Mr. Ruiz was out at the bars, they would sit and watch the children, drink a few *cervezas* or some *pulque*, and Yolanda would tell her about her job.

"She says her life isn't exciting. But Yolanda's, it was like the *telenovelas*. Drama and sex and..." Bobby searched for the word. "Mischief. She says that you shouldn't think that Yolanda wasn't a good mother. She took good care of Juan. She says you're not a woman, you wouldn't understand. Although, I've always thought of you as a bit of a woman. She says it's a mother's job to do what's necessary to protect and feed and clothe her children. Yolanda was a good mother. She did the necessary."

"Did she ever mention the name Jack?"

On the word *Jack*, Mrs. Ruiz smiled and nodded. Bobby listened and translated. "Jack? Yes. But not for a long time. Not for years."

"What did Yolanda say about him?"

"She liked him. She described him as older. Dignified. He was a customer. He paid, but was different. That's why she remembered the name. Jack. She pronounces it *Yack*. She says he treated her well."

Bobby listened intently and then continued. "Here's where it gets interesting. She says, when Yolanda got pregnant, she stopped working. From when she started showing to two months after Juan's birth. And when she went back to hooking, she didn't go into *El Norte*. She only worked here in Mexicali. She stopped talking about *Yack*."

I created a timeline in my head. Tried to get everything in the right order. Pop was a regular of Yolanda's. She got pregnant. During that time Bobby had said they stopped bringing girls to Morales Bar. When Yolanda was ready to go back to work, she's stuck in Mexicali. Pop and Yolanda lose communication. Then Pop gets sick the first time. In and out of surgeries. Hard to stay in touch with anyone. He learns he's dying. He has unfinished business. But it didn't answer the big question. Did Pop know about Juan?

I was just about to ask another question when my cell phone rang. It was Tomás.

He spoke quickly. "Jimmy, if you're still at La Ciudad Perdida, if you're still in Mexicali, leave. Now. Get over the border."

"Why? What's up?" I said, looking at Bobby.

"There's a chance Alejandro is on his way over there."

"Alejandro?"

Hearing the name, Bobby gave me a pair of raised eyebrows.

"What happened? You have second thoughts?"

"I don't get second thoughts. I make mistakes, but I don't second guess. First instinct's always the best, even if it's the wrong thing. I underestimated that *hijo de puta*. Apparently he wasn't as out cold as we thought. What is it you hillbillies say? He was playing possum. Little Piwi had put him in the back of his own van, was going to drive to the edge of the town and burn him out."

"Jesus, Tomás. You sure you want to be talking about this shit on the phone?"

"You watch too much television. I didn't think Little Piwi could be got. But all it took was a couple of Alejandro's boys. As Little Piwi was getting out of the van. Must've followed from the shoot. Two *vatos* shot him up pretty good. But it'll take more than a couple of bullets to stop that *buey*."

"How did...?"

"While he was lying there, he was texting or calling or something. Fucking technology, it's like a French maid. When it's not working for you, it's fucking you. Tons of ways to get a message out quick. Don't know when he woke, but he could've heard where you were headed. He can't find me, and he knows it. He's going to come after you."

"Thanks for the warning," I said, giving Bobby a nod toward the door.

"I'll take care of this problem, but it's going to take a little time. Require some organization. He knows I'll be looking. He'll be thinking it's him or me. He's right. It's him. That doesn't mean he's not going to do some damage. Like Little Piwi. I'll get him. Try to stay alive."

I hung up and turned to Bobby. "We got to go."

Mrs. Ruiz promised to look after Juan, at least until I could figure out what to do or what was supposed to be done. I vowed to return in a day or two, not sure if that was a reasonable possibility. I gave her all the money in my pockets, about thirty dollars. She seemed more than satisfied with the amount. I gave Juan a final look.

Bobby and I hurried back toward my truck, winding quickly along the muddy path.

"I don't know why we got to run. Dude's got a glass jaw. I ain't afraid of him," Bobby said.

"Bobby, you aren't afraid of anything. That's the problem. He's past fisticuffs. You going to punch his bullets out of the air? Some shit you're supposed to be scared of. Being scared of things keeps you alive. Even tigers are afraid of shit."

"What are tigers afraid of?"

"I don't know. Dragons," I said.

"Tigers are pussies," Bobby said with a laugh. "You see what I did? Pussies, like pussy cats. Tigers are cats, right?"

"Yeah, Bobby. I got the joke."

I rounded a shack about to hit the main drag when I spotted Alejandro. He had two *vatos* with him, both of them short and thick with shaved heads. All three carried baseball bats. I could also clearly see a revolver in Alejandro's waistband. I ducked back behind one of the shacks before he saw me and held out an arm to stop Bobby. He poked his head around the corner and then ducked back.

"You were right. Fucker brought a gun," Bobby said. "Total puss move."

"Those *cholos* are probably packing, too. How we going to get to my truck?"

"I'll decoy. Let them see me. They'll chase me. I duck 'em, and bingo-bango, I meet you at your truck."

"That's your plan?"

"I wouldn't go so far as to call it a plan." Bobby smiled. "But that's what I'm going to do."

I glanced back around the corner. Alejandro was talking to the two young men who had followed us when we first entered the *colonia*. They pointed in our direction, and before I could duck back, my eyes met the stare of one of Alejandro's men.

"Fuck" summed it up.

Bobby didn't hesitate. He jumped right into the main drag, middle fingers flying. "*Órale, maricón! Chinga tu madre,*" he hollered, and then he took off in the opposite direction down the muddy road. Alejandro and his two men whizzed past a few seconds later. Unfortunately, one of the men glanced my way. He stopped and yelled some breakneck Spanish. The other *vato* stopped. They both turned to me with sadistic smiles. Alejandro, oblivious and focused, continued after Bobby.

I took off, winding quickly through the narrow paths and praying I didn't slip in the mud.

I glanced over my shoulder. They were behind me, but I had put some distance between us. The smaller problem was that I had no idea where I was going and whether or not a dead end was in my future. My makeshift plan was to try to make a wide circle back to the main drag. As long as they chased me as one unit, I had a chance. If they split up, I'd have to slow down to avoid being ambushed.

The bigger problem was that I was a smoker with no endurance. Also, I was out of shape and extremely hungover. I couldn't run much farther without passing out. After forty yards I had a stitch in my side, my lungs burned, and I had a vinegary taste in the back of my throat. I told myself that if I survived, I would get a gym membership.

I needed to hide. I needed to blend in. I needed a weapon. I needed to not be there.

I turned a corner quickly and found the first open doorway. I almost brained myself on the low entrance, but I ducked quickly into the small board and mud structure. Thankfully, it was empty. One entrance, no back door, no windows. I leaned against the wall, waiting for my two pursuers to pass. Sweat dripped from my face, stinging my eyes. My heart raced like a dying bird's. I gulped in air, close to hyperventilating. I scanned the room for anything useful. A shovel leaned in the corner.

I heard the two men rush past, their breathing heavy. I counted to five, grabbed the shovel, and ducked my head out the door. Rather than going back the way I came, I followed them for a few steps. If I were them, I would split up soon—one of them continuing forward while the other headed back.

Shovel plus surprise beats bat. At least in theory.

I found a good hiding place and waited. The space between the two small structures gave me enough cover to avoid being seen while giving me ample space to swing the shovel.

Two gunshots cracked sharply in the distance. Bobby. What had I gotten him into? I could already hear him telling me that he had gotten himself into this on his lonesome. That he was a grown man and he wasn't my responsi-fucking-bility. But if he got hurt? That would be too much.

I hadn't realized how much standing in an alley waiting to attack another human being with a farm implement could increase one's introspection.

Footsteps approached, walking not running. Not footsteps really, but the sucking sound that boots make when they're pulled from mud. Slow, cautious steps. I gripped the wooden handle tightly, knuckles turning white. I didn't realize I was clenching my jaw until I felt the pain in my teeth. I tried to relax, but the situation didn't allow it. I didn't want to turn the corner and reveal my position just yet. I needed surprise. I had to rely on my hearing. I held my breath and closed my eyes.

One step. Another. Then nothing. He had stopped. He was listening too. Had he heard me? Had I made a sound? Had I moved? I kept completely still, icy sweat leaking from every pore. My right leg shook uncontrollably. I felt on the verge of losing control. I heard him spit. He was close. But was he close enough?

His boot sloshed as his next step landed. I swung the shovel and watched the blade arc at arm's length. It gained speed as it reached the corner and I stepped out. In the fraction of a second he had to react, his eyes bulged in surprise. He was taller than I had thought. The shovel connected flat with his shoulder. The blade turned on impact and cut through his cheek, slashing the meat of his face. Blood sprayed with the path of the shovel, absorbed and lost in the mud at our feet.

The man's feet slid from under him and he landed hard on his back. He still grasped the bat in one hand, the other hand reaching for the flapping gash on the side of his face. I stood over him, ready to hit him again. He let the bat roll from his fingers and held up his hand in surrender.

"*No más?*" I asked.

He nodded, bloody bubbles rather than words exiting his now-misshapen mouth.

Looking away from what I had done, I noticed laundry hanging from a line nearby. I grabbed a small dish towel from the line and handed it to the prone man. He held the towel to his wound.

A noise turned my attention to the end of the narrow road. The other *vato* stood thirty yards away. He was breathing rapidly, taking in the scene before him. His eyes fixed on mine.

We stared at each other. Literally, a Mexican standoff.

The man at my feet hit me in the knee with his bat. The nerve. He knocked me to the side, but not down.

"Fuck you," he gurgled in English.

I stood up straight, my weight shooting sharp pain through my knee. The man at the end of the row put his head down and charged like a rhino. I kicked the man on the ground in the side on principle, and then I took off. At least now I was going toward my truck. Even if a berserk man with a baseball bat was chasing me.

I ran maybe fifty yards before my knee screamed. That wasn't going to work. Fuck it.

I turned and stood my ground. Shovel versus bat. Advantage bat, but I didn't have a choice.

The man kept coming full steam, bat over his shoulder like a battle-ax in a Frank Frazetta poster. I grabbed the handle of the shovel wide with both hands, holding it like a quarterstaff and preparing to parry his blow. He reached me, swinging the bat. I feinted a block, sidestepped him, and let him sail past me, hitting nothing but air. For good measure, I hit him in the back with the flat of the shovel as he passed. It pissed him off more than it hurt him, but I had to take what I could get.

He turned and we circled each other. One good swing and he'd be able to break the shovel in half. I had reach, so I took a couple of quick jabs at him with the blade of the shovel. He easily knocked them away.

I had brawled enough in my lifetime to know that violence didn't have to be emotional. Some people got angry. It took away their focus. This was a fight, so I thought about fighting. The mistake too many people made was that they thought about the end of the fight instead of the middle. The middle of the fight was where the end happened.

I found my answer. I was going to use my weakness to my advantage.

He took his swing. I held up the handle of the shovel, letting him hit it dead center. The handle broke in two, splintering the wood. While he was at the end of his swing, I brought one half of the handle down on his foot. The sharp splintered end sank deep into the top of his shoe. He screamed as I brought the shovel blade up quickly and connected with his chin. He dropped to the ground, conscious, but in too much pain to care about me anymore. When he reached for his foot, I could see the tip of the wood sticking bloody out of the rubber sole of his boot.

I had learned my lesson. I didn't stick around to help.

Four flat tires. At the time I found no amusement in the unavoidable irony of my now worthless truck in front of the rainbow wall of tires of La Ciudad Perdida.

Bobby wasn't waiting for me. With two downed attackers in my wake, I didn't think it prudent to stick around. I took a quick breather, taking just enough time to quell the rising sick in my esophagus. Filled with adrenaline, my heart raced and my head sang. After a minute and with my faculties under control, I lit a cigarette, threw up, and limped west into the heart of the city.

I turned back to my truck, not expecting to ever see it again. What was the life expectancy of an abandoned truck in a Mexicali slum? My guess, two hours or night, whichever came first. Driven off or stripped, the city would even eat the bones. I was going to miss that piece of shit.

An hour later, Angie picked me up at the only landmark I could find on the west side of Mexicali. A McDonald's on Avenida Yugoslavia. I used loose change to buy something called a McNifica. It looked like a Whopper and tasted like septic waste. I left a series of messages on Bobby's voice mail. I still hadn't heard from him when Angie drove me back over the border into Calexico.

"What's going on? Where's Bobby? What happened to your truck?"

"I don't know where Bobby is. My truck is gone," I said, trying not to snap at her from my frustration. "Give me a bit. At least until we get to the house. I have to think. I have to get things straight in my head."

"Until we get to the house," she said, obviously unhappy.

"I need to call Buck Buck. I was going to call information, but I don't know his first name. He's always just been Buck Buck. I know his last name is Buckley. Do you know?"

"I don't want to be a smartass," Angie said, "but I think Buck Buck is his real name. Did you try it?"

I gave her a look and called information. Sure enough, Buck Buck Buckley was in the fucking book. I called and left a message. In the age of cell phones, I still had to wait. "Buck Buck, it's Jimmy Veeder. Grab your brother and head to my house. Bobby's in trouble. If you got a gun, bring it."

Angie gave me a sharp look.

I stopped her. "I know. When we get to the house, I'll explain everything."

Back at the house, I didn't explain a thing. Instead, I went straight to the hall closet and took out Pop's shotgun for the second time since I'd been back. I rolled the functional antique Winchester out of the Mexican blanket. I cracked it open, both barrels empty. Snapping the break-action back into place and feeling the weight of the shotgun, I felt invincible. I found a box of shells on the shelf in the closet. Bird shot, but it would have to do. I would have preferred a couple of deer slugs. I wrapped the shotgun back up and headed for the door.

Angie had watched me without a word, but she grabbed my arm as I tried to pass. "You better tell me what stupid shit you're about to do."

"Bobby's in trouble," I said.

"Bobby is always in trouble," she said with no humor in her voice.

"Angie, I got him into this."

"And now you're going to get him out? That's not a plan. You said you didn't know where he was. What are you going to do? Until I know exactly what's going on, you're not taking my truck anywhere. Especially not Mexicali with a shotgun."

I pulled my arm away, but had no argument.

She continued. "At the very least, wait to hear from Buck Buck and Snout. Don't do this alone. Tell me what happened. Bobby's usually the last guy who needs saving. Think about it. Think about Bobby. Put the shotgun back. We'll wait. I don't know what's going on, but running out of the house with a gun and no plan isn't going to help him."

I said nothing for a minute.

"Fucking Bobby better be okay," I finally said, defeated.

Angie took the shotgun and shells from my hands and walked them back to the closet.

I didn't know what to do with myself. When I have a task to accomplish, I have focus. But when things are unsettled, I am completely lost. I contemplated taking a shower, but the thought of Yolanda's body floating in the cistern kept me filthy. This kind of waiting was torturous, but Angie was right. Reacting wasn't good enough. I needed to think.

I put a bunch of ice cubes in a Ziploc, grabbed a beer and my cigarettes, and sat on the living room floor with my back against the wall and the ice on my knee. Angie silently brought me a coaster and an ashtray. I hadn't even known there were coasters in the house. She sat across from me and waited silently.

I needed to figure out what to do about Bobby. Should I have stayed? If I had, what would I have done? Angie was right again. Bobby was much better at taking care of himself than I was. But those gunshots. He could be trapped in La Ciudad Perdida, shot or dead. I needed to call Tomás.

In all that, tickling at the back of my brain was a little Mexican kid named Juan. Ill-prepared to get my head around Pop having a son, I tried to keep my mind on Bobby. But the kid kept creeping in there. That face. Those eyes. Did Pop really have a son other than me? It was crazy. Couldn't be. I had to find his relatives. Relatives other than me. If I was a relative. What a fucking mess.

It finally sank in. Angie was right. I couldn't do this myself. I needed help. All the help I could get.

"You ready for the whole story?" I asked her.

She nodded. "Let me grab a couple more beers."

So I laid it out for her. I told her everything. From the beginning. From Pop's request, which she knew about, to Yolanda's body, to this trip to Mexicali and the possibility of Pop having a son. The only thing I left out was how Pop died. That would always be mine.

It took about a half hour to get it all out. The storyteller in me kept wanting to embellish, but I did my best to keep to the facts. By the time I finished, the room was dark.

Angie stared at me, expecting more or absorbing what she'd heard, I'm not sure.

"Fucking shit" was Angie's response. "What in the holy hell are you going to do?"

"Exactly," I said.

At that moment, the door swung open. The bang of the door against the wall resounded throughout the big room. In the fraction of a second I had to react, I pushed Angie behind the couch and grabbed the poker next to the fireplace, the only weapon within reach.

I rolled into a crouch, ready to attack.

In the doorway Bobby laughed at me. I didn't recognize him at first, covered from head to toe in partially dried black mud, but his machine-gun laugh was unmistakable.

"You scared the shit out of me," I said. I put the poker back and helped Angie up to a sitting position.

"Are you okay?" I asked her.

She nodded and then looked up at Bobby. "What the hell happened? You smell like a colonic."

Bobby shrugged. "Long story. Dude chased me. Took a couple of shots. Missed, obviously. Shit, I haven't been shot at since I was a kid. I got all serpentine. Bobbed and weaved. Kept to the nooks, ran through the crannies. Ditched him, but I was hell and gone west. Part of Mexicali I ain't never been before. Only found one way to get back. At a shitball tamale stand, I hooked up with some illegals taking the plunge and rode the waves of the New River.

"I guess that wasn't as a long story as I thought."

I was surprised to see Griselda walk in past him. She continued the story. "The Border Patrol caught him as he climbed out of the river. Because of all the pollution and disease coming in from Mexico, agents won't go anywhere near it. They just sit on the bank and wait. Catch the ones they can. Double-thick rubber gloves and surgical masks. It's a nightmare. But apparently, Bobby was big enough to be a keeper."

Bobby added, "Couldn't stop puking. Pretty sure I puked up a corndog I ate in junior high. River smells like a baby shit omelet. *La Migra* gave me a ton of hassle. Thought I was a smuggler, a terrorist. Figured I couldn't be up to no good. They had that look in their eyes. The one they get right before they tonk you with their Maglite and perform a cavity search. I called fuck this and got them to call Gris 'cause she's all legit and could vouch for me. She worked her magic. Got me released." He winked. "I don't think she hates me."

Griselda punched Bobby on the arm.

She turned to me. "Bobby said you'd explain. I need to know exactly what's going on. I need you to be straight with me. This is a murder investigation. If you've withheld information, I need to know. Why was Yolanda at your father's wake? I don't want to get too cop on you, but I need everything that has happened and what you're planning to make happen or what might happen. We're on the same side."

I looked at Bobby.

He shrugged. "I wouldn't fuck with Gris. I'm going to hose off. Scrub some of the encephalitis off. Sounds like you two are overdue a chat. You can trust her, Jimmy," Bobby said. "Oh, and Gris, that's Angie. Angie, Gris." He closed the front door behind him. Angie and Gris half-smiled at each other.

I turned to Griselda. "How much did Bobby tell you?"

"I didn't bother to listen. Can only believe so much of what that troublemaker says. Start from the beginning."

I looked out the window and watched a buck-naked Bobby hosing himself off on my front lawn. He spent an inordinate amount of time on his genitals. Both Angie and Griselda followed my eyes. Their laughter broke some of the tension, and I retold the tale for the second time in an hour.

NINETEEN

"You know what the old *campesinos* say." Tomás spoke evenly on the other end of the phone. "The gopher digs the hole. The snake eats the gopher. Then the snake lives in the hole. The owl eats the snake. His turn in the hole. Finally, the rain comes. It drowns the owl. The animal, it doesn't matter. They live. They die. Only the hole remains."

"I didn't know the old *campesinos* said that," I replied after too long a silence. "And I don't have a clue what the hell you're talking about. I don't know what that means. Pretty though."

"Alejandro isn't anywhere. None of my eyes have seen him. He's deep in that hole, but he'll come out. He can only hide so long. The rain is coming."

"What about you? Aren't you hiding?"

"I'm not hiding. I'm different. I'm untouchable. I continue with my business, but more carefully. With more support."

"You think he'll come after me and Bobby?"

"Cross the border? Take some massive *huevos*, but that's one pissed *chingon*. And them two *maleantes* you messed up, they ain't so happy either. I got word to my people that work the border. Spread some money to the boys in green. Unless he jumps the fence, I'll be able to warn you if he heads north."

"That'd be a lot of risk for little reward, don't you think?"

"Jimmy, you stuck a piece of wood through a mother-fucker's foot. I don't know how they respond to that kind of thing in your world, but Mexicans don't let that shit go."

"I still got some shit to deal with down in Chicali," I said, thinking about Juan only to the point where I had no idea what I was going to do.

"Coming down here would be ill-advised. If it doesn't require your personal attention, send someone for you. You come down here, he'll come at you. Won't take him long to find out. All it takes is money to control the law on both sides. This is serious shit, Jimmy. You try to sneak in, you better be extra careful."

"Can I talk to him? Work something out?"

"It was past talking the moment your fist hit his face. You can't look for his reaction to be logical. There ain't no logic in Mexico. I warned you. He's dangerous. Dangerous to me, too. Tired of playing second. He's going to use this to make his move. Sooner than he wanted, but this was the, what do you call it?"

"Straw that broke the camel's back?"

"No, the idiot who punches Mexican gangsters for making stupid jokes."

"Yeah, that's me. It's not a party until I punch a Mexican."

"Alejandro doesn't have my friends. As long as I've got my friends. As long as they're happy, my business partners. The plaza, the cops, the priests, and the players. I'm good. He'll find help from the unaffiliated talent pool. Their quality and quantity will depend on how much money he's banked. I'll know soon enough. Because one thing is certain—he's coming."

"Then what happens?" I asked.

"People die."

When I came back inside, Bobby, Griselda, and Angie had made their way into the dining room. They each had a beer in front of them, and it was church quiet. I glanced at Bobby as I sat. He wore Pop's terrycloth bathrobe and distractedly played with the sash.

"Seriously, bro," Bobby said, looking up. "It's a fucking sauna in here. Is the heat on? I'm sweating like a Youkilis."

"Air's broke. These are all the fans I got. Sorry."

"What'd Tomás say?" Bobby said, eyes back to the sash.

When I had relayed the events to Griselda, she had been very aware of the activities of Tomás Morales. He seemed to have established himself as a slippery player in the criminal enterprises on both sides of the border. Nothing specific, but connections to every criminal and most crimes. On hearing Tomás's name, Griselda showed obvious interest. I had a feeling that any information I gave her about him would be stored for later use.

I lit a smoke. "Tomás had nothing. Keeping an eye out for Alejandro. He seemed to think that if he tried to cross the border, one of Tomás's guys would see him."

"He's got people in the Border Patrol, too?" Griselda said, shaking her head.

"Looking forward to seeing Alejandro again," Bobby said. "That asshole's got a beat down on credit."

"I just want this to end. For Alejandro to leave us alone."

"Leave *us* alone?" Bobby said. "He shot at me. Tried to kill me. And if you hadn't gotten all MacGyver with that shovel, and I'm not totally convinced that actually happened, you'd have a couple of bat-sized dents in your *cabeza* right now. Let him come. I got some king-size hurting to put to that punk."

"This isn't the time for a war. There's too much to figure out. If you want to get back at him, fine. Not now. Revenge is a dish best served cold."

"Revenge is a what? What does that mean? What the fuck are you talking about?"

"It's a quote."

"Best served cold? What? Like stab him with an icicle? Or use ice bullets."

"What? No. What are you talking about?"

"No, no. You may have something. Think about it. Ice bullets would be completely untraceable."

Angie made a loud, exasperated grunting sound. Bobby and I turned to her. After a few seconds with her eyes closed and frustration in her voice, she said, "Boys, can we save the moronics for some other time?"

Griselda laughed, putting her hand on Angie's arm. "I was going to say something, but I was curious to see how stupid these two could get. They completely exceeded my expectations."

"He started it," Bobby said, pointing at me.

Angie gave Bobby a hard stare. "The only thing that matters right now is that boy. What's going to happen to him? What are you going to do?"

It took me a moment to realize that she had turned to me and was waiting for an answer.

"I don't know," I said. Then for no reason other than complete impotence, I repeated, "I don't know."

"Well, until you know, there's nothing else for you to do or think about. You have a problem. Solve it. Nothing you can do about this Alejandro. Work on what's in front of you."

"I don't even know for certain if that kid's Pop's kid."

"Then that's where you start. Find out," Angie said. "Have a paternity test done."

"You need blood or something for that. I just put Pop in the ground. I'm not going to dig him up."

"All I'm hearing is excuses," Angie said, not hiding the aggravation in her voice. "You don't need blood. You have all your father's things. If there's a hair in his hairbrush, that'll do. Long as it's the whole hair with the follicle, it works just as well. You can compare it to one of the boy's hairs."

"She's right," Griselda agreed.

Bobby chimed in. "DNA, dude. It's all CSI and shit nowadays. I saw an infomercial for a home paternity tester. Three hundred bones. A little steep, but if you need to know, you need to know. Erik Estrada said it takes like a week to get the results. He was wearing a lab coat in the ad, so he probably knows what he's talking about. Not everyone gets to wear a lab coat. I was even thinking of getting one. You know, just in case."

"In case of what?" Griselda asked.

"In case I needed one."

Four beers later, Griselda was off on a rant. "It's only been a day. One day, and it's already falling apart. Me, the case, the body, everything. My bosses, they're pushing me to file Yolanda as an accidental death. Dove season. Election year. Bureaucratic bullshit. Like that's a reason. They know it's a homicide, but they don't think I can solve it. What they're thinking is, what's the point? Why bother? An open murder isn't what they want on the books. Better it's just another dead Mexican. Won't make their stats. Get lumped with all the other dead wetbacks." She drained her beer. I went to the fridge and brought out four more.

"That's fucked up," Angie said.

"Couldn't put it better." Griselda nodded.

"So fuck 'em," Bobby said. "Let's catch the mother-fucker our own damn selves."

"Thanks, Bobby." Griselda laughed.

"I'm serious. Just 'cause that's not how it's done don't mean we can't do it. You said it yourself—they're going to quit. Going to bury it. Maybe I'm all revengey right now with that prick, Alejandro, on my brain. But too much fucked shit has happened. Some bastards need a severe ass-kicking to balance out the bill."

Griselda laughed. "I had a couple too many beers. I was venting, not looking for help. This is serious police business. It's my job."

"You mean, the job they're not letting you do," Bobby said. "You let this here farm boy get a little Columbo on this shit, and you'd be doing the job you're supposed to. Hey, look, I don't want to get you fired or shot or whatever they do, but I don't see the harm in me looking into it."

"Actually, there is," Griselda said. "It's called interfering in an ongoing criminal investigation."

"But if they close the case—you said they were going to close the case—if they close it, what am I doing wrong? I wouldn't be fucking any ongoing nothing. There wouldn't be no investigation. Is it illegal to ask people questions?

"It had to be someone who was at Morales Bar. This is the middle of nowhere. No other reason to be this far out of town. Not like there're people just strolling by. I made that list. We got us some suspects. You're in, right, Jimmy?"

"No way, Bobby. This is all you. I'm sorry about Yolanda. Hell, I feel responsible, at least in some way, but she's dead. You said it before, dead is dead. I went to get her last name, find her family, and look what happened. Griselda's right— we don't know what we're doing. And Angie's right, too. There's a little boy without parents. He was going to have a hard life before his mother died, but now…"

"He's fucked," Bobby finished my sentence.

"Mrs. Ruiz said Yolanda was about to go back to Guadalajara. Head back south with Juan. That she had raised enough money to go home. Where is that money? She wouldn't've kept it at her house. Wasn't no lock on the door."

"Wasn't no door on the door," Bobby said.

"She was killed right before she was going to leave?" Griselda said.

"Too much of a coincidence? You think the money has something to do with her death?" Angie said.

"Money usually does," Griselda replied.

At that moment for the second time that night, the front door flew open and slammed against the wall with a loud crash. I turned, my heart beating out of my chest.

Buck Buck and Snout stormed into the house. I had completely forgotten that I had called them.

They stood just inside the door ready for battle, their faces streaked with a rough estimation of camouflage makeup. Buck Buck had a Remington pump-action shotgun, finger just outside the trigger guard. A shotgun shell bandoleer draped across his torso, a sombrero on his head, and a nub of cigar in the corner of his mouth: the psycho bandito look. Behind him Snout had two revolvers holstered cowboy low on a gun belt on his hips. He held a recurve crossbow with a bolt nocked and ready. In his shorts and tank top, he didn't have a look. Unless batshit crazy was a look.

They both breathed heavily, staring at our quorum. Their dramatic entrance had taken everything out of them.

I turned to Griselda, who had her hand on her sidearm. "They're with us."

"Of course they are," she said, not showing any sign of relaxing.

Explanations and introductions were quickly made. Buck Buck and Snout's disappointment was childlike. All that preparation and Wallyworld was closed. Bobby gave them the rough recap. They were ready to head south, amped for a fracas. They almost convinced Bobby to join them. His instinct said fight, but Bobby stuck by his brain and used every ounce of restraint to convince them that now was not the time. Even if he didn't believe it himself. I knew he was doing it for me.

While he talked them down, I spent my time convincing Griselda not to arrest the moron twins for scaring the hell out of her.

As Buck Buck was leaving, he said, "You need us, you call again. We're always ready for action. Probably not used to it in the city, but country folk look out for each other."

"I grew up here too," I said, not sure why I was defending my rural origins.

"All right, Jethro. Just saying, you want, Snouter and I'll camp out outside. Sentry duty. Or we can go on the hunt. Just like in *Hawaiian Hellground*."

"What's that?"

"Mack Bolan."

"Who?"

"The Executioner? It's a book. *Hawaiian Hellground*. Number 22. I'm surprised you don't know that, being an English college major and all. Thought they'd teach you literary shit."

"I ditched Literary Shit 101."

Griselda and Bobby left soon after Buck Buck and Snout, leaving me and Angie alone in the big house. Not much had been decided on, but beer and exhaustion adjourned the meeting.

I had settled on two clear objectives: One, stay away from Alejandro. And two, figure out what to do about that kid. The talking was over for now. It was time to do some heavy figuring.

"You okay to drive home?" I asked Angie.

"Nope." Her eyes were at half-mast.

"I'll throw some clean sheets on the bed in back. I usually just hit the couch anyway."

"Are you going to go again?" she asked.

"What? I'm not sure what you're asking. Go where?"

"Your father died. I'm sorry. But that's why you came back. For Jack. That's done. Are you going to leave again? Are you leaving now?"

"You're drunk. If you want to talk about this, let's do it tomorrow. I'm not going anywhere tomorrow. I still have the house and the land and this thing with the kid, so…"

"That's not an answer. You didn't answer me. Are you leaving?"

There was silence between us. But her patience trumped my discomfort, so I answered.

"I don't know."

"You don't know," she said.

"A lot has been happening really fast. I'm just trying to get to morning. Hoping that when I wake up everything will be clearer."

"You don't know?" Now it was a question.

"I'm definitely not leaving soon."

"When you go, where to? What are you going to? Are there people there? Are people waiting for you?"

"I just said I don't know. I honestly don't."

"You know, you haven't once asked me what I've been up to. What I've been doing in all this time since we saw each other last. But I'm going to tell you. After we stopped our thing, after like six months, to be honest, I didn't really think that much about you. Maybe here and there, yeah. But not like a lot. I liked us, what we had, a lot, but you move on. Then I had seriouser relationships, moved away, moved back. But when you walked into my work the other day…"

She trailed off, leaving a thick silence between us.

"What?"

"I don't want you to leave."

I stared at her, trying to conceal the warm hum that rose through my body. She stared at me like she wanted me. Her body drunkenly tilted forward.

She smiled. I knew that smile. It was slightly mischievous, but mostly it was decisive. Like Angie had made a decision and she found that decision amusing. That smile had always frightened me.

"You're drunk," I said, trying to end the line of conversation.

She nodded, agreeing. "We haven't been alone in this house together since we were in high school."

She was right. I laughed at the quick memory of those times. Why couldn't we stay young forever?

"Do you remember the last time?" she asked, the smile ever present.

"Only every day since I left."

Angie leaned in and gave me a vicious hug that made my healing ribs ache. I did nothing to stop her or show my pain.

After a minute she let go of me, punched me hard on the arm, told me to fuck off, and walked to the back of the house. I watched her until she turned into the back bedroom. I went to the linen closet and grabbed some clean sheets and pillowcases.

"Sorry again for the air-conditioner. I hope it's not too hot for you," I said as I walked into the bedroom.

Angie sat on the edge of the bed, her feet not quite touching the floor. She was completely nude, leaning back slightly with her legs crossed and her arms on the bed at her side. Her brown skin brought back memories that I wanted to climb inside.

"I hope it's not too hot for you," she said. That was no accident. She knew how turned on I was by lame jokes. She was really pressing.

Wanting to stare, but trying not to, I looked down at my feet. I tentatively set the sheets on the corner of the bed, conscious that I was staying outside her reach. "A little too hot," I said.

She coyly patted the side of the bed next to her.

I tried to lock my eyes on hers, but I couldn't help taking another peek at her breasts. And the rest of her body. Maybe a little more than a peek. Angie appeared to have improved with age. She was a strikingly beautiful woman. I tried to stay on her face, but I was a man, goddammit.

"Not when you're drunk," I said.

"I'm not that drunk," she said, that drunk.

"Yes, you are. Scoonch back on the bed. I'll tuck you in. You can dream about me. That's the best I can do. All the nasty dreams you can handle. You want to try this some other time, both of us sober, we'll see what happens, but not like this. Not today, not right now. Drunk sex should be a break from sober sex, not a replacement. God, you look great. I can't believe I'm saying this, but I'm going to leave before I do what I want to. Jesus, your body looks… Good night."

"I want you to stay," she said.

I left the room, closing the door behind me. The devil on my shoulder screamed, "What the fuck are you doing?" That's how I knew I was doing the right thing.

TWENTY

Sometime in the very early morning, Angie slipped in next to me on the couch. There was just enough room for her tiny frame, one leg twisting around mine. She wore one of Pop's dress shirts. The odor of her alcohol sweat and Pop's closet made a confusingly familiar potpourri. I put my arm around her, nothing more. And I did that primarily for her safety, as she was precariously close to falling off the edge. Her grip around my chest held firm.

The next hour was heaven and hell. The heaven of being close to Angie, filled with that first-date anticipation. Our bodies close. Her skin warm. A lifelong memory happening in the present. The hell was in trying to do everything in my power to not get an erection. I felt like a boner would send the wrong message and potentially ruin the moment. I'm more of a romantic than I let on.

Wide awake and needing a distraction, I went back through the time I had spent with Yolanda. It was important to me that I could still see her face. Her living face, not the one at the bottom of the cistern. That one would be with me forever. Her brief but important cameo in my life deserved to be remembered.

I thought back to the first time I saw Yolanda alighting from Alejandro's van. Marveling at her sheer presence. The morning we spent together, the quiet ease. Our time spent not in conversation, but in moments. The way Pop's face lit up when he saw her. I knew it had been something more than a roll in the hay. Far more important than I'll ever know. Without intending to, she forced me to realize that I didn't know Pop as well as I thought. That night after she visited Pop, it wasn't the last time I saw her. I saw her at Pop's service. But our final private moment was when we said good-bye that night. That light kiss and a hint of regret as she stepped back into Alejandro's van. Like she was aware of the finality in our good-bye.

She didn't have her overnight bag.

My body reacted to the revelation. I tried to sit up, but my arm was completely asleep from Angie's weight. I had to lift it with my good hand and shake it until the pins and needles came and eventually blood returned.

When Yolanda went to meet Pop and when she was at the house, she had a small overnight bag with her. But in the back of Alejandro's van, she hadn't been carrying anything.

If she had simply left her overnight bag, I would have seen it. It would be on top of the mess. If she hadn't forgotten it, there was only one other possibility. She had left it on purpose. She had hidden it. She had planned to return for it. At Pop's service, she had come to pay her respects, but had she come for something more? To retrieve her bag?

Where was it? What was in it?

I shook Angie very lightly, eliciting little more than a deep groan and a stinging punch on the arm. I awkwardly tried to slide from under her, getting more groans but eventually slipping out and rolling onto the floor.

I crawled into the kitchen and made coffee as quietly as I could. My labors at silence were moot, as the popping of shotguns clamored outside. Apparently the early bird doesn't just get the worm, but it gets killed for the effort.

When I sat down with my first cup of black coffee, I went through it again. Yolanda had her bag when we left Harris Convalescent. I distinctly remember her holding it in her lap on the drive. Her pose had been so demure. I could picture it clearly. What about when we had arrived at the house? Bobby had been there. He and I left for a few hours. Gophers. Digging holes. She would have had plenty of time to hide it.

There was something in the bag that hadn't been there when she first arrived.

Why wouldn't she take it with her?

Alejandro. He was her ride. If whatever it was had any value, she couldn't have trusted him. Nobody could trust him. Whatever it was, she was afraid that Alejandro would take it from her. Maybe he had a habit of checking her purse. So she hid her purse to retrieve it later. And with Pop's death, her first opportunity arose.

It could be anywhere. The house was huge and full. You could hide a hippopotamus in plain sight among the clutter in any room. I finished my coffee as the dread of searching the entire house sank in. It would take days, even weeks. Looking for something that might not even be there.

Then I saw it. I was staring at it. Right in front of me. Not the overnight bag. The flowers. In the middle of the dining room table. They were wilted and dead, but when Yolanda had placed them there, they had been fresh and beautiful. I hadn't looked closely at the white, bell-shaped flowers until that moment.

I knew that plant. We called it ditchweed. I don't know its real name. It grew wild all over the Valley. Finally, my past experiments with hallucinogens had a practical application. In high school Bobby had heard from either someone's cousin or a dog-eared copy of *High Times* that you could get high from eating it. In a constant state of teenage boredom, that was expert enough for me. I had smoked oregano, licked frogs, and drank two bottles of Robitussin on similar information.

The oregano and frogs yielded nothing. Robing is comparatively expensive for little reward. And I wouldn't recommend ditchweed, unless you consider a rapid heartbeat, dry mouth, the inability to pee, and constipation a good time. If you do, have at it.

Of course Yolanda couldn't hide it inside. She needed to know that she could get to it. The house could be locked. I wasn't in on the secret. If she left it in the house, even hidden, I might still have found it. But outside. It was obvious I wasn't that diligent about the yard work. It was easy to hide something where no one was looking.

I threw on my boots and walked out into the warm morning. I lit my first cigarette of the day, feeling the synapses pop and clarity rise. The shotgun fire felt like it was inside my head, loud and close. I looked to the rising sun on the horizon to see the silhouettes of a dozen hunters in the fields and on the ditch banks. They plodded through the dirt with little joy, raising their shotguns regularly to fire into the air. On the second day of dove season, killing had become routine.

I began at the water pump and then walked around the perimeter of the house, eyes to the ground.

Sure enough, at the side of the house against the short stucco wall was a patch of ditchweed. Only a few of its distinct white flowers still remained. Getting closer to the plant, the smell hit me. I had forgotten how pungent its odor was. The flowers smelled like rotting garbage.

I got on my knees, examining the area for I'm not sure what, but knowing I had to look. It's not what was there, but what wasn't. I found a freshly dug hole. A hole just big enough to fit an overnight bag in.

I ran my fingers through the still-visible thin lines in the dirt made by the small hand that had dug the hole. Whatever Yolanda had hidden, whatever she had dug up the night of Pop's funeral, it was gone. And most likely, it had gotten Yolanda killed.

I lit a cigarette and watched the hunters against the sunrise. About a half dozen cigarettes later and still in the same position, I figured out who I needed to talk to.

"Angie?" I whispered softly, loud enough to wake her, but not enough to scare her. She rolled a little onto her side and wiped at some spit at the corner of her mouth. She blinked her eyes open and stared at me like she had no idea who I was.

"I drank too much," she said. "My brain hurts me in my brain."

"I need your truck, and you need to come with me," I said.

She rolled back over and pulled the couch cushion over her head.

"There's coffee. You want me to get you some coffee?"

She made a grunting sound, indicating that she was now bored with this conversation.

"I'm not going to leave you here alone, and I have to go. You have to get up."

She lifted the cushion and squinted at me. "Have you considered fucking yourself instead?"

I said, "Alejandro is out there. He's a little erratic, to say the least. I don't know if he knows I live here. I doubt if he'd try anything in the middle of the day, but I'm not going to take that chance. I ain't leaving you alone in the one place he might show up."

Angie's eyes opened big, her hand coming to her mouth.

"What? What's wrong? " I looked over my shoulder, expecting to find someone standing right behind me. The room was empty. I turned back to Angie.

She said, "I tried to fuck you last night."

I smiled.

"Oh my God. I'm just remembering. Oh God. How fucking embarrassing."

"You failed, so it's cool. Forget about it."

"Go. Take my truck. Let me be mortified by myself."

"No way. What about Alejandro?"

"In case of psycho, use shotgun," she said and covered her face back under the cushion.

"I'll get your clothes," I said, standing up. "Where did you leave them? Oh yeah. I believe you left them on the bedroom floor when you got all naked for me."

That woke her up. The cushion hit me in the face. And a fist gave me a charley horse, only because it missed my nuts by two inches.

"I need to know what Pop was keeping from me," I said to Red the moment he answered the door.

Red Fidler filled the frame of his front door and stared at me with overt boredom. He rolled his tongue around in his mouth, sucking at something between his teeth.

"I need some answers," I said.

"Well, James," he said, "when a man and woman love each other very much…"

"Funny. If he told anyone what was going on, he told you. You were Pop's best friend. His lawyer, too. What did you bring him that day I saw you at Harris Convalescent?"

Red answered with a disinterested stare.

I brought out the big guns. "Did you know he had a son?"

That got an eyebrow raise, then, "I'm looking at him, aren't I?"

"You know what I mean. Did you know he had a son in Mexico?"

"Why don't you come inside and I'll explain the intricacies of client/lawyer confidentiality? I can elucidate for you why I am not going to tell you a thing about anything."

"You're going to get lawyer on me? Your client is dead. It's time I knew."

Red squinted past me. He nodded toward Angie, who had her eyes closed and her head against the passenger window of her truck. "Ask your girlfriend in too. You might not remember, having been gone so long, but it gets a touch hot out here in the desert. Hate to see her melt."

"She's got water. Told me she needed to sweat a little. I asked her twice."

"Good for you. Took me a time to learn the hard way. Woman tells you what she wants, you listen."

"Especially this one. She hits."

"Son," Red said, "they all hit."

Red's house was meat-locker cold, the recirculated air simultaneously stale and brisk. It smelled like beef broth and dead flowers. He led me to a side room that had been made into a home office. It didn't look like he used it much. The only thing on the desk was a half-finished crossword. I sat in the folding chair across from the desk as Red fell into his worn brown leather chair.

"Now what is it you think I'm going to tell you?" Red said.

"That day I saw you, I need to know what you brought to my father's room. What did he ask you to bring him?"

He said nothing. His face offered me nothing. This wasn't a guy I wanted to play hold 'em with.

"I think whatever it was got someone killed," I said.

That got a reaction, but not much of one. He picked up his pipe and cleaned the bowl with a small pocketknife. "I heard about the whore. Real shame. Heard it was some sort of accident."

"Don't know who you heard that from, but I saw the body. I carried her out of that water. Not a chance in hell.

Yolanda, that was her name. The whore's name. She was murdered. Don't matter if they bury it. That's politics bullshit. I'm talking truth. Someone killed her."

He nodded. "And that has what to do with you? To do with me?"

"You brought something to my father, which he gave to Yolanda. I'm convinced of it. Whatever it was got her killed. You're keeping something from me. Keeping a dead man's secret. It makes me wonder what else you're hiding. I just told you I know about the kid. Is there something else?"

"I am keeping a dead man's secret because the dead man asked me to. His secrets died with him. If he didn't want you to know, let it go at that."

"One of those secrets is out. If my father had a son, that changes things."

Red knocked the pipe against the rim of his trash can and then examined it. "Look, I get it. You found that girl's body. You feel responsible. That's noble in its own dumb way. But you're not responsible. It's just a bad coincidence. As far as the kid goes, you're even further removed."

"So you knew."

He blew into the stem of the pipe.

"You're not going to tell me?" I said.

"That's right. I'm not going to tell you. My word means something."

I stewed, trying to figure my next move.

Red continued. "You got to remember, I've known your father longer than you've known him. We went through a lot of doors. I owe more to our friendship than any- thing you got. You're his blood, but he was like mine. If your father wanted to tell you his secrets, he would have. Why can't you respect that? Nothing you do will change anything."

That hurt. Because about some things, he was right. Pop told stories. I had a slew of true and elaborative tales from Pop, but there were a lot of gaps in there. The stories were ribald tales, hardly personal. I was digging in a place that Pop had deliberately and successfully kept away from me. Pop had attempted to settle his relationship with Yolanda before he died. The problem was that he thought Yolanda would be long gone with her son. That she would be happy and safe in Guadalajara, not dead in a concrete cistern and her boy abandoned.

Red had Pop's secrets, and all that left me was stories.

"Is Mrs. Fidler around?" I asked.

"She's in the back. Tending to her roses or her sweet peas or something. You want to say hello? She'd love to see you."

"I don't know all of my father's secrets, but I know some. I may not've come back to the desert, but Pop and I talked on the phone, wrote a lot of letters."

Red laughed. "So you're going to put the screws to me? That it? You got something on me? You're going to blackmail me? Honestly, you might be giving me my first opportunity as an old geezer to call someone a whipper-snapper."

"If I have to, I will."

"I don't know what you think you know, but there ain't nothing you can blackmail me with."

"How long you been married?"

Red paused, giving me a curious, yet cautious look. "Forty years in November. Sweet of you to ask. I'll tell you where we register. Probably Crate and Barrel—she loves that junk."

"Forty years? That's strange. Because I remember Pop writing me and telling me a story about you and him in San Felipe. Something about a bottle of *mezcal con gusano,* puppy love, and a surprisingly convincing transvestite. But I thought he said that happened thirty-five years ago. I still have the letter, so I can always check the date."

He kept his poker face, but a bead of sweat ran down his temple. And in this icebox, I knew that meant I had touched a nerve.

I continued, not wanting to let him off the mat. "Even if Pop was tight with his secrets, he seemed to be pretty open with yours. You two went to the dog track in San Luis Rio Colorado like twenty years back, right? As Pop's story goes, you ended up selling your wedding ring to some Mex *usurero* to cover some bad bets on the little ponies. Made for a hell of a good story. So you said Mrs. Fidler's in the back? I think I will say hi. What'd you tell her? You lost it? Got mugged?"

I stared at him. He stared at me.

After several moments, he said, "You were always a little fuck."

"Yeah," I agreed.

Red packed the bowl of his pipe, taking his sweet damn time to get it just right. When he finally had the pipe lit, he said, "I'll tell you everything, but that's how it's going to be. Every damn thing. You really want that? You want every detail? You really want to know all your father's secrets? Your father was my friend, my best friend. Don't mean he couldn't be a bastard."

"What I want isn't important. I need to know."

"I was there the day you were born. Day your mother died. You knew that, but you didn't know her. You never knew them as a couple except in a photo. I was in the waiting room with your father. Can still see him sitting there. His face blank, his body like the air was taken out. Dumbly holding a handful of cheap cigars. Hell, cigars. A different time. Known your father fifty years, more. That's the only time I ever saw him cry sober. He was scared and destroyed and even happy. Every feeling a man can have and he was feeling them all at once. He was completely broken. With a responsibility he wasn't ready for. A loss that cold-cocked him and a burden he hadn't wanted. I'm talking about you, James."

I listened, feeling heat rise to my face.

"When Big Jack met your mother, he was in his fifties and she was twenty-six, twenty-seven, young. Even at that age, Jack was wild. A bachelor, a drinker, a gambler, an up and down troublemaker. Those stories he told you, I bet you got the toned-down versions. Son of a bitch found trouble at every turn. But it's not like he was stupid. Don't know no one that read as much. He knew things. A good man, but it was like his back was always against a wall. Least the way he acted. He had been on his own so long, he didn't know better. He didn't know but surviving. A lot of Depression kids like that, but none more than Big Jack. Your mother, Barbara, she tamed him.

"Jack loved your mother. That is a fact. She was the only thing to that point, up until you came along, that he ever gave a good goddamn about. Least as I could tell. I mean, we were friends, but only to a point. He was completely devoted to Barb. You have to be when you're facing that kind of age difference. It wasn't like she was marrying him for his money. He didn't have none. Never was that good a farmer. At first, people talked, but the talk died as soon as people saw them together. They could see it. They glowed with it. Everyone wanted what they had. They had something that was so good, it had to end in tragedy.

"On the day you were born, Barbara was taken away from Jack. It wasn't a possibility that he had ever contemplated. Your birth was supposed to be a blessing, not a curse. To his credit, he never blamed you. But in that single moment, his life changed drastically. He had known he was going to be a father. He had come to terms with that, but he was of a different generation. He had waited to marry. Waited even longer to have children. And when he decided to have a kid, it was because it's what Barb wanted. He wanted to give her everything she wanted. She wanted a kid, she got it. The plan, spoken or implied, was she takes care of you, raises you. He does the father stuff: works, plays catch, goes to games, teaches you to swear, punishes you, goes hunting, fishing, and the rest of the father things. But without her, when it was left to him, he didn't want the job.

"In one of his lowest moments, he even talked about getting rid of you. I ain't saying this to hurt you, just making you see how hard it was. How hard the decision was. We talked a lot about adoption. Believe it or not, I was the one who convinced him to keep you, to raise you. I think he would've come to that conclusion himself, but he was scared like you wouldn't believe.

"From what I can tell, you're like him in a lot of ways. Jack had spent life prior to your birth avoiding responsibility. Hated the idea of being forced to do something. But every time he was given responsibility, every time the opportunity arose to prove himself, he took it seriously and did the work. He never walked away from the responsibilities he couldn't avoid.

"So, little James comes along. Jack gets over the initial shock, accepts the responsibility, and goes about being father of the year. He did it as much for Barbara as for you. Went from selfish to selfless on a dime. Whatever you needed you got. While at the same time, he gave you all the independence you could handle. Let you make your own mistakes. You were a smart kid. Got your father to thank for that. Could've probably used some church, but overall, you seem to have turned out okay. Even the wild streak is there in you. He could only teach you what he knew.

"But the fact was, there were times he hated being a parent. Didn't show it, but he goddamn hated it."

I'd had enough. I had to break in. "You're full of shit, Red. For twenty, thirty years, Pop was just acting the parent, but the whole time he despised it? You expect me to believe that shit?"

"You ain't listening. I didn't say he wasn't a good parent. I didn't say he didn't care about you. I didn't say he didn't love you. What I said was, he hated being a parent. You think you got to like doing something to do it right? He didn't hate you, he hated the job.

"But in the whole time you knew him, he wouldn't never let it show. Maybe even got to liking the job after a bit.

"You didn't know him younger 'cause you weren't born. You never saw that wild side, except maybe once or twice in passing. But you would've chalked that up to too much tequila at a wedding.

"When you left for college or wherever the hell you went, Jack went back to his old self. He didn't need to act any part anymore. He knew you weren't coming back. That you had grown out of the Valley. That you would end up in Los Angeles or Berlin or some important place. You had become a man. And while he would always be your father, there was no longer any job requirements associated with the position. He had no responsibilities. So he went back to who he was when I first met him. Only difference was now he was seventy-something. Wasn't like he was going to let something like age stop him.

"Being old might've even made him wilder. What is it? Closer to the end than to the beginning. Dying wasn't exactly a surprise.

"He knew he wasn't going to get married again. He was a man, he had his, you know, he still liked women. But he had never had any interest in women his age.

"I know you're one of those sensitive, political correct kids, but we grew up in a time when going to a Mexican hooker wasn't considered cheating. You wouldn't tell your wife, of course, but you never felt guilty neither. Used to joke, call it 'a side of beans.' You know, 'Let's go down to Mexicali, grab a few beers and a side of beans.' Just a good time. Times have changed. Now whites marry Mexicans and

Negroes and Orientals and all kinds, but that wasn't how we thought of things. We weren't racist. It was just the way it was.

"I knew. Your father knew. Everyone knew you could find some brown at Morales on weekends. Hell, Big Jack was right across the road, nothing easier. He'd just walk the thirty yards, shoot the shit with Morales for a couple of hours, have a few. I don't know if he told you some of their stories, but they go back, too. Morales and your father were no-joke trouble in the fifties. Night comes, the *señoritas* show, nature takes its course.

"Then maybe three, four, five years ago, the times I'm there I started to notice he's no longer interested in variety. Not that I could ever tell that much difference between two Mexicans. But anytime I see him with one of the girls, it's the same Mexican, the same girl. Hard to forget. She was taller than the rest of them. That Yolanda that got killed."

"You knew her," I said.

"When I saw her at Harris, I knew her right away," he said. "I never trusted her. No different than any other Mexican, far as I could tell. Figured she was angling to get on this side of the border. To live the Mexican Dream. The Mexican Dream is the same as the American Dream, but you got to get out of Mexico first.

"Maybe it was her age. Maybe it was something that I couldn't see. I mean, she obviously looked nothing like your mother. But the way Jack acted, it was the same as when Barbara was alive. She calmed him.

"Other than money, I couldn't figure what was in it for her. Sure, he paid her, but it wasn't enough to buy loyalty. And that's what she gave him. In fact, at Morales I never saw her with anyone else. So either he was throwing money at her or she wasn't eating.

"Then she gets pregnant. What better way to get your hooks into someone. Hell, that's the reason I got married way back when. How do I know he got her pregnant? Your father told me. I was still his best friend. Still am, far as I'm concerned. At first I thought it was just a trick. Was it even his? No reason to believe different. What does he do? Only thing he could do. He let her go."

I shifted in my seat, feeling the image of my father fade like a photograph left in the sun.

"What was an old man going to do with a Mexican hooker and a kid? He cut off all contact. Mexicans pop out kids like oversexed rabbits. What was one more? Your father knew he couldn't do it again, go through what he went through with you. He wasn't going to marry her, and he wasn't going to raise the kid. So the best thing was to make it crystal clear that she no longer had a place in his life.

"To her credit, she didn't belabor it. She took it well. Didn't ask for money. Didn't scream and throw a tantrum. And that was that—they went their separate ways. No anger. In fact, it was touchingly understanding. I started to think maybe I was wrong about her.

"Then the cancer came and the cancer spread. Jack reevaluated. He started seeing the end come into sharp focus. He needed to make things right. Across the board.

"Jack almost didn't tell you he was dying. That's why it took so long for you to find out. He wanted you to go about your life. That was important to him. But in the end, he knew the right thing to do was tell you.

"You came back, James. You don't know how much that meant, because he knew it wasn't easy for you to do. It doesn't matter whether you wanted to come back or not, it only matters that you did.

"After that, there was only one more thing for Jack to make right. Yolanda. But he didn't know where she was. I looked, but didn't have any luck. Mexicali's changed quite a bit since my day. You were his only hope. I was surprised how quickly you found her, although it looked like you took your lumps along the way.

"Which brings us to the end of the story. I wish it had a better punch line. You told Big Jack that you found Yolanda, he contacted me. And against my counsel, I brought him some money. Some money he had set aside. That's what I brought to your father. Nothing exotic, just cash. If that's what she was killed for, it's a goddamn shame."

"How much did you bring?" I asked.

"Just shy of eight thousand dollars," he said.

"Eight...? That doesn't make any sense. I mean, sure, it's not twenty bucks. But who would kill someone for eight grand?"

"Someone who would kill a person for a lot less. Someone who would kill a person for nothing," Red said.

TWENTY-ONE

"I'm not going to bother with any kind of DNA test," I said.

Angie turned to me. "Don't be an asshole, Jimmy. You can't ignore this and pretend like something that *is* happening isn't happening. What good does not knowing do?" She cocked her arm to hit me.

"Hold up, Tex Cobb," I said. "Let me finish."

She drove her truck down a dirt road faster than I would. The truck kicked up enough dust to quickly envelop two dove hunters walking on the adjacent ditch bank. Angie had some color back in her cheeks and was starting to look like she'd pull through.

"I was about to say, I accept that Juan is Pop's kid. Don't need a DNA test 'cause I know that's true. Red pretty much confirmed it."

"What are you going to do?"

"I don't know."

I could feel Angie looking at me, but I kept my eyes straight ahead.

"What don't you know? Seems like there's only one thing to do," Angie said. She turned her truck down Orchard Road, my house in view.

"I don't know what I'm going to do. I haven't decided. I got things to think about."

"The only thing you should be thinking about is that kid."

"Believe me," I said, "I am thinking about that kid. And I'm not going to make any decisions half-ass. This isn't small shit here."

She shook her head, a humorless smile on her face. "You're just going to take off again."

"Don't tell me what I'm doing. I don't know what I'm doing. I haven't made a decision to do nothing."

"I think you have," Angie said.

She pulled her truck into the circular driveway. As she rolled to a stop, something caught my eye across the street at Morales Bar. Something with a heart-shaped window. Alejandro's van was parked in front of the bar.

"Fuck, fuck, fuck me," I said, ducking down in the seat. My back spasmed from the angle as I tried to keep my head below the level of the dash.

"What? What are you doing?" Angie asked.

"Keep driving. Don't stop. Hopefully they're inside. Get out of here. That van. In front of Morales. That's Alejandro's. He's at the bar. Or he might be in the house. Waiting for me."

"Where should I go?" Angie looked worried, but not panicked.

"Not here. Anywhere. Doesn't matter. Just go. Head into Holtville." I peeked over the dash in time to see Alejandro and another man walk out of the bar. Alejandro's yellow cowboy shirt glowed in the morning sun. I ducked back down quickly. "That's him."

"The guy coming out of the bar? Which one?"

"What're they doing?"

"The canary cowboy is staring right at me," Angie said, concern in her voice. "Now he's getting in his van. Him and the other guy." I stayed down, feeling the car make a sharp left out of the driveway and onto the road.

"Don't turn around. In the rearview, are they following?"

"Shit," Angie said. That was all the answer I needed.

I had found Bobby's number on my cell phone and was in the process of dialing.

"Floor it," I said. "If they got a gun…"

"A gun?" Angie practically screamed.

I tried to remain calm. "Yeah. Don't let them get close. If they got a gun, which they do, you can't let them close enough to get a shot. Or they could push us in a ditch. I'll get us out of this. I know these roads. At least, I think I remember them."

"You better," Angie said. Both her hands white-knuckled the steering wheel. She leaned forward in her seat, willing the truck to accelerate.

Bobby picked up. "Yeah, Jimmy, I'm kind of busy here. Got me in the middle of some shit."

"Angie and I are in trouble."

"Shit, fuck," Bobby yelled. "Hold on, my leg is on fire."

"What? Did you say 'on fire'?"

Angie turned to me quickly. "Fire?" She glanced at the rearview, then back at the road. She was twitchy and scared. I felt useless.

I listened to a barrage of swearing and rustling, the phone obviously not close to Bobby's ear. "Bobby!" I yelled. "Bobby!"

Eventually, Bobby's voice came back on the line. "Sorry, bro. I forgot I had this burn permit. Got a field of Sudan on fire in front of me. A little out of control. Fucked my pants up. Shit burns fast, got away from me. What up?"

"Where is Griselda?"

"She went up to Calipat to meet Yolanda's autopsy guy. He was coming in from Palm Springs." Calipatria was in the north of the Imperial Valley, forty-five minutes away even if she ran the lights and siren.

"Alejandro's on our ass. We're heading up Orchard toward town, about a mile before the overpass, Angie and me. He's right behind us in his van. My Winchester's at the house."

"That motherfucker. Where's your truck gun?"

"I'm not in my truck. It's gone in Mexicali. And even if I was, I don't have a truck gun," I said, trying to clearly communicate my annoyance.

"Can you make it into town?"

I looked behind us. The van was closing the gap. The guy in the passenger seat was leaning out the window. "I don't know. I don't think we'll make it. It's too straight a shot."

"You're south of the overpass? Turn onto Hunt Road, right, go east. That fucking dirt road is so fucked up and rutty, it'll be like a bouncy castle inside that beaner van."

I turned to Angie, pointing to the approaching dirt road. "Take a right on Hunt."

She nodded quickly. Her tongue stuck out a little bit between her lips in concentration.

Bobby was still talking. "You see a field burning east? Out by Bond's Corner?"

I looked to my right. I didn't need to look long. Smoke rose up from the horizon in a dark blue-gray plume. It was the only field burning. Maybe eight or ten miles in the distance. "Yeah, I see it."

"Hunt will take you all the way there. Right to us."

Angie took the right onto Hunt Road so hard I thought the truck was going to flip on its side. She hit the gas, the truck fishtailing and accelerating quickly. Hunt Road was a tractor road, wide enough for two lettuce trucks to pass, but with wheel ruts over a foot deep in places. Angie's truck bounced and bucked, but her F-150 was built for this kind of ride. I turned around. The van had to take the turn slower. It was still following, but it started to grow dim in the truck's dusty wake.

"Making the turn put some distance between us," I said to Bobby and Angie simultaneously.

"I got Buck Buck and Snout here," Bobby said. "You make it to us, and you're golden. We'll be waiting for that rat bastard."

"Drive toward the fire," I told Angie, pointing at the smoke.

Bobby said, "When you're about to hit the smoke, honk three times. See you in a few. Got some firearms to load." He hung up.

Angie kept her foot on the gas the whole way. We ran every stop sign, leaped intersections, and almost went into a ditch, but the van never got any closer. I kept my neck craned out the rear, watching the van about a quarter mile back. That was only a twenty-second advantage, but as long as we kept that distance, we were safe enough.

I turned to Angie. She was deep in concentration, but I swear I saw a hint of a smile.

In less than ten minutes, we were at the burning field. Up ahead I could see where the smoke crossed the road. It was nothing like the dust behind the truck. The smoke was solid, no light penetrating its mass. It was like driving directly toward a fifty-foot-tall gray wall.

"Straight?" Angie asked, considerable doubt in her voice.

"Set the wheel as best you can—don't turn it. Close your eyes and pray," I said. I reached over for the steering wheel and honked three long beeps just as we entered the dense smoke.

For a full eight seconds, there was nothing but dark. The smoky redolence was thick even within the closed windows. It even felt like the smoke killed all sound. Like being underwater. No sense of movement or time. There's nothing quite as ball-shriveling as driving seventy miles an hour and having no clue what's one foot in front of you.

Then we were through. As abruptly as when we had entered. The world hadn't changed. It was just more road and fields. Angie had stayed straight as an arrow, the truck tires straddling the center line.

The truck passed Bobby, Buck Buck, and Snout standing at the side of the road, spaced out about ten yards from each other. Shotguns to their shoulders, they aimed at the cloud of smoke, waiting.

"Pull to the side," I said, pointing to Bobby's Ranchero and Buck Buck's truck.

Angie pulled the truck to the side, skidding to a long stop and pulling behind Bobby's Ranchero. We both turned in our seats to see the show. The van would be coming through the smoke at any second.

Any second.

"Stay in the truck," I said to Angie.

"No argument here."

I got out, my eyes glued on the giant black cloud. Fires still burned in the field, the flames almost invisible in the brightness of the day. My eyes stung from the smoke and smoldering ash.

Any second now.

Bobby gave me a glance. I gave him a shrug.

We all stared at the smoke and waited.

Then, out of the smoke, we saw the faintest glow. Diffused by the smoke and almost imperceptible, two glowing headlights inched forward and then stopped still inside the just-visible edge of the smoke.

I walked to Bobby. He head-nodded to a shotgun on the ground a few feet from him. I picked it up, my eyes never losing their focus on the headlights.

"Can they see us?" I asked. "I couldn't see a goddamn thing inside that shit."

"Don't matter," Bobby said. "They know we're here. *Pendejo* can smell a trap. Good on him."

Buck Buck yelled, "You want I should fire a warning shot over their bough, captain?"

Snout laughed.

Bobby walked to the middle of the road. He held his arms out to his side, the shotgun held firmly in one hand, daring Alejandro to try something.

"Come on, motherfucker," he yelled. "Let's get this done."

Slowly the headlights receded. The van backed up and disappeared into the sunless pitch.

For ten minutes, we waited for the van to come barreling through the smoke at any second. That was how Buck Buck ended up putting a big hole in the grille of our former fourth grade teacher's Olds. It really was an accident. Buck Buck was on edge, and his reflexes were quick. A car came through the smoke. He turned and fired.

Mrs. Knipp was shaken up. That tends to happen to eighty-three-year-old women when you fire a shotgun at them. To her credit, she pulled over slowly despite the steam from her exploded radiator.

She stayed in the car. When we ran to see if she was okay, she rolled down the window and the first words out of her mouth were, "Buck Buck Buckley. I should have known. That day I caught you playing with yourself behind the cafeteria, I should have known you'd eventually try to shoot me."

Bobby and I laughed until she gave us a glare. She was serious, like this had been inevitable.

I thought Buck Buck was going to cry. He spent the next five minutes promising to take care of all the repairs personally and anything else she needed.

"Please don't tell my mom," Buck Buck pleaded.

"I didn't tell your mother when you wouldn't stop flashing your pecker at Peggy Miller at recess, did I?"

"No."

"What did I do? What did I tell you?"

"You told me the next time I took it out, you would snip it off. Then you took out your scissors and cut them in the air. And then I peed myself."

"That's right. And you stopped."

Buck Buck nodded, as if he had learned a valuable lesson. I missed the moral, but apparently Buck Buck and Mrs. Knipp had a far more complex relationship than I had ever realized. I had also forgotten how much of a little perv Buck Buck had been.

Eventually, Buck Buck helped Mrs. Knipp into his truck and they headed into town.

Because we didn't have a war room, Bobby and I made do with the tailgate of his truck. Our strategy session consisted of drinking beers from Bobby's cooler, calling Alejandro an original combination of expletives, and throwing rocks at a nearby telephone pole.

As the excitement waned and her hangover returned, Angie crashed and fell asleep in the front seat of her truck. I found a blanket behind the seats and did my best to shade her.

Snout went back to tending the burning Sudan grass. Despite my vocal reservations, he kept his shotgun strapped to his back. Apparently, "no fucking Mexican cocksucker was going to fucking catch him with his fucking dick in his fucking hand." With arguments as strong as that, I'm surprised Snout hadn't joined the debate team in high school, instead of regularly drinking stolen butterscotch schnapps under the bleachers during third period.

When Griselda's patrol car roared through the thinning smoke, Bobby and I dove for our guns. Snout flipped his shotgun to ready. I guess we were still a little jumpy. Luckily, Buck Buck was already on his way to town and all our reflexes sucked. We recognized the two-tone sedan with blue and red lights on top before we accidentally knocked out a couple of shots.

"I put in a call for the van. Sent it out as a 'wanted for questioning' since he didn't really do anything. Probably back in Mexico, but it should come up if he tries to cross again. All we have is the vehicle. He can easily use another car, so you best still be on your guard." Griselda had joined us in the back of Bobby's truck and grabbed a beer from the cooler.

"I ain't going to keep looking over my shoulder," Bobby said. "That shit's going to end."

"If you're planning on doing something illegal or stupid or both," Griselda said, "I don't want to hear it. I'd rather you kept your stupid on the inside."

"I'm just saying," Bobby said. "This is bullshit, that's all. Fucking bullshit. That's all I'm saying."

"Mr. Morales," I said.

"What about him?" Griselda asked.

"Angie and I saw Alejandro coming out of the bar. He knows Mr. Morales is Tomás's grandfather. He might've gone over there to get information about Tomás. Or to…?"

Griselda downed her beer and jumped to her feet. "I'm on it."

"I'm coming," I said.

She paused for a moment, but it didn't take much thought. She shrugged and motioned to her patrol car. "If you're coming, let's go."

I turned to Bobby. "If Angie tries to go off on her own, don't let her. Make sure you or Snout go with her. If it's Snout, no crazy-ass shotgun. A pistol, fine, but nothing too big. Next time I see him, he should still have all nine of his toes."

"I'll be done with the burn in an hour," Bobby said. "My house, *carne asada*, lunch."

I nodded, ran to Griselda's car, and hopped in. The car was moving before my door closed.

On the drive to Morales Bar, Griselda updated me on the progress of Yolanda's murder investigation. Griselda drove ninety miles an hour with one casual arm on the window like a Sunday drive. Considering the events of the day, she even let me smoke in her patrol car. So long as I gave her one of my cigarettes.

"Still fighting to keep it a homicide. Blunt force trauma, coroner said. The wound was deep. From the photos, it doesn't look like it could be from the fall. Hoping when we comb the bottom of the well, we find a rock or whatever that did it. We find that, we find a bit more of the story. There's a lot of broken concrete around the pump."

"I don't need the details," I said. The image of Yolanda's dead eyes and wet black dress returned.

"Sorry. I do that. You get lost in the job sometimes. Desensitized is what they call it. All the crazy you see becomes normal, and normal becomes crazy."

"Probably why you're with Bobby," I said, smiling.

"I know that was a joke, but probably right. Maybe. I know I can't do normal. Whatever that is."

I shook my head. "I can't even figure how things have escalated to the point they're at. I track it in my mind, but I can't find where it went nuts. Not too long ago, I was spending my days trying to make my dying father laugh. And before that, doing shit all."

"Life's crazy, yeah?"

"Where're you with Bobby's list?" I asked.

"Just getting started. The way things work down here is, I got my cases, but I also got my regular shifts. So while I'm doing my interviews, a lot of them on the phone which isn't optimal, I also got to drive the ditch banks and help lost hunters. Without time and resources, I'm trying my best to keep Yolanda from getting lost in the system."

"That's something."

"I'll work the interviews. Everyone I can find. But a lot of people were there. And a few Mexican nationals, I'm going to have a hard time talking to. Including your friend, Tomás. On top of it, everyone was intoxicated. I drew up a timeline. The doc placed the time of death at between one thirty and two in the morning. I'm focusing on finding the people who were unaccounted for then."

"Based on what?"

"People's accounts. Foggy, drunken memories. Bobby gave me a starting point. And Mr. Morales seems to have a practically photographic memory for the events inside his bar. Whether he's been drinking or not."

"Somehow that doesn't surprise me."

Griselda continued. "I got no reason to believe this was anything more than one person. So, I'm taking what each person says, who they saw, what they were doing, and cross-referencing everyone's story. It's going to take some time, but it's already starting to give me a picture, at least from what we got so far. If two, three people say they remembered, say, Mike Egger playing pool the whole time, then I take that as gospel. He's off the list."

"Taking the nicest and Catholic-est guy on the face of the earth off a list of possible suspects, that's big news."

"Just an example."

"So, the gazillion-dollar question. Who's not accounted for?"

"Yeah, that's what sucks. Almost everybody. Including you and Bobby, Buck Buck, and Snout. I think I've scratched like five people off my list. So far the real problem is figuring out who all was there. I got three or four high school kids that nobody can ID. Most likely from Calexico, but who knows. Then there's another half dozen out-of-town hunters and a few field-workers. The bar was open and serving. If I hadn't been on duty, I would've been there. And I never even met your father."

"It was a good wake."

We pulled into the empty dirt lot in front of Morales Bar. Both Griselda and I cautiously got out of the patrol car. The constant volley of distant shotgun fire played soundtrack to our approach. Griselda kept one hand on her sidearm. She turned to me.

"Get back in the car," she said.

"Fuck that," I countered.

She gave me a stare and shook her head, but didn't say or do anything to stop me. With one hand on the door, Griselda nodded her head silently as if counting to herself.

She quickly opened the door and entered the dark bar, pistol still in her holster, but unsnapped and ready. The door closed behind her. I yanked it open and followed her into the hot, empty room.

While Griselda gave the room a visual once-over, I found Mr. Morales behind the bar. On his back. He was alive, but it looked like he'd been worked over pretty good. His right eye was swollen closed, and dried blood painted his face coming from one ear, his nostrils, and the side of his mouth. His broken right arm was bent at an unnatural angle that made me recoil.

I leaned down next to him and started when his head turned to me, showing a bloody jack-o'-lantern grin. "Fucking pussy hit like my great-grandniece."

It was unsettling to me that this was the first time I'd ever seen Mr. Morales smile.

"Here," I yelled at Griselda.

She ran to my side, cringing at the sight of Mr. Morales.

"You better get an ambulance down here," I said.

Griselda nodded, took one more look at Mr. Morales, and ran outside.

I leaned in, putting one hand on Mr. Morales's shoulder. I was afraid to move him, but I wanted him to know that I was there. "We got help coming," I said.

He shook his head and then spit a bloody gob against the back of the bar. His voice was quiet, but strong. "Who's going to work the bar? I ain't never closed in over forty years."

"That'll get figured out. Can't worry about that."

"Who's going to work the bar?"

"Okay, I'll find someone. Jesus Christ."

"Who?"

"I don't know. Someone. I'm starting to understand why they beat your old ass."

"Not that fucking Bobby."

"Shit. I'll find someone. I have no fucking idea. If no one else, I'll do it."

"Okay."

"Finally."

"You can keep it shut during the day, but come six or seven, I want them doors open. Don't fuck it up," he said.

"What's to fuck up?" I said, insulted.

"It ain't as easy as you think."

"Sure. How does it go? I give the customers money and they give me beer, right? Or, oh, it's so confusing," I said. "I know you're all beat to shit and all, but where did you learn how to ask for favors?"

"People show up, the doors are closed, they won't come back."

"It's covered. You probably look worse than you are. You're going to be fine."

"I know I'm going to be fine. This wasn't my first hiding. My arm hurts like hell and I'm going to piss blood for a week, but past that." He started to sit up, but thought better of it and lay back down.

"Was Alejandro looking for Tomás?"

"Of course, *estúpido*. If he hadn't punked up and brought another *cabrón*, I would've got a few more punches in. Tagged him a pretty nice one."

"You tell him anything?"

"What's to tell? I don't know where Tommy is. Wouldn't've told him anyway, but I ain't had nothing to give. Gave me the beating 'cause he was scared."

"Yeah, he looked real scared when he was chasing me."

"Shit scared. He's playing tough, but he knows that Tommy is going to kill him. Makes him dangerous, yeah? Knows he's cornered. Can't just leave town 'cause where the hell'd he go. If he has money maybe. Mostly he knows he's got to stay and die, so he's going to die fighting."

"But he's the one coming after us, after you."

"Try to understand it. He got no choice. I know my grandson. Alejandro can't hide in Chicali, and he can't go *mano-a* with Tommy. He's going to look for some angle, some back alley, some last ditch. He's scared. Should be, too. Tommy ain't the kid you knew."

"Yeah, I kind of got that."

"*Mi hija*'s boy, he ain't afraid to be what they call *pocho*. An American playing Mexican when he needs to. Heard someone use the word Trisket 'cause it's nothing but a brown cracker. Tommy, he ain't got the past. The Life. You grow up like Alejandro, in a *colonia* near the dump, scraping by, selling fucking gum, stealing scraps—you don't got hope to hold you back. You only got survival. Doing what you need to stay alive. Tomás thinks he has a future. Alejandro knows he doesn't. He's got nothing to lose."

"You sound like you feel sorry for him."

"Kid like Alejandro, he couldn't be anything 'cept who he is." Mr. Morales shook his head. He closed his eyes. "Damn, my balls hurt."

Griselda walked back inside. "How's he doing? I got an ambulance coming up from Calexico. Ten, fifteen minutes."

"Hey, sweetness, honey, *muchacha*," Mr. Morales said to Griselda. "Be an angel and pop a beer for me."

"He's going to be all right," I said.

They put Mr. Morales into the back of the ambulance. He refused to leave until I once again promised that the bar would be open for business that evening. After the ambulance drove south, Griselda and I walked across the street to my house.

"This has gotten out of hand," Griselda said.

"You're telling me?"

I had no idea what to do. For the time being, I was going to grab my stuff and stay at Bobby's until we knew what was going to happen with Alejandro. I also grabbed two boxes that Angie had marked "Jack's Papers." If I was going to hole up, I'd need something to read. Why not dig into my father's past and explore his innermost secrets?

The flames rose a foot, ignited by the dripping fat of the *carne asada*. The meat sizzled on the barbecue as Bobby flicked at the thin strips with a pair of tongs. He took a mouthful of beer and spit-taked it over the flames. The smoky steam filled his backyard with a savory aroma.

I sat with Angie, Griselda, Snout, and Buck Buck, each of us on lawn chairs around a plastic table. Each with bottles of beer in our hands. In the center of the table was everything we needed for our meal: flour tortillas in a warmer, guacamole, homemade salsa, chopped onions, cilantro, and a cooling earthen pot of refried beans. It all looked and smelled so good that nobody faulted Snout when he stuck his two fingers in the beans and scooped out a mouthful.

When Bobby finally brought the big plate of sizzling meat to the table, we were all so famished that for the next fifteen minutes not a single word was spoken.

All communication was made through pointing and grunting, combined with facial expressions that suggested the continuum from gastronomic bliss to "Ouch, I just bit the inside of my cheek."

When food tastes that good, you want to savor it, but your mouth won't let you. It's uncontrollable, acting on its own. I didn't even stop chewing when I bit my finger trying to jam the fat end of a burrito into my mouth.

Nothing like the simple pleasure of good food to put things in perspective. Well, not really. Even filet mignon and caviar isn't going to make a person forget that there's a homicidal Mexican in a canary-yellow shirt looking to bleed you.

TWENTY-TWO

Sated and full of meat, I lounged on Bobby's sofa and closed my eyes. The food and lack of sleep threatened to carry me away. If not for my damn brain, I might have snuck in a nap. No such luck. It had its own agenda. It wanted to examine my life.

For the last ten years, I had never planned more than a week ahead. That's the way I liked it. I wasn't attached or tied down to anything. Not to places I lived or even the people around me. I had people I cared about. But that didn't mean I couldn't walk away. The people and places would always be there. No reason I had to be. Just like with the people in the Imperial Valley. It didn't matter how long I was gone. They would be there when I returned.

I had never had a job that I wouldn't have left at the drop of a condescending remark. I had never had a boss that I wouldn't tell to fuck off, if they got mouthy. That's the beauty of a shitty job. There was always another slightly less shitty job waiting. I was just smart enough and just stupid enough to get by doing a hundred different menial chores.

But now I was home. Back home and contemplating staying. Some of it was beyond my control. I now owned a house. I owned a farm. I had three hundred and sixty acres of arable land. I owned all sorts of crazy shit that I had never wanted. Hell, I owned an antique tractor that hadn't run when I was a kid and was still sitting in the exact same spot on the edge of the property. What the hell was I going to do?

"What're you thinking about?" Angie leaned over the back of the sofa, looking down at me.

"Nothing. Stuff," I said.

I moved my legs just in time as she jumped over the back of the sofa and slid onto the cushions. She grabbed my legs, put them on her lap, and looked at me with that damn smile.

"Sorry I got you mixed up in my bullshit," I said. "Pretty fancy driving back there."

"I watched a lot of *Dukes of Hazzard* as a kid."

"Seriously, if anything had happened to you, I don't know what. I'm sorry. I didn't mean to pull everyone down in this hole with me."

Angie smiled. "What's happened has happened. We're all grown-ups. If we wanted to walk away, we would. Only person you're responsible for is you." She looked at me for a few seconds. Her smile vanished. "You and that kid."

I pulled my feet off her lap and sat up. "Do we have to do this now? I don't want that put on me, Angie."

"Juan is your father's child. When your father died, when his mother died, the only person he has is you. If you don't help, who will?"

"As soon as this business with Alejandro is done, then I'll concentrate on figuring out what to do with the kid. He's safe where he's at. Safer, at least. Doesn't make sense to do anything now. I don't know when or if Alejandro'll try something again."

"You're really thinking about leaving him down there?" Angie said, a little too snide.

"I don't know, Angie. I don't know what's best for him. What I'm going to do."

"You'd leave him down there. Without a mother or father?"

I didn't say anything, hoping that was hint enough that I was no longer interested in talking about it.

"I know you," Angie said. "I know what you would have done twelve years ago. And there's no reason you'd do anything different now."

Angie stood up and left the room. The air felt thicker, more difficult to inhale. The food in my stomach turned to acid and weight. I closed my eyes, feeling like even more of a failure.

I woke up about an hour later. The house was quiet, the room still warm and bright from the afternoon sun.

Next to the front door were the two boxes of Pop's papers. I slowly sat up, letting the blood settle in my body. I carried the boxes to the edge of the sofa and sat back down. In an overly dramatic way, I put my hand on the lid and peeked inside. It looked like letters, manila folders, Christmas cards, pretty much any paper that had handwritten messages on it. Some bills, as well. I set the lid on the cushion beside me.

I picked up a red envelope resting on top. Looking at the return address, it was from an address in Portland, Oregon. I didn't recognize the name: Samuel Eliason. The postmark told me it was from 1972. Inside was a birthday card with a cartoon stripper on the front. Inside was a bad pun. It was signed *Sammo* in a man's block letters, no message.

What kind of insight was I supposed to have gained from this? Had I just lifted back the veil and seen into Pop's true nature? It could be anybody: an army buddy, a business acquaintance, someone from high school. What was I looking for? Secrets? Something that would tell me something about Pop that would ultimately tell me something about myself?

I felt like an asshole.

I put the letter back in the envelope and tossed the envelope back in the box. I replaced the lid and then gave the box a light kick.

My phone rang. It was Tomás. I had left a message while the paramedics were putting Mr. Morales onto the gurney. That had been hours before. I was surprised that it had taken him so long to get back to me.

I had expected Tomás to be angry or at least show some kind of emotion, but either he had had time to process the events or he just wasn't the kind of guy to give anything away. He was all business, planning, and tactics. He felt Alejandro's insult (his word) of attacking his grandfather, but only chose to look at it as an expression of Alejandro's combat strategy.

"I agree with *mi abuelito*. The *pendejo* sounds desperate. He's, what would you say, gasping at straws." I didn't correct him. "Going after someone as harmless as *Lito*, or even chasing after you. He's attacking whoever he can put in front of him. Because he knows when he faces me, it will be too late. An easy target is at least a target. You can't shoot what's behind you. It's a respectable approach. Proactive."

"I'm surprised he didn't kill Mr. Morales."

"Would've cost him too much. Going to cost him as it is. But if he had killed him, I don't know."

"How much more can it cost him? You're planning on killing him."

"In Mexico, there may be little quality of life. So at the least, you do your best to maintain a quality of death. If he had killed *mi abuelito,* his death would have been poor and endless."

"Jesus. So what do we do now?" I asked.

"We? *We* don't do anything. I am in the process of taking care of this shitstorm that you started. You should do nothing, stay away from this, go about your life. Maybe be a little more careful, but just go back to whatever you were doing."

"I wasn't really doing anything," I said.

"Then go back to your nothing," Tomás said. "You have no idea what this is costing me. Shifting my attention to a speck of nothing like Alejandro has caused a loss of focus on my primary profit centers. I have enough to consider without protecting you. You cannot help me.

"When he needs extra hands for heavy work, Alejandro hires the same five or six men. Two of them, the ones you shoveled, they aren't going to know anything. They were out of the picture before he went gone. Some friends, I'm told, have information about one of the others. Once we find him, I'll be that much closer to Alejandro."

"I'm supposed to just sit around and wait," I said.

Tomás answered sternly. "I'm not mad at you, Jimmy. But I need you to respect my position."

I didn't know how to respond to that, so I didn't. "I promised your grandfather I'd keep the bar open for him. If you need me, that's where I'll be."

"Better if you dug a hole and climbed inside."

"Don't like that idea. Planning on going down there and slinging some beer. Don't think Alejandro would expect me to be there. Besides, I can bring my own security."

"You promised him?" Tomás asked, considering it.

"He wouldn't get in the ambulance until I did."

There was about five seconds of silence. I chose not to fill it.

"Safe a place as any, I guess. Public. Keep that *pinche* Bobby Maves around. Much trouble as he is, he's got a good taste for war. You want, I can send Big Piwi down."

"There's a Big Piwi?"

"Little Piwi's *hermano.*"

"Is there a Medium Piwi?"

Tomás laughed. I was glad to have reduced some of the tension between us. Tomás said, "Stay out of trouble. This *mierda* with Alejandro will be over soon. After that, we'll talk about next."

"Is there any way that all of this can end without people getting hurt? Without someone getting killed?"

"Probably," Tomás said after a brief silence. "But that's not the current plan."

"*Dónde está Señor Morales?*" or "*Tú no eres Señor Morales*" were the only greetings I got from the Mexican customers before I handed them their Budweisers. From the white clientele, I got the English versions of the same questions as I served them their Coors Lights. I was amazed at how clearly divided beer choice and race coincided at Morales Bar.

I gave each person the short answer, and word quickly spread among the patrons about the attack on Mr. Morales. In Spanish and in English, the only topic of conversation at Morales Bar for the first hour was the *cabrón* that attacked Mr. Morales and what each individual would do if he ever saw the culprit. I started to wish that Alejandro would try something, picturing him charging into the room, only to face a barload of drunk enemies.

As time progressed, I felt safer and safer. So much so that I told Snout and Buck Buck to get off the roof where they had stationed themselves without my provocation. They joined Bobby in the corner and set to steady drinking. All three with their eyes on the door.

Three hours into playing bartender, I found a groove. It was a good rowdy crowd, and everyone was there to forget their day. After the talk of the attack on Mr. Morales, much of the conversation shifted to the dead girl across the street. It seemed that many of the people in the bar were there the night of Pop's wake. They each told their story. I caught snippets of opinion, observation, and straight-up bullshit.

"Mike and I were playing pool the whole night. Remember seeing some hot broads, but I couldn't even say if I saw the one that died. Heard she was a whore. Not surprised she got killed. They know what they're doing. They know the risks."

"*Si permanecemos en la República, nosotros nos moriremos de hambre. Así que venimos al Norte, y ellos nos matan. Si usted es un mexicano, usted no puede ganar.*"

"Someone told me she was shot five times. I don't remember hearing no shots. But with all these fucking hunters around, who could tell. Shit, maybe it was a accident. My brother once shot me twice on accident. Least he said it was a accident."

"All the drug shit down there—before you know it, that violence going to make its way over the fence. Next time, it ain't going to be just a Mexican that's dead, I'll tell you."

"*Yo no recuerdo nada. Bebí tanto, fui afuera de enfermo. Vomité en el lado de una camioneta anaranjada. Y entonces me desmayé.*"

Bobby gave me a whistle and held up his empty beer bottle, smiling. Like he was expecting table service. I flipped him off, but he didn't see me. He was facing the door and his expression had changed. So had Snout's and Buck Buck's. I don't know if I've seen awe, but that was probably as close as I would get.

The gigantic Mexican ducking under the doorway was the biggest man I'd ever seen, and I spent three months in Tonga. He was about two inches under seven feet with forearms bigger than my thighs. The strange thing was that under his prominent brow, he had a gentle face. Even with the five teardrop tattoos under his left eye. It was a gentle face, but it was nowhere near friendly. It was like his face was trying to fool everyone into thinking he wasn't an enormous monster. He was. He looked like he lived under a bridge and ate live things.

Everyone in the bar had stopped what they were doing and were looking directly at him. Nobody moved. People froze, beer bottles halfway to their mouth. I felt like I had walked into a cartoon.

He nodded at me and walked toward the bar, his eyes focused on my face. I did and said nothing. He reached into his pocket. I felt a thimbleful of piss escape my body. I heard the high-pitched slide of chairs from the corner where Bobby was, but I didn't look away from my new friend. I slowly put a Budweiser on the bar and shot him an insincere smile. I kept my other hand near Mr. Morales's shotgun, although I doubted its efficacy on this target.

"Big Piwi?" I hoped.

He opened a cell phone and touched a few keys with his massive chorizo fingers and then handed it to me. I slowly put it to my ear, expecting it to be hot to the touch. Big Piwi drank from his beer, his pinkie sticking straight out.

"Big Piwi will drive you," Tomás said without greeting.

"Drive me where?"

"Where he takes you."

"I thought I was laying low. I thought I was supposed to stay out of this," I said.

"I didn't ask you a question, Jimmy. Big Piwi will drive you," Tomás said, his voice strained. "If I tell you to do something, I have a good reason. And I expect you to comply. I am your friend, but that will always come second to my interests."

"Not really how I would define friendship."

He ignored my comment. "We found one of the men we were looking for. We've been asking him questions. He tells us some things, but not others. About Alejandro and that. Here's the thing. He asked for you."

"For me?"

"He asked for you. By name."

"Who is he? Do I know him?"

"That's what you're going to tell me. He keeps saying he has something he'll only tell you. We've been persuasive, but he has been equally adamant," Tomás said. "Big Piwi is an excellent driver." He hung up.

I handed Big Piwi the phone. He crushed it in his hand and threw it on the ground. A bit over the top, but effective. That'll keep anyone from tracing a call.

Big Piwi was as loquacious as his brother. I tried asking about Little Piwi's condition in both English and Spanish, but only got a surly shrug. I asked him where we were going and got even less. When we drove across the border into Mexicali, I wasn't surprised. I verbally expressed my concerns. He nonverbally expressed his lack of concern by ignoring me completely.

A Mexican police officer opened the gate leading into the chain-link and concertina wire protected parking lot. Big Piwi parked the black SUV in front of a door that turned out to be the back entrance of the *Policia de Mexicali* precinct building. Big Piwi nodded his head toward the door and got out of the car. When he saw that I hadn't moved, he looked back inside like I was a child or an idiot or a child that was an idiot.

I said, "You might not understand, *usted no comprendo*, but this gringo is slightly uncomfortable around the Mexican police. *No me gusto la Policia de México.* If Tomás wants to talk to me, we can do it in the car."

"You think you have a choice?" were the only words Big Piwi spoke. It sounded like the roar of a semi-articulate, tattooed mastodon.

I got out of the car and followed him to the door.

The interior paint of the hallway was a chipped and peeling institutional green. It was dimly lit, and the air was thick like a gymnasium locker room. I couldn't see past Big Piwi, who ducked under each of the hanging bare bulbs that lit our path.

Most of the doors that connected to the hallway were open. As we passed, I looked into identically furnished rooms. No variation on the presentation: a long table, a wooden chair, and nothing else. There didn't appear to be any other people around.

Big Piwi stopped, and I walked into his back. It was like walking into a wall made out of creature. He stood in front of a closed door and pointed at the knob. All the taciturn, cloak-and-dagger procedure had succeeded in creeping me out.

"After you," I said.

He shook his head.

"Can I ask you something?" I said.

He shook his head.

"Are you afraid of Tomás?"

He didn't shake his head.

Until that moment Tomás Morales had not scared me.

A cold chill shook my body. I had seen Tomás in action. I had witnessed his impassive pragmatism. We had discussed the murder of a man. But there was still a part of me that couldn't help but to remember that kid with the briefcase.

It took that moment for me to realize that the child was gone. That was the past. And the past meant nothing.

Standing in the hallway of that Mexican police station, I felt like I had fallen back into a dark hole that I couldn't climb out of. I was back in the cistern. I felt a surge of panic. I was back underwater, fighting Yolanda's lifeless body in an effort to breathe. I couldn't reach the surface. The only chance for escape was to dive deeper. Deeper into the darkness and black muck.

I opened the door and walked into the small room.

A powerfully built Mexican man sat at the wooden chair with his hands tied behind his back. His feet were bare and his skin was shiny with sweat. Blood and saliva ran from his mouth and stained his stubble and the front of his torn shirt. He cried and smelled like piss.

On the other side of the table, Tomás spoke with two uniformed police officers. He glanced at me, but continued to give whispered orders. The two men hurried out of the room. Tomás walked to the far corner and waited for me to join him.

"His English isn't great, but you should be able to talk to him," Tomás said.

"Who is he? One of Alejandro's guys?"

Tomás nodded.

"What have you been doing to him?"

Tomás ignored me. "Some information led the local police to Alejandro's suspected location. The Mexican authorities performed a raid on the building, protecting the public from what they considered to be imminent criminal activity. They missed Alejandro. He was already gone, but three of his men were there. This is one of those men."

"What happened to the other two?"

"What do you think?"

I looked at the beaten man in the chair. I wondered if he considered himself "the lucky one."

"What does he want to talk to me for?" I asked.

"Your name arose," Tomás said. "Apparently, Alejandro was putting something together that involved *Yimmy*. As ridiculous as this sounds, he thinks you can save him."

We both turned to the man in the chair. I put a hand on Tomás's arm. "This is seriously fucked up, Tomás. Torture? I don't know if I can be a part of this."

Tomás looked at my hand until I let go. "You don't know if you can be a part of this? Jimmy, shut the fuck up." He turned back to the man, argument resolved. "*Muchacho? Estás listo? Este es* Jimmy. *Él habla muy poco español. Hablas inglés?*"

The man stirred and looked at me. "Jimmy?"

"I'm Jimmy."

"*Él es un asesino. Él me matará,*" the man said, turning to look at Tomás. His voice was wiry and strained, unnatural to his build.

"Who is going to kill you?" I asked.

"He is to kill me," the Mexican man said to me, but his eyes were still on Tomás.

Tomás said nothing.

"He isn't going to kill you," I said.

"Can you stop the devil?" the tortured man said. "Can you?"

"I don't know."

"If he is to kill me, you will not find him."

"Then I will make sure you are safe."

"If you want to find him."

I turned to Tomás. He nodded.

"I won't let him do anything," I said. "I give you my word. Tomás Morales will not harm you. Not if you tell me everything you know. Where is Alejandro?"

"*No sé.*"

"In English," Tomás shouted. Seeing the big man cringe made me cringe.

He dropped his head, as if the weight of it was no longer bearable. "I no know."

"You just said that you can help me find him. Why did you want to talk to me? How do you know my name?"

"Alejandro," he said. "Alejandro, he say, nothing stop Tomás Morales from the killing. Alejandro in Mexicali, he know he *es muerto*. Tomás Morales, *él ve todo.* Alejandro say he cannot be Mexicali. He run. *El Norte, no?*"

"Okay. Alejandro wants to leave Mexicali. Where's he going?"

"*Sí,* Alejandro go to Los Angeles, San Diego, yes?" the man said.

"Great, but where do I fit in?" I said.

"*Dinero.* He wants your money."

"What?"

"He, Alejandro, is not to leave until you give his money."

"What the fuck are you talking about? *His* money? I got news for him and you. I ain't got no money. And if I did, I wouldn't be giving Alejandro *centavo uno.*"

"This is all he talks about. Jimmy will give me the money. Jimmy have the money," the man said. "The money to begin *negocio en El Norte.*"

Tomás looked at me. "There something you're not telling me?"

I shook my head. "Okay, for the sake of argument, let's say I have money. How is he going to get my money? Why does he think I'd give it to him?"

"Just before *la policia* come, Alejandro to go," the man said. "Alejandro to go to get the boy."

In an instant my stomach tightened into a fist, filling with gravel and snot.

"The boy?" I asked.

"Alejandro, he to go to La Ciudad Perdida."

"Oh shit."

"He was to go to get the boy." The man began crying again, mumbling what might have been a prayer.

Now I understood. *If he is to kill me, you will not find him.* He wasn't talking about Alejandro. He was talking about Juan. He was saying that I would never find Juan.

Tomás stepped in and said, "The boy? What does that mean? What boy? Jimmy?"

I heard Tomás talking, but the meaning didn't sink in. All I could hear was the beaten man's words.

He was to go to get the boy.

Get the boy.

TWENTY-THREE

Tomás called the officers back in the room and told them to send a squadron to La Ciudad Perdida. I told him about Mrs. Ruiz and Juan and where they were within the *colonia*. He remembered the directions he had given me the day before and repeated them to another couple of officers. The bustle of activity took less than a minute.

Tomás took me into an adjoining room. It was the same institutional gray-green with a desk, a couple of chairs, and a couch. He pointed to the couch. I sat down. The fabric felt damp and warm. I lit a cigarette with a quivering hand.

"Who is the boy? Who is he to you?" Tomás asked. "Why am I only hearing about this now?"

"He's Yolanda's son. The dead woman's son."

"What does that have to do with you, Jimmy?"

"He's also my father's child."

"Your…?" He did the math in his head.

"I didn't know he existed until yesterday. Fuck, that was yesterday. It wouldn't've been difficult for Alejandro to figure out why we went down to the *colonia*. Find out who we talked to. Talk to them. A gringo in that slum gets looks. So does a shovel fight. Nobody but a few people know about Pop, but he could've figured that the kid was important to me. Probably thinks the kid is mine."

"If he's still at La Ciudad Perdida, my men will find him."

"Why would he try to take him?"

"Money," Tomás said. "There are no other reasons."

"I don't have any money."

"A lot of Mexicans, especially poor Mexicans, believe that all white people, all Americans, are rich. And comparatively, they are. I doubt if Alejandro's plan is overly structured or thought out. He's not a deep thinker."

"What the fuck is he going to do with Juan when he finds out I don't have any money?"

He patted my shoulder and walked back into the interrogation room. He spoke softly to one of the remaining guards, who immediately left the room.

Tomás returned, standing over me. "If he is in Mexico, we will find them. If not, we have our new *amigo*."

Four cigarettes and a stomach ulcer later, Tomás's cell phone rang. He had a long conversation in Spanish that was too fast for me. I caught a few words, but no meaning. However, Tomás's disappointment was clear.

Tomás hung up. "No Alejandro. No boy. They found the old woman. She had been beaten. She was, is unconscious. I have a doctor on his way. But even awake, I don't think she'll tell us anything important. Only confirm what we know. Alejandro has the boy. And they are gone."

"Fuck," I shouted, my head ringing from the volume.

Tomás continued. "They are gone, but close. He will have to contact you. If he wants your money, he will need to make arrangements to get it. The boy will be safe until then."

"And Alejandro will be safe as long as he has the boy."

"Now you see why they call it a Mexican standoff."

The man was offering his terms. "*Sé donde esta el chico.* I will tell where he takes the boy. We were to, *cómo se dice* '*encontrarlo.*' I know where he takes the boy. *Pero no hablaré aquí. Debo ser libre. Tengo un primo en Calecia.* My cousin in *Calecia.* Bring me to *mi primo,* I will tell you."

I took Tomás to the side. "Can you get him over the border? Can you get him to his cousin?" My body surged with adrenaline. I could feel myself shaking and frantic, unable to completely control my nerves.

"I can get people over the border, yes. But we aren't going to bring him to Calexico," Tomás said calmly.

"But—" was all I got out.

"We will find them," Tomás said. "Alejandro has not contacted you. He is most likely on the move. We have time."

"Are we just going to wait for him to call? What about this guy? He has the information we need."

"Exactly. And he is going to tell us. In this room. Right now. He is going to tell us where Alejandro took the boy. He was supposed to meet them. He knows and he will talk. He does not make the rules," Tomás said. "I make the rules in Mexicali."

Big Piwi walked into the room and set a case of mineral water down on the table. He took his place directly behind the shaking man.

I turned to Tomás. "You going to make Italian sodas? We're wasting time. You need to stop being the big boss and do something to find them."

Before Tomás answered, the man interrupted, emphatically chanting, "No, no, no." His frightened eyes stared at the mineral water. His voice rose and dropped to the rhythm of his breathing. The volume arced in rolling waves with each desperate breath.

"He will tell us. Ten, fifteen minutes. He will tell us."

"What are you going to do, Tomás?" I asked.

"*Tehuacanazo.*"

"What does that mean? I don't know what that means."

"There's really no good translation," he said, ominously playful.

Tomás picked up a bottle from the case and leaned toward the man. "*Dónde está Alejandro? Dónde iría él? Dónde se ocultaría?*"

"*No. No. Mi primo en Calecia.*"

Tomás turned to me, smiling. It was a smile that no man was meant to see. A smile that was supposed to be hidden beneath an executioner's mask. Not sadistic, but implacable.

Tomás said, "He thinks he can get what he wants."

"Maybe he doesn't really know," I said. "He's trying to stay alive."

"He knows."

"He also knows that you aren't going to let him live, which gives him no incentive," I said. "I don't want Alejandro to do anything to that boy, but I don't know if I can let you kill this guy. I mean, torture? He's just this fucking guy, some lackey chump."

"He understands that this is a part of his life."

If I hadn't been so disturbed, I would have laughed. "That's not an argument, that's insane."

"He knows that today is his last day," Tomás said. "When the sun rises tomorrow, he will no longer be. It's fascinating to watch. Nobody knows how they will conduct themselves with that knowledge."

"Then why doesn't he just tell you? Get it over with? He's obviously scared shitless of whatever you're about to do."

"It's what you said. His knowledge keeps him alive. As long as he owns what he knows, he lives. Even if it's only to buy a painful fifteen minutes. If he tells me his secrets, then he is a dead man. At least, that's how he thinks. Nobody goes to their grave easy. They all cling to life by their fingernails."

"I told him I wouldn't let you kill him."

"I heard you tell him that," Tomás said. "When you came here, you wanted to make sure that you were safe from Alejandro. I wanted to make Alejandro cease to be. You now have a different problem. I don't. I want to find Alejandro for the same reason. I intend to use the most effective methods regardless of your concerns."

I wanted Tomás to get mad. I wanted him to yell. He was so calm. He showed no emotion. It scared the hell out of me.

"We're friends, Tomás. As a friend, I need your help, yes. But as a, I don't know, as a human being, I can't let you kill a helpless man."

"He is only helpless right now."

"Killing him will not help the boy. I know that."

Tomás looked down at the ground for a moment. "Why do you only call him 'the boy'? Or your father's child?"

"What do you mean? You're changing the subject."

"He is your brother, isn't he?"

"Yeah. He is my brother." And as I said it, I realized that was the first time I had used that word to describe him.

He is my brother.

"Are you willing to do anything to get your brother? Are you willing to do anything to protect your brother's future?"

My mind raced. I barely heard the questions.

My brother.

"Are you willing to do whatever it takes?"

I stared silently, but I knew the answer.

"You're going to find out," Tomás said and gave Big Piwi a nod.

Big Piwi grabbed the man by the neck with one hand, his other hand on the front of the chair. He picked both the man and the chair off the ground and slammed them onto the table, crushing the man's bound hands beneath him. The sound of grating bone on wood made me wince. The man screamed, bound and on his back. He tried to struggle, but had no leverage. Big Piwi slid the man's head to the edge of the table by his hair and held him, one hand on the chest, the other on his forehead. The man's body writhed, but Big Piwi's grip was firm, the man's head tilted back and still.

Tomás unscrewed the cap of the mineral water. It burped a little gas, bubbles rising to the rim. A little bit of water ran over the side and Tomás's hand. He walked to the table and stood over the man, whose face and ears glowed bright red.

"*Dígame,*" Tomás said to him. Then he poured the mineral water into the man's nostrils.

The man screamed, water and pink saliva spraying from his lips. The muscles in his neck tightened and clenched. The compressed violence of choking. Tomás let the water pour from the bottle, the man's nose overflowing, his sinus cavity full of caustic water.

I turned away, but without the image the sound was more distressing. The man's muffled, gurgling screams fighting for volume, but dying in liquid. The sound of a man drowning. Drowning in the desert.

"*Dónde?*" I heard Tomás ask.

The response was more smothered cries.

I walked out of the room, closed the door, and retreated down the hall until I could no longer hear the man. Except in my head.

I sat down on the ground, lit a cigarette, and inhaled deeply. It gave me no comfort, only a burning feeling in my chest and stomach. A part of me knew that I deserved the pain.

Fifteen minutes later, Tomás was standing over me. "The carbonated water has no lasting effect. It is only pain. More brutal people in the south use gasoline."

I said nothing. Thinking about the man and the building I was in. This was all being done within the parameters of the "law." My fear of Mexican jails had been reaffirmed.

"We must go. You must go. I will give you the information on the way. Alejandro is no longer in Mexicali. I know where he is, but I don't know for how long."

"I can't go anywhere until I know that he's going to be okay."

"He? Who? Him?" Tomás asked, looking back over his shoulder.

"Yeah. What's going to happen to him?"

"Let's go. You have the advantage on Alejandro. Don't squander it. Your brother's life."

"No, Tomás. I'm trying to hold onto something human here. This isn't something I can walk away from."

I took a couple of deep breaths.

"It's not just about saving Juan. It's about what happens next. If I'm going to take care of my brother, if I'm going to raise Juan, I can't be the kind of man who lets an innocent man get killed."

"Innocent?"

I held my stare at Tomás.

Finally Tomás shook his head. He gave me the same look you give to a child when you finally give in and buy them that ice cream cone.

"For you, Jimmy."

He held out his hand and helped me to my feet. Tomás put his arm around my shoulder and walked me back to the interrogation room. Big Piwi had set the chair back on the ground. The man was slumped over and appeared to be semiconscious. Water, blood, and saliva dripped from his mouth and nose. Tomás nodded at Big Piwi. He grabbed the man by his wet hair and lifted his head up. The man opened his eyes to slits and stared vacantly at Tomás.

Tomás grabbed the man under the chin and spoke slowly and clearly. "*Este hombre acaba de salvar tu vida. Tienes una hora para dejar Mexicali. Si oigo que usted ha vuelto, tú morirá después de mucho dolor.*" He used Spanish that even I could understand. The man had an hour to leave Mexicali. He could never return or he would be killed.

Tomás turned to me. "Happy?"

"Not the word I would use," I said. "Where is my brother?"

TWENTY-FOUR

"The Oasis," Tomás said. "That's where Alejandro took the boy."

Tomás and I sat in the back seat of his SUV. Big Piwi drove, his mass wedged behind the steering wheel. He barely slowed to give a nod to the Border Patrol officer working the crossing. Membership has its privileges.

"The Oasis," Tomás repeated.

"What is that? Like a bar? A night club?"

"No. It's a problem. It's in Gordons Well."

"That's in the sand dunes on the way to Yuma, right?" I asked, remembering the name from my youth. "There's nothing out there. How can he be there? The old plank road and a bunch of quads and dune buggies."

I took out my pack of cigarettes. I could feel Tomás watching me as I fumbled with the torn opening at the top of the soft pack. As I dug my nails into the filter end of a smoke, I looked up at Tomás. He gave me a brief head shake. I put the cigarettes back in my pocket.

Tomás said, "It's the south end of the Algodones Dunes. Runs close to the border. Right where the All-American turns north. A remote point of entry without the danger and inconvenience of crossing the canal. Some of the dunes are in Mexico. It's a serviceable place to cross. But only for the well-equipped. Very dangerous for anyone else."

"I know where you're talking. It's nothing but sand. There's no shade, let alone anywhere to hide," I said. "But I got a feeling if it's got a nickname like 'the Oasis,' I'm about to find out what's what."

"In the old days, Gordons Well might have had a well. Now it has a geothermal plant."

"That's right," I said. "I went on a field trip out to one of them when I was in fourth grade."

"And it's not just any geothermal plant," Tomás said. "But the crookedest little geothermal plant in the world."

By the time Big Piwi had pulled into the parking lot of Morales Bar, Tomás had given me the lowdown on the Gordons Well Geothermal Power Plant Project (or the GWGPPP, if you can believe it).

Commissioned by the Department of the Interior in the early seventies and run by a joint effort between the state of California and Imperial County, the power plant ran quietly and efficiently for its first thirty years of operation. Until the last couple of years. It seems that three years ago, due to the power plant's proximity to the All-American Canal and the San Andreas Fault line, there were concerns about the effect the plant was having on the Imperial County water supply. The EPA came in and in a surprising display of efficiency began their testing and issued a temporary delay of all energy production at the facility. That temporary delay became indeterminate when they found high mineral counts, particularly sulfur and phosphates. The engineers and employees of the GWGPPP were redistributed to the other power facilities in the area, leaving a skeleton crew of security guards to mind the plant.

The security staff proved to be both entrepreneurial and original. Nobody knew how it started, but those remaining men at Gordons Well went into business for themselves. And they didn't open a lemonade stand.

Location, location, location. The men at Gordons Well realized that the forty-acre power plant could function as a welcome refuge for a select group navigating the desert. Its remoteness provided both privacy and convenience. Since the christening of "the Oasis," drug traffickers, coyotes, and all variety of smuggler had used the facility as a safe haven from the desert and the authorities. For a price, of course.

The rules were simple. Pay the toll and you are welcome. By the day or by the hour, rates were adjustable. At congested times, four or five groups would use their services simultaneously. While they tried to keep rival groups apart, conflicts had been known to arise. Violence was discouraged; however, it was often difficult to avoid. The unwritten rule was that any troublemakers were banned from returning. At least the ones that weren't buried somewhere in the dunes.

The Oasis guards had created a business that was to everyone's advantage. It was in nobody's interest to upset the balance. The criminals who used their service couldn't replace the guards, and the safe haven saved them time and money. Most were eager to pay. As long as nobody got greedy, everybody would profit. The services were simple: time out of the sun, food, and water. But more importantly, they were Switzerland, an accepted neutral country where you could hide your gold or yourself. As long as you had the money.

In fact, Tomás had admitted to using their services himself. He avoided specifics, but I got the impression that he was a frequent flier. And for that reason, he could not help me in my apprehension of Alejandro and Juan. As much as he wanted to get Alejandro, he didn't feel justified in violating the trust that he had developed with the Oasis guards.

Tomás said, "Once it's gone, it is never coming back. The desert gets more treacherous to cross with each year, and the Oasis plays a vital role. Not only for my personal business. The impact on my relationships would be damaged. If word spread that my actions caused the closure of the Oasis, it would be costly.

"You cannot call anyone for help. No police. No *La Migra*. Nothing. No one. Their participation would not only jeopardize the life of the boy, but mine as well. The people that rely on the Oasis are many and unmerciful.

"The best I can do is to ensure that Alejandro remains within the perimeter. There is only one road into the facility. I can promise that Alejandro never leaves the dunes. But getting your brother back, that's up to you."

As I got out of the back of the SUV, I turned to Tomás.

"That guy," I said, "the one that you tortured for this information."

"What about him?"

"You lied to me, didn't you?"

Tomás didn't say anything.

"You're going to kill him, aren't you?"

"No," Tomás said, glancing at his watch. "He's already dead."

It didn't take long to give Bobby, Buck Buck, and Snout the abridged version. Sobering them up was a different story. Whose bright idea was it to leave them in charge of Morales Bar?

And that's how I ended up sitting in the passenger seat of Bobby's Ranchero, heading east on Highway 8 toward Yuma. I wished we were going to Yuma instead of a crooked geothermal power plant somewhere near the halfway point. Bobby was banging his head to some Molly Hatchet tune that wasn't "Flirting with Disaster," steeling himself for whatever was to come. I would have turned it down, but I knew better than to touch the original Philco in Bobby's ride. Snout and Buck Buck were behind us in Buck Buck's pickup.

I had my posse and we were equipped, hauling trailers carrying two ATVs and two dirt bikes. And in the back of Bobby's Ranchero were duffel bags filled with every weapon we could find. We were armed to the teeth with all things explosive, ballistic, sharp, and deadly. There was even a sword in one of the bags. A fucking sword. If I wasn't so juiced on my own fear, if this wasn't really happening, if a small boy's life wasn't at stake, I would have felt ridiculous.

It was just after midnight with only the slimmest slice of moon. I looked at the desert, dimly illuminated by the stars. The scrub and chaparral devolved to sweeping barren sand dunes in the blink of an eye. The change was not gradual, but severe. Even in the day, there would be no visible indication of life.

The song ended, and Bobby turned the dial on the radio to a low roar. His hand trembled slightly. He caught me looking, made a fist, and gave me a light punch on the leg.

"Give me a smoke," he said.

"You don't smoke," I said. "And definitely not in your baby." I stroked the dashboard.

"Shut up and give me one."

I shook a cigarette out of the pack and handed it to him. He rolled it in his fingers and then gave it a long sniff. He put it in his mouth unlit and sucked on it.

Bobby laughed to himself. "Remember when we found that pack of cloves in junior high? Smoked like all of them in an hour. That's the highest I ever felt, 'cause I never felt nothing like that. All spinny and laughy. Then I puked out my spleen and both my intestines until I was heaving air and what tasted like my own piss. Kept me from smoking no more. The smell of cloves still kills me. Hell, I smell pumpkin pie and I get queasy."

"That's what cloves are for," I said. "It's like the cigarette fairy plants them for dumb kids like us to find."

"All that shit we did. All the trouble we got in. When people talk about memories, that's the shit they're talking about. All the crazy shit. Hell, most of the time, all I remember is laughing. Laughing our asses off. But I got no idea what we were laughing at."

"You're my best friend," I said, matter-of-factly. "You know that, right?"

"I never forgot," he said.

We didn't say anything for a minute or so.

Done with the silence, I turned to Bobby and said, "You going to smoke that thing or just fellate it until it grows from a king-size to a 120?"

He gave the cigarette a long look and then handed it back to me. "You're right. Can't let a car this cherry get all smoky."

"Thanks for doing this," I said. My tone had turned serious without my conscious consent, bringing us back to our current situation.

"Didn't even have to think about it, bro. Uncle Bobby can't let anything happen to his favorite new nephew."

Knowing we were close, I felt the need to go over the plan. To go over our reasoning. To just go over everything for the millionth time. I needed to make sure that as crazy as this was, that crazy was best.

"We're doing the right thing, right? Tomás is right, right? Alejandro won't do anything to Juan until he talks to me. If he wants my money, then he has to call me to get it. And if we can get to him before he calls, he'll be completely off guard. He won't know what hit him. We have the element of surprise. He thinks he's in his Fortress of Solitude, but we're about to hit him right in the Batcave."

"Okay, I'm going to interrupt you right there. The Batcave thing was too much," Bobby said. "Calm it down. Have a drink."

He handed me a flask. I wasn't sure that was a good idea, so I took a quick swig. The tequila burned, painfully mollifying.

Bobby shook his head and said, "Griselda is going to be pissed we didn't go to her. It's not that this shit is illegal—she's used to that. It's just insulting. Like we don't trust her. I know Tomás said no cops, but fuck him if it means helping the kid. Seems like they're trapped. We call the cops, the cops show up."

"Yeah, the Imperial County Sheriff's Department deals with hostage situations all the time. Their negotiator probably doubles as the janitor."

"More qualified than us," Bobby shrugged.

"You've been to one of those plants. There're like ten big buildings. Scattered. That gives anyone any length of time to get rid of any kind of evidence. The cops show up, Alejandro just ditches the kid. All they got him for is being here illegally. They chuck him back to Mexico like a too-small bass. And Juan's body is hidden in some pipe deep in the heart of the plant. Plenty of nooks and crannies. Nooks big enough to hide a 747. Don't get me started on the fucking crannies."

"And we can get in and out without being seen? We're like ninjas now?"

"Better chance than any cop or government fucker who don't give a shit about my brother."

"Griselda gives a shit."

"I didn't mean her," I said.

"What makes a Mexican woman want to be a cop? Crazy. Girlie likes a challenge."

"You two work, don't you?"

Bobby laughed, easing a little of the tension. "When and if she finds out, she's still going to be pissed. Maybe even more pissed than when I tried to do it with her in the front of her patrol car with a drunk *cholo* passed out in the back."

"That never happened."

Bobby gave me a look that told me it might have.

I said, "How about you do what I'm going to do with Angie. Keep my mouth shut. If we get Juan back safe, she ain't going to care about any kind of bullshit we pulled. Right now, they don't even know Alejandro took him, that he's in any kind of danger. Let's get him back. Let's worry about that. First we make sure everyone's okay. Then we make up a solid lie."

Bobby gave me a look out of the corner of his eye. "You going to lie to Angie?"

"No," I admitted.

"You love her," Bobby said, poking me hard in the ribs.

"I never said I didn't," I said. "I never said I stopped."

"That's awesome, bro."

"Okay, thanks. But suddenly, I feel like I just walked into a tampon ad. I love the shit out of her, but it's time we put on our man pants."

"Let's crank it up."

Bobby quickly turned up the dial, and Bread's "Baby I'm-a Want You" blared from the speakers.

I gave him a look, but he just shrugged, saying, "Mix tape." We let it play, not so much banging our heads as gently swaying.

We pulled into the large dirt expanse of the Imperial Sand Dunes Recreational Area just outside of Gordon Wells. In any season other than summer, there would be dozens of

RVs and tents scattered in the make-do parking lot. But in early September, only the hardcore fanatic braved the thousand-degree, no-shade heat to ride a man toy in a giant sandbox. That night there were two RVs and a pickup with a dune buggy on a trailer. A bonfire burned at the north corner of the hardpack. From the look of the men around the campfire, my guess was that the RV occupants were hunters wisely using this as spillover parking. Because it was not an official campground, there were no fees. And while the dunes had no life, the All-American Canal banks a mile away were solid dove killing grounds.

We parked as far away from the other vehicles as possible, staking our claim at the southeast corner. The Oasis was about a mile through the dunes where the sand leveled out and gave way to scrub.

If we took the single road that led to the Oasis, we'd be detected. Surprise was our only advantage. We were going to have to approach the facility from the back. Through the dunes. A direction no one would be expected to take, even if they weren't expecting anyone. Whoever was going to the Oasis would either come from the west road or from the border to the south. We were going to hit it from the north, trekking at night Boy Scout–style and using the stars to lead us until the lights of the facility became visible.

The noise of the bikes and quads would telegraph our arrival even at a half mile. So we would have to walk them through the sand, using them only as our getaway.

Bobby and I got out of the Ranchero and untied the tie-downs holding the vehicles onto the trailer. Buck Buck and Snout pulled up next to us and got out, doing the same thing. Snout gave me a big wave and a smile. Buck Buck farted loudly and then laughed. I loved those idiots.

When I had asked them to join me, the entire conversation had gone like this:

Me: "Fellas, Alejandro took Juan."

Them: "Let's go get him."

Me: "It could be dangerous."

Them: Laughter.

Walking uphill on the side of a sand dune is hard enough, earth giving and sliding down right under your feet, the ground like liquid. Sinking calf-deep, it's hard to maintain balance while at the same time making any kind of forward progress. But when you're also trying to walk a dirt bike through the porous sand, it feels next to impossible. When I tried to show off by mentioning what a Sisyphean task this was, Bobby agreed that it was about as much fun as having an STD.

It took a disastrous first dune for me to get the hang of it: don't go straight up, but at a gradual, zigzagging angle. In the deep sand, the wheels did little good. I ended up dragging the bike most of the way. Buck Buck and Snout didn't have any better time with the quads, but they weren't complainers and muscled through it.

Downhill was easier, but that's because it consisted mostly of falling, sliding, and burying myself in the sand at the bottom of each dune. Gravity fucked with me coming and going.

It took the better part of two hours to travel what I guessed to be about three-quarters of a mile. Tomás's directions were predictably perfect. We followed Orion's belt and whatever the group of stars to the left were (he had only drawn them). Cresting the top of a particularly bastard dune, the Gordons Well Geothermal Plant came into view. Its yellow lights illuminated the desert haze around it.

We all sat down on the sand, the eerie glow of the multi-structure complex creating a hypnotic effect. It was hard not to think about what would happen next, and I assumed that's where everyone else was. With all the necessary preparation, I hadn't had much time to think. Which was probably a good thing.

Bobby broke the silence. "We're going to have to kill Alejandro."

My mind raced to come up with an opposing argument. I didn't have much luck.

Nobody said anything for a minute.

Buck Buck finally broke the silence. "It is what it is."

"There's got to be another way," I said.

"World won't miss him. Be a better place, more than likely," Bobby said.

"Is that our decision?"

"Tonight it is," Bobby said.

I sat on the sand, absorbing the truth of it. There was no way that Juan, Angie, or I could have any peace if Alejandro was still around. He would always be a threat. And right now with Juan as his hostage, I knew that he had to go.

I dug my fingers into the sand, letting the grains run over the back of my hand. I slowly lifted it, letting the sand run off. I kept a small pile on the back of my hand and then brushed it off.

We said nothing for ten minutes, passing a flask around and staring at the lights of the Oasis. I almost jumped when Buck Buck broke the silence.

"I got so much sand in my butt crack," Buck Buck said, "I could shit a castle."

Snout laughed and then said, "I got so much castle in my shit that I could sand a butt crack."

It didn't matter that it was more about the fear and exhaustion. At that moment Buck Buck and Snout were the funniest men on the planet. I laughed with them, Bobby joining me soon after. The laughter was contagious. Very quickly I couldn't even remember what I was laughing about. I was laughing at the laughing. And every time I tried to stop, every time I tried to catch my breath, it only made it worse. A whole new wave of hysterics rose. I almost rolled off the hill I was laughing so hard. Trying to wipe away the tears, I stuck a fingerful of sand right into my cornea. It stung like hell, but only made me laugh harder.

But even in my hysterical state, I couldn't shake the nagging foreboding. The Big Laugh always seemed to bring tragedy with it.

TWENTY-FIVE

Apparently there wasn't a whole lot that one could steal from a decommissioned geothermal plant. Or at least that's what the scant security measures suggested. A chain-link fence surrounded the grounds. Little more. No razor wire. No dogs. None of those cool red laser beams from the movies. Just crappy schoolyard chain-link. Easily climbable chain-link.

Snout was pissed. He was the one who had lugged the bolt cutters through the dunes.

There was no visible movement on the grounds of the facility. Not even wind. On the trek through the dunes, I had created an image of a movie POW camp with guards walking the perimeter. In reality, the guards were probably sitting in an office somewhere, drunk and reading pornography. If they were awake at all. It wasn't like they were expecting us.

The five main structures of the power plant didn't exactly loom over us as much as they squatted. Three massive warehouse-type buildings abutted two enormously wide, but short smokestacks. The warehouses had loading docks and multiple doors. My guess was that these were where the generators were housed. Catwalks, staircases, and pipes connected all the buildings like an enormous hamster cage. There was even a strange wheel. Its function was beyond me. A double-wide temporary office stood on its own just south of the main facility.

The floodlights were blindingly bright, their hum the only sound. I was glad I hadn't bothered to get decked out in black. I would've stood out even more.

We left the motorcycles and quads out of sight in a gully about fifty yards from the north fence. We hid beneath a long windbreak of tamarisk.

"According to Tomás, there're only two, three guards at any one time. But no way of knowing how many people they're housing," I said. "Tomás said coyoteing dips in the summer. But a lot of smugglers use the Border Patrol's aversion to the heat and getting out of their trucks to their advantage. You got to love a wily criminal's ability to adapt.

"The guards are definitely armed, but it's not like they're badasses. They're just regular guys who had a good idea. They'll be interested in protecting their investment, but probably not enough to get hurt. They shouldn't give us any shit, as long as we just fuck with Alejandro."

"We can try talking to the guards first," Bobby suggested, surprisingly nonviolent.

Buck Buck and Snout laughed.

"Don't got nothing to offer," I said. "Alejandro paid them. And from what Tomás suggested, this service don't come cheap. Especially if they see he's got a kid with him. I ain't got money like that."

"They've got to be thinking that's his kid and he's on the run," Bobby said. "If they know they're accomplices in a kidnapping, maybe they'll balk."

"You're talking about Guantanamo candidates. Their list of felonies is long and federal. Who knows who they've let into the country?"

"If I were them and knew what was what, I'd leave Alejandro, the kid, and us dead in a ditch," Buck Buck added.

"Easiest way to get rid of anything," Snout seconded. "Bury it in the desert."

Because getting in was simple, most of our plan was about getting out—and getting out quickly. We used the bolt cutters after all. If we had to leave in a hurry, which seemed inevitable, then a big hole in the fence was easier and faster than a climb.

Although light filled most of the compound, there were still enough pockets of shadow that we could stay out of sight. Not that there was anyone looking. We still hadn't eyed a single person.

The plan was to split off. Buck Buck and Snout would take a look in the far warehouse building. Bobby and I would check out the double-wide and then hit the nearest warehouse. If all went smoothly, which none of us were planning on, we would meet at the northwest corner of the middle warehouse and go in together.

We would communicate only in an emergency and by text message. I can safely say that this was the first time that I was glad for that particular technology. And the first time I had found a unique function for it. Who knew that texting would be a boon to covert infiltration?

As Buck Buck and Snout made their way across the grounds, Bobby and I quickly investigated the double-wide.

No light came from the windows. It was either empty or its occupants sleeping. It didn't take us long to learn which.

The snoring shook the walls. The man-made vibrations had both weight and girth. Bobby gave me a wide-eyed look, impressed. There could be only one person in the office. Nobody else could have slept through that kind of storm. And if anyone were awake and not stone deaf, they'd have woken up the beast or gone insane. It sounded like someone was strangling a nine-foot-tall goose.

Bobby slowly rose and peeked through the bottom corner of the window. He ducked back down, shaking his head. It wasn't Alejandro. I wasn't surprised. I don't know why, but I hadn't figured him for a snorer. We continued to the nearest warehouse building.

Bobby and I crouched in the sunken truck ramp of a wide loading dock. Multiple rolled steel garage doors and a couple of standard doors led into the building. Concrete and steel were the predominate building materials. None of the main buildings in the facility had windows. That was obviously a problem. That meant we were going to have to enter the building Monty Hall–style without any idea of what was behind door number one.

We worked under the assumption that the Oasis guards and their guests had a level of overconfidence in their safety. Why guard doors if they weren't expecting anyone to come through them?

We didn't even know which buildings were being used to house people. However, we did know that if we came in contact with anybody, we'd have to improvise. Bobby had a recently modified sawed-off, and I had Pop's shotgun. That made improvising a little more interesting and, in some ways, predictable.

I did a sloppy stomach roll up onto the four-foot-high loading dock, neither graceful nor particularly quiet. Bobby made it look a lot easier, shushing me as he rose. We walked slowly to one of the rolling doors. Very gently I put my ear to the steel, trying to get a sense of any activity within the building. I waited for what felt like a full minute, but was probably closer to twenty seconds. I heard nothing and shook my head. Bobby head-nodded to the standard door twenty yards away. Bobby put his shotgun to his shoulder, pointing the barrel to the ground. I put my hand on the doorknob, waiting for Bobby's signal.

Bobby took three quick breaths and then nodded. I turned the knob. It was unlocked and made a loud click as I pushed the door in an inch. I cringed from the sound and then quickly opened the door. Bobby slipped in. I followed him into the darkness, lifting my shotgun.

We stood in an abandoned office that now appeared to be used as a storeroom. It was filled with boxes, but thankfully, no people. I kept the door open a couple inches for the light. There was only one other door. It led further into the building.

"It's like playing Doom," Bobby whispered. "We can only go forward."

"There's nothing about this that's a game," I said. "Not a fucking thing."

"Settle, Jimmy. We'll get the kid back."

"This isn't a game," I repeated.

"You keep telling yourself that." And with that, Bobby opened the door and moved quickly into the deeper darkness beyond.

Once I closed the door, it was pitch black. And while we had flashlights, it didn't feel prudent to turn them on. That was until I almost brained myself on a low pipe. My head made a distinct coconut sound that made me think of the Three Stooges. The four of us were kind of like the Stooges. And if we were, I'm pretty sure that made me Shemp.

Rubbing the bump on my head, I listened into the darkness. It was dead quiet.

Bobby whispered, "Ain't nobody going to just sit in the dark like this. There ain't nobody in here."

I had to agree. It was like being blind, seeing nothing but black with your eyes wide open.

Bobby turned on his flashlight and gave the building a quick sweep. The interior of the structure was the size of an airplane hangar, the beam of light swallowed by the darkness after thirty yards. A massive dormant generator filled the center of the structure. The rest was pipes. Lots of pipes. Big pipes. Little pipes. They were everywhere. Even an engineer would have a hard time figuring out all their functions. I'm convinced that some of them had no function, but were only there to complete a certain industrial aesthetic.

"Let's walk around, make sure," Bobby said.

I nodded.

"Did you nod?" Bobby asked. "Cause in the dark, nodding don't communicate dick."

"I nodded," I said.

"I just nodded back," Bobby said, and then he walked deeper into the building, waving the light into the corners.

I kept my shotgun at the ready, trying to maintain focus through fear. The pipes and shadows made hallucinatory beasts as the light passed. I concentrated on Juan.

Five minutes later, we were waiting at the northwest corner of the middle warehouse. Hidden in the shadows of some rusted equipment, Bobby and I waited for Buck Buck and Snout. The quiet was as alarming as every slight sound.

Five minutes after that, still no Buck Buck and Snout. I gave Bobby a tap on the leg with the barrel of my shotgun. "You think something happened to them?"

"They're too dumb to get caught."

"Sometimes I'm not sure if you hear the things you say," I said.

The not-so-quiet vibration of Bobby's cell phone echoed from his front pocket. Bobby smiled and dug it out. He read the face.

"The boys say they found a tunnel. Think it leads to the smokestack things. They're going to check it out and we should go in here ourselves."

"They texted all that?" I leaned in, trying to read the message.

"No. It just says, 'Found tunnel.' And 'tunnel' is spelled wrong. I inferenced the rest. 'Found' is spelled wrong, too."

Second verse, same as the first. We entered into the building the same way as the previous warehouse through the office door, assuming correctly that the layout would be identical.

Four stained mattresses lined the floors. Half-eaten bags of pork rinds littered the floor next to juice boxes and empty beer cans. A bucket full of piss and soft shit gave off an ammonia stench so strong my eyes watered. I stood completely still for a moment and concentrated on not puking.

The air was thick with flies. The sliver of light from the half-open door sparkled off their iridescent bodies. The poorest man's fireflies.

Bobby lifted the collar of his shirt over his nose and mouth. He put a hand on the knob leading into the warehouse. He blinked tears from his eyes and opened the door.

I followed him into the light.

It took me a long second to realize the difference from the other warehouse. The lack of darkness. Every light was on in the building, the maze of pipes and equipment sharply visible. I wiped the tears from my eyes with the back of my hand. I turned to Bobby to say something, but stopped when I saw his finger on his lips.

He walked slowly along the wall of pipes that made one side of the makeshift hallway along the perimeter of the building. It turned into a winding maze, but my tour of the previous warehouse gave me some sense of direction. I followed closely behind Bobby, keeping the barrel of my shotgun trained at the ground. With each step scattered noises grew louder. Some kind of machine was running. An engine or a venting system.

We continued slowly toward the sound. Cold sweat dripped from my hair down the middle of my back. I was jonesing for a cigarette.

We rounded a corner. Red light. Bobby and I froze.

It wasn't a machine. It wasn't Alejandro or Juan. It was seven tattooed and scarred South Americans huddled on the ground in deep sleep. Their rhythmic breathing softly purred in the hollow space. The innocence of their positions made them appear angelic. The black guns that each of them clutched in their listless hands ruined that effect.

One of the sleeping men had a yellow, red, and blue flag tattooed on his arm. I made a mental note to look up the country of origin when I got home. That is, if the same man didn't end up killing me.

Green light. Bobby and I took a quiet step back. Not quiet enough.

Flag Tattoo opened his eyes. He stared at us with that early morning glaze. Seeing, but not yet comprehending what was in front of him.

"*Quién?*" he mumbled.

We didn't hang around to answer. Bobby and I hauled ass back the way we had come. I had to keep one hand on Bobby's back to keep from tripping over him.

As we neared the office door, the rustle and voices grew louder behind us. Swearing and barked directions in Spanish. But the voices weren't loud enough to hide the sound of a different group of voices in front of us. While the voices behind us were belligerent, the voices in front of us were laughing and seemingly unaware.

Five armed Mexican men stood at the office door. The very same office door that was supposed to be our exit out of the building. The Mexicans stared at us with amusement and surprise when we rounded the corner and came into view.

Bobby stopped. I tried to hit the brakes, but slammed into his back and fell on my ass. I scrambled to my feet.

The Mexicans laughed at my pratfall. Then they noticed our shotguns. Then they heard the voices behind us. Then they stopped laughing.

Bobby looked behind us, voices and footsteps growing loud. He turned back to the Mexicans and trained his shotgun to the ceiling.

He shouted, "*Llene tu manos, hijos de las chingadas,*" and fired two quick rounds. The deafening sound rang in my head and echoed throughout the building.

The Mexicans hit the deck, reaching for their guns. The footsteps behind us stopped.

Bobby took off back toward the South Americans. No time for questions, I followed and prayed he had a plan.

The moment we were out of view of the Mexicans, Bobby fell to the ground, crawled under the nearest pipe, and scuttled out of view into the center of the building. I didn't need an invitation. I dove under the pipe right behind him.

We crawled quickly, staying below the maze of pipes. At points the squeeze was so tight that exposed bolts tore at my shirt and back. We kept moving. I focused on the soles of Bobby's feet, my face inches away, keeping pace. Even when his heel brushed my chin, I made no attempt to broaden the gap.

It didn't take long for the firefight to commence. It was a hell of a thing to hear. The Mexicans had obviously pursued us and ran smack-dab into the South Americans. As everyone's gun was cocked and ready, all it took was one itchy trigger finger and war was declared. Not enough time for it to occur to anyone to use their shared language to ask where the gringos hightailed it to. From under the pipes, it sounded like the end of the world. The blast of arms and the tenor ping of ricocheting lead.

I had no sense of direction under the pipes, putting my complete faith in Bobby. With the volume and echoes, for all I knew, we could have been going toward the gunfight. It was like all my senses had been stripped away.

Bobby led us right to the office door.

With the gunfire at our backs, we tore out of the building and ran across the length of the loading dock toward the north edge of the building. As we turned the corner of the warehouse, we literally ran into Buck Buck and Snout. We almost knocked each other down and shot each other simultaneously.

"What the fuck is going on in there?" Buck Buck loud-whispered.

"Not now," Bobby said.

He motioned for us to follow and took off toward the first warehouse. We stayed along the north edge of the building. Back at the loading dock, we jumped into the truck ramp and quickly found the safety of darkness. We all sat with our backs to the concrete, breathing hard.

I had a good view of the double-wide and saw the light go on in the office. We were deep enough in the shadows that I had little concern of being detected. Nobody would be looking in our direction anyway with the violent popping of gunfire in the distance.

"Who the fuck is doing all that shooting?" Buck Buck asked.

"Fucking drug smuggler convention in there," Bobby said.

"We're here. Who they shooting at?"

"Each other," Bobby said.

"Nobody in the back warehouse," Snout chimed in. "Sorry, Jimmy. Didn't see no kid."

"Could be more people in the middle one. These are big buildings. We didn't exactly get the complete tour," I said.

"We can't go back there now," Bobby said.

"How many you talking about?" Buck Buck asked.

"Enough. Like a half dozen on each side. That is, if there are only two sides and some other group of scumbags didn't feel left out and join in," Bobby said.

"Probably a few less by now," Buck Buck said.

"We can take 'em," Snout said.

The door of the double-wide flew open. While we were well out of sight, we all still ducked out of instinct. An impressively fat man buttoned his shirt as he stepped out of the office. His red face and peeling bald head telegraphed his time in the desert sun. He shouted into a walkie-talkie.

It didn't take long for two other guards to show. A heated discussion with a lot of pointing and shouting followed. With the gunfire continuing in the middle warehouse, the three men stood in a close huddle and discussed their plan of attack. Baldy was in charge.

One of the men went into the double-wide for a minute and came back with three serious guns. I don't know firearms well enough to say what kind, but they were action movie serious.

Even with the guns, they made no move. Why would they? Whatever was happening in that warehouse wasn't their fight. It looked like the plan was to wait it out, assess the damage, and take it from there. These guys were smarter than they looked.

With the guards standing there listening to the show, we were trapped in the darkness of that truck ramp. We were safe and out of sight, but the floodlights between us and the fence were too bright to allow any escape. And we hadn't found Juan yet. I couldn't speak for the other guys, but I had no plans to leave until I found him.

The men lifted their rifles toward the warehouse. Someone approached out of view. There was yelling back and forth. While the guards kept their guns aimed, they let the man approach.

It was Alejandro. He was carrying Juan. He held his hands out as much as he could with Juan in his arms. He approached cautiously, even doing a pirouette to show them he wasn't armed. They lowered their rifles, but their body language never relaxed. Drug smugglers shooting at each other in the distance will do that.

Baldy motioned for Alejandro to go into the double-wide. Alejandro asked a few questions, but only received shrugs and curt responses in return. Visibly frustrated, Alejandro and Juan entered the trailer. The door slammed shut. The three guards remained outside, still in discussion.

Like popcorn in a microwave, the gunfire slowed to sporadic bursts. Then stopped. Nothing for a minute. Then one quick shot. And again. After fifteen minutes of complete silence, the guards huddled again. They came to some kind of agreement and walked very cautiously, guns at the ready, toward the far warehouse.

I gave Bobby a look. He nodded. Buck Buck woke up Snout. I counted to thirty and then lifted myself out of the truck ramp. Glancing in the direction the guards had gone, I saw nothing. I motioned for the guys to follow. We walked quickly but quietly to the double-wide, stopping just below the window.

I crept up to look, but Bobby pulled me back down. I threw him a glare, but he shook his head and nodded to the door. Keeping low, Bobby and I crab-walked to the door. Bobby pounded on the door, saying nothing.

"This is bullshit," Alejandro said through the door. His voice grew louder. "I ain't paying no full price. *Lo jodiste. Chingadas* shooting, not what I paid for. Wanted to get shot, I would've stayed in *La República.* You better have some discount…"

The moment Alejandro opened the door, Bobby and I had him by his shirt. We pulled hard. He landed face-first on the ground, immediately attempting to scurry to his feet. I put my foot on his back, and Bobby stepped on one of his hands. Alejandro yelped, flailing his arms and bucking his body.

Buck Buck didn't need to be told what to do. He ran quickly up the steps into the double-wide.

Alejandro yelled loudly. Bobby kicked him in the head, and I dropped to one knee onto the middle of his back. He arched and moaned, the wind knocked out of him. Gasps took the place of volume.

Buck Buck came out holding Juan in his arms. He wasn't overly gentle, obviously not accustomed to carrying a child. Luckily Juan was subdued. His eyes were huge. But after this recent adventure with Alejandro, he seemed like he was just going to go along with whatever happened.

"Get him out of here," I said. "Take one quad, one bike. Don't wait for us. Get the kid as far away from here as you can. Bring him to Angie. Don't tell her nothing. Just tell her to look after him. Go!"

"What about him? You?"

"I got it. Go," I said.

Buck Buck and Snout took off toward the hole in the fence. Juan looked confused, but stayed silent. Buck Buck made fart noises into Juan's ear until he started laughing. It took them less than a minute to be completely out of sight.

"You should go too," I said to Bobby.

"The fuck," he said, ending the debate.

Bobby pulled Alejandro's hands behind his back, running a zip tie around his wrists. I took off my boot, pulled off my sock, and shoved the sweat-soaked sock into Alejandro's mouth.

By the time we hefted Alejandro to his feet, I could hear the sound of the quad in the distance. Alejandro struggled and threw elbows, but three short punches to his ribs pacified him.

Voices rose in the distance. I closed the door of the double-wide. Bobby and I dragged Alejandro around to the back, out of sight. We threw Alejandro to the ground. I sat on his hamstrings, holding his ankles down with both hands. Bobby sat on his lower back, his back to mine, one hand pushing Alejandro's face in the dirt, the other lifting his arms to the point of pain. The voices of the guards grew louder as they approached.

"Knew something like that would happen. I been telling Bub. When we got Colombians, we got to keep them apart. Motherfuckers are serial-killer crazy," one guard said. "Not like there was a clear winner. What a mess. Wonder what the fuck started it."

"You hear engines? Like bikes or quads? Out that way."

"Fucking cares? Unless they ride in here, let them have their fun. Too hot to ride in the day—probably just a couple jackasses getting stupid."

"They might have heard the shots."

"You ever been on a quad? Can't hear shit above the motor."

"What the fuck we going to do now?"

"Grab the fucking mops and buckets like Bub told us to."

With the sound of the office door opening, Bobby gave me an elbow to the back. After a moment the voices returned.

"You take the mops and that cleaning shit. I got to find some rubber gloves. I ain't going near none of that blood. Who knows what disease those fuckers carrying?"

"Where you think the Mex with the kid went? They was just here."

"Who the fuck cares? He paid up front."

Alejandro started to kick with his legs, but I had him pinned. Bobby pushed his face harder into the rocky ground. He stopped struggling.

"Found 'em," the guard exclaimed. And we listened to them talking bullshit as their voices receded and they returned to the warehouse.

Bobby and I rose. Alejandro squirmed like a fish on a ditch bank.

I took a look around the side of the double-wide. The guards were gone.

With a foot in each hand, Bobby and I dragged Alejandro facedown across the pavement and hardpack to the hole in the fence.

Bobby slipped through the chain-link and then grabbed both of Alejandro's heels and roughly pulled him through. I followed and we dragged him to the cover of the tamarisk.

"Now you can take off," I said to Bobby.

"What?"

"I can't ask you to do this," I said.

"You don't even know what you're going to do."

He was right. I didn't.

"Exactly why I should be here," Bobby said. "I started this with you. Whatever happens, we're doing it together. You can fuck yourself if you think different."

It took some doing, but we got Alejandro on the back of the quad. Luckily he wasn't a big man and comfort wasn't a concern. With enough baling wire and duct tape, anything is possible. We treated him as cargo, laying him over the back above the rear axle. He would have to flex his neck slightly during the ride or his face would scrape against the tire.

I took the quad, Bobby took the bike, and we headed back toward the lot and Bobby's Ranchero. We followed the stars, or at least tried to. I tried to attack the situation and figure out my next move. But no matter how hard I tried, I couldn't get a fix on it.

At what I assumed to be the halfway point, I rode into a gulley and stopped the quad. After about fifty yards, Bobby turned and saw that I had stopped. He rode the dirt bike back to me and killed the engine. The silence of the desert was a sharp contrast to the Oasis and the bikes.

"You trying to ditch me?" he said.

"Wasn't thinking about you. I'm just not sure what happens now," I said.

"Slapdash, but not half-ass, brother." Bobby tried a smile.

"The Veeder promise," I said with little joy.

We undid all the tape and wire that held Alejandro in place. One cheek was black from where it had grazed the back tire. Bobby and I dragged him off the quad. I didn't see any more need for the gag. There wasn't a living thing within earshot that could hear us or give a shit. I took my sock out of his mouth. It was saturated pink.

On his knees with his hands still zip-tied behind his back, Alejandro looked up at me and Bobby. His face was scraped and bloody, sand sticking to the dark red wetness. The front of his shirt was shredded, revealing his abraded chest.

If it was anyone else, I would have felt sympathy. But Alejandro wasn't the kind of guy who brought that out in a person.

"Motherfuckers. You're dead, motherfuckers," Alejandro spat, proving my point. I kicked him in the stomach. He bent over, heaving a mouthful of yellow liquid.

I leaned down. "That's the best you can do? Threaten us? Fucking idiot, this isn't a movie. There's no one to impress out here. We're going to talk."

"Fuck you," he countered. I kicked him in the stomach again.

I looked over to Bobby.

He shrugged. "You're doing fine."

I said, "We're going to let you go. But I set the terms."

Bobby gave me a look.

Alejandro spit on the ground and opened his mouth to speak, but said nothing. That was a start.

I laid it out for him. "You can't go back to Mexicali. You know that. Hell, you can't stay anywhere near here with Tomás looking for you. That works for me because it looks like I'm staying down here. After tonight I don't want to see you again. I'm taking the Imperial Valley. You can have anywhere else. The fucking whole rest of the world, for all I care.

"I'm trying to unfuck this situation. If Tomás wants, he'll find you and kill you. Matter of time, you know it. Who knows how far his reach goes? I can tell him to let it go. He'll listen to me. If he's convinced you're no longer a threat, he'll listen. Right here, right now, one-time offer. I'm giving you an out. All I got to know is that this bullshit is over."

Alejandro rolled his neck around, cracking it. "I can go?"

"Yeah."

Alejandro turned to Bobby. "Like that? I walk out this desert, *soy libre.*"

"Whatever Jimmy says." Bobby nodded.

"Where the fuck I'm going to go?" Alejandro spat.

"You were heading to LA," I said. "Go there."

"You get that from Rocio? Tomás get him to talk? Gave me up," Alejandro said with a hint of regret.

"It's not like you got options. You see where we're at, right? What's out there? Tomás wants you dead."

"Fuck that *pocho cabrón.*"

"Don't start that shit again. Easy solution. Go to LA."

"What I'm going to do there? Wash dishes in a *pinche taqueria?* Rather you fucking shoot me. I ain't starting over. All the money I had is gone. I ain't got shit. Used it all with them fucking Oasis *pendejos.*"

"That's why you grabbed Juan? For money? You grab a fucking kid?"

"You do what you do. Shit, give you credit. Didn't even give me a chance to call you. Hadn't figured the ransom shit and all that, but here I fucking am. Fucked in the fucking desert. You got over on me."

"What made you think I had money?" I said.

Alejandro shrugged.

"Do I look like I have money?"

"You're white, ain't you?"

"You aren't dumb. Might act it, but you got a better reason."

Alejandro smiled at me. "I know fucking farmers. Farmers hate taxes. Always got cash. Need cash to pay illegals, so you make a couple of hay deals maybe. Keep as much shit off the books you can.

"That *puta* got money off you. Don't know if she black-mailed you, if she stole it, whatever. She got your money. She got it, I can get it. Anyone got eight grand cash sitting around, they got to got more."

I froze.

"Jimmy?" Bobby asked.

I held my hand straight out to Bobby without looking at him. My body was stock-still. I lowered my hand, walked to the quad, and got my shotgun. I broke it open and checked both barrels.

Alejandro smiled at me. "She worked you. A fucking *puta.*"

"And you're a fucking punk," I said and hit him in the face with the stock of my shotgun. He landed on his side in the sand, his shoulder audibly dislocating. He yelled in pain. I put the barrel of the shotgun to his head.

I turned to Bobby. "He killed Yolanda."

"Do it," Bobby said.

Alejandro mumbled at my feet, and then he started laughing. I kept the barrel of the shotgun a few inches from his head.

"Something funny, asshole?" I said to him.

"I didn't have to kill her. She would have given the money. I could've just took it. Didn't even need the money really. I wasn't even supposed to be there. Went to give Tomás a message. Saw her across the street."

I interrupted him. "You think I give a shit about why you did it or what happened? I ain't the police or some fucking detective. I don't care why or how or any of that shit. All I care about is that you killed her. That she's dead because of you."

"You ain't going to shoot me." It was a statement.

I didn't answer. I didn't need to.

"I'll wait by the bikes," Bobby said, turning and walking through the thick sand.

"You can't do it. Go with your friend. You ain't hard enough to kill no one."

I glanced over my shoulder, making sure that Bobby was out of earshot. "I'm going to let you in on a little secret. Something no one else knows."

I took a breath, not sure if I was ready to say it aloud.

"I killed my father."

371

I waited until his expression changed in acknowledgment that I wasn't bullshitting.

"I killed my father. And I loved him."

Alejandro said, "I should have…"

I pulled the trigger.

I didn't push the quad driving back through the dunes. Bobby drove the dirt bike at my side, maintaining whatever pace I chose. When I slowed, he slowed. When I sped up, he sped up. Bobby stuck by my side, no matter what.

Driving slowly along the crest of a dune and staring out at the starlit inclines of sand, I tried to convince myself that I was on another planet. A planet of nothing but sand like the movies they shot out there. A different planet. Because on earth, I had killed two men. I had traveled all over the world, but it wasn't until I came home that men died by my hands.

It took me a minute to get Pop's face into my mind. It's amazing how quickly something that familiar fades. Luckily the image that came to mind wasn't the drawn features of his disease, but the laughing countenance of Big Jack. The Big Laugh. It made me smile. What had he said? You can't save a man's life. You can only postpone his death. Or hurry it along.

Then the thought of Yolanda rushed in there. Unfortunately, it was the sight of her at the bottom of the cistern. Alejandro had taken her life far too early. For nothing. For no reason. For that alone, I felt little guilt for what I had just done. He had destroyed a life, and that impact was going to carry down to Juan. I took from him what he took from her. It was simple.

And now I was going to try to undo some of the damage by looking after Juan. It wasn't a matter of responsibility. I had no problem shirking those. It wasn't out of duty. It was Pop's mistake, not mine. It was simply that I could do a tiny bit of good. If I made the effort, Juan could have a chance. A life. He could have opportunity. For all the shit that went down, he deserved at least that. I couldn't save the world, because I didn't give a shit about the world. I gave a shit about a handful of people, and Juan was now one of them.

In the distance a flat surface exposed itself in the star-light. Something angular and out of place in the sand. There weren't supposed to be corners in the dunes. I squinted at the shape, trying to make it out.

I turned to Bobby and said, "Does that look like a fort to you?"

But he couldn't hear me over the sound of the engines, pointing a finger at his ear. When I turned back, I could no longer find the shape in the sand. Just as well. Some things were meant to be buried.

Like a good friend, the desert keeps its secrets.

TWENTY-SIX

The aroma of wet grass filled the air. The alfalfa smelled sweet and good.

I walked the row the full half mile, looking out at the expanse of three-inch-high grass. The growth looked even with no thin spots. It still had some time before the next mow, but I was doing my best to be attentive to my new vocation. Still getting my farming legs beneath me, I found that I could be incredibly protective of my crops. I doted on them when all they needed was time to grow. I wasn't comfortable calling myself a farmer yet, but I was doing the work and I could see myself doing it for a while.

It was the first day under ninety degrees since I'd been back. The Imperial Valley had skipped fall and made a dash right to winter. The hot, muggy, and buggy days had passed. Finally the desert climate shifted to the kind of weather that brings the snowbirds down from up north.

Walking the field, smelling the hay, and feeling the sun, I couldn't imagine being anywhere else. It was a strange feeling. I wanted to be there. I wanted to see this all through.

I walked back slowly to my truck. My piece-of-shit Mazda. The one I had been forced to abandon in Mexicali. In a frightening display of his reach, Tomás had retrieved my truck from a Mexicali chop shop's maw. When I saw it parked in my drive, it sent chills through my body. The stock gearshift knob had been removed and replaced with a scorpion in clear resin and there was a small statue of the Virgin Mary glued to the dash, but that was the only evidence of its absence.

I took my time and picked up the occasional rock that had no place on the beautiful dark soil of my farmland. I placed the stones in the front pocket of my jeans. I'd give them to Juan when I got home. Currently rocks were his favorite toy. For all the brightly colored plastic shit I bought him, a few scraps of wood, a cardboard box, and a pile of rocks was all he needed to entertain himself for hours. Simple tastes. Like me. Like his father.

That's what I called myself. His father. Not just on paper or for simplicity's sake, but that's the role that I was trying to fill. I was trying to be everything my father had been for me.

Tomás had helped me with all Juan's paperwork. More official than the real thing, he had promised me. According to the birth certificate, Juan was born in the same Brawley hospital that I had been born in. I was listed as the father and Yolanda as the mother. Once we had the birth certificate, all the other paperwork fell into place. No one ever doubted it. After all, the kid looked like me.

I hadn't found any of Yolanda's relatives in Guadalajara yet, but I hadn't given up looking. I was considering going down there and poking around. That was, if I could convince Bobby to join me on another misadventure.

Bobby and Griselda were still going strong. While she had to have guessed that something not quite legal had gone down, she never asked. Yolanda's murder eventually went into the "Inactive Investigations" categorization. Officially unsolved to this day. At least, on paper.

I buried Yolanda next to Pop in what I had learned was a plot Pop had bought for me. It hadn't been a practical purchase or a morbid one. It was the product of some kind of three-for-two deal that he had gotten when my mother died. Yolanda would forever be on one side of Pop, my mother on the other. I think he would have liked that. The two women that he loved. And although I didn't really know either of them, I was convinced that they would have gotten along and liked it, too.

My cousin Mike got me up-to-date on the farm and the status of the crops. He helped a lot at first, but I was close to the point that I was pretty much on my own. Pretty much. With his help and Bobby, Buck Buck, and Snout, I almost had everything under control. It amazed me how much time my friends were willing to give. No matter the time or task, their usual response ended up being either a shrug or something along the lines of "You'd do the same for me." In the city people bitched when you asked them to help you move. Out here a neighbor would help you shovel shit for eight hours without batting an eye and still pick up the tab when you went to dinner.

Angie had been staying at my house a lot lately. We were taking it slow, but quickly enough that we were having fun. She acted like it was to help me with Juan, but there was still something very strong between us. I'm not sure if our history made our relationship stronger, but it made both of us feel like we'd already made it through the tough part.

Nobody had asked or said a word about Juan. Maybe there was gossip floating around, but nothing had gotten back to me. I had shown back up, gotten myself a Mexican three-year-old, and nobody cared. Luckily, most people are so involved with their own lives that they couldn't care less about mine. It didn't matter, because once most people met Juan, they fell in love. He's a funny little guy.

The biggest surprise was that I hadn't thought once of leaving. That was a first, but there wasn't another place that gave me the people or things I had in the Imperial Valley. It was home, and it was where I needed to be. I chose my responsibilities and loved every one of them. I don't think I'd changed, because I don't think people can. But I'd learned to enjoy what I thought I couldn't.

I drove my truck into the circular driveway of my house. Angie and Juan stood up from the sandbox that I had made for him. Angie dusted the sand off her shorts, watching Juan run to my truck on his stubby little legs. He was on me the moment my feet hit the packed dirt. I grabbed him under the arms and lifted him high above me. His laughter filled the air. He had Pop's laugh.

ACKNOWLEDGMENTS

It takes a rare friend to take the time to read an early draft of a first novel. I couldn't have finished this book without the support and feedback of Michael Batty, Jim Furgele, Greg Eliason, and Pete Allen. Thanks, guys.

A big Inca thanks to Jaime Arze for not only reading the book, but making sure that I didn't embarrass myself with my ninth-grade Spanish.

I was very fortunate to be a finalist in the Amazon Breakthrough Novel Award competition in 2010. There are far too many people to thank individually. But from the judges to the voters to the Amazon staff, I could not have gotten this book published without you. Thanks.

Thank you to Alex Carr and everyone at AmazonEncore for taking a chance on this country boy.

To Richard Drew, I have never given you nearly enough recognition or thanks for your quiet, yet constant support. So here it is. Thank you. Everything that you've done for me has not gone unnoticed or unappreciated.

Mom, your love and support are a constant that I rely on every day. Sorry for all the swearing in the book.

And finally and forever, the love of my life, my wife Roxanne. You are my best friend, favorite critic, and biggest fan. I would be nowhere without your love, understanding, and friendship. I truly love our adventure together.

Dove Season was written at Beulahland in Portland, Oregon.

ABOUT THE AUTHOR

Photograph by Roxanne Patruznick, 2011

Johnny Shaw was born and raised in the Imperial Valley on the Calexico/Mexicali border. He received his Master of Fine Arts in screenwriting from UCLA. In addition to his work as a screenwriter and playwright, he owns a used bookstore and teaches writing. He lives in Portland, Oregon. *Dove Season* is his first novel.

Visit Johnny at www.johnnyshawauthor.com